Lucy Sweet was born in 1972 in Hull, but hasn't let that stop her. She got her first writing job at 19 and is a regular contributor to a wide range of publications as a journalist and cartoonist, including *Punch*, the *Independent on Sunday*, the *Express* and the *Sunday Times*. She lives in Glasgow with her husband, where she currently juggles multiple careers as a girl-about-town columnist, magazine editor and struggling musician. *Have Love Will Travel* is her first novel.

HAVE LOVE WILL TRAVEL

Lucy Sweet

BLACK SWAN

HAVE LOVE WILL TRAVEL
A BLACK SWAN BOOK : 0 552 773018

First publication in Great Britain

PRINTING HISTORY
Black Swan edition published 2005

1 3 5 7 9 10 8 6 4 2

Set in 11/13pt Melior by
Kestrel Data, Exeter, Devon.

Black Swan Books are published by Transworld Publishers,
61–63 Uxbridge Road, London W5 5SA,
a division of The Random House Group Ltd,
in Australia by Random House Australia (Pty) Ltd,
20 Alfred Street, Milsons Point, Sydney, NSW 2061, Australia,
in New Zealand by Random House New Zealand Ltd,
18 Poland Road, Glenfield, Auckland 10, New Zealand
and in South Africa by Random House (Pty) Ltd,
Endulini, 5a Jubilee Road, Parktown 2193, South Africa.

Printed and bound in Great Britain by
Cox & Wyman Ltd, Reading, Berkshire.

Papers used by Transworld Publishers are natural, recyclable
products made from wood grown in sustainable forests.
The manufacturing processes conform to the environmental
regulations of the country of origin.

For Gracie, to read when you're older

Thanks to the Sweet family for never insisting I get a proper job and enthusiastically supporting everything I do, no matter how dodgy! Big thanks also to my agent Susan Smith and Gail Haslam at Transworld for their unwavering enthusiasm. Also to Anna Burnside for keeping me supplied with freelance work while I was writing it, Jayne Rowe and Mark Stewart for early encouragement and advice, and to top ladies Jane, Sarah, Kristina, Kelly and Rozanne, who are a constant source of inspiration and booze. Cheers to proper writers Annie Caulfield and Karen McLachlan for advice and contacts, and finally a special thank you to my husband Ian, who put up with my constant whining for over a year.

Part One

EDINBURGH

He gazes wistfully out of the window. We're in a restaurant. No, we're in a diner. We're just about to leave town and we don't know where we're going, but we've got to hit the road.

A waitress in a pink uniform idly pours coffee and stares at his godlike beauty. The sunlight turns his sandy blond hair and tanned forearms to gold. He reaches his hand across the table. His lips are set in a neat pout, curling up at the edges, idly amused. He fixes me with a sizzling blue stare.

'Tell you what,' he says. 'Let's have an adventure.'

Outside, the long stretch of road shimmers in the heat, waiting for us to conquer it.

'I love you, Jane,' he says, kissing me.

'I love you too, Brad.'

'Darlin', would ya stop thinking about me for five seconds and hand out these leaflets, ya skivin' wee slapper!'

Camp David ballet dances towards me and gives me a pile of leaflets with a wink and a game-show-hostess flourish.

'Love ya really, babe,' he says, pinching my cheek.

11

'Do this for me and there'll be a dirty great bonus in your pay packet next month, if you know what I mean! Heh heh!'

I smile weakly. He shrieks and clatters off like a deranged spinning top.

Knobhead.

I watch as his bendy frame disappears through the entrance of the tourist office, (or the gateway to hell, as I like to call it) and stare dolefully at the slab of glossy paper sitting on my lap, advertising 'The Ghost Walks of Edinburgh'. An unconvincing *Scooby Doo*-style ghoul is superimposed on a photo of a gravestone, advertising 'horrific graveyard encounters' and 'midnight excursions into the realms of terror' (starts 8.30 p.m.).

Brad waves his hand limply and melts away.

Bollocks.

I gaze wistfully out of the window. Instead of shimmering roads there's damp concrete, broken gutters, sodden grass.

Smoothing my 100 per cent polyester tartan skirt, I skulk out of the empty staff room and into the main office, busy with tourists making urgent enquiries. The slow-moving, recycled air buzzes with muted 'Where do Is' and 'How do I gets'. Everyone is present and correct at their workstations. Kelly is tapping her dinky little fingernails on her keyboard, simpering and primping her ginger perm. Dumb Paul is at the Citylink desk, looking gormless. Sophie bends her big pastel backside over a filing cabinet. Fiona recites something off her screen in a monotone, as if she's reading back an order at Burger King. Val's just dialled an outside line and is clearing a very important backlog of phlegm from her throat. Everybody wears the uniform: white shirt, regulation tartan and a perky ID badge with a thistle on it. It's a touching scene of industry and professionalism and it makes me want to gouge my eyes out. Over in the shop the tinny sound of Scotland The Brave is singing out from the bowels of a novelty tartan teddy bear.

I walk out slowly from behind the counter, avoiding the pleading eyes of the desperate, damp customers. If I can make it through here without being asked a tedious question about bus timetables I'm going on my lunch early. And I'm not sitting in this dump eating a sandwich while Val and Sophie discuss their ovaries, either. I'm going to treat myself. I'm going to pull out all the stops and have chips on a bench in the rain.

Kelly throws me daggers across the room, sensing my presence with a hawkish twitch of her big ginger head. This operation obviously calls for a high level of stealth and discretion. I mustn't draw any more attention to myself.

OK, Jane, just get it over with, stuff the leaflets in the box and make a run for it. Easy does it. Walk inconspicuously across the room. Just try not to look like you work here, or speak English. Pretend you're Slovenian.

I clutch the flyers tightly to my breast, covering up my 'Hello, My Name Is Jane' tag, and arrange my face into an Eastern European scowl. Soundlessly I slip through the queue, blind to the confused faffing of the tourists. I whisk past scratchy anoraks and dripping umbrellas, hands clutching maps, mouths demanding attention, advice and something to do to pass the time.

God, tourists get on my nerves. They're like babies – always lost, always needing assistance, always staring stupidly at a fixed point in the distance with their mouths hanging open. Don't they have homes to go to?

13

OK, keep walking. You're doing a grand job. Nobody's noticed you so far. Try not to breathe too loudly. Only five more steps to go.

I quickly slot the leaflets into the rack and do a speedy tidy-up, keeping my face steely and foreboding. I wonder if a commando roll into the staff room might be too over-the-top. I decide to play it cool. No sudden movements. The only sound I can hear is my shallow breath and the static swish of my hideous A-line skirt. I slip undetected through the queue. Nearly done it . . . two steps away from the counter . . . only one more to go. Oh yeah, I'm good – I should be in the frigging SAS. Slovenia, dix points – chips here I come.

'Excuse me, dear, could you tell me how I'd get to Holyrood Castle?'

Bollocks.

'So I says to her, ah'm no wantin' to give you a hard time, sweetheart, but you've got to stop staying out all hours and carrying on. You're only 15 and you'll end up in trouble, an' ah'm no gonnae be the one left tae pick up the pieces.'

'So what did she say?'

I bite the corner of a BLT, full of depressed lettuce and charred, cold bacon. Even if it tasted of anything, I wouldn't be able to tell. The staff room, with its brown cord carpet and clashing blue chairs is choked with dense cigarette smoke and the stink of stale coffee grounds. Today's conversation has thankfully bypassed Sophie's reproductive system (yesterday there was talk of discharge while I was eating cottage cheese) and instead Val and Sophie are discussing Lindsey, Val's errant stepdaughter. Poor Lindsey is getting a right pasting, but as far as I can tell her behaviour is perfectly normal. If I had to come home to Val's wheezing frog face I'd stay out all night too.

'She never says anything. She just locks herself away in her room.'

Sophie is listening intently, her face constipated with concern.

'She's reacting to change in the only way teenagers know how,' she says, oozing an oil slick of empathy onto the floor.

God, look at her hair. All Eighties flicks and streaked like Lady Di. What does she do? Go into the hairdressers with a Royal Wedding teapot and say, 'I want it like this'?

'It's a very difficult time. I know, I've been there.'

You wouldn't think that Sophie was the powerhouse behind this tourist office. But she's the boss, all five foot one of her, wrapped in a cosy swaddle of puppy fat, always putting on the kettle and asking if you fancy a chat. I suppose she's all right, but that homely stuff just makes me feel uncomfortable. Next to her I'm a nasty, unmanageable, six-foot cactus, while she's something pink and fragrant you could put on the windowsill in a nice little pot. She's so . . . nice. Nice nice nice.

'I think she's probably got a lot of residual anger about her real mum. Have you tried talking to her about that?'

There's a pause while Val tries to figure out what residual anger is.

'Well, I don't know anythin' about her real Maw, apart from she was a bitch.'

I roll my eyes into the back of my head, seeing orange stars and making myself dizzy. Outside the rain is turning to drizzle. My first summer in Scotland has

15

been a washout. It rained in June, July and most of August. Soon it'll be September and then I'll get itchy feet and that Back To School feeling – the yearning for a new pencil case, new friends, a new life.

I aim my sandwich wrapper at the bin. If it goes in, then I'll definitely get another job. Something to do with the Arts. A gallery assistant, maybe. Eventually I'll be running my own place and have a loft in the meatpacking district in New York and I'll start wearing polonecks and horn-rimmed glasses and be fabulously wealthy. 'She's a very exciting new artist,' I'll say into my state-of-the-art mobile phone, framed by a back-drop of brightly coloured canvas. 'Reminiscent of the New York School, but with a visceral grafitti-style twist. We've already sold three and we've got interest from Saatchi. Har har, yes I know, who hasn't? But seriously, this kid is going to be shit hot. Har har.'

Hmm, maybe not. Something, anyway. Anything. Anything but dozy bleeders holding maps upside down and who couldn't find their own arse with both hands. Right, here goes.

I lob the sandwich wrapper across the room just as Camp David bursts in. Deflected off the door, it bounces limply through the air and flips back at me, covering my already hideous tartan skirt with an in-criminating mayonnaise stain.

'Hiya, ladies! Is this a proper witches coven or can anyone join in? What are you talking about? Shaggin'?'

The Val and Sophie counselling session breaks up and they beam at him. You'd think he was funny the way they carry on.

'We were just talking about what a stud you are, Dave.' Val grins, almost flirtatiously, lighting her sixty-fifth Superking of the day.

'Val, you filthy wee TART! Don't start without me, then. I wanna hear it all. Hiya, Jane – what's that white stuff all over you? Don't tell me, it's . . . ugh! UUUUUGH! What have you been doing? You dirty beggar!' He breaks into a gale of laughter, almost shoving me off my chair. He's convulsing with mirth, going puce. He frantically waves his arms around and slaps his thighs.

'She's . . . it's like . . . it's . . . sp . . . un . . . k! Hahaha!'

Sophie, unable to hide her amusement, tells David to behave himself and offers me a tissue. I feign a game smile and get rid of the mayonnaise as he rolls around in his seat with his fist in his mouth. I can feel a hot rash creeping up my neck, the last thing I need.

'Just need to go to the shops,' I mumble, getting up, blushing, smiling stupidly. 'Does anybody want anything?'

Sophie and Val shake their heads and lift their eyes to heaven.

'Ignore him, Jane.' Sophie soothes. 'You know what he's like, a total crackpot!'

'It's fine, honestly,' I say with false brightness. My teeth are dry from my fake OK-you-got-me grin, and my lips are about to buckle. 'See you in a bit.'

I leave them goggling indulgently at Camp David's increasingly pathetic seizure and close the door. Behind it, the muffled hysteria continues. They're laughing at me.

'God, Dave,' I hear Val croak. 'What are you ON?'

I'm going to get a sign to put above the counter: *You don't have to be a twat to work here, but it helps*. I try to contain the stinging feeling. Oh well, just another day at the office. This is my tenth shitty job since I left college five years ago, so I should be used to

17

communicating with morons. I try to pull my face into some kind of neutral expression, but there's a nerve ending going haywire in my chin and I've got something in my eye.

I wander back through the main room, pulling my jacket over my name tag and keeping my head down. From here I can feel Kelly's green monster eyes on me, two sharp little knives in my back. The minute I arrived here she hated me, and nothing I've done since can change her mind. It's like we're biologically incompatible: cats and dogs. But at least I can see it in her face. I can tell that the others just wait until I've left to rip into me, changing the subject when I walk into earshot and smiling too innocently, like caught-out kids.

At least it's stopped raining. Walking down the steps, past the stream of people and cars and the strangled din of the bagpiper on the corner, I find the driest bench in Prince's Street Gardens and perch on the end of it. The bench is soaking and splintered, dedicated to a man called Geoff Dixon, who died the day I was born: 5th November 1977. I'm sure it must be a bad sign but I can't be bothered to figure out what it means. 'He loved Edinburgh.' It says. Hmm. Can't say I'm with you on that one, Geoff.

I turn away from the ominous plaque towards the Waverley shopping mall, and watch the parade of tourists walking along the pavement above me. They look exhausted, festival-fried, but they're manically laughing and eating ice cream, terrified of not having a good time. A millipede of Spanish schoolchildren carrying Day-Glo rucksacks passes by noisily. Someone who looks suspiciously like my dad, but thankfully isn't, wanders past wearing a jester's hat. I wouldn't recognize him now anyway, it's been so long. (He's probably deep in the South American jungle, trying to 'find himself' and living off earwigs.) To complete the scene, a braying student theatre group run around on the wet grass dressed in Shakespearean costume, bothering people with flyers and ringing a hand bell. I'm beginning to despise this place. Out of the corner of my eye the Scott Monument gives me the middle finger.

I light a diet cigarette and raid my brain for Brad. Lovely Brad. I left him at the table, kissing my fingers, being all sun-kissed and gorgeous. We were going to go on an adventure, but now he's buggered off without me. The mayonnaise has left a noticeable oily stain and I stink of Val's bricklayer's fags. Hanging about by a bench across from me, there's a trendy girl with a catalogue-model boyfriend who looks like he's stepped out of a Gap ad. She laughs and teases her perfect beau as he flinches from the wasps bothering the litter bin. I wonder what her name is and how she got to be so happy. I wonder if she likes the same things as me. I wonder if they'll feel sorry for me and let me slavishly hang around with them wearing my manky tartan uniform. Good-looking boy pretends to strangle her and she laughs, showing sweet pink gums. It's obvious they're having lots of really great sex and exist in a shiny world of parties, brunches and chill-out rooms. Then two painfully hip girls approach, one small and dark, the other tall and blonde, wearing denim skirts and tight washed-out T-shirts. One wears yellow and blue trainers, the other a pair of pointy Mary Janes. They all embrace, a riot of white teeth and Toni&Guy haircuts, and go off to some fabulous engagement, possibly sponsored by Diesel.

I mash out my fag on Geoff's wooden arm and steel myself to go back. I wish I had some friends. It wouldn't matter so much about Camp David or Kelly if the people at work weren't the only people I ever see. When Lizzie was here it was all right. I've known her since school, and when she said I should move up to Edinburgh it sounded like an exciting thing to do. She'd been living up here for two years, working for some international law firm, and told me I'd love it. I thought, Why not? It was as good a place as any. I'd been living in Manchester since college and it was getting boring anyway, so the idea of a new place, especially one with its own incomprehensible accents and funny banknotes, was pretty appealing. At first it was great – I extended my overdraft and dossed about for a bit, tagging along, being the novelty new friend, making myself part of her circle, a group of perfectly pleasant, impeccably well-brought up girls who liked to let their hair down after work. I acquainted myself with the pubs and clubs and takeaways and stayed with Lizzie in her girlie, overpopulated flat in Marchmont, on a very glamorous old mattress in the kitchen recess. The fun only lasted two weeks, though, until the company Lizzie worked for asked whether she would transfer to their new office in Australia, starting in a matter of weeks. It was a promotion, too good an opportunity to turn down, she said. I feel like I'm deserting you, she said, but I shook my head and said she must go forth and conquer and all that, even though I was dying inside. She offered me her room in the flat as a consolation prize, but the thought of living there without her seemed weird. Anyway, I didn't want anyone to think I wasn't go-getting or thrusting or independent. So I left the flat, rented the first place I could find and got the tourist office job. As Lizzie got caught up in packing and visas and stuff, suddenly Edinburgh didn't seem so brilliant after all. It was handsome but uptight, far too touristy, and you had to ask for salt and sauce on your chips instead of vinegar, which for some reason became a cause of bizarre, homesick, irrational fury (sauce! Who do these people think they ARE?). I felt like a spare part, wary of relying too much on Lizzie and her crowd, but drawing a blank everywhere else, especially at work, where Kelly sat there glaring at me like a sinister baby orang-utan. At Lizzie's leaving party a month later, right under the banner I'd made that said Bon Voyage in glittery bubble writing, she said, 'Don't worry, this lot'll look after you.' With the confidence of someone off to bigger, better things, she waved across the room to her pissed, cavorting mates and I knew that none of us were going to stay in touch. Without Lizzie as the focus of attention, they simply didn't need me. I went for lunch once with Rebecca, who was a trainee barrister, and it was like pulling teeth. She talked about work and there was a hair in my penne arrabiata.

'Hiya, Kelly,' I say pleasantly, hoping to diffuse the wrath of the ginger demon. 'Are you off on your lunch?'

'Do you know what happened to those brochures?' she snaps.

Kelly stands in the corridor near the cloakroom with her fat fist on her hip, looking like she means business. Her hair is extra bouncy today, spritzed into jaunty marmalade curls that make her look like she's about to do a dance routine with Daddy Warbucks. She stinks of her vile signature perfume, Eau de Skunk.

'What brochures?'

'The ones I asked you to send out about two weeks ago. The ones Lunn Poly say they haven't GOT.'

Her piggy eyes, rimmed with clownish green eyeliner, narrow even more. It strikes me that she would look right at home in a military uniform, standing on a balcony and firing a gun into the air. Somewhere along the line she's decided she's the boss and I'm her skivvy. We stand there at loggerheads, staring at each other with barely suppressed disgust. Kelly thinks I'm weird and possibly a lesbian, I think she's repulsive. One of us is right and it isn't her.

'Oh, *those* brochures? Oh, I'm sure I sent them. Maybe they, er, got lost in the post or something.'

They're sitting under my desk, glowing in my mind's eye like nuclear waste.

'I know I sent them. I definitely sent them,' I say, my face instantly heating up. 'There must have been a postal strike or something.'

'Jane, you didn't because they're sitting under your desk. I saw them when I went to the toilet.'

Her snout curls in triumph. This could be bad. She's going to either squeal to Sophie or torture me with it for ever. I look at the floor, caught out. Then out of the blue, a picture of Kelly on the toilet, straining to do a dump, pops into my head, and a huge embarrassing guffaw rises in my throat. I swallow it.

'I'm sorry, Kelly. I'll send them today.'

'You're not sorry, and you better had,' she growls. 'It's been two weeks and I'm getting phone calls. Why can't you just try a bit harder? I mean, it's not like it's difficult to put a few stamps—'

Sophie bustles past, wearing a serene Prozac smile.

'Everything all right, ladies?'

'Yes, Sophie, thanks. Just . . . you know . . . chatting.'
Kelly giggles nervously.

What a crawler.

I must have been making a face because she goes on
the defensive and starts poking my shoulder with her
manicured stumpy finger.

'I'm trying to be professional,' she hisses when
Sophie is out of earshot. 'Why can't you do the same for
a change? God, Jane, your attitude stinks. You just
don't care. Nobody asks much of you round here, you
know. Cut me some slack, OK?'

With that she's away, all puffed up at getting the last
word.

'OK. Sorry,' I say again, and I start walking away in
the opposite direction. She's right about one thing, I
don't care. I get paid £5.50 an hour – why would I?
Perhaps sensing my bad attitude, she spins round and
gives me a slow fifteen-year-old girl dirty look, starting
at my shoes and ending in the evil eye.

'You've got a huge hole in your tights, you know.'
She smirks gleefully. Then she piddles off, her heels
going clickety-clack on the lino.

I look down and, sure enough, there's a huge moon of
white flesh on my calf, probably the work of Geoff
and his bench. My heart plunges into my shoes.
Bitch. I grab a magic marker out of the staff room and
fill it in.

'Jane, isn't lunchtime over?' says Sophie, poking her
head round the door, the smile never leaving her lips as
she clocks me inking my leg.

'Yes, Sophie, I was just—'

'Well you'd better scoot, the office is packed out.'

'Yes. Right.' I dither, putting the lid back on the pen,
my face burning. What am I doing? Sophie stands

there, watching me with a baffled smile, until I leave the room.

This job makes me feel like I'm a big overgrown school girl, the one with holey tights who's so frigging dozy she's got to stay back until she's twenty-five. I went to university, y'know. OK, so I only got a 2.2 in Media Studies, but none of these dimwits would be able to write a dissertation on 1920s German Expressionist cinema. They're the kind of people who laugh at babies falling off cliffs on *You've Been Framed*. I perch on my chair, ergonomically designed to give you lumbago, and wiggle my mouse into action. I glance across at Fiona, the only person round here who hates her job as much as I do. She's on the phone, twizzling her hair with a pencil. When she sees me she sticks the pencil up her nose, rolling her eyes around in mock stupefaction. I roll my eyes in solidarity and mimic blowing my head off with a gun. The clock says 2.07 p.m.

'Next please,' I say, doomed.

In between the tides of confused and confusing customers, all I can see is Kelly's big head and those green-rimmed eyes, cold and beady like a pair of frozen peas. I get the message, fat arse. Why don't you just make a voodoo doll and stab it with a pair of scissors? Hire a plane and write, I HATE JANE DARLING across the sky for all I care. She's such a little fart. I bet she's never been anywhere or done anything. I bet her mummy and daddy dote on her and make her cocoa and she goes to bed in a sea of fluffy bunny rabbits and teddies. Little do they know that under that pudgy dimpled exterior beats the cold, black heart of a monster.

Stop STARING! What is her problem? She does it all

24

the time when I'm doing the most mundane things. Yesterday I was shaking a sugar sachet before I put it in my coffee and she may as well have been taking notes. Sometimes she isn't even sly about it either, she just goggles at me, like I'm some bizarre curiosity – a pink hippo or a bearded lady. Maybe she's in love with me and can't deal with her confusing urges. Whatever, I just wish she'd knock it off.

I turn my chair 45 degrees in the opposite direction and address the endless line. Even with my back turned I can feel her leaking waves of pure hatred.

I really shouldn't care less about this; she's a small, rubbish, thwarted person who puts posters of Will Young up on the staff pinboard, who's never been told to shut up and get over herself, who has the sexual allure of Basil Brush and a highly unattractive streak of megalomania. She can't pronounce bureau de change properly, either. Plus, she's about two feet tall and her shoes are shit. But although I could easily grind her into dust, the fact that she can't even bear my presence makes me feel pathetic. I want to beg her forgiveness and ask her what it is I'm supposed to have done. Despite everything, some miserable, needy part of me wants her to like me.

All this and it's only ten past two.

My next customer is a woman with big teeth – English, posh, annoying.

'Can you tell me about the ghost tours?'

2.12 p.m.

American couple – pushy, vaguely seedy.

'We need tickets for the Edinburgh festival. Can you buy them here?'

2.25 p.m.

25

Clueless bloke – cheap sunglasses on a jaunty fluorescent string round his neck.

'Do you sell maps?'

2.27 p.m.

Idiot in a tracksuit.

'Where's the castle?'

2.30 p.m.

Young Swedish girls, full of irritating Scandinavian outdoor pertness.

'We like to walk so we would like to have information of some walks please.'

2.48 p.m.

Myopic family of four, sharing grim genetic make-up. Husband possibly a kiddie fiddler.

'Is this where you get tickets for the bus?'

2.52 p.m.

Swarthy Spanish fisherman type. Quite nice.

'I wish to find out more about Inverness.'

3.02 p.m.

Total fuckwit.

'How long is the Royal Mile?'

3.03 p.m.

'Book me a hotel. NOW.'

Rendered senseless by inane questions, I barely register the customer's face. He's rude, that's for sure, but my brain has turned to mid-afternoon mush and I can't even bother to be offended.

'Certainly, sir. What kind of accommodation do you require?'

'A hotel. In Edinburgh.'

Oh, yeah, you're funny. I sigh and glance up at him. He's thirtyish with dark, neat stockbroker hair: good-looking if you like that sort of thing. Pierce Brosnan without the charm. He reminds me of a posh leather wallet stuffed full of tenners – tanned hide, reeking of money. Probably a dot com millionaire or something crap like that. I focus on my computer screen.

'Three star? Four star? Five star? Big hotel? Small hotel? Central? Out of town?'

I can feel his eyes drilling into my head.

'Look, I don't care.' He snaps. 'I want a room for the night, preferably somewhere in Edinburgh. Preferably somewhere with a roof. And a bed. If that's not too much trouble, *dear.*'

I bite the side of my cheek. Don't call me dear, you public school wanker.

'Quick as you can, please.'

Right, Pierce, that's it. I'm going to put you in the worst hotel in Britain. Rats will nibble your knackers while you're asleep, cocksucker.

'The Bellevue is very nice,' I lie, tapping briskly on my keyboard. 'A stone's throw away from Princes Street.'

'Well go on then. I haven't got all bloody day,' he harumphs, facing away from the counter, obviously far too important to address me directly.

What a tit. I find the number and pick up the phone. Even calling the Bellevue makes me feel like there's a layer of dirt on my skin. The only reason we deal with them is because Queen Victoria once walked past it or something. The line clicks and sizzles as the proprietor snorts catarrh into the mouth-piece.

'Hello, Jane from the TIC here. Do you have any rooms available tonight?'

'No,' he hacks. 'Full up all week.'

'Full? Are you sure?'

I'm dismayed. Pierce sighs dramatically and runs his

fingers through his hair. My masterplan foiled, I drearily return to my database.

'The Bellevue is f—'

'Yes, so I heard.' He snaps, increasingly irritated. 'Come on then, try another. It's not rocket science. Get me somewhere else. Today, if possible. God almighty, how hard can it be?' he whines, bringing his fist crashing down on the counter. He's wearing a Rolex, the flash git.

I find, annoyingly, that I've started shaking. I want to smash my monitor over his obnoxious head. I phone the Hilton, the Marriott and the Holyrood. Full. Now he's had his hissyfit, he wanders off to flit moodily through the postcard carousel and ponder the unfairness of life. The Grand, the Grosvenor, the Apex – everything is booked solid during August. I beckon him over; he's fuming.

'I'm afraid they're all full, sir. Would you like me to try B&Bs?'

He stares at me as if I'm a turd.

'Jesus Christ. Are you telling me there are no hotels in this town at all? What's this?' he says, waving a flyer irritably in the air. 'The Balmoral. Tell you what, that's a hotel. Try it.'

I pick up the phone, but he grabs it off me and slams it down.

'No wait, since you're so useless, why don't I phone them?'

He flips open his mobile and punches in the number. I feel like blubbing and my chin has started to go again. He stalks back to the postcard carousel to give the Balmoral a piece of his mind. From his outraged reaction, it looks like they're full as well. Across the room Kelly has been watching the drama unfold from her desk. She may as well be holding a bucket of popcorn and a hot dog. I stare at my screensaver, trying to stop the babyish tears from escaping, watching an inappropriately jolly thistle pinging across the screen. Eventually he hangs up and marches over.

'This is a pathetic excuse for an accommodation service,' he says quietly, trembling with anger, pointing at me. 'It's not like this anywhere else. They employ people who can do their jobs.'

I take a deep breath, and for the first time I look properly at his self-consciously expensive clothes and his mean, overblown act and a wave of weariness hits me. 'Oh . . . fuck off.' I sigh, clicking my mouse and deleting his request.

'Jane, when you're dealing with difficult customers it helps to maintain a sense of perspective.'

Sophie is regarding me with Paddington's Hard Stare. She's no good at looking tough. Especially when her office is a mess of pink fluffy picture frames and baby photos.

'He patronized me, he called me useless, he grabbed the phone off me—'

'Yes, but YOU are a professional,' she says, waving her candy-coated fingernail in my face. 'If you feel in any way compromised come and get me or David. Don't take it into your own hands and for heaven's sake don't swear at them. It makes us all look bad.'

I wish everybody would leave me alone and stop pointing at me. I cross my legs. The hole in my tights has become shamefully large, revealing a smaller circle of magic marker and a ring of white flesh, like a target. I quickly cross them back again. Sophie goes to the cabinet and digs out a file, probably filled with my previous transgressions. All my faults catalogued and underlined in red ink.

'You're a bright girl, Jane. You could really get on in the tourism industry if you applied yourself.'

The very idea of getting on in the tourism industry fills me with horror. I'd have to wear a neck scarf. I sigh and rub at a biro mark on my finger.

'Do you like your job?' she asks, writing something in my file with a ridiculous Loch Ness monster pen.

I click into automatic. 'Yes. Of course I do. It's very interesting and varied.'

'It's more than that, Jane. We are the front line. The first point of contact. People are disorientated, in a new place, and your job is to be the first friendly face they see. If you're not friendly, their view of Edinburgh will be tainted. And not just Edinburgh, the whole country. It could be the difference between them visiting every year or never coming here again.'

Oh please. What does she want me to do? Shave my muff into a map of Scotland?

'I'm sorry, but he was just rude, Sophie. He wasn't disorientated.'

She heaves a great flustered sigh that makes her matronly bosom rise alarmingly.

'That's not the point. Unfortunately we get difficult people here all the time and you can't afford to lose your cool.'

There's a silence as she writes something down in big loopy hairdresser handwriting. I look around her office. Photos of her children, Hector, Barney and Mia, crowd the walls and pinboard. Rugrats flailing on the carpet, beach balls with currants for eyes, distant shapes playing on swings. Mr Sophie is conspicuous by his absence, but there's something about the photographs that I can't help but envy. When she leaves work at the end of the day, she's got somewhere to call home. In one picture she sits on a sofa surrounded by her children, eating lollies. The kids are covered in red sticky juice, but they're all laughing at some off-camera joke, genuine peeing-themselves laughter, and Sophie is laughing too, her cheeks pink and her hair endearingly ruffled. Maybe she'll take pity on me and adopt me.

'I'm going to have to give you a written warning,' she says with a constipated sympathetic expression. 'I'm sorry, but it's procedure.'

A cold feeling grips my stomach. I mean, I'm not exactly employee of the month, but a written warning?

'But—'

She silences me with a wave of her Nessie pen and carries on writing.

I look down at the hole in my tights, which has now become a symbol of my utter failure. I am a wretched human being. Sophie scribbles away furiously. What's she writing? *Jane Darling is a loser who will never come to any good. Incapable of doing even the simplest tasks, she will slither along the path of life.*

I can't even do a crap job properly. It's easy, all I have to do is give out flyers, phone up hotels and smile occasionally, and I can't even do that. If I ever see that bastard again I'm going to kill him.

'Can I ask you something? Are you happy here?' Sophie oozes, her head tipped to one side.

The unexpected question jolts me out of my murderous thoughts.

Am I happy?

'What— do you mean in my job?' I stutter.

'No, I mean, in general.'

The sight of Sophie's steady gaze, her rounded, lived-in face, her Marks & Spencer mumsy clothes, suddenly make me want to break down and hide in her skirts.

Am I happy?

Well, let's see. I don't know. I haven't really thought about it. I know I don't like Edinburgh much. Although when I think of the splinter in the park bench and my poky little flat and Lizzie's friends who never called and Kelly's grimace, I realize that I don't hate Edinburgh half as much as it hates me.

Sophie's eyebrows are upended with concern. She's so kind. What has she done to deserve me? All I do is think terrible thoughts about her haircut.

Hot tears start coursing down my cheeks. I try to wipe them away, but they're determined to come, puffing up my eyelids and making a red-nosed fool out of me.

Sophie, now in her element, whisks a tissue out of a nearby box and hands it to me.

'Oh, Jane. Don't cry,' she coos, making me cry even more. A gallon of molten snot dribbles attractively down my face. I'm racked with spectacular heaving sobs, a total basket case. What's the matter with me?

Sophie waits until I've stopped gushing, which takes for ever. She sees that my tissue is soaked and gets me another.

'God, I'm sorry.'

'Oh don't be sorry,' Sophie says in a cheerful horsey voice. 'I've got three kids – I'm not afraid of a bit of snot.'

I let out an embarrassed snort of laughter, blowing the aforementioned snot out of my nose in an alarming green bubble the size of Mars.

'Tell you what, I think you need something to get you going. The Scottish tourist board has a stand at the Destinations travel fair in London, and I think it would be a good idea for you to go down for a day. Get some ideas, regenerate some enthusiasm, come back with a new sense of purpose. What do you think?'

I wipe my nose. A day off. In London. Stroll round the travel fair, do some shopping, take in a show. Maybe that would be just the thing.

'Yes. Yes, that would be lovely. Thank you.' A smile cracks my dry lips.

'OK, good. Susan Chater from the tourist board has asked for an extra pair of hands, so I'll put your name down. Kelly will be doing a short Powerpoint presentation at one o'clock and you'll be her right-hand woman, there to answer any questions and help with brochure handouts. It's a high-profile event, so we'll need you to put on a sunny smile and a brave face and do us proud. Is it a deal?'

Sophie leans forward, grinning expectantly, all crisp and efficient.

I sniff and blink.

Kelly's dogsbody?

'Er—'

Sophie raises her eyebrows, but there's a hardness behind her expression. Something tells me that if I decline this kind offer, I'll be out on my arse.

'Sounds great. It's a . . . deal.'

'Brilliant. You'll go next Monday. You'll have a fantastic time, I guarantee it.'

Yeah. Brilliant.

Anyway, where was I? Oh yes, Brad and me are in the car and we're cruising along on an empty road, a sweet breeze coming through the window. Warm wind tickles the back of my neck and there are no people and no buildings for miles around, just trees, grasses and scorched earth. I'm wearing immensely cool shades and trying to find a good song on the radio. The only sound is the purr of the engine. He puts his hand on my knee for the first time and my thighs go up in flames. He looks sideways at me and it's obvious we're both thinking the same thing. He's suddenly serious and he stops the car and then . . . shit!

'Fair maiden, come thither and see our show at the Pleasance, for gadzooks it is excellent entertainment.'

I take the flyer off the foppish student actor and keep walking.

'Hark,' he calls after me. 'There is a fearsome hole in thine tights!'

I cut across the gardens and onto Lothian Road. My flat is a fifteen-minute walk from here in Tollcross, but I'm so insanely itching to get out of my uniform I might just take it off in the street. What a terrible day. The sky is still blank and oppressive, as if a giant in a pair of grey Y-fronts is sitting on the city. My armpits are sweaty, my long dark hair hangs in clumps.

I can't believe I've got to go to London with Kelly. When I told her, her face fell somewhere below her gusset, which turned out to be the highlight of the day. Maybe I could leave her in Lost Property at King's Cross.

After the Usher Hall, the festival crowds thin out, replaced by Edinburgh locals who would cut their own throats to avoid third-rate street theatre. Their faces are passive, they carry supermarket bags and keep their heads down. They all look downtrodden as hell. Is anybody happy?

I suppose they are. They must be. I'm sure that the people who live in the flats opposite me are happy, all sitting in their cosy, lit-up boxes, eating dinner, feeding cats, doing ordinary things. I watch them sometimes from my casement window in the roof, and feel rather spectacularly sorry for myself, isolated in the attic like a trapped princess with one of those cones on her head. A heavy, tired feeling weighs on my shoulders. I wish I hadn't cried in front of Sophie. She must think I'm a drip. She's probably going to tell Val about it and they'll start analysing me over coffee and cigarettes, just like they do with Lindsey and their fallopian tubes. 'Jane has a lot of residual anger. She's also a complete wuss.'

I think at least Fiona is on my side, though. She's a woman of few words, but her hatred of Kelly far surpasses mine. She calls her 'carrot flaps' and has been known to steal things out of Kelly's lunchbox because she's already got an arse the size of Germany. Although, for all Fiona's griping, I think she might secretly be One of Them. After I'd been in Sophie's

35

office she came to see what all the fuss was about and I could tell she was dying for some gossip. When I told her what I'd said to the customer, she squealed, 'Good for you, girl. Fuck 'em,' then slapped me on the back and gave me a Chewit. I felt like we were allies, the two most clued-up people in the office against the rest of the drones. Somehow I thought she'd keep it to herself, but no. She slinked off and five minutes later Camp David appeared. 'What's all this?' he twittered. 'I want to probe you, Darling. Spill it. Tell me. Tell me everything you said and everything Sophie said and don't miss a thing, Miss Thing!'

I dunno. I don't want to think about it any more, I'm exhausted. I can barely get my key in the lock. I begin the long climb to my hole in the roof. I need a bath and a beer and a boyfriend.

'Hello, dear.'

At the sound of my footsteps, my downstairs neighbour emerges on the pretext of buffing her brass door fittings. It's Queenie, a woman of indeterminate age and smell.

'Hi, Queenie.'

'Have you had a good day?' She whistles, polishing furiously. I notice she's wearing a bizarre pair of slippers with mop heads attached to the soles.

'Oh, you know.'

'One of those, eh? You don't seem very happy, I must say.'

Oh sweet Jesus. Not you as well.

'Well, at least you're young.' She cocks her head to one side and squints at me through her bottle-bottomed glasses. 'And you've got a lovely figure. Put a bit of make-up on, smarten yourself up a bit and you'd be a real catch. Have you got a boyfriend, dear?'

I stand there open-mouthed, wondering if I heard right.

'Er. No.'

'Well, don't you worry, one'll come along soon. They always do. You won't be on your own for long.'

'Actually, I quite like being on my own,' I protest.

'Oh, nobody likes being on their own.' She sniffs, matter-of-fact.

There's a pointed silence, punctuated only by the swish of her duster. I can see my distorted form in Queenie's gleaming doorknob, an ugly oversized head receding into an elongated, boneless body.

'Yes, well . . . I'd better go.'

I start making my way up the stairs.

'Love turns up when you're least expecting it, dear. One day you're just minding your own business and DOOF!' she slams the palm of her hand against her storm door, sending thunder echoing up the stairwell. 'It knocks you flying.'

'Oh, right . . . OK. Bye!'

I dart up to the top floor.

Mad old bat.

Once inside, I dump my bag in the cramped square hall, squeeze into the bedroom and scramble out of my tartan truss. I pick up my crumpled uniform with my foot and kick it viciously into the washing basket. Sitting on the unmade bed in my pants, I catch sight of my reflection in the mirror and make a thorough, unflinching survey. Lank hair, skinny frame, dark circles under my eyes, bony fingers, chapped lips. Jesus, Jane, Queenie was being kind. You look like a heroin addict. You've got to do something about it. You could organize a ghost tour and be the scary madwoman in the attic.

I drag a brush through my hair and give up when I hit a knot. Nobody's going to see me, are they? Pulling on jeans and a threadbare kiddies T-shirt advertising the joys of Blackpool Pleasure Beach, I sideways shuffle into the bright red living room and duck into the cheesy yellow kitchen, narrowly avoiding a low-hanging roof beam. My flat, a fathomless collection of odd angles, sharp edges and garish walls, is always trying to stun me into submission. 'Compact and quirky,' the agency said, but it's actually just fucking deranged, partitioned by lunatics and painted by colour-blind midgets. I've lost count of how many times I've knocked myself senseless on the doorframes. If it were a person, it would have been bundled into the back of an ambulance and sectioned years ago.

I open the fridge, the door whacking into the wall. There's something lurking in the salad drawer that really stinks, but I'm too scared to find out what it is. As I slam the fridge shut, a photo becomes dislodged from its magnet and flutters to the floor. It's a younger version of me and my friend Ali, being bad girls at college in Manchester, looking like we're at the tail end of a disastrous hair-dye experiment and gurning over pints of lager. I stare at it for a minute, marvelling at our bright wide eyes and ridiculously young caramel-coloured skin. It was taken six years ago, but it feels like twenty. Ali lives in Newcastle now with her husband Liam, who is the youngest partner ever in some respected architecture firm. They have holidays in the Maldives and high-tech kitchen appliances. I bet her salad drawer doesn't smell of rotting corpses. She works in a gallery and she's a proper adult with a house bigger than a postage stamp. She's the one with the thrusting job in the Arts, not me. I always wanted to be like her. She was smarter and funnier and braver and prettier than me. She knew just what to say. I smile at the memory of us, drunkenly customizing second-hand clothes, wasting lipstick on unsuitable boys, trying and failing to start a band. A million ideas that didn't quite come off.

I crack open a beer and collapse on the rickety futon in the living room. Looking round the room at my things – books, a Dansette, a box of old albums, a leaning floor lamp with a swirled orange shade from a car boot sale, a photo of me and my dad at Flamborough Head when I was eleven with a haircut like a fruit bowl – and I start to feel a bit better. The alcohol rushes through my bloodstream, making me floppy and relaxed, and the shitty day melts away. I put a record on and light another low-tar, low-taste Silk Cut.

You know – burp – I'm really not so bad.

Compared to Kelly I'm a real catch. And I'm not awful at my job, I just had a lapse of concentration, that's all. And what Queenie doesn't know is that bitter single women make up a significant part of the population these days, so it's not like I'm unique. They're everywhere you look, speed-dating, internet chatting and buying meals for one. Being lonely and unsuccessful is no longer considered a stigma, it's a lifestyle choice.

I open another bottle.

Anyway, fuck 'em all. Kelly cannot shake me, Sophie cannot sack me, Camp David cannot make any more jokes about spunk at my expense, and as for you, Pierce Cocksucker, you will go to hell with a red hot poker shoved up your stockbroker arse for even daring to call me 'dear', for I am Jane Darling, independent woman extraordinaire, good-looking if only she'd put some make-up on, talented in all directions if only she could make up her mind what to do, but a good person nonetheless, underneath the bile and the whining and the bollocks. Yes, one day nobody will mess with me and I will laugh at this dismal episode in my life. 'Doing a crap job in a place I hated and having no friends was the making of me,' I'll say to my new celeb pals while I'm fanned by a scantily clad Latino house-boy. 'I worked in this awful office with these ghastly people. Had to wear tartan! Ha ha ha! But you know, it toughened me up and now look at me. I'm a rockstar artist actress millionaire astronaut.'

I'm pissed.

I sway to the kitchen to get another beer and pick up my notebook, a fat thing full of random clippings and pictures ripped out of magazines for forgotten reasons. Along with my dreadful song lyrics and my innermost shallow thoughts about people I fancy and my evil drawings of people on the bus, I write a list of things to do.

THE PLAN

1. Get another job. This is of utmost importance and will save sanity. Try any of the following: The Arts, Journalism, Publishing, Internet, TV etc. Buy newspaper with jobs in it. This will probably help. DO NOT FORGET: YOU ARE QUALIFIED IN MEDIA STUDIES AND CAN TYPE
2. Get some friends. You can do this by . . .
a. Enrolling in a night class. Do something like photography or life drawing, where you might meet exciting people and nude men
b. Advertising in the paper

c. Hanging around in clubs looking shifty

3. After London, tell Kelly where to stick it. If she tells Sophie and Sophie sacks you, then perhaps fate is trying to tell you something. You are obviously made for greater things

4. Try to do at least one new thing every day – don't get into a RUT, or you will end up like One Of Them. Go to the zoo, go to the pictures, read highbrow books, go to gigs on your own. It is not GOOD ENOUGH to sit on your arse while life slips away. Put yourself about a bit or nobody will notice you're here!!!

I read it back and am amazed at how easy it seems. There are all kinds of things I can do to make things better, but I've just been too preoccupied with other nonsense to do them. If I stay focused and try to tackle my plan point by point, then I should actually have a life by the end of the week. How hard can it be? I get a rush of high self-esteem and purpose and my head feels impossibly giddy. Simple! I rifle through the newspaper, looking for things to do tonight, places to go, people to see. The future seems so clear and crammed with possibilities that I want to get onto it straight away. I've got ants in my pants. I can't believe I've been such a lazy trout. I'm going to get a shower and go out and get a life, I'm going to be who I want to be for a change, rather than caring what everyone else thinks. This is the start of the new me. Hurrah!

At my feet, the phone starts ringing. I pick it up. Before she even opens her mouth to speak I can hear by the way she exhales her cigarette smoke that it's . . .

'Hello, Jane, it's your mother. Are you all right?'

41

Uh. Optimism implodes, planes come crashing out of the sky, time grinds to a halt.

'Hiya.'

'You sound funny? What's the matter?'

'Nothing.' I huff, collapsing into surly teenager mode.

'Well, what have you been doing?'

'Nothing. Working.'

'Right.' I can hear her dragging on her cigarette, the liquorice paper sizzling at the end. She smokes those brown, metre-long menthol ones. She'll be sitting in the chair by the window, legs crossed. After a hard day on her feet at Barbara's Blooms, Babs will be in her mules, fiddling with the fried ends of her perm and flipping the insole against her heel in time to the theme tune to *Ground Force*.

'What have you been doing?' I ask to fill the gap.

'Oh, it was a nightmare today. I've got two weddings on Saturday and they both want gerberas, but I don't have enough and the distributors in Holland say they can't deliver until Monday. I've got enough in storage for one bridal bouquet and one set of altar flowers, but Becky reckons I'm going to have to spread them between the two, fill it out with something else and hope for the best.'

Blaarrrrghraaaghblurrrrrrgh. I absently doodle a picture of a lighthouse perched on a rock, shooting its rays into the air. In the beam I write 'BORING' in big receding letters. Then I cross it out, feeling guilty, and write 'BARBARA' instead.

'I'm hoping that no-one will notice if we fill them out with freesias and a bit of gyp, but people are picky, aren't they. Mind you, Becky is usually right about that kind of thing, so I suppose that's what I'll do.'

'Oh yes, hmm.'

Saint Becky is always right. Sister Becky of The Immaculate Floral Arrangement. Most people would leave home at the age of 23, but not her. She stays in Leeds, helping Mum in the shop and being the model daughter, while dozy Jane goes off and makes a mess of everything. She never says it in so many words, but there's always this invisible choir of angels singing somewhere in the background when it comes to Becky, and a big clanging note of disapproval for me. She knows I got the bad genes. I'm my father's daughter. A loose cannon, an unexploded bottle rocket. Stand back and let her go off on her own.

'So how's work?'

'OK. Sophie's sending me to a travel fair in London next week.'

'London?' she gasps. 'Well, that's good, isn't it? She must think you're doing well.'

I'm seized by childish irritation. 'It's just a crappy job, Mum. I'm not particularly bothered what she thinks.'

Babs sighs and lets out an exasperated growl.

'Please don't be so negative, Jane. You're bloody annoying. If you don't like it what's the point? You should come back home rather than hanging about up there on your own.'

I scribble on the pad furiously, making a rip in the paper.

'I don't want to come back home. It's fine.'

'You don't sound fine. You sound miserable and . . . drunk. Are you drunk? Maybe you need a bit of time to figure out what you want to do. I just want you to be happy.'

AARGH!

'I HAVE figured out what to do. That's what I was

doing before you phoned. Look, Mum, it's my life and I'll figure it out by myself. And I'm not drunk, I've just had a few *well-deserved* beers after work. I don't know why everyone keeps on at me. I'm not a complete failure.'

'All right, keep your hair on, I didn't say you were,' she whines. 'I just think it'd be a good idea to come home for a week or so, that's all. Have a holiday, catch up with some of your old friends, relax for a bit. You haven't had a day off in months, no wonder you're crabby.'

I'm not CRABBY! I want to scream, which would only confirm aforementioned crabbiness. Instead I jump up from the chair and sit down again in a powerless, frustrated way.

'Anyway, it's just an idea, that's all,' she says, sighing. 'Give it a think.'

There's a lull in the conversation. I can only hear the dull thud of my heartbeat in my ears.

'Hmm. Yeah. Maybe. We'll see,' I say, hoping she'll drop it. Suddenly I feel a great weight pushing down on my head from getting up too quickly. All I want to do is go to sleep.

'Anyway,' she breezes, 'have you got anything else planned?'

My head is suddenly full of custard and I can barely process an answer.

'I don't know. I might go out on Friday night with Fiona.' I lie. Fiona has a host of friends who always come into the office, dragging her away to pubs and stuff. She wouldn't want me getting in the way. She'd no more invite me out on a Friday night than put a bucket on her head and sing the Bulgarian national anthem.

'Well, that's nice. You have a good time, darling. Are you eating OK?'

'Yes.'

From here, I can almost hear the Swamp Thing calling from the salad drawer. Remnants of last night's chicken chow mein congeal above it. Next to that is some yoghurt from 1976.

'Don't worry. I'm fine. Say hi to Becky for me.'

'Will do. I'll phone you next week. Take care, love,' she says, as if she'll never see me again.

'Yeah. Bye.'

I put the phone down and bury my face in a cushion. Why do I suddenly feel like an ill-equipped ten-year-old?

Oh, I don't feel like going out any more.

The train passes wind-blown cliffs near Berwick-upon-Tweed, lashed by waves that are the same salty grey as the sky. I wonder if I could discreetly pan Kelly's head in with the emergency hammer and throw her into the sea.

'Well, *I* think David's a TOTAL laugh a minute,' she blabs, hoping to get a rise out of me.

It's 7.35 a.m., as if there was ever a good time for this.

'The other day he said to me, "You know, girlfriend" – he always says that, like, in a Ricki Lake type of way: "GRRRLFRIEND" – he says, "You've got hair the same colour as a Bottychelly." So I was like, what? And he says, "You know that bird with ginger hair coming out of a seashell." I was like, what are you ON? He says "Bottomjelly did a painting of a woman in a seashell – she was a ginger." I didn't know what he was on about! He's MAD!'

Social nicety prevents me from slapping her with a copy of *Hello!*. Besides, it's too early. I give a polite laugh in response and hope she'll go away.

Since we met this morning she's been making a concerted effort to be nice and chatty, and somehow it's worse than the green-eyed staring. Although I may have spoken too soon. A minute later Kelly starts fiddling with her gold hoop earring and regarding me slyly. I try to read all about Martine McCutcheon's new kitchen, but my eyes keep sliding off the page. Kelly keeps on at her earring, frowning at me curiously, as if she's working out a hard sum. She eventually gives up and takes a sheaf of paper out of a pocket in her laptop bag, shuffling it around on the table efficiently. She looks like she's about to start reading the news.

Martine has a busy life, I note, but still finds time to cook her favourite meal, roast lamb and mint sauce.

Kelly switches on her bossy, professional tone.

'Right, we're going to Stand U132, and we'll have to report to Susan Chater as soon as we arrive. It'll probably be the same as last year, I should think. We've got the presentation, which should be about an hour, so you help me with that. Last year this guy called Dan came down and we had such a good time. He was really nice, but then he left to go to college. You got his job.'

I sense that this is a source of immense disappointment.

'So afterwards we make ourselves available to passing trade, do a handout, then we can have a quick look round. The train leaves at six thirty, so we have to make sure we leave about an hour before. We'll arrange to meet up at five to be on the safe side . . .'

Martine has lovely granite work surfaces. She finds it difficult to find love because she works very long hours, but when she's relaxing, she likes nothing more than making brunch for friends and family.

'Are you listening?' Kelly snaps.

'Yes. Leave at five.'

'You'd better give me your mobile number in case we lose each other.'

Chance would be a fine thing. I tell her my number and she types it into her phone – bip, bip bip. I hope I'm not going to live to regret it – she might start crank calling me in the middle of the night, threatening me about brochures.

'Last year's Destinations was brilliant,' she continues. (Did Kelly mention she went last year?) 'They've got all kinds of things to do. You can go to Africa World, and Caribbean World . . .'

I tear myself away from Martine's cuisine and realize I'm interested.

'There's even a champagne and seafood bar,' She reveals.

'Really?'

'Yes.' Kelly's on a roll now. 'And there's a celebrity theatre. They have loads of travel writers and presenters giving talks. Michael Palin's going to be doing a talk about Cape Horn at half past four.'

The air between me and Kelly seems to have warmed up considerably. Maybe she isn't such a big poo bag after all. Her pudding face is animated, pretty even.

'Wow,' I say, genuinely enthused. 'I just thought it'd be a bunch of trade people talking shop. Hey, we can get pissed and get Michael Palin to show us his Horn.'

Uh-oh.

There's an exaggerated pause, during which the man on the next table frowns at me over his copy of the *Financial Times*. Kelly's eyes narrow.

Tumbleweed blows across the table.

You could hear a pin drop in Newcastle.

Her face ices over and she leans towards me confrontationally.

'I don't think it'd be a good idea to drink while we're supposed to be working, do you, Jane?' she warns. 'It's not very professional. Maybe save it for the train on the way back.'

She pops her papers back in her bag with a little flourish that makes me want to rip her head off.

Hmm. That went well. I take a sip of stewed train coffee, which tastes like it was brewed in a tramp's pants. Kelly, now a ball of frustration, busies herself with her handbag, a smart black leather affair with organized compartments. She takes out a compact and inspects herself, then starts piling on orange face powder, sweeping it over her cheeks. How old is she? She could be my age, but the way she acts she could be in her forties. Fiona told me she lives with her mum and dad in Costorphine, the posh suburban part of Edinburgh, which is why she's got such a stick up her arse. I could have guessed as much. I wonder if she's ever been in love, or taken drugs, or clattered down the street in a shopping trolley wearing a comedy hat. She coats her thin, prissy lips with peach lip gloss and rubs them together. I notice that her mouth curls in a natural sneer, designed to find fault, bore you and generally piss on your chips. Botticelli? Mussolini, more like.

'Jane, I'd be grateful if you left most of the talking to me, if that's all right,' she says, snootily. 'I'm more, you know, experienced than you. I just want everything to run smoothly.'

'Fine,' I say, watching another train thunk past the window. 'Doesn't bother me.'

She inspects herself in the mirror again, then sighs and shifts about all kinds of ways in her seat.

'Don't you ever wear make-up?' she asks, with a sharp edge of annoyance in her voice.

'What?'

'You KNOW,' she says. 'Lipstick? Eyeshadow? Mascara?'

'Only when I'm going out.'

'I see. You'd look quite nice with dark eyes, I reckon. Kind of a smoky look. You should make more of yourself.'

'Mmm.' How about a black eye, Kelly? Want one of those?

I turn the page of my magazine and fixate on Santa Palmer-Tomkinson's baby shower at a top Belgravia hotel. Good turnout of double-barrelled names. Sebag-Montefiore, Monkton-Fitchett, Twattington-Smythe . . . there's a mountain of designer baby clothes and a cake in the shape of two bootees and a rattle. 'Just adorable,' says the bejewelled Lady Vincent of Bath and Wells, who looks like a battery chicken with an overactive thyroid.

I look up briefly, surprised to find that Kelly is still banging on.

'But that would be for night. I reckon for day you'd suit just a touch of foundation, a bit of mascara and perhaps some brownish eye shadow, with some clear gloss or rose pink to emphasize your lips. And maybe your hair could be a bit more . . . styled.'

It dawns on me that Kelly thinks about this a lot. She probably has a plastic Girl's World representation of my head at home. What does she care?

'I just reckon it would make you feel better about yourself. You've got a bone structure lots of girls would kill for. I mean, no offence, Jane, but you don't seem to care much for your appearance.'

I can't begin to think what to say next.

So I come up with a scathing and well-considered retort: 'Oh, OK. Well, er . . . right.'

There's an uncomfortable silence. Gum. Gum will stop me screaming. I take a tab from my pocket and rhythmically chew in time to the rattle of the train, eyes fixed on the landscape. I try to conjure up Brad. He would stride down the aisle towards my seat, wearing a tight little T-shirt and jeans that perfectly advertise his mighty fine arse. Then he'd grab the back of my head and give me a big dirty kiss in front of an astounded Kelly. 'She's beautiful just the way she is,' he'd say. 'Unlike you, pork breath.'

Kelly goes back to rummaging around in her handbag, without a trace of embarrassment. In fact, she seems to have cheered up considerably. Then she starts humming a song that sounds suspiciously like Westlife in a mangled cat voice. I have to get away from her.

'I'm going to the buffet car. Do you want anything?'

Kelly's face lights up.

'Ooh, can you get me a chunky KitKat and a packet of McCoy's?'

Oink. 'Yeah sure. What flavour?'

'Er . . . smoky bacon, if they've got them.'

Figures. I walk down the train carriage, feeling trapped. It's going to be a long, long day. Even at the buffet I can smell her skunky perfume, which seems to have welded itself to the insides of my nostrils. 'You don't care much for your appearance, do you, Jane?' What a cheeky cow.

I toy with the idea of stamping on her KitKat. But it wouldn't do any good. I feel so repulsive. The man in charge of the buffet doesn't even look at me when I order. The person in the queue next to me pushes past as if I'm invisible.

When I get back, Kelly's on her mobile, gassing away, probably bitching about me. I hear her giggling and saying, 'She said this' and 'She said that' in a quiet hiss. When she sees me, she looks momentarily guilty.

'She's here, do you want to speak to her?' Kelly mouths the word, 'David.'

Oh great. She hands me the phone.

'Well hello, DARLING!'

'Hello, David,' I say in an artificially upbeat voice.

'What colour knickers are you wearing?'

'What?'

'Grey and baggy or a THONG?'

'What?'

'Ooh, you tease! Well I hope you're having a good time without me. You two dirty birds on the loose in the big smoke, it doesn't bear thinking about. I'm so jealous. Kelly tells me you're looking fabulous today as well.'

I glare at Kelly, demolishing her crisps like a gannet.

'Mmm. Don't know about that.'

'Ooh, you've got a sexy husky voice, Darling. Mmm. I could really get into this phone-sex malarkey, it's giving me quite a thrill. Talk dirty to me . . . uh! Yeah! You're turning me ON! UUUUUUUUHHHH!'

'Er, I'd better go. Talk to you soon. I'll just put you back on to Kelly. Bye.'

I hand her the phone and slump into my seat, praying for the day to be over. Kelly is burbling into the receiver, but I don't hear what she's saying. They're probably concocting other new and interesting ways to humiliate me. Outside there's a rolling backdrop of trees, forests, rivers and pylons. Reflected in the thick glass I can see a distorted double image of my face, with grotesque grey skin and pinched lips. An ugly old cow chewing the cud.

London is absolutely sweltering. King's Cross is a greenhouse and the second we get off the train Kelly turns into Pol Pot and starts barking orders, even though I can tell she's panicking and has no idea where she's going. With her dumpy frame and too-brisk walk, she seems hopelessly out of her depth in a big city. I trail behind her as she navigates the underground with all the urban sophistication of Elmer Fudd, getting snarled up in the turnstile, standing on the wrong side of the escalator, bending her ticket. I feel fleetingly superior and cosmopolitan in comparison. By the time we get to Earls Court, Kelly has worked herself up into an indignant fury.

'God, that was a nightmare. London people are so pushy,' she says. 'Last year we got a cab.'

'Oh, right. OK.'

(Don't care. Not listening.)

As I follow Kelly into the vastness of Earls Court I feel the misery of the train journey slowly recede. I might be starting to have a good time. The exhibition is so much bigger and flashier than I'd expected, each stand promising carefree times in distant lands. Thrills and excitement await in the Rocky Mountains, love blossoms on sandy beaches, pulses race on the pistes. There's a fibreglass elephant in Africa World and a replica of a desert island with real palm trees. The cool air-conditioning is laced with the smell of coconut suntan lotion. Suddenly it hits me. What am I doing wasting the best years of my life in a tourist office when I could be having a proper adventure? I should be *in* the brochures rather than giving them out. I could be anywhere. Eating noodles in Tokyo, striding confidently through the Kalahari desert with a bottle of Evian, whitewater rafting up the Zambezi. Why am I torturing myself?

I wander past the glossy posters, seducing me with their shiny leisure possibilities, and feel an epiphany coming on. All I need to do is save some money and go somewhere. Get on a plane and a few hours later I'll be on the beach, drinking a cocktail. Why didn't I think of it before? What's a photography class or a personal ad in a magazine compared to paradise? Edinburgh's not the only place in the world. Why the hell am I living in a cupboard in a roof and working in a boring job with a bunch of arseholes? I could be the toast of Kontiki. I could be rustling my grass skirt in the direction of some surfer pinhead with a huge gleaming board.

'Hurry up, Jane. Susan will be waiting for us,' Kelly squeals, racing ahead.

AND, if I ran away then I'd never have to see Kelly again. Yeah! Excitement flutters in my chest. A rather attractive man on the Kuoni stand hands me a leaflet and my fingers brush against his. It's the first physical contact I've had in ages and it brings on a completely unwarranted buzz of desire. I walk past in slow motion in a breeze of Ambre Solaire and look at the flyer – two people languish on a sand dune gazing at a deep red sunset. I can taste freedom. It's just around the corner. I can escape.

'Ah, at last. Helloo, I'm Susan Chaterrrrgh. I'm the deputy managerrrggggh of the Scottish tourist boarrrd.'

Just around the corner, my bubble is cruelly and suddenly lanced with a kilt pin. I realize I've reached our destination and I'm trailing about a minute behind Kelly, who is standing as if waiting for a military inspection. In the Scotland section fragrant wafts of Ambre Solaire are replaced by a rather unpleasant mossy odour. It could be coming from Susan Chhhhrrrghhhghr. She's a humourless figure dressed in a dull green blouse, standing proudly next to a dummy of William Wallace in a glass case. He looks marginally more feminine. She surveys my rumpled clothes with a mixture of fascination and horror.

'I thought yooood be cominghh eargggghlier. Well, I sooopose you'rggghh hereggh nooo. Kelly, deaaargh, your tableggh is oover thereggh if yoo want to set yourself up. If you need technical supportggh then give me a shout. What's yourgggh name?' Susan regards me with suspicion and I realize she's talking to me.

'Eh?'

'Susan, this is Jane,' Kelly schmoozes. 'She's my assistant today.'

How far I have come in life. Assistant to a five-foot-nothing orange-haired gonk with a laptop and a Napoleon complex. Susan, who has remarkably large nostrils, sniffs disapprovingly.

'Well took yourggh bloouse in properly dearrggh. You look like a traamp.'

'Pardon?'

'You might want to sort oot yoor hairgggh in the mirrrorrrr, too.' Susan looks worried and starts wringing her hands.

'Come on then, Jane. Don't just stand there. We've got to set up!' Kelly chirps. Jittery and confused, I rake my hand through my hair and trail after Kelly. We go behind a curtain with 'Scotland' printed on it. A sign says 'Edinburgh, Tradition and Invention. Presentation 1 p.m.' It all seems quite important and organized. Inside the makeshift room a large table is set up with bottles of Highland Spring and press packs. On the felt-covered wall there's a blank screen. I thought Kelly would just be fruitlessly waving her laser pointer as passers-by flicked things at her, then I'd hand out three flyers and make myself scarce. This is like the frigging United Nations.

'Is this for the public, then?'

Kelly sighs and speaks slowly, as if I'm a small, uncomprehending child.

'No. A group of delegates from Air Canada are having a tour of the exhibition and Susan has organized this talk to try and persuade them to establish a new direct route to Scotland.'

'Oh,' I say, feeling unstuck. I stopped paying attention after she said the word 'delegate'. 'Sophie didn't tell me anything about it.'

'Didn't she? Hold that, will you?'

Kelly hands me a black box with a scart plug sticking out of it. She begins expertly attaching cables to a projector as I stand there uselessly. My mouth has gone dry.

'So what do I do?'

'Just back me up, follow my lead. I've worked it all out, so if anybody asks you anything, you politely deflect the question and let me take control. Susan is bringing some people from Edinburgh airport and the Aviation Authority, then they'll give a talk. We'll go through it quickly before they arrive.'

'OK.'

For the first time ever I feel grateful towards her, relieved that at least *she* knows what she's doing. Kelly looks convincingly professional. She suddenly seems taller, her face is kinder and her fingers have gone from thick pink sausages to nimble digits, capable of complicated technical feats. I feel every inch her junior. I straighten my skirt as best I can, wishing I'd bothered to iron it properly.

'Don't look so worried,' Kelly says, looking genuinely hearty. 'Just smile. I've got it all under control.'

The Canadian delegates eventually shuffle in, sporting various degrees of baldness and shades of grey, followed by a smartly dressed woman with a helmet of hair the colour of peanut butter. Behind her Susan Chatergggggh gurgles her way through another incomprehensible sentence, spraying the Aviation Authority people with genuine Scottish spit and trailing the sinister mossy smell. Kelly greets them all with supreme confidence, shaking hands, introducing me and suavely directing them to their seats. I feel utterly bemused, as if I've just woken from a coma and found myself at a cocktail party.

'Jane, would you hand round the brochures, please?' Kelly chirrups.

'Uh, yes, absolutely.'

'Welcome to Edinburgh,' she jokes, addressing the room with twinkling, polished efficiency. 'Well, not quite. But today we're going to try and recreate it as faithfully as possible, as well as bringing some of its fascinating history to life.'

Kelly might be a stumpy windbag, but she seems to know what she's doing. I look around the room, smile pinned on firmly, and mechanically hand out the information packs – glossy slabs of utter shite.

'Jaaaane. Ah don't have a brooooouchooooore.' Susan Chrrrrrgh burbles from the end of the table, waving her hand in the air as if she's drowning.

'Oops, sorry,' I chirp, leaning over to pass her one. As I reach out, I knock over an unopened bottle of water with my left boob. From the other side of the table, one Canadian, a man in his fifties with a leathery tan, winks at me. Oh God. Repositioning the water with the minimum of fuss, I sit down next to Kelly and smile at her idiotically.

'So,' Kelly says, sending me a warning look. 'If you all have your literature to hand, I'd just like to start with a wee bit of history. Now, the first thing you probably think of when you hear the name Edinburgh is the castle.'

An image of the castle, taken on a crisp autumn day, flashes up on the screen behind her.

'The site where the castle stands has been a fortification since 6AD, maybe even earlier,' says Kelly. 'Malcolm the third used it as a royal residence in the eleventh century and nowadays the oldest existing building in Edinburgh is St Margaret's Chapel, built in the twelfth century.'

Click. There's an image of what looks like an old shed, covered in lichen, possibly Susan Chaterrrggh's house.

'It was named after Margaret, Malcolm's wife, who was known for her generosity towards the poor. She brought piety to Scotland. Margaret's son, David I, built the Abbey at Holyrood, a mile to the East along the Royal Mile.'

Click. A photo of the Royal Mile.

I shift in my seat. God this is boring. Couldn't she jazz it up a bit?

'The castle and Abbey became the anchor points of Edinburgh, and a thriving town grew up alongside the road between them, connected to Leith, Edinburgh's port and trade link to the world. By the end of the fifteen hundreds,' she blabbers, 'the population of

Edinburgh grew and it was established as the capital of Scotland. Back then the city was very different from what you see today.'

Kelly clicks again, but something has gone wrong with her laptop, and the screen shows an error message.

I look around at the already glazed eyes of the Canadians. One is doodling something on his notebook. I feel like I should do something. Kelly is getting red in the face, frantically tapping at her mouse.

'Sorry about this,' she squeaks. 'Just some gremlins. Won't be a minute.'

There's a terrible 30 seconds of dead air as she fiddles with the keyboard.

'You see, Edinburgh is built on volcanic rock,' I blurt randomly. 'The site where the castle stands is actually a massive dormant volcano.'

I notice a look of alarm from Kelly.

'Oh don't worry, Kelly, it hasn't blown up in ages,' I joke stupidly, trying to relieve the tension.

There is a smattering of relieved Canadian sniggers and a snort from Chhgggrrr. Suddenly the mood shifts. Kelly smiles at me murderously.

'ANYWAY, the reason the city has changed so much is this . . .' I carry on, strangely incapable of keeping my mouth shut. 'Initially, in the fifteen hundreds, the people of Edinburgh were so paranoid about having their city invaded that they built really tall tenements near the castle for protection. Some of them still exist, but a lot of them became slums and had to be demolished. The thing is, because the volcanic rock is so hard and difficult to build on, it was cheaper and easier to build the new city on TOP of the foundations of the old buildings. So underneath the present-day city there's a ghost town, a never-ending network of streets and alleyways. It's said that some of them are even haunted.'

I sit back and realize there are five pairs of rapt Canadian eyes staring at me. Kelly's mouth hangs open in a rather unladylike fashion.

'Haunted?' asks the woman with the Sunpat hair.

'Well, of course, it depends what you believe,' I say, warming to the subject. 'But in a particularly grim period of the city's history, the town council were so at their wits' end about how to contain the bubonic plague that they locked any sufferers into a part of the underground city called Mary King's Close. There were hundreds of them, trapped in tiny rooms and left to die from their terrible, OOZING wounds. It was unthinkable. Since then, there've been reliable sightings of strange and disturbing phenomena. In one incident in the early twentieth century, a priest and his wife stayed in one of the disused rooms. She was woken in the night by a terrifying clanking noise, and all she could see were thousands of thin, pointy knives and forks dancing in a bizarre formation. I mean, I've been there and I'm telling you, it's REALLY creepy. People think that Edinburgh is just tartan and shortbread, but there are all kinds of intriguing secrets beneath the surface. You just have to know where to look.'

Jesus. What am I ON about?

One Canadian man with bushy eyebrows shudders delightedly.

'Ugh. That's freaky!'

'Not that I want to put you off.' I laugh, nervously, worrying I might have ruined everything. 'Things are much more civilized these days. The only knives and forks you see are in the restaurants. And we don't lock

60

people in dungeons any more – not if they behave themselves, anyway.'

Oh I'm an idiot. Kelly is glowering at me. I've ruined everything. But the Canadians and Susan Chaterrrrgh must have completely retarded senses of humour because they're all laughing.

'So, can you visit these places?' asks one.

'Yes, there's a guided tour every day,' I mumble, picking up a leaflet from my pack. 'Here. Don't go on your own, though.'

The Canadian flashes a toothpaste grin and thanks me, throwing a satisfied glance at Susan, who is practically beaming.

Kelly's screen is now fixed and showing a picture of Leith docks.

'Thank you, Jane, for your contribution,' Kelly sneers. 'Edinburgh is also interesting for its shipping industry . . .'

I stare at the table and bite my lip. I'm going to pay for this, I can tell.

'For God's sake, Jane, what the hell was THAT about?' she growls, winding a wire round her fist and making it into a noose. The room is empty again, airless, fugged up with Canadian cologne and an undertone of Susan Chaterragggh's sweaty tights.

Here we are again, back at square one. If Kelly were a cartoon she'd have two jets of steam parping out of her ears.

'What?'

'You KNOW what.'

'I was only trying to introduce an element of titillation and intrigue,' I protest as Kelly makes a cat's anus with her mouth. 'People love those ghost tours. They like gore. At least they were entertained.'

'Are you saying I wasn't entertaining?' she huffs.

'No. I was just trying to make it a bit less . . . dry.'

'What, by talking about OOZING?'

'Well I think they might have enjoyed it.'

'That's not what I told you to do. Anyway, forget it. Go and get a box of brochures.'

She whips the curtain aside like a pantomime villain and stalks off. For the next half hour she doesn't say much, so I assume I'm in the doghouse. She's so prissy, I think to myself. Everything has to be done her way. We hang around, giving bored passers-by leaflets that they immediately shove into the nearest bin, until Susan Chaterrrrggh appears, having dispatched the Canadians. Susan tells us we've done a good job, praising my entertaining and 'highly original' contribution. Ha! I sideways glance at Kelly, but she's got her teeth gritted as if she's being impaled on a spike. Then my new mate Susan takes Kelly aside and they talk for ages. Kelly's probably trying to crawl up her arse, complimenting her on the colour of the table-cloths and the accessibility of the plug sockets, so I carry on dishing out leaflets until Susan comes up and sets us free for the day. She still seems ridiculously chuffed and even pats me on the shoulder, showering me with a fine coating of spittle.

'See,' I say to Kelly, following her back through the curtain and watching as she puts her laptop back into its bag. 'They liked it.'

She grunts and fiddles about with the zipper. I pick up an unopened bottle of Highland Spring from the table and wait for her to finish faffing about. She stops, her shoulders slumped.

'What's the matter?' I ask.

Kelly's back is a blank wall cut in half by her bra, which I can see plainly through her blouse. She's breathing strangely, like an overexerted horse. Suddenly she spins round and turns on me.

'You are so insensitive! Why couldn't you have let me take the lead? All Susan talked about was YOU! I've worked for MONTHS to get this right and you come along and spoil everything, as usual. Do you think that had something to do with you putting me off with your stupid comments? I told you to leave the talking to me!'

'I'm sorry, I was just trying to help . . . you were . . . your . . . thingy was broken.'

'Can't you take anything seriously? Is everything a joke to you? Is everything just an excuse for you to take the piss?' She raises her chin defiantly. 'Answer me this, Jane. What do you care about?'

'What do I . . . ?'

'You don't seem to give a toss about your job, and as far as I can see you don't seem to like anything or anyone. You SABOTAGED my presentation. Why are you even here? Come on, what's the point?' she demands. Her chubby arms are folded tightly in front of her.

There's a fat, bruised silence. I can hear music from the interactive exhibition next door: bagpipes playing a supremely dreary version of 'Flower Of Scotland'.

She doesn't buy my bolshy, don't-give-a-fuck exterior any more than I do. Kelly's suspicious beady eyes are burrowing directly into my soul. I feel like a slug, left to shrivel under a mountain of salt.

Why am I here? What *is* the point?

I don't know, I just don't know.

My vision is blurring with tears. Please God, don't let me cry in front of Kelly.

'Sophie's such an idiot. Why did she have to invite you?' she wonders aloud, snapping her case shut. She stands there, wounded and insolent.

'I didn't mean to . . .' I begin, trying to keep it together. 'I'm going to look round the exhibition now.' I say slowly. 'See you at five at the Caribbean Island.'

Kelly loses some of her confidence and her arms drop to her sides.

'Yeah that's right, run away.' She sneers unconvincingly.

I walk off, my eyes prickling, waiting until I get to Ireland before I wipe them on the back of my sleeve. What a complete bitch. Everything aches. I traipse around the hall, feeling sorry for myself. My stomach is tight, my feet are swollen, my head is pounding. Across the vast room I can see the fibreglass elephant, but it looks in need of Prozac. Faded, crumpled people trudge through a carpet of leaflets, bins overflow with burger cartons. The air is full of fatigue and irritation, most of it coming from me. Kelly's words echo in time to my steps. 'What-do-you-care-about . . . why-are-you-even-here.'

I can't do anything right.

I need to sort myself out.

She's right, after all, isn't she? If you don't like anything or anyone, what *is* the point?

I walk the earth for a while, through Africa and Europe, and it feels depressingly small.

My mouth is bone dry. I need a drink.

As if by magic, the Wines Of The World stand looms up in front of me, an oasis in the desert. Empty plastic cups litter the counter and amateur wine tasters, degenerates and alcoholics hang around it, sampling the tiny freebies. Worming my way through the crowd, using my tried-and-tested Slovenian-stealth technique, I cadge a few drinks from the rapidly diminishing trays. I empty a plastic pint glass containing napkins and slosh five different samples into it. Then I neck it, leaning against a fake wine barrel spewing plastic grapes and vines.

Relief. Warmth floods through my body. I relax and let my mind swim. No Kelly or Susan or David or Sophie or Mum or Queenie, no Edinburgh or Leeds or London. I'm neither here nor there.

I sway backwards and forwards for a long time, staring into space, brain completely disengaged. A pleasant vibrating sensation, probably from the wine fridges, lulls me into a trance.

Soon I become aware of a rumbling noise. I'm starving. Maybe I should have some food. My stomach has started eating itself. Who am I again? The last thing I ate was a sandwich on the train, some dismal ham affair that cost a fiver. That was about six hours ago. Did the ginger whinger say something about a seafood bar? I set off, a bit wobbly, trying to find some tasty crustaceans. I start walking in the direction of the Caribbean, but my legs want to take me to Asia. As I wander aimlessly through the crowds, all those amazing adventures start to look woefully tacky. I pass Kuoni man again, but he isn't even fit. In fact, he looks like Peter Beardsley. How could I have been taken in? The last day of the travel fair is winding down – some stalls have closed, others are taking down their advert boards and dismantling their tables. I notice some of the gaudy posters are stuck up with drawing pins, ripped at the edges. Dazzling stretches of coastline are creased and torn, a suntanned bikini babe, tipping her head back and laughing, has a fold in her face, making her look deformed. Happiness can't be bought, why did I think that? Come to the white beaches of Barbados and get sand in your crack. Broken bones on the piste, have your handbag nicked in Greece, get the squits in St Moritz. You never really get away from it all. Things follow you around like a bad smell.

'Jane! It's past six o clock! I've been phoning you for the last ten minutes.'

Kelly, sweating Eau de Skunk, grabs my arm. She's purple and flapping, beside herself with panic. Have I really been away for two hours?

'Have you? My phone's on vibrate. Oh,' I say, realizing my mistake. Wine fridges indeed.

'We'llnevergettoKingsCrossintimetocatchthetrain we'regoingtomissit,' she gabbles. I stand there, motionless, unable to work out what she's saying. She hops from one foot to the other as if she needs a wee, and I smile vacantly.

'It's rush hour,' she pleads randomly. 'Where've you been?'

'Uhhrr.'

'Are you DRUNK?' she howls. 'Oh well, that's great! Come on!'

She forcibly hauls me towards the exit. I'm surprised at how strong she is. I allow myself to follow the slipstream of her hideous perfume, quite enjoying being someone else's responsibility. Then we're in the cool, calm interior of a taxi. London slinks by slowly, a blur of grey buildings, red buses and phoneboxes, office workers in shirtsleeves, wilting in the heat. I'm parched. I fumble in my bag for the bottle of water I nicked, but it isn't there. The traffic is terrible; we must only be going at about three miles an hour. Kelly jiggles about in her seat, frantically craning her neck to see out of the side window, the back window and the wing mirrors. As if looking worried is going to get us to the station any faster.

'The traffic is terrible,' I casually observe.

Kelly stares at me in anger and disbelief.

'I'm sorry,' I slur. 'I was just saying.'

She's furious, her face wild.

'You knew we were booked on the six thirty.'

'I lost track of time.'

She wants to hit me. If I were her, I'd want to hit me. I really am a rubbish anti-social person. What has Kelly ever done to me? Glared at me a bit. Pointed out a few home truths. Told me I should smarten myself up and put on some eyeshadow. Not exactly high treason. The cab judders to a standstill. It's twenty past six and the station is on the other side of London.

'It would probably have been quicker on the tube,' I volunteer.

There's a sour silence.

'God, you really are a fucking loser, aren't you?'

The words come from the back of her throat and sound low and strange, as if she's possessed. I've never heard Kelly swear – I wasn't even aware she knew how. Maybe she'd say sugar or bugger, but never that, never in a million years. I open my mouth to apologize, but the world is so loaded against me that there's nothing I can say to redeem myself. Kelly's right. Tomorrow she can tell everyone about my unprofessional behaviour and Sophie can sack me and I'll be out of their lives for ever. Someone else will replace me who doesn't get wankered at travel fairs and swear at customers and Jane Darling will be history, her name tag melted down and her tartan uniform recycled to make musical oven gloves.

*   *   *

At 6.40 p.m., I'm standing outside WHSmith in King's Cross, keeping away from her. Kelly is inside buying magazines and various things to cram into her gob. There's another train at seven anyway, so all is not lost. And I paid the cab, which cost a not inconsiderable amount, in the hope of clawing back some self-respect. It didn't make me feel better, though.

I watch the board flickering. There's a train to Leeds in five minutes. I'm tempted to just get on it and go home. Go back and work in the florists, like Babs wants me to. It'd suit everybody else down to the ground. But at 6.45 I'm still there, rooted to the spot like an obedient dog, waiting for Kelly to come out.

'It's platform fourteen,' she says as she clatters past. I trail after her. Fiona's right, she really does have an arse the size of Germany. If she was on the motorway she'd need a police escort. I wonder if Kelly and I will ever patch things up. Maybe if I ran up to her and grabbed her flabby buttcheeks with both hands she'd laugh uproariously and we'd become lifelong friends. 'Do you remember when we went to London?' she'd laugh, years from now. 'I thought you were a twat, but then you gave me a wedgie and I realized you were all right.' I feel like doing it, anything to defuse the situation.

Perhaps not.

Instead I dutifully board the train. Inside, cleaners finish off tidying up the debris from the previous passengers, cramming well-thumbed magazines and food wrappers into black bin bags. The carriage is stale, the seat cushions puckered. Kelly leads the way and chooses a seat carefully, neatly placing her bag in the luggage rack. I sit opposite and dump mine on the table. I sneak a look at Kelly, who is studiously ignoring me.

'I'm sorry. I didn't mean to spoil everything.'

She shrugs and starts flipping through *Cosmo*.

Right. Fine.

Seems like Brad is the only person who likes me at the moment. I close my eyes and try to find him. We're in the car, no, a hotel, let's not beat about the bush. A cheap motel room with a vibrating bed? No, too tacky . . . maybe just an ordinary hotel room . . . he's standing there and I'm on the bed . . . no I'm standing up . . . aw, shit.

I can't get comfortable.

I wriggle about, trying to find a position I can sleep in, and put my elbow on the arm rest.

A sharp point jabs my arm.

I look down.

There's a book down the side of my seat.

Interesting.

Maybe I'll read while Kelly sulks all the way to Edinburgh. I prize it out and put it on my lap. Its black cover gives nothing away. I open it and a photograph slips out. It's a monochrome profile of a man. I glance up at Kelly, but she's oblivious, engrossed in an article about Botox. I flick through it. It's a pocket diary for business appointments, about the size of a postcard. But it hasn't got any appointments in it. Instead, the week-to-view boxes are overflowing with tiny, elegant, sharp handwriting. Some pages are covered in detailed drawings and doodles, others are left blank. At the back there's a thin plastic pocket stuffed with receipts and bits of scrap paper. A faint thrill goes through me. On the inside cover is the name Richard Miles. For some reason my heart lurches with recognition, as if it's someone I know. I scan the carriage and platform for anyone who might be the man in the photo, but there's nobody.

Wow.

He's a fox.

What a weird thing to find. It's almost like a joke. A handsome man has dropped into my lap.

Oh shut up, Jane. It isn't yours. Give it to a member of staff.

His handwriting is perfect.

Give it to a member of staff.

He's gorgeous.

Richard Miles. Who is he?

Kelly sighs, licks her finger and turns to the horoscopes. I catch her eye and she looks away. The tannoy crackles into life.

'Ladies and Gentlemen, welcome to the nineteen hundred hours GNER express service to Edinburgh, stopping at Peterborough, Doncaster, York, Darlington, Newcastle, and Berwick-upon-Tweed, due to arrive in Edinburgh at twenty-three fifty-eight . . .'

The train backs out of the gloomy station and the carriage is electrified by late evening sun. The sudden light blinds me and the diary burns in my hands, promising the world.

I feel very, very weird.

Everything seems magnified and jittering with life. The celebrities in Fiona's paper are winking, made up of a million tiny points of ink which dissolve and reform as she flicks the pages. I can feel the hairs on my arms standing up to the almost imperceptible draughts she makes as she moves from the showbiz section to the horoscopes. Val's cough, which sounds as loud as the one o'clock cannon, bounces off the hollow chrome of the chair legs and clatters through my bones.

This is . . . this is . . . I don't know what it is.

Tuesday 8th February

On the way to work today I played a game – the one where you ask the universe a question and wait for the world to give you a sign. It could be anything, magpies, black cats, superstitious crap like that. I was feeling pissed off and lonely so I asked it, 'When will I find somebody?' and waited . . . I got 'Danger'. Then I got 'Caution', then I got 'Stop'. Suppose it serves me right for playing it on the train. Don't know what I was expecting it to say. 'She's behind you?' Anyway, I'm an idiot to think I can control the world and make it do what I want. I can't even control my own life. I wish I could just turn round and say STOP, too. But it's so beyond me now that I need divine intervention, I need a miracle. Sometimes it feels like my life's a terrible plotless film, straight to video, not even good enough for channel five, and whoever's directing it should be shot. I've lost my way and I'm sick of it. I want my close-up. I want my reward. I want to be in charge of my own destiny rather than at the mercy of everyone else, but I just don't know where to start.

Underneath, he's drawn an accomplished picture of a magic eightball. In the window, he's written, 'Ask Again Later.'

'What are you reading?'

Val sidles up to me, chuffing away on one of her navvy fags.

'Nothing,' I squeak, slamming the book shut.

'Is it dirty?' she leers. She blows such an enormous cloud of chemical blue smoke into the air that it looks like the aftermath of a gas explosion. For a moment I can't breathe, but such trivialities as breathing don't seem to matter right now.

I stare dumbly at her.

Richard Miles can draw, he can write, he's creative, he's rebellious, he's a shot of adrenalin. He's amazing.

I want to meet him.

I don't think I've taken my hands off the diary since I found it. It's like it's talking directly to me. Every time I open the book I feel closer to him. Every time I read a page he tells me a secret. Instead of shutting things out, he writes down his thoughts fearlessly, trying to make sense of his life. He gets right down to the nitty gritty and sees through the bullshit. He's honest with himself. Exactly what I should be, instead of sitting here, day in day out, just existing, staring at Kelly's pissed-off, curdled milk face and worrying about what everyone thinks of me. My nerves have been doing a stupid jig ever since I found it. In the photograph, he's poised and frowning, a beautiful specimen with strong fine bones and full lips, but he seems tired and troubled. He looks like he's reaching out for someone. He looks like he's waiting for something to happen.

Maybe he's waiting for . . . me.

No.

I blush and feel like an idiot for even thinking it.

'Well you're a ray of sunshine, I must say,' Val wheezes.

I stash it away in my bag and hide it under my seat, in case Val decides to stick her nose in. Fiona starts crunching noisily on her breakfast – a packet of salt and vinegar Hula Hoops. Sophie is peering intently at me, stirring sugar into her coffee. She taps her spoon against her mug three times. I dimly watch her do it, ding ding ding. The mug is an intense, flaring yellow, bearing the side-splitting slogan: 'No Coffee, No Workee.'

'Are you all right, Jane?' she asks, concerned. 'You look a bit pale.'

'Oh . . . yeah. I'm fine. Bit tired.' I smile.

'Long train journeys are a drag, aren't they?'

'Yeah.'

Kelly waltzes in. She throws me a disapproving look and I immediately tense up. Today she's looking spectacularly evil, her curls scraped severely into an air-stewardess bun.

'Morning Kelly,' Sophie chirps. 'How was yesterday? Jane tells me it all went well.'

Kelly puts her handbag on the hook and chews a wasp. Please. Please keep your trap shut. Please don't say anything incriminating.

'Yes, it did. They were quite impressed with the presentation, by all accounts.' She walks past me, ignoring me, and busies herself with the kettle.

'Excellent. Well, Susan was singing your praises from the rooftops. She said Jane was very entertaining and funny, and that you provided a good solid structure for the talk. She said you were an excellent double act!'

I cringe. I can't see Kelly's expression, but I can feel her hackles rising. Fiona laughs, spraying a jet of half-chewed Hula Hoop onto the showbiz section. Behind her paper I can see her choking and fumbling for her asthma inhaler.

'It wasn't exactly like that,' Kelly huffs. 'It was serious work.'

'Yes. Kelly did all of it. We weren't the Two Ronnies, or anything. I didn't do anything really,' I defer, worried the conversation might take a turn for the worse and I'll end up getting bollocked again.

'Well, what matters is you worked as a TEAM,' Sophie clucks. 'I'm very proud of my clever girls. Hey, we should call you the Two Ronnies from now on. Kelly, you can be the short one with the glasses.'

'They've both got glasses,' Val chimes in, watching me cagily.

'Have they?' says Sophie.

Fiona is gutting herself, a rustling, pink-faced, breathless mess. Our eyes meet and I allow myself a tiny smirk, but Kelly catches me and throws me a blood-chilling, you're-out-of-a-job glare. The rent is due on my multicoloured hovel soon. I fix my gaze on a piece of blackened chewing gum trodden into the lino and try to stop the corners of my mouth from trembling.

'Jane, don't look so preoccupied,' says Sophie. 'Give yourself a pat on the back.'

'Och, she's away with the fairies today,' Val pipes up. 'I wouldnae be surprised if she was in LOVE.'

Oh my God! Suddenly panic-stricken, I look at Val's gurning know-it-all mug. Her short, grey perm sits on top of her head like a scouring pad. It's all fags and bingo and Bacardi Breezers to Val. Cocks and fannies. What does she know about love? Shut it. Just shut it!

'I'm not *in love*,' I say, hoping I don't sound rattled. Behind her, Dumb Paul, who I didn't even notice had come into the room, is watching me with mute interest.

'I've been reading this book and it's quite . . . complicated.'

'Oh, I love it when you get so into a book you can't put it down,' gushes Sophie. 'I was reading that, what's it called, John Grisham thing. Oh, what was it? Anyway, it was great. I got so engrossed I forgot to pick Hector up from nursery. He was standing outside holding his drawing of a dinosaur for half an hour before the teacher phoned me. She was fuming! I thought she was going to call social services.'

The subject changes to Hector's life-threatening nut allergy, discovered during an ill-fated family visit to a nougat factory, and I'm off the hook again. I don't know what to do about this man. Passages in the diary are etching themselves onto my brain. He keeps saying he's lost. On the 27th of July he's written, *I'm trying so hard but I'm lost. I'm unravelling.* The loop of the 'g' trails off into a wobbly line, then twists into a dark, impenetrable scribble. For some reason it makes me want to cry. I wrap a strand of my straggly hair round my finger and let it fall loose.

'What's it about?' Sophie asks, and I realize she's talking to me.

'What?'

'The book, what's it about?'

'Oh. I don't know. I don't know yet.'

'I cannae be bothered with aw that crap,' says Val, picking the potatoes out of her ear. 'I'm no really one for mysteries. Cannae stand the suspense.'

Right, OK. Richard is sitting on the train, doing his usual commute, his refined profile silhouetted against the window. I'm sitting across the aisle from him and the diary is in my bag. I keep feeling his gaze on me, a strong, unmistakable heat, and I know it's him, I know. I turn to him, gathering the courage to speak. Feeling lightheaded I sit down next to him. I can't believe I'm doing this. He's radiating warmth, he smells of sugar and spice and all things nice. 'I think this is yours,' I say and I give him the diary, my hands shaking. He looks down at it and blushes, then looks at me with dark, dark eyes, eyes you would die for, eyes that could inspire reams of shit poetry, and says in a soft, quiet, intelligent voice. . . what would he say?

Oh, this is getting ridiculous.

The canteen smell of Queenie's old-lady dinner wafts through the floorboards. I'm trying to dye my hair and piece together enigmatic strangers at the same time and I can't sleep or eat for thinking about it. Two days, it's been, and I'm nearly dead. Fate has flung us together and I feel like I have to do something about it.

I've scattered all the receipts and bits of paper from the diary across the floor, hoping to avoid staining the edges with hair dye. I feel guilty being so morbidly interested in his personal details. If anyone I know saw me doing this they'd put me away. I stuck his photo on the wall, but took it down again feeling like a stalker. Something tells me it's only a matter of time before I start putting it under my pillow, kissing it and changing my name to Mrs Miles.

Aside from his articulate writing skills, his prolific sketches and dreamy black irises that seem to be looking into the future (*our* future! Oh shut up, Jane), here's the concrete evidence. A ticket for a gig in London for a band I've never heard of called Starlette. They sound like a feminine hygiene product. Then there's a receipt from what looks to be a rather posh restaurant in Newcastle, paid by Mastercard – £62, generous tip – and on the back of it, in his spiky, restless hand, is written '8 p.m. (Monument Metro)'. An e-mail address is scrawled hastily (drunkenly?) on a torn cigarette packet – Saraholsen@shark.net. A girlfriend? Sarah Olsen. Sara Holsen. S. Arseholen. Did he take her to dinner? I imagine a Danish blonde stunner wearing a fishtail dress, looking hungrily at Richard as she devours a steak with her pointy shark.net teeth.

Two tube tickets, one to West Hampstead, one to Tottenham Court Road. A train ticket to York from Edinburgh. Plus a tattered, twisted strip of what was once a business card from Copley and Weir Publishing of Brewer Street W1. Is he a writer? A failed writer maybe? Finally, there's a credit note for £50 from a shop called Kaleidoscope in York. On the back there are tiny detailed drawings of sultry girls and funny, long-necked cats.

It's a flimsy map pointing nowhere. According to these things he likes music, lives in Newcastle, York or London, might be a fantastic or rubbish novelist, might have a girlfriend, eats like a king, doodles like an angel and looks like a god.

Eat your heart out, Miss Marple.

I feel a pang of unreasonable jealousy about Sarah Arseholen. Is she prettier than me? Are they going out? Does she look like his drawings of women, with flowing locks, statuesque bodies and come-to-bed eyes? Apart from several meanderings about how he's destined never to find a woman who'll understand him, he doesn't really get too specific about his love life, except on Sunday the 14th of March. Then it changes – his writing is frantic and passionate, scattered with spelling mistakes and changing from capitals to lower case at bizarre intervals. He's talking about some woman or other, someone who sounds like a total nightmare:

She wanted me to tell her what she wanted to hear, so I said, OK, I'll lie to you if you think it'll make it any better. She pAced around the room in her underwear in this self-conscious, historyonic way, and the whole thing felt like a GaME, as if she was re-enacting a scene in some shit film or an epsiode of FREiNds or something. She just kept going on about me being THE ONE, but we'd only been going out for two weeks and I was sick of her already, so i told her the TRUTH. Pepole need to know the truth, don't they? It's kinder in the end. I'm usually good at letting people down. I kNOW what pissed her off, though, I knew what she was after and I called her bluff, and that's what she couldn't stand. She was after a sperm donor. She'd already cristened our children before I'd made a move. ARGH! [drawn in Hammer Horror lettering.] *Save me and mankind from the clutches of career-frazzled jane Asher wannabees with an eye on the main chance and a HOuse in The Country and 2 point 4 Jocastas and Jaspers – acessories, just part of the quest to HAVE IT ALL with a cherry on top. My feeLings didn't have anything to do with it. In fact, I'm surprised she didn't come at me with a TURKEY BASTER!*

Later he adds, in a smaller, calmer hand:
She left a message, apologizing. Games, games, every time.

After that there's no mention of any sperm-pilfering women – he's back in his own little universe playing magic eightball, putting the world to rights, raging, sketching. Looks like he dumped her. But there are so many gaps. After 17th March, it goes quiet for a whole month, save an odd drawing of a fat duck (or could it be a stork?) on the 1st of May. If it is a stork, could that mean he's impregnated her? Has he been ensnared by Jane Asher and her bun in the oven? Did he dump the diary because he wrote nasty things about her and couldn't bear it if she found out the truth?

God knows.

My head feels sticky, and I realize I should have taken my hair dye off ages ago. Cold globs have collected at my temples and are dripping insidiously into my ears. After I bash my head against the bathroom doorframe, leaving a horrendous scar on the paintwork, I sit for a while on the side of the bath, dripping and wondering what to do. Questions rattle around my skull. Who is he? Did he leave the diary there on purpose so somebody would find him? Is he playing games with the world? With me? An unseasonal draught whistles through the tiny window, making me shiver. I feel weak. I don't think I can take much more of this. Maybe I'm more like Val than I thought; the suspense is killing me.

I stick my head under the tap and wash off the dye, then curl up on the sofa to stare at my paper jigsaw. My teeth are chattering. Downstairs, Queenie washes her single plate and teacup and settles down in front of the blaring telly. The last entry in the diary is dated the 18th of August, three days before I found it.

One day I'm going to be what I want to be. But loneliness comes up and bites you and you're all of a sudden TRAPPED BEHIND GLASS. That's how it feels. You're unable to reach out and touch anything or anyone. You can't see things for what they are because your too caught up in it to know what's best for you. I don't want to feel like this for ever. Last week I was treated with absolute indifference by a complete idiot and I couldn't stop thinking about it. It was like a real injury; it seared me and hurt me and wouldn't leave me alone. I know it was nothing, it was just some stranger, but I magnified it x1000000 and so it's there bubbling under, along with a thousand other small crueltys and injustices I've amassed like so many war wounds which are debiletating and confirm my uselessness. Every day I meet people who are so easily amused, and I know they hate me because I hate them back. There's no disguising it, the mutual dissaproval, it festers and grows and I'm always left out in the cold, looking in, even sometimes envying their stupidity and their ability to settle for what they've got, but usually just hating, hating everything.

Feeling so ugly, so pointless, so dislocated. Yeah, yeah,
Richard, poor you. Nobody loves me, everybody hates
me, might as well go and eat worms. Grow up and—

There's something a bit disturbing about the way it
ends halfway through a sentence. Maybe he's . . .
maybe he's dead. I push the thought away immediately, but a ferocious panic grips me. He can't be dead.
We've only just met! I pace around, my toes like ice on
the hard floor, trying to convince myself that no, he's
not the type to throw himself off railway bridges or gas
himself in his car.

I really, really hope he's not dead. He's so handsome.
It would be tragic. He's beginning to seep into my
consciousness in the most unusual way. It's like I AM
him. Everything that he thinks, I think too. Trapped.
Lonely. Ugly. Useless. In the background the record
player spits and crackles. My stomach grumbles and
I'm dizzy, confused and feel as if I'm about to throw up.
I have to get this sorted out. If I e-mail Sarah Arseholen
she might know where he lives then I can return his
diary. If I carry on like this for much longer I'll die of
some terrible nervous disorder. Yesterday Camp David
asked me something and I jumped out of my skin. The
only thing I've eaten for forty-eight hours is a Malteser.
I'll give the diary back, then I'll carry on with my life,
end of story. It's not worth it, it's not.

I'm lost, unravelling.

I stare at the floor and feel a lump rise in my throat.

I suddenly get an urge to gather every trace of him
and clutch it to my chest.

Later, when I've dried off and am feeling a bit less like
a mental patient, I do something I haven't done in

months. I phone Alison. It's time to stop avoiding her. Just because she's successful and I'm a peasant doesn't mean we can't be friends. But when I dial, even the ringing tone in the receiver makes me feel vaguely inadequate. It sounds state-of-the-art, as if it's part of an e-mail/photocopier/espresso machine combo costing a million quid. I look down at my phone, a touch button thing with a cheap ring that could shatter concrete. Babs got it as a free gift when she ordered a leather blouson from Kay's catalogue in 1994, and it was crap then.

Eventually Ali picks up, her round Yorkshire vowels muffled by something she's eating.

'Hello?'

'Hiya, Ali. It's Jane.'

'Jaaaane!' she splutters. 'Oof, hang on.'

The line is muffled and I can hear her laughing.

'Sorry, I just spat quiche into the mouthpiece . . . ugh . . . mmmffugggff.'

'Quiche? Oh, how the other half live,' I say.

'Yeah, exotic eh?' she says, through a mouthful of pastry. 'So how are YOU? I haven't spoken to you in ages! How's Edinburgh?'

'Oh, you know, OK. Still working at the tourist office.'

'Are ya? Enjoying it?'

'S'all right. What are you up to?'

'Oh, you know' – there's a pause, then some laboured swallowing – 'all right. Liam's got a new job so I hardly ever see him, really, but he loves it. He's a pig in shit. He gets this enormous salary and I spend it. I'm working at the Transmission Gallery. Exhibitions co-ordinator – sounds grand, but it's not at all. Let's see, what else? Finally done the house up after about a hundred years of living in squalor. Oh, I dunno, loads. You should come down and visit.'

Jealousy quietly eats away at me. I clear my throat, which seems to have seized up while she was talking.

'Well, that's why I was phoning,' I announce gaily. The words come out sounding too forced and over-rehearsed. 'I was thinking of taking a few days off and coming down to see you. Maybe go and see my mum, too. You know, have a bit of a holiday.'

'Brilliant!' Ali squeals, 'When?'

'Er, well, I'll ask about getting time off from work and then give you a ring to organize it. Would that be OK?'

'Course it would. Any time, you know that. How about next weekend? Or whenever. Hey, I can't wait. Bad girls back together again – aw, we'll paint the town red! It's been ages since I've had a really mad one.'

'Yeah, me too.'

We talk about various really mad ones in the past, or at least Ali does. She seems to have a photographic memory for embarrassing things I did when I was drunk four years ago. 'Remember when you were ape dancing to Oasis at the Dry Bar and Liam Gallagher walked in?' (yes). 'Remember when you defaced that Wonderbra poster on Palatine Road and gave the model hairy nipples?' (Er . . . no). Remember when you were sick outside the Abbey National on the corner of Market Street and Piccadilly and slipped in it? (NO). Some of it I have to drag out from the recesses of my memory banks, like the time I fell off a table in 42nd Street and hit my head, something that used to happen with almost monotonous regularity. But Ali could recite it all in chronological order, with dates and everything. She could probably tell me what kind of marker pen I used to draw the nipple hair with.

'So,' she says, changing tack. 'Are you still a single lady about town?'

'Er, yeah. Just about.' I falter, looking at the diary.

'Fab. Ooh, you'll have to tell me all your slutty tart stories.'

'Well, that should take about five minutes.'

'Aw, shurrup, I bet Edinburgh's not safe with you around, you slag. Come down here and we'll relive the good times. I don't get to flirt and mess about any more,' she whimpers.

'Well that's because you're married and you can never shag anyone else again,' I remind her.

'Hmm.' She giggles. 'Doesn't mean I can't perv, though. I could still pull if I wanted to, you know. I've still got it going on. The other day a tramp whistled at me.'

'Hey, I thought you weren't interested in other men. I thought that Liam was the most handsome man on earth,' I say, baiting her. It's true that Liam is shockingly handsome, a Calvin Klein model waiting to happen, with eyes the colour of chlorinated water and the perfect pecs of a lifeguard. Even when everyone was worrying that Ali might be getting married too young they couldn't help but admit that Liam was a real catch. Her own mother melts like a choc ice on a sun lounger when he comes within three feet of her.

'Yes, Liam is still as DREAMY as ever.' She sighs prettily. 'But just because I'm not buying anything doesn't mean I can't look in the shop, does it?'

'Yeah, well as long as you don't handle the goods.'

'Fnar.'

'Anyway, I'll find out when I can get time off from work and give you a ring to organize it in a few days. OK?'

'Great stuff. Hurray. Bad girls together again.'

'I'll see you really soon.' A twinge of excitement goes straight to my bladder and I hop from one foot to the other. 'I can't wait,' I squeak.

'Me neither,' she trills.

We do a bit of high-pitched girlie squealing and hang up. Out of the corner of my eye I'm struck by the sharp contrast of my new hair colour against my black T-shirt.

I don't know what's come over me.

What the hell am I doing?

But over on the sofa the pages of the diary flutter in the breeze through the open window, as if congratulating my decision.

'That's nice, Jane,' Fiona says, looking up from the paper.

'Ooh!' yelps Camp David. 'It's friggin' Nicole Kidman in *Moulin Rouge*. Hubba hubba!' He slinks up to me and slips an arm round my waist. '*Voulez-vous coucher avec moi ce soir?*'

Dumb Paul lets out a muffled Beavis and Butthead laugh.

Sophie raises one eyebrow and clears her throat.

'Very nice, Jane. What's it in aid of?'

'Och, Sophie,' David scolds. 'A fabulous gal doesn't need an excuse to get her hair done. Now, tell me, Nicole, does the carpet match the curtains? Eh? Eh?'

Val dashes her cigarette out in an overflowing cut-glass ashtray and gives me the once-over.

'Told you,' she says in a sing-song playground voice. 'It's a MAN.'

Camp David clutches his chest in mock horror.

'No, say it ain't so! Jane, how could you, when you know we're destined to be together. I stayed a virgin for you. Well if I can't have you, I don't want to live another moment on this wretched planet. I shall kill myself!' He picks up a biro and pretends to commit hara-kiri. Val and Sophie laugh. Kelly agitates her ponytail with an afro comb, watching haughtily from the sidelines.

'Who is he?' David demands, slumping to his knees. 'Is he better-looking than me? Has he got a bigger MANHOOD? Oh, just end it for me, Jane. I can't go on knowing that you're promised to another!'

'David, that's enough. Stop acting up and go and open up.' Sophie grins, throwing him the keys. 'It's very striking, Jane. Now everyone, get to work, you're getting on my nerves.'

My face is the same Autumn Scarlet as my head. I go into the office and fiddle with some box files for something to do. My foot catches against the rogue brochures under my desk. Camp David, keys jingling on his hip, throws the doors open and the morning sun floods in. I look up.

'Stay there. Don't move. It looks so good in the light,' he shrieks, making a frame out of his fingers and peering through it. 'Ravishing!'

Kelly comes in and sits at her desk, followed by Val, coughing like a consumptive tramp. David swaggers up to the counter.

'Now, Jane, we're having a work's night out on Friday and if you don't come I'll be very upset,' he informs me in all seriousness. 'Oh, and if you say no I'll tell everyone who your secret boyfriend is.'

I freeze. He eyeballs me. His expression is inscrutable, his small turned-up nose, dusty freckles and spiky blond hair all seem to be vibrating with evil, impish energy.

What does he know?

Val smirks, Kelly stares at me blankly. Did they get the diary from my bag? Have they been reading bits out and laughing? *Look at Jane and her imaginary friend –*

what a loser.' Camp David's squirrel-like face gives nothing away. I think I'm going to start whimpering. Either that or die.

'It's Ewan McGregor, isn't it, you dirty devil,' he says, smashing me in the arm. 'Leading him on; flashin' your muff on that trapeze. You should be ashamed of yourself.'

Val rolls her eyes and gets on with her work. Kelly is already busy typing, indifferent to David's antics.

'Ooh, the banter,' David twitters, a catchphrase from a comedy show I haven't seen. I'm too flustered to even contemplate the full horror of a work's night out.

'SO, will you come?' he asks, turning from the devil's spawn into an excited little boy.

'Yes,' I mumble under duress. I feel weak and exposed and I want to go home. I don't feel very well. I wonder if I should have a lie down.

'Top hole, Darling. Och, I'm so glad you're coming. It's gonnae be a humdinger, just you wait. You'd better get your gladrags on – I'm going as John Travolta.'

I struggle to grasp what he's saying.

'What?'

'Friday night. Seventies party. If you dress up you get in for nothing. Get your flares on grrrlfriend, and strut your funky stuff. Disco! "Disco Inferno"!'

David dances on the spot like he needs a shit.

I close my eyes.

People are so easily amused . . . says Richard.

When I open them again, David is on my side of the counter, jangling past me, torture finally over.

'What are you going as, Val?' I hear him say behind me. 'Albert Steptoe? Aha ha ha!' Val thumps him.

'Ya cheeky wee bleeder!'

I sigh and open Internet Explorer, logging into my

Hotmail account. The office is full of strange, jarring noises and foreign bodies. Over in the shop a group of teenage Spanish tourists are laughing uproariously at the Scottish novelties. I look up and see Fiona. She points at her head, points at mine and gives me the thumbs up, which is nice of her. I smile weakly but it doesn't make me feel any less of a circus freak. The Spanish tourists are shrieking now, oblivious to their volume, simulating lurid sex scenes with Scottie dog fridge magnets. 'Mirar el perro! Ay ay ay!'

I click on Create Mail and take the ripped piece of cigarette packet from my skirt pocket – not that I really need to look at the address, I already know it off by heart. My fingers hover over the keys. Dear Sarah Olsen, I found your address in a diary belonging to a man called Richard. No. I found a diary belonging to Mr Richard Miles and your address was in it. Um . . . sorry to bother you, I just wondered whether you knew the whereabouts of Richard Miles, you see I . . .

'AAAAAAY!'

There's a momentous scream and clatter as the shelf collapses on top of a Spanish boy, burying him under a ton of snowstorms, oversized pencils, stuffed bagpipers and assorted tartan crap. His friends tell him off as he rolls on the floor, but he's not hurt, he's bent double with laughter.

For fuck's sake, I'm TRYING to do something IMPORTANT.

I get up and march over to them, brimming with shaky anger. Terrified, they immediately start a scramble to pick everything up.

'Sorry,' says one, blushing, helping me lift the shelf. I grit my teeth and wave them away as politely as I can. They disperse, chattering madly, still giggling.

Grumpily I start the clear-up operation. While I'm rearranging the little tartan drummer girls in tubes so they face proudly to the front, I remember what Richard said in his diary about Edinburgh – he hated it even more than me. He wrote a scathing entry about visiting his friend, who was in some play or other. I thought it was funny. He said something like:

Edinburgh during festival time is a pit of amateur dramatic hell. There MUST be better ways to make a living than fannying around on stilts and juggling sprouts. Even people who have nothing to do with the festival turn into lunatics. On my way to the hotel I got acosted by a man dressed as a potato, giving out leaflets for a chip shop. I asked how much they paid him per hour and he gave me a dirty look through his little eye holes and turned his back on me. I couldn't believe it. I got a dirty look from a POTATO. I can't even get the time of day from a root vegetable.

Bless him. So sensitive. I'd protect him from rude root vegetables if only I . . .

As I pick up a vomitous set of coasters featuring a gold etching of Edinburgh castle, I sense somebody kneeling behind my left shoulder. I wait for them to go away, but the presence gets stronger, darker.

Something changes, there's a shift in the atmosphere. My breathing slows down. I'm suddenly aware of the electrical impulses in my chest, firing my heart, keeping me alive. I don't know whether the presence is real or not – surely I can't conjure him up just by thinking about him – but I can smell a fresh, enticing mixture of washing powder and spearmint and it's making me dizzy. Mmmmm. I feel intoxicated. I move my head a tiny fraction to the left, and there it is: a familiar jaw line; olive skin; full, soft, kissable lips.

Oh my God. He's here. It's him. How could this happen?

A hand comes closer to mine, fine-boned and capable, clasping a snowstorm. Inside the globe, glitter swirls around Edinburgh castle, casting a magic spell. I'm hypnotized. His mouth can't be more than inches away from my ear, I can feel his breath tickling my neck. Some chemical reaction is taking place and I'm completely powerless. I raise my chin and turn to face him. How did he find me? Do I just click my heels and he appears?

'*Hola.*' He smiles, showing uneven teeth.

'Urrr!'

I lurch violently backwards and fall sideways onto a musical plate. As 'The Bonnie Banks of Loch Lomond' plays merrily from under my skirt, I take in the full extent of him, garish yellow T-shirt, boyish stick-thin arms, the bum fluff and hungry leer of a hormonally charged Spanish fifteen-year-old.

'You are very beautiful woman,' he oozes, leaning closer. He must be about TWELVE.

'Jane, are you all right?' Fiona asks, watching the scene with barely contained hilarity.

'Yes, I'm fine,' I squeak, making a desperate face. 'Can you, er . . . give me a hand, please? There's been a bit of an accident.'

The song finishes rousingly in my knickers and I struggle to my feet. As Fiona approaches, my Spanish lothario scarpers, joining his cackling pubescent friends at the entrance.

'Well, Jane, you're a hit with the lads today. Isn't he a wee bit too young for you?'

'Oh, God, what a nightmare. I thought he was some-one else.' I giggle nervously, tidying up the shelf. 'It's OK now, he's gone.'

I give her a resigned isn't-life-mad look and she wanders back to her desk, throwing amused, confused glances over her shoulder as she goes.

I dust off the musical plate and set it back on the shelf.

I'm an idiot.

Why did you think it would be Richard, you stupid cow? He doesn't know you even EXIST. Order restored, I stomp back to the computer and close Internet Explorer. Fuck Sarah Olsen and Starlette and bloody train tickets.

Just stop thinking about him.

Think about something else. Do some work. I look over at Kelly. She's busy helping someone, all sweetness and light. The tightness of her hairdo lifts her eyebrows into pleasantly surprised arcs and she's got her flawless public persona cranked up to eleven, smiling beatifically at the customers. When she smiles, she doesn't look like such a pig. And a very small part of me – the almost microscopic part that gives a shit about being a tourist adviser – admires her confidence and immaculately pressed lapels. I decide to copy her body language and press my buzzer to graciously receive my first customer of the day. Two elderly women stagger up to the counter, sharply dressed in their Sunday best, already poised to ask a series of boring questions. A lead weight settles on my shoulders, but I valiantly struggle to stay awake long enough to serve them. Smile. Be Professional. You are the first point of contact.

'Hello dear, I wonder if you could help us. We're

here for the day from Pitlochry,' the first one explains.

'And we're hoping to have an adventure,' says the other with a mischievous glint. 'Something a bit out of the ordinary. Something a wee bit outrageous.'

An image of Richard shimmers in my mind. He's there, waiting, a wee bit outrageous, taking my hand across an unidentified table.

'Let's have an adventure.'

'So, well, what kind of things are you interested in?' I smile, pulling myself up and aping Kelly's ever-helpful, ever-ready attitude. 'Gardens? Monuments?'

'Ooh, no, that sort of thing's for old folk!' the first huffs, affronted. 'We were thinking of' – she leans over the counter and whispers – 'the Ladyboys of Bangkok.'

Her friend shrieks and wallops her on the arm.

'Margaret! Behave yourself! Och, sorry about her, dear, it's the drink. She's a bit, y'know.' The other makes a loopy gesture and crosses her eyes.

They both laugh, a long, sustained, rattling wheeze. I sit back, glad for an entertaining diversion. Hinge and Bracket are 80-year-old schoolgirls in support hosiery. I give them a Fringe brochure, explain the maps and numbers of the venues and where to get tickets. I am cooking with gas, firing on all cylinders. They're beside themselves, absolutely delighted.

'Ooh, isn't this exciting. There's so much to choose from. The world's your oyster here, isn't it? I bet there's never a dull moment.'

'Er . . . no, never,' I say, guiltily, thinking of all the wasted nights I've spent sitting on my lumpy futon and counting the dents in the woodchip wallpaper (106, for the record).

'Well, thank you, dear, you've been ever so helpful. Come on, Margaret, it's Bangkok or bust.'

Something approaching job satisfaction sets me aglow. Gripping the brochure they recede into the sunlight, an irrepressible silhouette against the glass doors, off to find adventure and cross-dressers.

Then everything goes quiet. All I can hear is the hum of my computer and the efficient click of fingers against plastic keys. Sarah Olsen, probably a well-groomed, bulldozing blonde who works in PR, will be sitting in front of her computer too, perhaps looking at an inbox full of e-mails from Richard. Bitch.

But he needs more than her. He needs direction. He needs me to help him.

The clock ticks slowly towards the end of another day, and then it'll be tomorrow, and I'll still be here, treading water, obeying orders, making sure everyone else has a good time.

How can anyone expect to find happiness if they don't take any risks?

Surely if two old ladies can journey into the unknown, so can I.

I'm going to go and see Ali, the sooner the better. And while I'm doing that, maybe I'll make a few detours and see if I can find Richard. He should have his diary back – it's the right thing to do, after all.

Before I can talk myself out of it, I get up and go to Sophie's office.

On the door is a sign that incongruously warns to 'Beware of the Boss', featuring a cartoon of an angry bulldog in a pinstripe suit, purple and sweating with rage. I can hear her on the phone, her soft voice rising and falling in a gentle croon. I knock and open the door. She's perched on the desk with her plump legs coyly crossed, wearing a pink powder puff of an angora jumper. Waving me in, she gestures towards the chair in front of her and pats the seat.

'Well, I just don't know what happened, Ken, I really don't. I can assure you we sent them out. Unless we order another batch from the printers, but that's going to be costly. I'm awfully sorry. Hmmm. We'll all have a proper look around to see if they haven't gone astray somewhere in the office. Speak to you soon, Ken. Bye.'

Sophie hangs up.

'Ken Dornie,' she explains significantly, as if I should know who the hell he is. 'The mystery of the missing brochures continues. You know, I wonder if they got sent out at all.'

A guilty feeling wriggles in my gut. I make a mental note to torch them as soon as I get back to my desk.

'Oh well, maybe Kelly knows something about them. We'll have a look.' She sighs, lost in thought. There's a long pause. The clock on her desk, a pink rubber thing in the shape of a startled fish, ticks loudly.

'What can I do you for, Jane? You know, that red is a very vibrant colour, I was saying to Val, I used to have hair like that, back in my wild days. You remind me a lot of my—'

'Would it be OK if I took Monday and Tuesday off next week?' I blurt nervously, seized with the urge to get to the brochures before anyone else.

'Oh well, I don't think we can spare—'

There's a familiar tappety-tap on the door and Kelly flounces in. When she sees me, she flinches slightly, as if bothered by a mosquito.

'Sorry to bother you,' she says, fixing Sophie with a brilliant grin. 'I just need—'

'Kelly, you don't know where those brochures got to, do you? You sent them out, didn't you?' Sophie pleads.

Kelly looks like she's suddenly struck with rigor mortis. She gives me a sly, sideways glance.

'Yes. We did, didn't we, Jane?'

I plaster on a fake smile and look kindly up at her.

'Yes, Kelly. We did. We definitely did.'

'Well they didn't arrive,' Sophie worries, getting panicky and playing with the telephone cord. 'How could they not have arrived? This makes us look very unprofessional.'

'Maybe . . . there was a postal strike,' I offer. Kelly shoots me an evil glare.

Sophie cocks her head with interest.

'Was there? I don't remember.'

'I think so. Wasn't there, Kelly?'

'Possibly,' she says, slowly drawing out each syllable of the word, her eyes narrowing.

'I'm going to look for them,' Sophie announces suddenly, springing to her feet with alarming resolve. I automatically do the same, getting between her and Kelly, who is nearest to the door.

'We'll look for them, won't we, Kelly?' I jabber. 'Sophie's probably got a MILLION other things to do.'

'Well, actually, I can't, I'm quite busy,' Kelly says, enjoying every minute of my torture.

'Oh well, NEVER MIND. Leave it to me,' I boom as Sophie advances towards us. I push past Kelly and walk briskly out of the room. Diving under my desk, I grab the box and whisk it away to the brochure library in the back. If I put them there I can mix them up with the others on display, and hopefully Sophie won't notice the mucky fingerprints of Jane Darling, the shiftless swine who can't even put a stamp on an envelope. As I heave it across the office I can feel the cardboard of the box straining under the weight of all that premium glossy paper, and suddenly it collapses, brochures slithering all over the floor, leaving a full-colour trail of shame. I try to gather them up, but the covers are so slippery they fall from my grasp. From the corner of my eye I see Kelly marching up to me. She's getting nearer, on the warpath. Oh bloody hell. Sophie is nowhere to be seen, not yet, anyway, but any minute now I'm going to see her pastel pear shape coming round the corner and she's going to catch me and I'm going to get mercilessly sacked and have to go back to work in Barbara's Blooms and spend the rest of my life making frigging funeral wreaths with my mum and Becky. I mean, this might not be the best job ever, but it gives me independence, pays the rent and gives me something to do and moan about, and don't tell anyone, but sometimes, in a perverted, masochistic, downright depraved way, I kind of . . . secretly . . . *enjoy it*. Oh God! She's nearly HERE! A film of clammy sweat covers my hands – Kelly is advancing, I'm fucked, I'm well and truly—

'What are you doing?' Kelly demands.

'Kelly, please, I'm sorry,' I snivel, an utterly pathetic specimen. 'I forgot to send them before we left. It was a mistake. I'm already on a written warning . . . please don't tell her . . .'

In my mind's eye the book of my misdemeanours has grown to gigantic proportions, my name scored through with one vicious swipe of the Loch Ness Monster pen. Jane Darling is out.

'Come on,' she barks.

Kelly makes a huffing noise and takes control, scooping up vast armfuls of brochures and stoutly carrying them into the back room. Carrying a flapping cardboard box, I follow her. With the upper body strength of Geoff Capes, she shovels them in a cupboard under the shelves marked 'Steam Engine Museum', slams the sliding door and locks it. She throws the little key behind her and it disappears into the deepest recesses of the magazine racks with a delicate plink.

'Have you found them, Jane?'

Sophie, seeming huge and unwieldy in her pink twinset, appears behind us and I yelp out in shock.

'I–I–I–I–I didn't . . .'

'No. They're not there,' says Kelly, standing now, cool and relaxed, flipping calmly through the library as if she's browsing the easy-listening section in a record shop. 'Only the ones for the office. As I said, we definitely sent them out. I clearly remember going to the post office with Jane myself. We almost did our backs in, didn't we?' she chuckles convincingly.

I'm impressed. Kelly has the scheming, underhand qualities of a serial killer.

'Yeah,' I gabble, still holding the cardboard box. 'They weighed a ton.'

Sophie is on the back foot, puzzled.

'Oh, OK. If you're sure. Bloody Royal Mail or Chlamydia or whatever they're calling it now. Oh well, I'll send Ken ten from the office and that'll just have to do.'

Sophie stands there for a while, frowning at the racks. Kelly looks at me. I look at Kelly. Her face is set in a blank, even smile, giving nothing away. Sophie comes to and claps her hands.

'Right then,' she says. 'What was I doing a minute ago?'

'I, er . . . I was just asking if I could get some, er . . . time off next week,' I shakily venture, knowing I'm pushing my luck. Kelly prickles and busily rearranges flyers for the Gretna Green Outlet Village.

'Oh, Jane, I'm not sure. We're stretched as it is.'

'It's just, my friend has got a job in er . . . Australia. She lives in London and she's asked me to come down for the weekend. I wondered if I could see her off at the airport on Monday night, then I'll get a train back on Tuesday morning. We've known each other for years, and I might not see her again.' I trail off, aware that it sounds completely sketchy.

'What's her job?' Kelly asks conversationally.

'Pardon?'

'Her job in Australia. What is it?'

'Er . . .' What's her job? I desperately ransack my brain for careers, but can only, for some reason, think of a lollipop lady.

'She works on the roads.'

'The roads?'

Sophie is watching me curiously.

'Yes. Traffic calming. I don't understand it really, but she's very good, she was headhunted.'

I have no idea what I'm talking about.

There's a nasty little silence as Sophie turns on her bullshit detectors. Kelly is pleased with this turn of events, I can tell. What's she playing at? Rescuing me one minute, landing me in it the next?

'Well, I don't know if we can manage without you at the moment,' Sophie says doubtfully. 'It's going to be busy right up until the end of September. And then we'll have to start gearing up for Christmas and Hogmanay. Sorry.'

I gaze at my scuffed black work shoes and the blue

office carpet, illuminated by a depressing strip light. Behind us, in the office, Camp David is still singing 'Disco Inferno'. Something inside me curls up and dies.

'I'm sure we'll be OK, Sophie,' I hear Kelly saying. 'I'm SURE we can get by without Jane for a couple of days.'

I look up. Kelly has her chin held high and a saccharine smirk on her face. Today's lip gloss is a ghastly shade of plum.

'Do you think so? Hmm . . .'

Sophie looks set to reconsider. What the hell is going on?

'I'll work overtime the weekend after,' I venture.

'It'll be fine,' Kelly soothes, watching me warily.

Sophie nods.

'Okey-dokey, you can have Monday and Tuesday off. And don't say I'm not good to you,' she says, poking me cheerfully in the collarbone. 'Now can we all stop standing around and do some work? The queue is enormous.'

She trots off. Kelly stays put, running a finger over the dusty shelf.

'Thanks, Kelly.'

'I think it'll suit both of us, don't you?' she says frostily, walking away.

I'm limp with relief. The future looks bright for the first time in ages. All I have to do is get through the work's night out on Friday and I'm free.

Richard's diary entry from 16th June drifts into my mind as I go back to my desk, happy, beaming, oblivious to the crowd of pestering, restless tourists.

Is it so wrong for a man to dream of being rescued? I've got this fantasy. I'm going about my business and all of a sudden I'm aware of a girl beside me. She's beautiful, a fair maiden with long red hair. She takes my hand, looks deep into my eyes and all the bad stuff melts away. She takes my hand and I know. I just know.

DOOF! Queenie bangs her Bluto right hook on my front door. She certainly chooses her moments. I've got to get dressed, I've got to get my bag packed for tomorrow, I've got to deal with the Safeway carrier full of festering ready meals and orange peel before it comes alive and tries to strangle me, and I'm half naked, wrapped in a flimsy towel, covered in glitter and lip gloss. I haven't got time for this. In fifteen minutes I have to be at Ziggy's Seventies night club, dressed as Frida from ABBA and wishing I was dead.

'Hello, dear. Ooh, you're in the altogether!' she screeches delightedly, holding aloft a suspicious foil-wrapped brick, which I fleetingly hope might be drugs but probably isn't.

'Sorry, Queenie, I'm getting ready to—'

'Going out, are ye?' she booms, staring at me un-abashed.

'Yes, in a minute.'

'Your hair's different. Hmm. Is that what the young people are doing these days? Brought you some fruit-cake – get your strength up. Look how skinny you are. Skinny Malinky long legs, big banana feet!'

I wonder if she might be pissed.

'My husband didn't like it when I wore lots of make-up. Said it made me look cheap. Nowadays, though, anything goes, doesn't it?' she mutters, peering at my clown face. 'Oh yes. Anything goes,' she adds pointlessly, sneaking a look over my shoulder. I follow her beady eye and see she's surveying my living room. A pile of variously folded and crumpled clothes sit next to a holdall.

'Are you doing a moonlight flit?'

'Er, no. Just a holiday. Couple of days down in England.'

She looks unsure.

'Och, what can you get in England you can't get here?' she moans. 'I went to Bristol once and it was a dump.'

Not wishing to discuss the aesthetic merits of Bristol all night, I slowly edge towards the handle.

'Listen, Queenie, thanks very much for the cake. It's very kind of you. It's just, I'm really late.'

'Aye, well, off you go. You have fun,' she says, her nose slightly out of joint.

'See you soon, Queenie, thanks.'

She hovers about, working a decrepit dishcloth between her papery fingers.

'You will be careful, won't you, dear?'

The question stops me in my tracks.

'What?'

'You won't get yourself into a mess, will you? I've seen plenty of young girls getting carried away and getting into all kinds of bother.'

What the hell is she ON about?

'I don't know what you mean,' I say briskly.

'There are a lot of funny people out there. I wouldnae want to see you get hurt.'

103

'Well, thanks for your concern, but I think I can look after myself.'

She stands there peering suspiciously at my hair, as if she's trying to work out whether I'm a prostitute.

'You won't find the man of your dreams with all that on your face,' she mutters to her dishrag. God, what a cheek, who does she think she is? One minute she's telling me to put on make-up, the next she's telling me to take it off.

'I beg your pardon?'

'Nothing, dear. Have a lovely weekend.' She smiles blandly and shuffles down the stairs.

I stand stupidly, holding the foil wrapper, watching her go.

'I'm in fancy dress,' I shout down the stairs, but she doesn't hear me.

Fruitcake.

I slam the door, chuck the brick into the kitchen with a thud and run into the bedroom cursing. I've already met the man of my dreams, you stupid old bag, and it's got fuck all to do with you. I dig out a pair of silver trousers and a bottle-green sparkly vest, remnants of the bizarre charity-shop purchases me and Ali used to make. Top it off with a crocheted hat, white vinyl handbag and white boots that I bought from a retro clothes shop and I'm ready. I stand for a moment in front of the mirror.

Jane, you're not a fair maiden, you're a lunatic.

God, I hope I don't accidentally bump into Richard tonight. I hope he doesn't live here and, in some awful twist of fate, see me cavorting around with Camp David and Kelly, dressed like a Seventies slag.

I decide to take the diary with me. It'll help guide me through the evening's undoubtedly awful proceedings.

I open it at a random page and he's holding forth on the general public, a bunch of people neither of us have much time for.

Collectively, people are stupid. When I go anywhere I can see it, the same dumb, foolhardy, misguided impulses that made religious cults and Pop IDol and the Labour party so popular. They need a leader, otherwise they're fucked. People don't think for themselves and it drives me insane, it really does. They just leave their brains at the door. I suppose that's just the way it is, but why can't there be less incompetents and more true originals? The world is full of people following the herd. I'm adrift in a sea of mediocrity! Instead of doing something for themselves, everyone wants the quiet life, so they can get on with doing what everyone else does. Leave the worrying to someone else. Most people can't even be bothered to have an opinion of their own. Am I the only person who can see that?

The paragraph is ringed with drawings of smack-addled sheep.

Reading it gives me a little thrill.

He's so . . . feisty.

I slot it carefully into the inside pocket of my slag bag. Then I grab my battered leather jacket, keys, money and fags, and leave my brain at the door.

Ziggy's is on Leith Walk, a scabby place painted black with chalkboards outside promising drinks at Seventies prices. It looks like the kind of club you might get stabbed in, or at least felt up by a lorry driver. The bouncers, a couple of ogres with shaved heads and neat beards, stand disconsolately in the drizzle, smoking. When they see me get out of the taxi, they straighten up and look like they mean business. I feel a right idiot wearing this get-up, and I can see them sharing an amused glance as I totter towards them in my white wellies.

'Mamma bloody Mia,' one of them says.

'Did you ask the Michelin Man whether you could borrow his boots?' asks his sidekick. I reach the entrance.

'Very funny,' I say, my feet already killing me.

'Are you sure you've got the right place, love? It's no Seventies night the night, y'know,' the first warns, suddenly stern.

'What?'

'Aye,' the other assures me. 'That was last night.'

They both stare at me. A car fizzes down the wet road and fades into the distance.

Did I get the wrong night? Is this some kind of hilarious practical joke? Are Camp David, Kelly and Sophie and Val going to poke their heads round the corner and start pointing at me? Look at Jane. She's such a twat. She totally fell for it . . .

'Really?' I stammer, hot humiliation beginning to course through my veins.

'Ha! Only jokin'. On you go.' He laughs, waving me in.

Fun-ny. Face prickling with embarrassment, I walk past a bored woman in the admissions booth and prepare myself to enter hell. The thumping strains of 'I Will Survive' rattle the entrance at the bottom of the sticky stairs. Even without X-ray vision I can see Camp David miming along to it, pretending to be Gloria Gaynor. I fight the urge to turn and run screaming into the street.

It'll all be over soon.

I play with my bag strap and feel the weight of the diary inside.

Look, Jane, just go in, have a few drinks, show your face and leave. You don't owe them anything.

I push open the doors and try to slip quietly into the fray.

It's just as I thought, only worse. The place smells of wet dogs and is half-empty, with dirty floor-length mirrors and a piddly disco ball. The bar is at one end and the lonely DJ is at the other, a balding middle-aged fart in a Hawaiian shirt. On the dancefloor a hen party of stilettoed women wearing distinctly un-Seventies devil's horns cavort around the bride-to-be, who is dressed in a bin bag with a pan on her head. I can see myself reflected on the opposite wall – green top, surgical boots, squiffy doily.

I look mental. This is not good. Oh, Christ, none of this is good.

Directly opposite the pissed-up hens is a mucky red velvet booth full of people from work. I spot Camp David first. His white John Travolta suit is so fluorescent under the UV lights that you could see him from space.

'DARLIN'!' he yells, showing teeth the same blinding colour as his suit. He looks sinister, like an unhinged TV evangelist.

'Hiya.' I walk over. As I get closer, they come into focus. Sophie sits in the middle, her hair flicked Farrah Fawcett style, with her elbows slumped on the table. She's laughing, a filthy machine-gun cackle. Dumb Paul sits practically on her knee, wearing a hippie wig and telling a convoluted, possibly dirty joke, which strikes me as bizarre, seeing as I've never heard him speak. Next to them, Val sips a glass of red wine while talking animatedly to Fiona, who listens intently, the bottoms of her trendy designer flares swishing as she jiggles her foot in time to the music.

They seem different, like a group of total strangers. Camp David comes looming out of the darkness towards me.

'Hi, Jane. Thank God you're here.' He smiles, taking my arm. 'You look fab. Come on, let's get a drink. This place is fucking awful.'

I wave briefly at the table, who screech back a welcome, and follow David to the bar. 'Now, what shall we have? They do this disgusting cocktail called the Jesus Christ Superstar. It's hideous, but we just HAVE to get legless – it's the only way.' He grimaces theatrically at the barman. 'Two Jesuses please. God help us all.'

'I thought you liked it here,' I say, wondering what on earth's going on.

'Never been before in my life. My boyfriend said it was good and now I'm seriously considering dumping the bastard. Have you ever been to Vegas?'

'Er, no.'

David never mentioned that he had a boyfriend before. The fact that he's in a real relationship is a bizarrely shocking admission. I assumed he just ran around goosing people and telling tedious jokes about cocks.

'I've, er, never even been to America.'

'Ha! No, ya daftie. It's this club in Leith, all Fifties – you get dressed up and it's fun and you dance to a big band. Well I thought it'd be like that.' He looks around, disappointed. 'Or at least a wee bit ironic, or a wee bit glam rock. Ziggy's, Stardust, Spiders from Mars, Bowie, y'know? But it's just a terrible backstreet pub full of skanky trollops.'

I stare at him, taken aback. Irony? Spiders from Mars? What IS this?

A Jesus Christ Superstar is deposited in front of me, 125mls of pink antiseptic gloop.

'Nice, eh?' He grins. 'Get it down you. It's the only way we're going to squeeze any fun out of this shitehole, babe.'

He flounces off, so I trail after him, back to the table.

'I've got Miss Darlink a drink so she'll be dancin' on the table showing her drawers soon enough.' He winks, reverting to type, acting his socks off for the assembled crowd.

'Jane,' slurs Sophie. 'Lovely outfit. Oh, I used to have a top like that years ago. Hey, hey, c'mere,' she says, smacking the seat.

I dutifully perch on the banquette.

'I've got a joke for you, what's worse than having a cardboard box?'

'Sorry?'

'Was worse' – she hiccups – 'than having a CARD-BOARD BOX?'

'I don't—'

'Paper tits! Aha! Ahahaha!'

Dumb Paul laughs so hard he nearly slips off his seat. Val makes a pained face behind her and returns to her conversation with Fiona. The music comes to a standstill as the DJ fumbles to put on another record. The hen-night girls boo.

'Great outfit,' Sophie says again, demolishing a gin and tonic. 'Sorry if I'm a bit leathered, I don't get to go out much 'cos of the kids, y'see. But it's been so long since I last went out on the town I've left the little bastards to fend for themselves. They'll probably be setting fire to the kitchen as we speak. Aha ha!'

I laugh along with her, wondering if Ziggy's isn't the gateway to a parallel universe.

Sophie goggles at me, her head wobbling slightly on her neck.

'Now listen, Kelly's going to be a bit late; she had to go to her boxercise class. I think that's it, innit? I dunno. Paul'll know – what's boxercise, Paul?'

'Not as bad as paper titsacise,' he splutters and Sophie erupts, spilling her drink down her stupendous cleavage, which is decorated with metallic stars.

'Oh look what you made me do.' She giggles, taking a handful of Paul's wig and wiping her chest with it. Paul, inches away from her almost visible nipple, seems to be having a fine time.

This is definitely not what I was expecting. I stare pleadingly at Fiona, who is curling her lip at Sophie's lurid antics. To my relief, she gestures for me to come over to her and Val's side of the table. Sophie, now trying to cram Dumb Paul's head into her bosom, doesn't even notice I've gone.

'Look at her carrying on, she's a total slapper.' Fiona shouts into my ear. 'All her kids have different fathers, y'know.'

I recall the photos in her office of her three children, Hector, Barney and Mia. For the first time I realize that none of them look anything like each other. What did she say to me the other day? Something about having red hair in her 'wild days'?

'No,' I gasp, watching Sophie rooting in her cleavage for a lost ice cube. 'I thought she was supposed to be Mother Earth.'

'Ha. Yeah, right! Mother who's shagged everybody on earth, more like. Don't go too near her, she'll probably try and give you one later.'

I finish my drink and feel fuzzy, disconnected. Sophie is a slut and Camp David has taste. Wonders will never cease. The club has started filling up – a large group of office workers dressed as the gangsters in *Reservoir Dogs* spills through the doors.

'Oh – my – God. That is SO seventies.' Camp David sneers queenishly, breaking out into a cheeky smile.

'Want another, Janey Waney?'

'Ooh, yes please.'

I give him my empty glass.

'Mr Pink's quite fit,' I whisper confidentially.

David throws his hands up with delight.

'That's *exactly* what I was thinking,' he shrieks, scooting off to the bar.

I feel a warm glow, possibly from the drink, which is super strong – no wonder Sophie is so pickled.

'Where did you get your top, Val? It's really nice,' I ask, trying to make conversation, the booze chasing through my body. I'm smiling inanely, but I realize I mean it. She's wearing a surprisingly tasteful embroidered hippy top, a pretty garden of delicate vines, flowers and leaves.

'This? I made it years ago,' she replies, offhand.

'What? Really?'

'Uh-huh,' Val confirms, lighting a fag.

'She used to do costumes for the theatre. Didn't you know?' Fiona offers.

I always just thought Val was a big walking cigarette – Nick O'Teen's sister – with a permanent plume of smoke coming out of her head. It never occurred to me that she might be capable of doing anything but inhaling and hacking up phlegm.

'I had no idea. That's brilliant.'

She gives me a suspicious look. I realize that I sound

111

like a patronizing infant school teacher and clumsily try to backtrack.

'No, NO.' I underline, making myself so loud and clear that she flinches. 'Really, it's brilliant! How come you never said you could do that?'

'Well, my darlin',' she says in a gravelly voice, 'you didn't ask.'

She shrugs amiably and starts talking to Fiona.

Oh.

Now nobody's talking to me any more. Fiona's eyes dart towards me apologetically.

Right then.

Sophie and Paul carry on their love tryst on the other side of the table. It's not surprising – my conversation isn't exactly sparkling. I'm self-involved, boring plain Jane with nothing to say, Jane who doesn't take an interest in anyone or anything, Jane who walks around all day with her eyes closed. Doesn't even bother to find out the most rudimentary facts about the people she spends all day with. Over the table, Sophie screeches at something Paul says – he's got his hand perilously close to her crotch. The hen-night girls link arms and stamp around the dancefloor, singing badly along to 'Wig-Wam Bam'. I pass the awkward moments by inspecting a possible transvestite on the other side of the club. He looks more convincing than me. I think I'm going to cry, something I'm doing more and more these days, leaking, blubbering, showing myself up in front of people who would really rather I wasn't there. My head's itching like crazy. Has my doily got fleas?

'PAUL! You dirty BOY!'

Paul's hand must have reached its intended destination. Ugh.

I head off to the bar to pay for the drinks, but Camp

David waves my money away. I smile and take a sip, but it doesn't make me feel any more at ease. After a minute I realize that he's gazing at me, a curious look on his face.

'You know, I can't quite figure you out, Jane Darling.' He frowns slyly. 'You intrigue me.'

I snort with laughter, pink stuff catching the back of my throat and coming out of my nose.

'Yeah, I'm very intriguing, me.'

Attractively I wipe pink snot on a bunch of napkins I find sitting on the end of the bar. The smell of fried food is ingrained in the paper. Nice.

'You are . . . you're highly mysterious. I can never tell what you're thinking. You don't say much, but I can tell it's always busy up there.' He points at my fore-head.

'Believe me, there's nothing interesting going on.'

'Oh, I don't know. I think you're a bit of a dark horse. What you doing? Planning your escape?'

'Yeeeah!' the hens applaud the song as it finishes. The seedy gangsters stand awkwardly by the dance floor, eyeing them up. I blush furiously.

'Maybe,' I say, wondering whether he really does know something about the diary. He might tell off-colour jokes and behave like a bit of a dick sometimes, but he's not daft. Maybe he's picked up on something. Maybe I've given something away.

'ANYWAY, I asked for "Sweet Jane", but they didn't have it.' David winks, motioning towards the DJ.

'Really? I love that song,' I say, shocked that he would request something for me. What does Camp David know about *Lou Reed?* The same person who only last week was singing 'Agadoo' and humping the filing cabinets?

'Aye, well, I thought you'd be into that kind of stuff.'

'Yeah. I never thought you'd be, though.'

'I'm a fuckin' connoisseur. You know, I've got an original copy of Peel Slowly And See by the Velvets, signed by Mo Tucker and John Cale, with the banana on it, *unpeeled*. It's probably worth a fortune, but I just couldn't sell it.'

If David started speaking Swahili I'd be less surprised.

'David, when you're at work, how come you're so . . .' I begin without thinking.

'So . . . ?'

'I just . . . at work you're . . . always acting really loud and outrageous, and I don't . . . I mean, I can't. . . . but HERE, I mean, you're pretty clued up . . . you're totally different.'

He looks confused and hurt.

Oh, great. Well put, Jane. Nice one. No more requests for you. Why don't you take your stupid crocheted tea cosy and go home before you offend everyone in the world?

Then he sighs, jangles ice cubes in his glass and scratches his chin ponderously.

'Well, Jane, cool just doesn't come into it in that office, does it? What am I gonnae do? Talk to Sophie about ma Nick Cave box set?'

'I suppose not, no,' I say, feeling utterly thick. *Nick Cave!?*

'SO, I do a bit of acting to pass the time. You know, it's just a wee routine to entertain the troops. I might be crap, and I know my humour isn't always to your taste – oh, sorry about the spunk thing, by the way, rather bad taste even for me,' he says, folding his arms. 'But let's face it, that job is dull as shit. If I didn't try to liven

114

things up we'd all die of absolute, mind-numbing, bollock-twisting, motherfucking BOREDOM.'

He breaks out into a wide, canny grin.

'That's true.' I grin back.

'But, if Madame would rather I clean up my act,' he says, sarcastically.

'God, no, you don't have to at all. I'm sorry. I'm just a bit . . .'

Lost and unravelling.

'I'm just not really feeling myself at the moment.' I finish.

'Och, I'm glad to hear it, darlin',' he says, raising an eyebrow.

'Ha ha.'

We share a wry smile.

'So, you were saying you think I'm cool?' he says, tugging his lapels and striking a pose. 'Does my un-peeled banana please you in ways you never thought POSSIBLE?'

Before I can answer, I hear the walrus cry of Sophie, effortlessly cutting through the music.

'Phwwooorgh!!' she hollers.

We both turn round.

My face falls.

My heart flips.

My knees go weak.

It can't be. I must be imagining things.

Standing at the door, bathed in a shaft of orange light is . . . is . . .

Kelly.

She's wearing a blonde wig, shiny blue trousers, a tank top, a crocheted hat, and white boots. She looks like a Womble in drag.

'Oh please God, no,' I say to no one in particular.

'Hey, Frida,' Sophie bellows at me. 'Meet Agnetha.'

We stare at each other across the crowded room.

This is it: my Waterloo.

Only Jesus can save me now. I neck my drink and attempt a smile, which is more of a disgusted contortion as alcohol burns my throat. Camp David runs up to her and greets her with a violent bear hug, but is soon accosted by Sophie, who staggers to her feet and waves drunkenly towards the dance floor. Meanwhile Kelly decides the best thing to do is to ignore me. She comes up to the bar with her snout in the air, avoiding my eye. The pale satin covering her thick thighs strains at the seams as she walks. The best strategy, I woozily tell myself, is to show no fear.

'Hi Kelly. We're BOTH in ABBA. S'funny coincidence, isn't it?' I slur.

She pretends she hasn't heard.

'You should try the Jesus Christ Superstar. It tastes like shit but it does the trick.'

'I don't like alcohol.' Kelly sniffs piously.

'Don't you? I never knew that. Seems there's a lot of things I don't know about round here. People are full of surprises, aren't they?'

'What are you talking about?' she spits.

'Oh, nothing. I meant, like, I didn't know you did boxercise. Was it good?'

Kelly flinches and orders a diet Coke.

'Thanks SO much for helping me out earlier with the brochure thing. I'm sorry about that, bit of an oversight. You were great, though, like a trained assassin or something. And you're an ace liar,' I jabber. I light a cigarette and get a headrush. The multicoloured bottles behind the bar swim prettily in front of me. I soon

116

realize that didn't sound like much of a compliment. She looks like she might punch me. All that boxercise must mean Kelly's upper body strength is pretty good. She could get me in a headlock before I could say, 'Chiquitita.'

'Oh, I didn't mean it like that. It's just . . .' I begin.

'Jane, just leave me alone,' she growls, elaborately fanning my smoke away.

'Eh?'

'You've caused enough trouble for me at work. Don't ruin my night out, OK?'

She stomps off.

There's no need to be rude, I think, watching her backside wobble away like two puppies in a sack. I said sorry, didn't I? What the fuck is wrong with these people – ignoring me, pushing me aside – don't they think I have feelings?

Suddenly I'm filled with righteous indignation.

I go after her and tap her on the shoulder.

'Hey, now wait a minute, Missy, I'm just trying to be friendly. I'm trying to . . . to make amends, and you . . . you . . . Mrs . . . Mrs Stick up Your Arse, you can't even find forgiveness for a teeny tiny bit of . . . of forgiveness in your heart. Well what does that make you?' I say, the words spilling out all over the place in no meaningful order.

Her eyes, clear and sober, regard me with a mixture of fear and contempt.

'I'm not a bad person,' I whine quietly. 'I'm not. Give me a break. Cut me some slack.'

Kelly stabs her straw in her juice and sighs.

'Stop acting like a child,' she scolds, with a patronizing edge to her toffee-nosed Edinburgh brogue.

'I don't act like a child,' I protest childishly.

117

I look over at the dancefloor, where the Dogs are prowling amongst the Hens. By the DJ booth, Sophie is blabbering to the bald Hawaiian-shirted guy while he stares vacantly at her breasts.

'I try to help you, you know,' she says, after a while. 'I do my best, but every time you mess it up. You don't seem to want to get anywhere in life. You're quite happy just bumming along, waiting for the world to make decisions for you. I don't understand you. I don't want to be a part of that, and I don't want you to drag me down with you. I'm an independent professional. I'm interested in being a success, not a failure. I'm on the ladder,' she declares pointedly.

The smug way she lectures me, sounding like a motivational mouse mat, makes me seethe. Amongst these grown-ups, Kelly seems naïve, suburban, silly – a spoilt kid up past her bedtime.

'I'm not a failure,' I stutter. 'At the travel fair I tried to help YOU.'

She doesn't reply, tilting her piggy nose to the sky.

'Anyway,' I blurt, 'at least I don't still live with my mummy and daddy.'

Cheap shot, but what the hell.

She bristles and turns away.

I walk off and go back to the bar for drink number three. Kelly has a knack for making me feel terrible. Her comments splinter and lodge in my head. I don't bum along, do I? She's a fine one talk about bums – in those trousers hers looks like a barrage balloon.

Anyway, I've got a degree. OK, so it's not a great one, but it beats her shit HNC in Travel and Tourism hands down. Admittedly my CV isn't exactly consistent: bar work, a spell at Starbucks, an ill-fated TEFL course in

Japan, assistant at a record shop, file clerk, fruit picker, more bars, a call-centre drone, a clumsy waitress, a brief spell doing unpaid freelance reviews for a city guide. Offices, pubs and temping. My job before this one was working for an agency in Manchester, getting paid to go through every newspaper with a highlighter pen, looking for any mention of the blue-chip companies that hired us. I had to be at work for 5 a.m. and couldn't stay awake past *Neighbours*. It sounded like a great excuse to read the papers and get paid, but it was boring as hell. The people who worked there – mostly depressed twentysomething graduates and embittered conspiracy theorists – could only stay a few months before having a nervous breakdown. I was there for six weeks before I lost the will to live.

Oh God, she's right. I do bum along. None of those jobs lasted longer than a couple of months. Nothing I've ever done comes to anything.

'All right?'

Fiona is standing next to me.

'Yeah. Want a drink?'

'Yeah, OK. If Kelly's been giving you shit, just ignore her.'

'Easier said than done,' I say dully, catching the eye of the barman, who's engrossed in a flirtatious conversation with a woman who looks like Popeye.

'Two Jesuses,' I slur.

He wanders over and starts making lame Tom Cruise-style cocktail manoeuvres to impress her. Fiona and I share a private smirk.

'I've worked there much longer than Kelly, and she still tries to tell me what to do,' Fiona offers matter-of-factly, picking a silver thread off her jumper.

'I can't do anything right,' I say. 'Generally. Ever.'

'Well, you're the rising star of the tourist office. Kelly can't stand it, that's all.'

'Eh?'

'Cheers,' she says, taking her glass off the bar. What's she talking about, rising star? We clink sticky pink glasses.

Fiona takes a sip and gags.

'Jesus Christ! David should serve this stuff in his bar. It'd go down a storm.'

'His what?'

'Oh, some idea he's got to start a bar. Called Dick. You can imagine the decor.'

'Sounds er . . .' I murmur, staring at the row of depleted optics. 'He's got a lot going on, hasn't he? I didn't realize. So what about you, Fiona? What don't I know about you? What do you want to do? With your life, I mean.'

She seems taken aback, shocked even. This is an end-of-the-night conversation and it's not even eleven o'clock. I'm hammered.

'I've no idea. What about you?' she counters.

I can feel myself getting flustered. Just because you don't know your arse from your elbow, doesn't mean everyone else is the same.

I plough on blindly.

'Well, I dunno. I mean, do you ever think about, you know, running away and starting again? Just totally following your instincts wherever they take you?'

Fiona, wearing a very serious expression, considers the question at length.

'Yeah,' she says eventually. 'I think about it sometimes. But then I think I could just probably start again without running away.'

The music rumbles on behind us, a funky bassline winding into the distance.

'I WANT to run away. I just want an adventure, you know?' I sigh. 'I want excitement and romance. A change of scene. Blah, blah, blah.'

My feet are actually itching. Tomorrow seems too long to wait to find Richard.

I stare at a sticky stain on the bar and push the viscous gloop with the tip of my finger. When I look up, Fiona is regarding me with worry and confusion, as if I've told her I'm about to commit suicide. I shouldn't have said anything. It's too close to the bone. People will start asking questions.

'But you only just got here,' she says.

We stare at each other. Fiona's tomboyish haircut has a haphazard purple stripe sprayed in it. Her wide mouth is punctuated with dimples. She looks like trouble, the kind of girl who could climb a tree. *You should stop worrying about Kelly and get to know her*, scolds a voice that sounds a lot like Babs, deep in the recesses of my drunken skull.

'Yeah. Hey, maybe we should get jobs at David's gay bar,' I dribble, trying to lighten the mood.

'Yeah.' She smiles, sipping her drink. 'Mind you, he probably won't employ anyone who doesn't have a twelve-inch knob.'

'We could wear strap-ons. Or we could be the cigarette girls. Fag hags.'

Fiona rolls her eyes and giggles at my crap joke.

'Girls,' David cuts in, flinging his arm round my shoulder.

'Jane,' he gasps urgently. 'I hate to break it to you, but Sophie's just requested "Dancing Queen".'

Fiona looks grave.

'Oh, yeah, sorry. That's actually what I came over to tell you,' she cringes.

Whoever's directing the film of my life also, it would seem, directed *Muriel's Wedding* and should be shot. I bash my head on the bar.

'Oh great. Is Kelly in on it?' I ask.

'Don't think so,' David replies, biting his lip with fluorescent teeth.

'No,' Fiona confirms. 'In fact, this could be pretty funny. I don't think Fat Arse has ever been to a club in her life.'

I watch as Kelly stands uncomfortably on the fringes, fiddling with her smart black handbag and looking out of sorts. Part of me suddenly feels sorry for her, but I soon get over it.

Inevitably, the strains of ABBA come bursting forth. Sophie jumps up and down in the distance, trying to attract my attention, her boobs juddering wildly. She's already got hold of Kelly, who has started to struggle, as if she's being taken hostage by terrorists.

'Well, I suppose I'm drunk enough to do it,' I say, downing my drink to make sure. Fiona rubs her hands together vigorously and cackles.

'Kick her ass,' she squeaks.

The pink stuff runs into my stomach, burning. Richard, carefully stashed under the banquette in my bag, watches me with suave interest.

'OK. Here goes.'

There's been a now-or-never feeling about this doomed disco every since I arrived, so I decide to go in guns blazing. No point in being a wallflower. I strut towards the dancefloor with Fiona and David following, and take Kelly's arm for a quick tango. Kelly has two flat feet and stumbles uselessly along with me, too shocked to offer resistance. I whisk her around until she's dizzy, throw her back and catch her before she falls backwards, all the while mouthing the words in a horribly over-the-top, flirtatious fashion, which I can tell is making her feel ill. I croon meaningfully at Kelly as she wishes she'd never met me. Everyone is laughing, or looking on with hearty approval, which just makes me act up even more.

This place isn't so bad. The booze is swilling joyfully around in my bloodstream and I feel lit from the inside, supported on all sides by Sophie, Camp David, Fiona, Val and even Dumb Paul, who clap and whistle around us. Just behind them, I catch the eye of a good-looking boy with a shaved head who's also clapping appreciatively, and I smile, a glittering, fabulous, 500-watt disco smile. I *am* the dancing queen. The lights roll and flip as I fling Kelly around and the mirrors are a twinkling blur of flailing limbs and satin.

Kelly is putty in my hands, a useless lumpy amateur compared to me and my panther-like prowess. I'm in total control of her, twisting her around and bending her backwards like the helpless springy ballerina in a music box. We waltz and pirouette and spin and spin and spin and then, as if by magic, I . . .

Fall over.

At first I tip backwards into someone and feel arms reaching out to grab me, but they don't catch me and instead I slide down the soft wall of their body. It's a fleetingly enjoyable sensation before the floor comes reeling up towards me at an odd angle and smacks me on the side of the head. I'm lying on my back, the ground rocking strangely, and I see stars, a million refracted mirrors and a white light coming towards me.

I see a shadow and wonder if I'm dead.

Then I realize I'm not dead, because the shadow has a shaved head and is asking me if I'm all right, and the white light is Camp David's suit, and the person next to Camp David looks awfully like Kelly, although it can't be her because she actually looks concerned for my welfare. My back is killing me.

'What's your name? Can you say your name?' the shadow asks. Dazed, I bring him into focus. He's the one I smiled at, the one who was clapping. He looks like a dashing doctor, a concerned brow, a kind face, a firm bottom lip that for some hysterical reason I feel like sinking my teeth into.

'Jane. Sorry. Ow,' I mumble, laughing to myself, the pain in my head making me whimper. 'Who are you?'

'This is Dan Holm,' says Camp David. 'He's my friend.'

'Oh for God's sake, this is no time for introductions. Jane, can you count to ten for me, backwards?' A voice I identify as Sophie bellows in my left ear, bringing me harshly back to reality. Her cleavage is full of winking, suggestive sparkles.

I sit up dizzily and the whole place is looking at me, waiting for my brains to leak out of my ears. Then I realize that I've fallen at an awkward angle, and my silver jeans have split at the crotch, revealing to all and sundry the grey knickers I've had since I was about 17. Camp David suppresses a falsetto shriek when he sees what a state I'm in and mashes his fist into his mouth, but whether his face registers amusement or alarm, I can't really tell. Why did I have to wear my worst trolleys? Clutching my back, I clamber to my feet, and Kelly of all people reaches out to steady me. Everything feels different, altered. The hens are gone, and I can see

124

a more sophisticated crowd, who are sniggering behind their hands at me. One person is, inexplicably, dressed as Adam Ant. A dull ache starts up in my head.

'It's fine. I'm fine. I just didn't expect,' I say, trying to regain some dignity and shakily brushing dust off my spangly top. I can taste something chemical and metallic. Maybe if I went to the toilet I could climb through the window and escape.

'Are you sure you're all right? I thought you were knocked out. You gave us a fright, you mad tart,' squeals Camp David, trying to guide me to the booth. 'Ooh, Dan, get Darling a drink. It's an emergency!'

'Honestly, I'm fine. I'm going to the toilet.'

'What day of the week is it?' Sophie slurs, shaking my shoulders.

'Friday.'

There's a pause as Sophie tries to figure out what day it is.

'Is it? Isn't it Saturday?'

'I'll be back in a minute.'

I excuse myself from flapping tourist officers in Seventies garb and escape to the ladies', a dingy room covered in brown tiles, scratched with nail files and blotted with lipstick. I stand at the sinks. What an idiot. Can't keep a job, can't dance properly, can't make friends, can't do anything without falling on my arse. My mascara has crawled underneath my eyes and down my cheeks. I can feel a bump rising on the back of my head. I must have bitten my tongue as I fell because there's blood in my mouth. Kelly *hates* me. My vision is blurred with tears.

I stumble to the middle cubicle and lock the door. On the back of the stall in eyeliner someone's written, 'This place is crap.'

I try to conjure up Richard, his profile, his words, his sketches, anything to remind me that there are higher, more beautiful things in the world than acting like a complete tosser in a Seventies club. But all I can remember is a bleak entry from the middle of January:

There's no such thing as a good friend. You're on your own. Trust people for a second, and they'll take advantage of you.

No matter how hard I try to bring him to life, his face can't be animated. It's frozen in the photograph, chalk white against grey.

Richard? Where are you?

A rush of heat and music comes through the door and someone walks in. I hear Kelly calling my name.

There's a long silence. I'm too embarrassed to speak. We both wait, listening to the running of water from a broken cistern.

'I didn't mean to do it,' she says finally.

I stare darkly at the sanitary bin.

'Didn't mean to do what?'

'Push you. I didn't mean to do it so hard.'

The bump on my head is throbbing in time to the music outside.

'But you *did* mean to push me?' I say.

'I didn't mean to,' she says again, whinier this time. 'But you were spinning me round really fast and I wanted to stop.'

I inspect Kelly's feet under the door. Her white boots are streaked with grubby black marks. Her feet are tiny. Cloven hooves.

'Oh, I see.'

The rushing of the water continues, but muffled now. My ears feel full of cotton wool.

'Are you OK?' she asks, feigning concern.

'Yeah,' I say eventually.

She stands there for a while. I stay still, thankful for the barrier of the cubicle. Lulled by the swooshing cistern, I drift into a numb stupor, imagining myself part of the fixtures and fittings. My eyes are stinging.

'Why are you even here?' I think I hear Kelly say, but she's gone.

When I finally emerge, as together as I'm ever going to be, the DJ has sweat rings on his Hawaiian shirt and is playing 'Agadoo'.

'I'm going home,' I announce on my way to pick up my bag. The back of my throat is dry and the disco lights are so bright they're splitting my skull. I'm feeling sorry for myself on an epic scale. All I want to do is lie down and wait for tomorrow. When I get home I'm going to ceremonially destroy this daft outfit, change my name and go and live in Uzbekistan.

'No, You can't go,' Camp David yells. 'Dan just bought you a drink. He's really sorry.'

Dan looks apologetic.

'I'm really sorry.'

'What for?' I ask, wondering if I might be concussed.

'I should have caught you, but I missed,' he mumbles.

'No, it's not your fault,' I say, not really listening and glancing over at Kelly, who is cagily avoiding me like a wildebeest pretending to ignore a lion. 'I have to go, honestly.'

David suddenly slings his arms around me and hugs me. I'm enveloped in UV rays. His neck is warm,

Kelly and the club go away. Everything is immediately peaceful. I think I'm going to cry again.

'Now listen,' he whispers, 'you've got to stay and finish your drink because I say so.'

'But . . .'

'Ah, ah, ah . . . what did I say?' Holding me at arm's length, he fixes my doily, licks a finger and pokes it near my eye, wiping off a crust of eyeliner.

'Ow! But why?'

'Dan's my friend,' David says, wiggling his eyebrows suggestively, 'and he wants to meet you. Oh my God, Sophie's buying a round for the first time in years. Better be offski,' he barks, mincing off to the bar at the speed of light.

I stand there with Dan, David's 'friend'. He smiles sheepishly and offers me a Jesus Christ Superstar.

'It's a double, if that helps,' he says.

'Thanks.'

Dan is tall and eager to please. He's wearing a black T-shirt and nondescript jeans. He's handsome in a chiselled, gay kind of way, with sandy brown hair cut so close it reminds me of sealskin. My first instinct is to touch it, but that would be really weird. I wonder if he's the boyfriend David was slagging off earlier – they seem close.

'So,' I say after a long pause. 'How do you know David?'

'I used to be one of your lot.'

One of whose lot? I wonder. A heterosexual? A girl? A fuck-up from Leeds?

'I used to work at the tourist office,' he explains patiently. 'I left last year. Went back to college.'

'Oh, right. I didn't realize,' I try again. 'And what are you doing at college?' I ask, as if I've learned how to

128

converse from a Fifties etiquette manual. I'm really quite drunk and brain damaged and I really must go home. My thought processes are virtually non-existent.

'Media studies. I'm hoping to be a film critic.'

'Ha!' I say bitterly. 'Yeah right. You and everyone else. I did media studies and look at me now.'

He looks at me now and backs away slightly.

'Yeah, well. I'm, er, writing a couple of reviews for a film magazine at the moment, so hopefully something might come of it. You never know. I've got to go down to London to meet the editor and have a chat next week.'

'Oh. Right. No. Oh God, I didn't mean . . . Wow, I mean that's great. You could be the next Barry Norman,' I burble, overdoing it. 'What did he used to say? Not a lot? Oh no, that was Paul Daniels.'

He's looking at me as if I'm insane, which possibly I am. Bongos are pounding in my brain.

'Dan, I'm sorry, I think I need to sit down.'

'Does your head still hurt?' He smiles.

'Yeah, a bit,' I whimper.

'Come on.'

He offers the crook of his arm and we stagger to a booth in the corner. His weight is reassuring – I suddenly feel like my body has disappeared and I'm just a mess of tacky clothes and caked, dribbling eye make-up. I could blow away in the wind.

'Can you count to ten backwards?' he asks, taking the piss out of Sophie.

'No, never seemed much call for it.'

'That was some fall. She nearly sent me flying, too,' he says, frowning across at Kelly.

'Yeah, well, we don't get on very well. She's a mingebag,' I murmur.

'Ooh. A technical term, eh? Well, yeah, she is. Sometimes. She used to be like that with me. I remember when we went down to the Destinations fair once, she gave me such a hard time.'

A dim memory of Kelly waxing lyrical about my predecessor floats to the surface.

'That was you?' I ask. 'I went with her this year. She gave this talk and I spoiled it by telling this story about peasants with boils which everyone else thought was great. Then I went to the wine-tasting stand and got pissed. She wasn't very pleased.'

'Really?' he grins. 'Well, I coughed once during the presentation and I thought she was going to slam my bollocks in the laptop.'

I laugh and my cranium resonates with pain.

'But she's OK, once you get past the head injuries. When she shouts at you and tries to knock you out it means she likes you,' he says dryly. His long fingers pick tentatively at a beer mat on the table. 'She can be quite kind sometimes though. She's only nineteen, you know. She's just an ambitious wee kid who gets ahead of herself.'

'Nineteen? Really? Is that all? She seems about forty-five.'

We sit there a while, watching Kelly awkwardly talking to Fiona while Fiona pretends to listen.

'So Frida,' he says, surveying my outfit. 'How do you like Edinburgh? Is it better than Sveeeden?'

I'm no expert, but his Scandinavian accent is pathetic. He tips his head to one side like an inquisitive budgie. He's cute. I suddenly feel entirely at ease with this ridiculous person.

'Well, I dunno. Not much. It's a bit up itself sometimes, isn't it? All these dried-up old ladies and blokes with papooses, and people arsing about on stilts. And I really hate the festival. It's just . . . amateur dramatic hell,' I say, quoting Richard. Coming from me, it sounds silly.

Dan pulls a face.

'Aw, come on, it's not that bad. You can see all kinds of things – Peruvian nose flute players, naked line dancers, there's even a transsexual mime version of Die Fledermaus on at the Pleasance. What's not to like?'

'Is there?'

'No. Have you ever been up Arthur's Seat?'

'No.'

'Have you ever been to Portobello?'

'No.'

'Have you ever been to the Botanic gardens and seen that big palm tree?'

'No. How big is it?'

'Fucking enormous! You're crap. You need showing around,' he says with an impertinent smirk.

'I am not crap. Get lost.' I smile, not looking at him.

'Everyone from Leeds is crap. It's a fact.'

'How do you know I'm from Leeds?' I ask suspiciously.

'Na ne na noo ne nam neeeeeds?' he mimics back in a high-pitched voice. It seems perfectly acceptable to lamp him for that, so I do. He feigns agony.

'Ooh, you're such a bitch. No wonder our lovely sweet Kelly tried to kill you with her bionic ginger fist.'

'Go back to your boyfriend and talk about soft furnishings,' I scowl, folding my arms and pretending to be interested in the carpet.

He sits back in his seat, grinning from ear to ear, watching me.

'What are you doing tomorrow?'

'Nothing with you.'

'Come on, I'll buy you an ice cream and show you my big plant.'

'Fuck off.'

'You've got a mouth like a navvy, you have. Bet you're common as muck. Look at you, dressed like a slapper.'

I give him the finger, unable to keep a straight face. This is fun. My headache and Kelly-inspired misery have disappeared, and my inhibitions have evaporated in a giant lake of pink alcohol.

'Even though you're a rude, disgusting cow, I'm still not taking no for an answer,' he says dramatically.

'I can't tomorrow. I'm going on an adventure. I've got a secret,' I whisper conspiratorially, warming to David's daft mate, lover, whatever. There's just no tension. I feel I can say what I like.

'Are you a hermaphrodite?' he whispers, leaning in close. His breath is hot against my ear and, inexplicably, makes the hairs go up on the back of my neck.

'No,' I say, rolling my eyes.

'Well come on, what is it? Are you one of them lezzas?'

'Nope.'

'Well, what then?'

I'm shaking with excitement. The thought of telling him about Richard makes me go all funny. Talking about him seems momentous – I've never even uttered his name to a soul. This feels earth-shattering, something I can't go back on. I'm about to tell a total stranger my secret. I can't hold onto it any longer, it's bursting to get out, and as soon as it does it'll become real, completely real. I hardly dare do it, but I'm drunk and Dan seems trustworthy enough . . .

'I found a diary on the train when I came back from London with Kelly,' I explain, my voice quavering. 'And it belongs to this man called Richard Miles. And I think,' I can barely get the words out, 'I think he might be . . . my soul mate.'

There's a terrible silence between us. The word soulmate, an overwrought, Mills and Boon word, hangs mournfully in the air. The whole thing sounds much more ridiculous than I'd anticipated.

'Are you serious?' Dan asks, still smiling.

'Yeah. I mean, honestly, I know it sounds stupid, but everything in it is . . . I don't know, somehow it all has something to do with me. It's like, I can't really explain it. He thinks the same thoughts as me, and he's lonely and angry and I feel like I can help him. I feel like we can help each other, y'know? I just found it lying there, and it was as if he was trying to reach out or something, send a message to someone who might understand. I have to try and find him, just to see whether I'm right.'

Dan clears his throat and frowns. All the life has drained from his face.

'So, what's in it?'

'Everything. Thoughts and drawings and stuff. He's really clever, talented and sensitive. It sounds insane, but I carry it around with me because it sort of guides me. Oh God, you think I'm a freak.'

'No. No, not at all.' He says, obviously thinking I'm a freak. I wish I could start the conversation from scratch and leave this part out. Enough about me, let's talk about you. Seen any good films lately?

'Have you got it with you tonight?' he asks, offering the small, encouraging smile people usually give to care-in-the-community patients.

'Yes,' I mumble.

'Can I see it?'

Dan seems genuinely interested, but there's worry in his voice.

'I don't know.'

'I'd really like to,' he says decidedly.

I look at Dan. His face is totally sincere. What the hell.

'Well, I suppose I've told you now. I may as well go and get it.'

So I go and get it. The bag is trapped between Sophie and Camp David on the opposite banquette.

'Just have to get something from my bag,' I say, reaching between them for the diary.

'How are you getting on?' David enquires.

'Yeah, fine. Wanted to show him something.'

'Ooh, steady on, Darlin', there are some things a lady should leave until her wedding night,' he says, raising one eyebrow and pursing his lips.

'Oh shush.'

As casually as I can, I walk over and give it to Dan, who handles it with care, as if it's a museum piece or an unexploded bomb. I don't even know whether I want to stick around for his reaction. My muscles have turned to soup.

'Look at the drawings. Aren't they good?' I twitter nervously. 'And here's the photograph of him. He's great looking, isn't he?'

Dan nods slowly. I can see a twitch start up in his jaw.

'I found all these receipts in the back. I've pieced them together and I think I might have narrowed down where he lives to a few places. I'm going to do my best to track him down.'

'How do you know that's him?' Dan asks, looking up.

'What?'

'How do you know he's the man in the photograph? That might not be him. It could be anyone.'

For a second the pain in my head returns, then vanishes again.

'I just know. Sometimes . . . you just know,' I say firmly.

He reads for a while. The DJ is playing 'Last Night A DJ Saved My Life' and singing smugly along as he clutches his headphones to one ear. Over at the bar, David is a phosphorescent streak. As he waves his hands around, jabbering to Fiona, he leaves faint tracers in the air. The room has taken on a bright, glittering, jangling quality – every surface seems alive and reflective. Disorientated, I try to focus on the shadows, where Sophie and Dumb Paul are snogging each other's faces off. I concentrate on the mechanical, washing-machine movements of Paul's terrible kissing technique while lights fly around me, as if I'm on an out-of-control carousel.

'So,' he says after what seems like for ever. 'Do you think he's like you?'

'Well, yeah,' I reply.

'Jane, I mean, I might be wrong, but I wouldn't say this guy has got anything in common with you at all. I don't really know you, but . . . he seems . . . a wee bit full of himself, doesn't he?'

'What?'

My breathing becomes shallow. I feel impossibly jittery.

'What do you mean?'

'Well, look here . . . 14th of February. "Tonight I'm going to go to a restaurant on my own, carrying a bunch of flowers, and order a really expensive bottle of champagne with two glasses. Then I'll just sit there, on my own, until all the loved-up couples start feeling sorry for me. I'll sit there until they're beside themselves with pity for me, until they can't concentrate on anything else but the fact that I've been stood up. Then maybe they'll know how I feel ALL THE TIME." That's just self-indulgent, isn't it? What's the point of that?'

'He's lonely,' I protest, picking at my thumbnail.

'And all this stuff about people being idiots, and him being the only one who understands what life's all about. I mean, that's so adolescent, it's the kind of thing I used to write when I was fifteen. And this,' he continues, really getting into it now as anger boils up inside me and I desperately try to stop myself from punching him in his stupid, big, inquisitive budgie head, 'this thing about his girlfriend trying to rope him in as a sperm donor doesn't really ring true, does it? It sounds like he didn't treat her very well and was trying to justify it to himself.'

I stare at him.

'You couldn't be more wrong.'

He draws back, for some reason surprised by my anger.

'Listen, Jane,' he pleads. 'It's just, you don't really know who he is. He could be anyone. He could be anywhere. What if you find him and he's a total nutter? What are you going to do then?'

The room is spinning. I can't believe I'm hearing this.

'I just don't think he's what you think he is. Even if you did meet him, I wouldn't get your hopes up. It sounds to me like he's got some funny ideas about women – all these strange pictures of girls with big tits, they're kind of weird. I just don't . . . get it.'

'What do you know about women?' I splutter with a

136

harsh, barbed edge to my voice that I barely recognize.

'Eh?'

'Oh, come on, you're gay. You'd think any pictures of women's tits look weird. You've no idea what you're talking about. Anyway, what do you care?'

I'm hyperventilating. My chest is tight. I feel like somebody has stamped on my heart. Why did I blow the secret? It was so perfect. Richard is pure, not like this grubby place with these disgusting drinks and horrible people trampling all over your dreams, everything sticky and old and broken and abused.

'I shouldn't have shown it to you,' I gasp, tears forcing themselves down my cheeks. I get up too quickly and stumble backwards. I'm immediately dizzy, and all I can taste is the hideous sweet Germolene flavour of the cocktails. I think I'm going to be sick. Bile rises up in my throat and I bolt out of the front door, up the stairs, past the bouncers and into a side street.

Crying and puking in my flimsy spangly top in a wet alleyway, near council dumpsters overflowing with bottles and chip wrappers, it occurs to me that I've really excelled myself this time. If Ali was around, she'd catalogue it and remind me of it for ever. But I don't want to remember this. I want to forget this place ever existed.

I lean against the wall, breathing in the damp drizzle, trying to calm myself down. I want to go to sleep and for this just to be a bad dream. Nobody said those awful things about Richard. I never got pushed over by Kelly. I was never here. The banging bassline inside the club makes the corrugated iron over the side entrance flex and contract. There's the shrill, cabbagey stink of rubbish, and something else, something feral – foxes or rats or rabid dog pee. I shudder involuntarily as someone walks over my grave. This city must be cursed. I can feel the other city, haunted and abandoned beneath my feet, catching up with me.

Soon I become aware of a figure standing nearby. It's Dan, holding my battered leather jacket and the diary. He's standing like an obliging waiter about to lead a customer to their table.

Shit!

The diary. I nearly left it. The thought makes me feel queasy again. I peel myself off the wall and lunge towards it. Even the things I care about most I can't hold onto for more than five seconds.

'Jane, I'm sorry. I didn't mean to make you cry,' he says quietly, offering me the book. I take it off him and grab it with both hands, falling back against a wheelie bin with a dull thud. I slip and kick over a waterlogged polystyrene carton half-full of bloated chips in curry sauce.

'Do you want me to get you a cab?' he asks.

'I can walk.' My voice sounds piercing and slurred, the voice of a drunken harridan. I pick an unsteady path through a mess of beer cans and spilt garbage.

'Please. Let me get you a taxi. You'll be safer.'

My boots are covered in curry. I'm a mess. I'm rubbish.

'I can go on my own,' I blurt. 'I'm a loser, you know. Haven't you heard? Ask Kelly. Ask anyone. I fuck everything up. I always have. I'm just a crazy girl who's in love with a book. Look at the state of me – I've got curry on my wellies!'

I take my jacket and walk away, out of the festering alleyway and into fresher air. I've no idea what I'm doing. I can't get a handle on what's happening at all. It seems easier to look at solid entities like the pavement.

Before I can even get my bearings or figure out which direction I'm supposed to be going in, the engine of a black cab is growling away alongside me and Dan has opened the door. The orange light of the 'For Hire' sign flickers in the rain. For want of any alternative, I get in.

'Bye, Jane,' he says, leaning on the roof. His face is dappled and blurred through the glass, but his stare is clear, trained on me. A red sticker on the half-open taxi window in the shape of an arrow helpfully points to him.

'For the record, you're not a loser. You're maybe a bit confused, and you've got a doily on your head, but I don't think you're a loser,' he says. 'And just so you know, being friends with David doesn't mean I'm gay.'

With that, he closes the door and the driver asks me where I want to go. I mumble my address and sink into the seat. Through the window Dan gives a resigned wave, his lips set in a tight, regretful smile. As the cab pulls away, I turn to see him still watching me, getting smaller and smaller. Silhouetted under the street-light, he looks suddenly heroic, his shoulders hunched against the rain like some Forties film star. I feel an ache of regret. He was only trying to be nice. Then I become aware of the sharp corner of the diary stabbing me in the chest, and I realize I'm hugging it for dear life.

Part Two

NEWCASTLE

Uh.

Urraggh.

My mouth is glued to the pillow.

A square of sharp sunlight leaks through a gap at the top of the curtains, and burns a hole in my head, which is stuffed full of ball bearings. Ball bearings with spikes. On the floor my bottle-green vest glints biliously, next to a pool of dirty silver trousers and one stray white boot splattered with something dubious and brown.

I feel like shit.

I've never felt this bad.

Jesus Christ Superstars are evil.

I slowly try to piece together what happened last night. I know I had some sort of embarrassing emotional crisis, but I don't know what. The diary. That guy. Dave? Dan. Dan was nice, but then he wasn't, and then what? How did I get home? Did he come back here?

Oh my God, is he here?

Raising my head hurts like hell, but I gingerly lift it off the pillow and squint around the bedroom.

He's not here.

I fall back down and catch my breath. Then I sit bolt upright, the world spinning out of control on its axis.

Is the diary here? Where's the diary?

I nearly expire with relief when I see it on the floor by my clothes. It's safe and well, unlike me. Inside it all the clues I need to find Richard are intact. And when I finally meet him, the unhinged, charity-shop jigsaw puzzle of my crap life might start to make sense. He's the missing piece. I know it.

I collapse back under the duvet and wonder whether I'll ever feel OK again.

Then I remember the bump on my head, 'Dancing Queen', Kelly admitting she pushed me. What a bitch. Camp David was being very strange. Was he trying to set me up with Gay Dan? Except he wasn't gay, was he? Or was he? I don't think so. I don't remember. I don't care. He said Richard was a nutter, that's all I know, and, oh God, I was sick. I was sick in the street. Classy.

I lie there listening to cars outside and the far too wholesome, loud drone of Queenie hoovering her carpet downstairs, bumping the vacuum cleaner against her skirting boards as she goes. Today I have to get on a train and scour the country. The enormity of the task doesn't bear thinking about. Tiredness pulls me under, but every time I give into it, I fall into such bottomless, deathly exhaustion that I panic and have to snap my eyes open again. The only thing for it is to get up. Drink a reservoir, try to eat, go to Newcastle, find ideal man, go home.

I stagger to the bathroom and look in the mirror. The person staring back isn't me at all, but someone out of the Addams Family, pale, with black and red ringed eyes. My teeth are coated in sugary varnish. Oh, Richard, if you could see me now.

Right, OK, tough measures are in order. My train is at midday, and it's now 11. I need to not look like something that was discovered in a peat bog a million years ago and I need to phone mum and tell her I'm coming down on Sunday.

I really can't be arsed talking to Babs. She'll be at work and in full customer-service mode, which involves putting on a silly posh voice and shouting. If I get Becky she'll use her puritanical sixth sense, twig I have yet another hangover and brand me an alcoholic. I can't win.

I fill the sink and wash my face, wiping off last night's smudgy eyeliner with my fingers. That guy Dan really laid into Richard. I trusted him, too, and he shot me down in flames. Well, I'm not telling anyone else. I can't risk that again. From now on, Jane, you will be inscrutable.

While I'm brushing my teeth, disjointed technicolour stills of last night flash before my eyes, like the pictures on a View-Master my Dad once bought me in Blackpool to keep me quiet. Kelly's scuffed boots under the door. Camp David's ultra-violet suit. Dan's face, head cocked to one side, laughing at my jokes. Sophie slutting around with Dumb Paul. The diary in Dan's hands as his mouth casually ripped it apart, twisting Richard's words into something ugly and unimportant.

I brush my teeth too hard and my gums start bleeding.

Forget it, Jane. Just forget it. Who cares what he thinks?

After two glasses of water and two Nurofens I decide it's now or never.

'Hello, Barbara's Blooms?'

'Hiya, Mum.' I croak, my voice three octaves lower than usual.

'Hello JANE! God you sound rough. To what do we owe this pleasure? Bye, Mrs Johnson, it'll be ready to pick up first thing Monday. Are you all right?'

There's a pause. I absently wipe my finger over the dust on top of the TV.

'Who are you talking to?' I ask.

'You, you dummy.'

'Yeah . . . I'm, er . . . coming down to see you on Sunday, if that's OK.'

'Really? Oh, LOVELY. That'll be eight pounds fifty, please.'

I hear the beep beep of the till and the faint rattle of the cash drawer.

'I'm er, just going to see Alison in Newcastle, and I thought I'd drop in.'

'Well that'll be nice, won't it? You haven't seen her for a while. Oh, I'm so pleased. Have you got anything smaller?'

'What?'

'How long are you staying?'

'Just the one night.'

'Thank you. See you again. Why don't you stay a bit longer?'

'I'm going to London on Monday.'

'Again? Why are you going to London again?' she asks, suddenly all ears.

The tube tickets from the back of the diary sit on the arm of my chair. One to West Hampstead, one to Tottenham Court Road.

'Oh, I've got to go and do something for work. The travel fair went well, so Sophie asked me to go down and er . . . do a presentation for this er . . . client.'

I mumble, cringing and writing 'bollocks' in the dust.

'A presentation,' she coos incredulously, as if I've just told her I'm going to the moon. 'BECKY!' she squeals straight into the mouthpiece. A fissure cracks open in my head, oozing molten lava, and my temples start to throb insistently. 'Jane, that's WONDERFUL.'

'Yeah, well, it's nothing really.'

'It's not NOTHING. Becky, Jane's going to London to do a presentation.'

Oh Jesus, shut up.

I hear Becky give a half-hearted, 'Oooh, get you' in the background. Even though it's a blatant lie, she could be a bit more enthusiastic.

'Things are definitely looking up for you, aren't they?' Babs gabbles. 'Well done. You know, it's about time something good happened to you. Exciting new opportunities are just around the corner.'

'Well, you never know.'

Babs starts banging on about her friend Joyce, who has a similarly dazzling career trajectory in the mortgage department of the Halifax, and my mind drifts. I imagine Richard sitting on the train, framed by the window, trapped behind Plexiglas. He's frowning with concentration, the words, *'When will I find someone?'* flowing from his pen. I'm standing on the platform and he looks up, and that's when our eyes meet for the first time. There's a spark of attraction, a sizzle, like a fly hitting an Insect-o-Cutor. In that split second our lives are changed for ever.

'Anyway, I'll give you a ring when I get to Leeds.'

'OK, love, see you then. Byeeee.'

I hang up, feeling in urgent need of hospital treatment. Wandering through to the bedroom, I pick up the

147

diary and the photograph slips out onto the floor. Richard, the opportunity to end all opportunities, lies on my threadbare rented flat carpet, reminding me why I'm bothering. He's so beautiful, ridiculously beautiful. The pose is iconic, burned into my consciousness. It's a snapshot of my future. But now I see a new impatience in the corners of his mouth, a fitful restlessness in the way he's sitting.

I am a man. I am a man who spends far too much time passing through. I am a man who stays in too many hotels and never even gets time to put his clothes in the drawer. I am a man who never settles down.

I need something real and permanent. I need somewhere to be. I need a home. I need somebody to hold me in their arms and make no impossible demands. I don't need advice, I don't need to be told (although people delight in telling me anyway) – I need peace and patience and kindness. I need somebody to pin me down.

A deep, desperate pang pulls at my heart.

I need a home, too, I need somewhere to be, I need something permanent. We're both unravelling, stumbling about in the dark, waiting for signs. How can two people be so alike and not have found each other? How can I have met so many small-minded, fake, self-involved people, and not you?

I look at the clock radio on the bedside table that says I'm going to miss my train, put the diary in my bag and fling myself out of the door, into the bright hallway.

On the first floor, I can see Queenie lurking, pretending to polish her already immaculate doorknob.

'Is that you away, dear?' she chirps as I walk past.

'Yep. See you next week.'

'Take care. Don't forget to come back.'

Chance would be a fine thing.

Edinburgh Waverley is packed with Saturday shoppers, spilling in from adjacent towns. West Calder, Burntisland – places I've never seen, places that could be horrible or picturesque or dull. The station screams at me – everything is really grating and intense, from a kid in a pushchair having a tantrum by the flower stall to the bing bong of the announcements. My train is waiting at platform nineteen, and I struggle along, trying to find my seat before my head explodes. Never again. My eyeballs feel like someone's taken them out in the night and played ping-pong with them. Even though I've sprayed, showered, plucked and brushed I'm still a dehydrated husk with a lump on my head the size of a grapefruit.

Unfortunately, instead of being blissfully empty with Egyptian cotton duvets and free eye masks, the carriage is packed, full of dithering bastards and whining kids. Already there are two people sitting opposite my seat – a middle-aged couple, him reading a copy of the *Daily Record*, her covering the table with an assortment of crap crisps, Puzzler books and a tartan Thermos. They both smell of gravy. As I put my bag up on the luggage rack, they tense up and glare at me territorially, as if I'm about to start taking pot shots at them with a crossbow. The reserved tickets on the back of their seats say King's Cross. Great. I sit down and he returns to his paper, while she watches me as if I'm something in a zoo, vacantly sucking on a boiled sweet. Why does everyone keep staring at me? I do everything I can to avoid eye contact. God forbid they should start talking to me. I just couldn't deal with a five-hour conversation about piles.

I shut them out.

OK. Richard, I'm all yours. Let's say he's here now. I'm just about to fall asleep and someone sits on the seat next to me. His thigh brushes mine and I don't even have to open my eyes, I know it's him. Still dozing – looking radiant, of course, not like something a pig farmer would scrape off his boot – I turn my head and our faces are inches away. As I come to, he's looking at me, a smile playing on his lips.

Just think, Jane, Richard might be on this very train.

The thought is delicious.

He's got to be somewhere. He might have been working in Edinburgh and be going back home to Newcastle, York, or London for the weekend. I imagine him tired and battered by the week's demands, his thick dark hair messed up after another sleepless night in a generic chain hotel, sick of coffee with UHT milk, sick of work and travel and in need of the love of a good woman. Called Jane. I glance briefly at the other passengers, but they're all either old or ugly or both.

I wonder what Richard does that involves so much running around. I've decided he isn't a writer. As far as I know writers just stay at home and work in their pants. But he's definitely arty – there's no way he's an accountant or a vacuum-cleaner salesman. I thought for a while that he might be some kind of investigative reporter, smashing international crime gangs and uncovering injustice in dangerous, unpronounceable countries, but I couldn't see his name in any of the papers. Anyway, those kinds of people don't have time to keep diaries. He could run a company, perhaps – a design consultancy or an architecture firm. It'll be something exciting, anyway, something creative. Something thrusting. I close my eyes again.

He's so vivid in my mind that I could reach out and touch him. His rounded top lip, his luscious lashes, the curve of his Adam's apple.

God.

Suddenly I feel a stab of lust so intense that I have to look over at Mrs Tartan Flask in case I've let out some kind of involuntary porn-star gasp, but she's gawping out of the window, crunching steadily.

Come on, Jane, concentrate.

You're here to find him, not to sit on trains thinking about shagging.

I search the station, the same way as I did on the day I found the diary. It's only been a week, but it feels like Richard's been in my life for ever. I already have his mind, now I need a body and a voice – living, breathing, physical proof. On the platform, people in a last-minute rush fret and faff with heavy suitcases and rucksacks. It's a warm early September lunchtime and the air is hazy and buzzing. A man with a mop of dark hair and a sky-blue shirt leans against the railings holding a paper cup. I suddenly feel free, like I've been let out of school early and nobody knows where I am.

Through the hungover haze I realize that this is a life-changing occasion. This is my date with destiny, my moment of truth. It's the beginning of a new phase in my life, a new me. Everything is full of possibility. I'm in an elevator, whizzing upwards towards an unknown destination, somewhere amazing and impossible to imagine, and I don't know when it's going to stop. My bad mood instantly evaporates and for a moment I'm delirious. A shiver goes through me, energy crackles around me, my hair seems loaded with static. Richard's out there somewhere, like some big glittering Christmas present, with my name on the tag. I can hardly wait.

Almost imperceptibly we start to move. The carriage creaks as the train gathers pace, and something flickers in the corner of my eye. For a split second I think I see that guy Dan running after the train, a blur of flailing limbs and shaved head, but when I turn round there's nothing, only the end of the platform receding quickly into the distance.

'He could be anyone. He could be anywhere.'

The sound of his voice, as clear as if he were sitting next to me, gives me a sudden knot in my stomach and I push it away.

Get. Lost.

Soon, the train pulls out of the station. I can feel the castle, the Scott monument's middle finger, the shopping centre and the tourist office, Ziggy's and my poky flat gradually disappearing brick by brick, until Edinburgh is gone.

'PIERS! What about this one?'

A loud-mouthed family of three, led by a harassed woman with a horsey face and starchy blouse, come bustling down the aisle carrying toys, a colouring book and a variety of bags and juice cartons.

'Is this seat taken?' the woman asks me inevitably, pointing at the empty chair next to me.

'Er, no. Go ahead,' I mumble.

Oh, great, this is all I need.

'Gaiaaaa! Gaiaaaa!' she wails. 'This one darling, there's a seat here. There you go, you sit here and mummy and Piers will sit on this one over here. Do you have your colouring book? Where's Piers? Piers, come

152

here, the lady wants to get past. Pick up your colouring book. Pick it up. Piers, behave yourself. Do you want to sit there, Piers? OK then Gaia, come and sit with Mummy.'

Piers is dressed in an expensively cut checked shirt and a pair of crisply ironed chinos. He could be mistaken for a very small off-duty banker on holiday in the Hamptons, were it not for the fact that he has a large streak of green snot dripping from his nostril. Damp-faced and grumpy, Piers decides to sit next to me and take high-pitched bawling to new levels. It's not exactly the romantic, mysterious thigh-brushing I was hoping for. I stick my finger in one ear and take my mobile phone out of my pocket. Ali said she'll meet me off the train and we'll go for dinner. I already know where I want to go. Richard's restaurant, the one where he spent £72 with Sarah Arseholen or some other unsuitable sperminator. It's called Café Bleu and it's on the Quayside. It's expensive, but I don't care. Anyway, I'm on holiday and Ali can afford it. Who knows? He might be there, dining handsomely but alone, and just about to order the main course. Which, unbeknownst to him, would be me, in the buff with a bit of parsley covering my extremities.

I text her to say I'm on my way. Next to me Piers cries inconsolably. Opposite, Mrs Tartan Flask is telling her husband to go to the buffet and get her a sandwich. It's all too loud. My head has started thumping again. I'm getting the fear. I'm going to have an aneurysm or a stroke or a heart attack. I'm having a brain haemorrhage. In a matter of seconds the lights are going to go out and I'm going to be dead.

'Piers, try to colour within the lines, then it'll be neater.'

Piers takes a crayon and scratches an angry red splodge over a jaunty picture of a mermaid, surrounded by seaweed and starfish. I decide he bears an uncanny resemblance to the kid in *The Shining*.

Redrum . . . redrum . . .

Fuck.

Stop it, Jane. Breathe, breathe.

OK, let's play a game.

Ask the universe a question and see what it says.

Right. Here goes.

Am I going to find Richard?

I look out of the window at unremarkable fields, scribbles of barbed-wire fence and derelict outbuildings. In the distance, behind a wave of pea-green hills, I can see the Forth Bridge. Tiny cars and lorries pass over it.

Give me a sign.

'Now that's not very nice, is it, Piers?'

We go by a train depot, where old carriages are rusting and dying by the side of the track. Some are sprayed with graffiti. One of them says, 'If You Want Sex Phone Jim on 09895 364174.' What kind of a sign is that?

More fields. More fence. Some sheep.

Come ON. Am I going to find Richard?

'NO!'

Piers lets out an anguished scream as Mummy takes the crayon off him. I turn round, my heart clattering against my ribcage. Me and Piers stare at each other, mutually surprised. His spiky eyelashes are studded with tears, his nose is a pink button mushroom. He looks at me pleadingly.

'No!'

'I'm awfully sorry,' horsey mum says, offering me

a sympathetic smile. 'Now, Piers, come on, don't be a baby.'

'No, no, no, no, no!' he wails. His mother scoops him up and carries him to the end of the carriage, where he continues struggling and squealing and yelling 'No' like a police siren. Across the aisle the ludicrously named Gaia is unfazed, kicking her legs up and down and singing quietly.

My entire body is jangling with shock. I sit back and try to calm down.

It's a stupid game anyway.

Richard said it himself, only an idiot would try to control the world and make it do what they want it to.

It doesn't mean anything.

Peace descends on the carriage as Piers is taken into the toilet. We pass a metal sign at the side of the tracks that says 'Edinburgh 50 miles', pointing in the other direction.

I'm just going to have to put myself in the hands of fate. I know I'm on the right track. If it's destined to happen, then he'll come to me. As long as I'm out there, vaguely following his path, if it's meant to be, we'll come together. We'll collide blindly into each other and no explanation will be necessary. If not, well . . . at least I tried.

I begin to lose myself in a daydream. I bump into Richard when I'm turning a corner into an unfamiliar street in an unfamiliar city, and there's that glorious second of impact, as my shoulder touches his chest and my hair brushes his neck and I'm dizzyingly close to him; we spring back and see each other for the first time, and it's like we've been asleep for years and suddenly we're awake. 'Sorry,' he says, but he's not and neither am I, and he holds my shoulders as if he's never going to let go, and I don't want him to let go, so we stay there for ages, just taking each other in, and then . . . and then . . .

Mrs Tartan Flask is watching me without interest, inserting a cheese and onion crisp in her gob like a letter in a postbox.

I cover my head with my jacket and try to go to sleep.

'Oh my God! Jaaaaane! I didn't recognize you. I was like, why the hell is that bird with the red hair waving at me? AAAAARRRGH! It's SO good to see you.'

Ali, wearing a spotty dress and a white Sixties raincoat, looks wonderful, and envelops me in an expensively perfumed embrace. Her dark brown hair is cut into a Beatle bob, and underneath her long fringe her eyes are rimmed with kohl. She could always pull off the daring, adventurous art-school look. If I tried to do it I'd look like Ringo's mum.

'Hiya, Ali. Thank God I'm here. That train journey was murder, I was sitting next to a screaming little bastard the whole way. Look at you. You look so grown up.' I smile, observing her well-tailored clothes, the single silver heart on a pendant, the way her round face seems more streamlined and composed. Her lips are painted sweetheart pink and her haircut must have cost a fortune. She looks every inch a success. At the other end of the evolutionary scale is me, stinking of old booze and underachievement, a neglected rag doll with the stuffing coming out of it.

'That's 'cos we *are* grown-ups. You look so different with that hair,' she gasps. 'Come on, let's get out of here.'

'Yeah, OK,' I gibber, my nerves shot to pieces.

156

Newcastle station is crawling with blokes dressed in humbug-striped football strips, drinking and shouting abuse at each other. One leers at me and says something to his friend, who laughs and shows a set of teeth like broken piano keys.

'On the batter last night, were you?' Ali says, grabbing my bag off me. 'I haven't been out in ages – I'm always too knackered. Where did you go?'

'Oh God, some awful Seventies place called Ziggy's. Went out with people from work. This horrible ginger girl pushed me over and nearly killed me and then I puked in the gutter.'

'NO! What happened?' Ali shrieks excitedly.

'It was someone from work. Kelly.' I grimace, thinking about Kelly's comical outfit, suddenly realizing how young and ridiculous she is. 'We were both dressed up as the girls from ABBA, and she's been winding me up for months, so I got drunk and made her do an embarrassing dance routine to "Dancing Queen" to show her up in front of our boss, y'see . . .'

In the cold light of day it doesn't seem half as tragic and overblown as it did at the time.

'So she got pissed off and pushed me and I hit my head and thought I was dead, and then I realized everyone was looking at me and my trousers had split in the crotch.'

Ali cackles filthily, which makes me laugh too.

'What? Did you show everyone your chuff?'

'No, worse than that. A pair of grey knickers I've had since I was about eight with "Monday" on written on the front.'

'Good old Jane – some things never change.'

Some things do, I think, as we pass the front of the station. With one eye, I scan the street for Richard.

157

'Anyway, it really wasn't very nice. And then I met this guy and it all went—'

'Who? Who?' Ali asks, doing an impression of a constipated monkey.

Oh, I'm so tight-lipped – I should get a job at MI6. Inscrutable to the last.

'Just this guy,' I say quickly, irritated at the interruption.' Anyway, I thought he was OK, but he was a tosser in the end.'

As the words come out of my mouth, I feel like I've told a lie.

'Anyway,' I continue, 'so we had this argument and I started crying and it was all a total nightmare.'

'Why did he make you cry?' she wonders, with concern in her voice.

Because he was horrible to me. Because he didn't understand. Why did he get so angry about the diary? He brought me my jacket, and he was kind enough then. He got me a taxi. *'You're not a loser,'* I remember him saying. *'Just because I hang around with David doesn't mean . . .'*

'Oh, it was nothing. I was just drunk – I would have cried at anything,' I say cheerily, trying to shake off a new feeling of uncertainty. This is a terrible hangover. I should have bought a bottle of water on the train, but the excitement might have been too much for Mrs Gravy to deal with.

'Aaaargh!' Ali bursts out, startling passers-by. 'Do you remember when we got caught weeing on Oxford Road by those policemen and I started crying because I thought we were going to prison?'

'Yeah.' I smirk, thankful for a change of subject.

'And you told them I was incontinent,' Alison recalls.

'Did I?'

'Yeah, you said I had a bladder condition. And then they asked why you were pissing in the street too, and you said that you weren't, you were "Having a rest". Near a puddle of wee.'

'I don't remember that at all.'

It strikes me that I'm not a very dignified person and I may have a drink problem. I have only vague memories of the night. Maybe we'd just been to see something at the Academy. I don't know. It seems so distant and fragmented that it might have happened to someone else.

'I remember it like it was yesterday,' says Ali, leading me round a corner to a street full of garages and lock-ups.

We navigate down a narrow flight of vertiginous stone steps covered in moss and puddles, down to the riverside. I feel so unsteady on my feet that I could pitch forward at any minute and fall catastrophically to my death. Maybe if I did, Ali would find the diary and Richard would eventually learn of my quest, standing darkly at my graveside, for ever changed and seething with regret. Which would be quite romantic if I wasn't dead.

'I know, let's go to Heaven.' Ali swoons. 'They do really good cake.'

'Mmm. Cake.'

'Cake is very fashionable this season. It's the new pie.'

'Mmm, pie. We're going out for dinner later, though, aren't we?' I quickly add, suddenly remembering the absolute necessity of scoping out Richard's restaurant. 'There's this place called Café Bleu I read about in the paper. It's supposed to be really good.'

'Ooh, get you! *Café Blue*!' she screeches, and I bristle, the tiny hairs on my skin leaping up in defence of Richard's superior gastronomic tastes.

'Why? What's wrong with that?'

'Well, it's a bit fancy schmancy, that's all. You used to live on Super Noodles and vodka. If it wasn't radioactive and didn't go off in the year 3000 you weren't having it.'

Hmm. It's true that I did live on the most appalling, inedible crap. My diet usually consisted of canned breakfasts and foil sachets of MSG and packets of custard-yellow nail clippings that swelled into macaroni cheese. There are probably tons of leftovers from my freeze-dried dinners lying in a landfill somewhere, refusing to die. Things have hardly improved since. No wonder she's suspicious.

'I'm different now.' I shrug, trying to make it seem less unlikely. 'I've been getting into cooking recently, actually, if you must know. I do a mean, er . . . risotto.'

'Really? What's in it?'

I think of my rotten kitchen, the festering carrier bag of rubbish I forgot to take out when I left, the funny smell in the fridge. What do successful people eat?

'Oh, wild mushrooms,' I announce, 'amongst other things.'

'Liam does the cooking when he's at home – I can't be bothered,' she says. 'But he only likes making stir fries. Things that make loads of noise and involve fire and chopping and making a big fucking mess. Typical man.'

'How is Liam?' A cosy image of them both in the kitchen, laughing and tossing beansprouts about, makes my heart sink.

160

'Oh, WONDERFUL as ever,' she says, skipping off the bottom step and throwing her arms out in stagy delight. She's glorious Technicolor in her red, yellow and blue polka-dot skirt, her cheeks smooth, rosy and cherubic, glowing with happiness. Next to her I feel like a badly drawn Czechoslovakian cartoon, all jerky movements and boiling lines. The reason I've been avoiding Ali hits me again all at once. She's perfect. She's in love, she's got a great job, a great house, a great life. She's not smug or self-satisfied; she's just done well. So why can't I be happy for her? Why am I such a bitter, uncharitable bitch? I realize that I want to see cracks, any evidence that things aren't as great as they seem – red-rimmed eyes, sneaky digs at Liam, rumbling discontent. Either that or slap her about a bit. How dare she be so nice and shiny?

'Since he got promoted they've kept him really busy. He's been away in Paris for a few weeks – he was helping to set up the French office,' Ali says, as she clickety-clicks down the street towards the Quayside. She's wearing a pair of red shoes I've wanted for ages but couldn't afford.

'Oh really?' I say, seeing my chance. Paris, eh? A hotbed of temptation, I would have thought. Three weeks is a long time to be away from the loving arms of the wife. Could it be that Liam has been indulging in a bit of *je ne sais quoi* with French ladies of the *nuit*? I search her profile for signs of bitterness, but she's looking straight ahead, smiling. There isn't anything except clear skies, sunny weather and hot woks. Everything's coming up roses.

'I took a week off and went out there to see him. Well, they'd put him up in this five-star hotel, you know, mints on the pillow, twenty-five-course meals, jacuzzi, the works – I was buggered if I was missing out on THAT.'

Yeah. Well. Hmm. Whatever. We walk under the struts of the Tyne bridge, and along the Quayside to the café. A fishy ozone smell comes off the river. As Ali tells a story of her culinary Gallic misadventures with a plate of calf's balls, I pray Richard will turn up. If he lived here, he would surely stay by the water. He'd have a cool warehouse flat with a picture window looking out on to the bridge, like in a TV programme I once saw. I peer up to one swanky apartment and wonder whether it's his house I'm looking at, and whether Richard and his things are behind the blank pane, a treasure trove of lost property just waiting to be claimed. I imagine him alone at night, frowning at the huge iron bridge, lit up in brilliant blue, all passionate, brooding and mysterious. Then I'm standing next to him, giving him the love and kindness and company he so desperately needs, while the streetlights glitter in the water. Finally we could both stop searching and find somewhere to be.

'God, look at the state of those two. Hey, Jane, do you reckon we'll look like that in ten years' time?' Ali hisses, shattering my romantic reverie by pointing at a pair of porky middle-aged women trussed up in flimsy vests and too-tight jeans. They're spectacularly sunburned, a surreal shade of tikka sauce, and both drip with catalogue gold jewellery. One of them, with frazzled blond hair and a hatchet face, is mindlessly pissed, stumbling around in a pair of cheap and nasty espadrilles.

'I'm gunna puke,' I hear her drawl, bending over to reveal a flabby arse bisected by a cheesewire thong.

This all-out ugliness – under Richard's nose, too! – makes me shudder.

'Ugh. That's horrible.'

'Welcome to Newcastle,' Ali says, rolling her eyes.

With some relief I notice that the café is much more civilised and seems to be geared towards curing hangovers. Blackboards scrawled with graceful chalk italics describe health-giving smoothies and obscenely unhealthy cakes. God, I'm in bits. Maybe I just need some sugar. Ali orders a huge queasy slice of chocolate fudge cake filled with black goo. I opt for ginger tea and an unfeasibly giant banana muffin I already know I'm not going to be able to force down.

As I put my jacket over the back of my chair, I see the corners of Dan's mouth turning down as he reads the diary.

'He's so adolescent.'

'God, you must have been really caning it last night,' Ali notes, squaring up to her cake, fork in hand. 'I hope you'll feel better in a bit, though. I wanted us to go out tonight. Don't you want to relive the heady old days of the Gobby Girls?'

The Gobby Girls was a name we were given by a guy called Andy who worked in the Union bar. He thought we were entertaining and used to spike our drinks for free just to see what we'd do. Once Ali fell out of the window and I wandered into the back of a flatbed lorry loaded with music equipment and nearly ended up in Birmingham with the National Youth Orchestra. Stupid stuff, but we were so unafraid back then. We didn't care what anyone thought of us. I look at myself now, always alone, always worrying, hating everything, and wonder what the hell happened.

'I don't know whether I'm feeling all that gobby after

last night,' I say. 'Nobody wants to see me dancing on the table with my knickers on my head any more.'

'Oh, I don't know,' Ali chews, cramming another oozing forkful of chocolate sponge into her mouth and making me want to puke. 'You've still got it going on. Bet there's plenty of lads out there who are just dying to see your knickers. It didn't bother you last night, did it?'

The humiliation of Ziggy's comes back to me again with stomach-churning clarity. Camp David stuffing his fist into his mouth when he saw my pants, Kelly pretending to apologize but probably victorious behind the toilet door, Dan's cynical words. How could he be so cold?

I feel sick. I'm going to faint.

Waves of anxiety grip me. My lips are numb. I try to steady my nerves by studying the blackboards, but the loops and curls of the letters just seem random, like spilled string. Then I notice. The cultivated, arty hand-writing isn't a million miles away from Richard's. In fact, it's eerily similar – the spiky 'a's; the tall, high crossed 't's; the strangely flowery twirl of the 'y's. As I look at it, the letters begin to rearrange themselves into phrases from the diary. Passion fruit mousse – '*people are so easily amused*'. Lemon frosted pudding – '*Lost and unravelling*'.

'It's nice in here, isn't it?' I say, hoping I don't have some kind of fit. I've never had a hangover like this before. I must be going mad. The blackboards are making me feel panicky. The writing could be Richard's. What if it *is* his? But how can it be? He wouldn't work in a café would he? He could own one, though (oh GOD, he'd look so cute in an apron!). The thought that he could be in some way responsible for

164

creating the banana muffin I've been reluctantly picking at for five minutes is so peculiar that I don't know what to do. I can't take my eyes off it. The craggy sponge suddenly looks like the surface of the moon.

'Yeah, it's great,' Ali is saying, a faraway sing-song voice in the distance. 'They do this sticky toffee pudding cheesecake which is just THE best thing EVER invented.'

I turn around. The guy behind the counter is skinny and sallow with a pock-marked face. He's about 30, around the same age as Richard must be, but there's no other similarity. I struggle to see round the corner to the open door of the kitchen, where people are laughing and talking.

'What's up?' Ali asks. 'Are you feeling OK?'

'Yeah. I've just got to go to the toilet,' I squeak with false cheer and stumble to my feet. 'Where is it?'

'Just over there,' she says, gesturing to a massive sign saying 'toilets', past the kitchen.

I put one foot in front of the other and do a passable impression of a normal person walking across a café. The small room is busy, full of young couples and cool types who probably spent their Friday night catching the latest Lars Von Trier at some art-house cinema, not wrecking their internal organs with pink gloop. I ignore them and keep walking, fixing my eyes on my goal. Beyond the illuminated doorway might be my destiny – Richard, with floury, sensitive hands, creating some mouth-watering delicacy, spinning melting sugar on the back of a spoon and skilfully arranging gooseberries. Hey, maybe that's why he said those horrible things about his girlfriend being like Jane Asher: they're rivals in the cut-throat world of baking. The doorway gets nearer and nearer. I can see an industrial oven and a gas hob. The strip lighting and stainless steel are blinding, and there's a figure, a shoulder, a leg, an arm, cut off by the doorframe, another person behind that. I can hear muffled conversation and the clattering of baking trays.

I slow down as I pass the kitchen and the world seems to slow down with it.

'Terry was askin' aftah you,' someone, a woman, is saying in a Geordie accent.

'Hor right ah burble burble err,' replies an incomprehensible man somewhere in the background. The possibility that Richard speaks like Jimmy Nail never occurred to me before. What if I can't understand a word he says?

'Aye right,' the woman yelps, and they both laugh, hers a witch's cackle, his a deep, resonant boom. I'm so close that I can feel the waves of heat coming off the oven. My knees are definitely on the weak side, my mouth has lost all its moisture. There's an over-powering scent of lemon zest and hot, yeasty sponge. My brain has turned to batter. I'm only a few feet away. The woman has long curly hair scooped into an untidy top knot, loose tendrils fan out like a fascinating under-water plant, but I don't care about her, I just want to see the person she's talking to, I just want a glimpse beyond her left shoulder. If it's Richard then I'll, I'll . . .

Sensing me loitering, the woman swivels round sharply with a suspicious look on her face.

'Can ah help you?' she asks.

'I . . .'

Behind her there's a man with a number-one haircut and a kindly smile. He folds his arms and tips his head curiously to one side.

'Are ya looking for the toilet?' she asks.

166

'I was just . . . I was . . .' I blunder, having to steady myself against the doorframe, suddenly powerless against a nervous, stricken feeling. Again Dan gate-crashes my vision, like the after-image of something bright, burned on my retina. I blink him away.

'Er . . . yeah.'

'Just down the corridor, dorlin',' the man says cheerfully before bending over to take something out of the oven.

The woman is still eyeing me like I'm a lunatic, which I'm starting to think I am.

'Oh, OK, thanks,' I murmur, stumbling backwards into the ladies'.

The toilet is mercifully cool and a brisk wind whips through an open window. Jesus, I'm losing my mind. 'Pull yourself together,' I whisper while splashing water onto my face and trying to stop my heart from bursting out of my chest.

'So what the hell have you been doing since I last saw you, anyway?' asks Ali, framed by a bad abstract painting the colour and texture of vomit. The card next to it says, '*Untitled (Chunks) 2003*, acrylic on board. £950.' We're in a bar now, somewhere called 45 Below, where everyone has a stupid haircut or stupid hat and looks like an MTV presenter. Richard isn't here – I've already checked. He wouldn't come near this kind of place, anyway, it's too trendy. He's far too deep to care about something as trivial as fashion. *Sheep*, he would say, *they're all just sheep*. I wonder what I must look like – tatty drainpipe jeans, a lumpy schoolboy parka, a striped T-shirt, Converse with a hole in the toe – the dress code of someone who's always hanging around on the sidelines being a drip.

167

'Just working, really,' I say, picking the label off my bottle of unpronounceable Lithuanian lager. Hair of the dog seems like the only thing for it now.

'Oh come on,' she says. 'A single girl running around in Edinburgh. If I know you, you'll have some stories. Spill.'

I've got a story for you all right, I think, picturing the diary buried deep in my bag.

'Not really. I'm getting a bit boring in my old age.'

'What?' Ali takes a gulp of beer and wrinkles her nose. 'You mean to tell me that you've been sitting in your flat for the past six months eating risotto and doing knitting patterns?'

Yes. But without the risotto or the knitting. I toy with the idea of making something up, based on things I've read in *More!* magazine – clubs, bars, one-night stands, hilarious tales of romantic misadventure, shopping. What *was* I doing? Before Richard came into my life I can't even remember how I passed the time. I think of the cramped flat and Queenie and my dull work skirt hanging up on the back of my door and draw a blank – it's as if I stopped existing altogether.

'I'm not that boring,' I mumble. 'I do . . . stuff.'

'What about Lizzie? Last I heard you and her were painting the town red.'

My old self, more optimistic and marginally less dishevelled, clambering up Lothian Road with Lizzie and her friends – the blonde one, the short dark one, the barrister, nice girls with nice names like Catherine, Emma and Rebecca – comes back to me briefly. Was that really only six months ago? The happy scene doesn't feel like it has anything to do with me: it's just a reel of someone else's Super 8 film, a rogue image deposited in my memory bank by mistake.

'Yeah, we were for a bit. Then she went to Australia. She got a job out there not long after I arrived. Her friends were OK, but I don't see them very much any more. They were a bit, y'know . . .' I say vaguely, waving my arms about.

'Oh, right. That's a shame.' Ali says, eyeing me doubtfully. 'So who do you hang around with now?'

Hmm, let's see. A ginger troll who tries to murder me and the old woman from downstairs who thinks I'm a prostitute.

'Hey, I got you a present,' I say, hoping to distract her.

I pull out a tartan garter that plays the theme tune to *Take The High Road*. I remember when we got these delivered – Camp David put one on his head, but the elastic couldn't stand the strain and it popped off and landed in the hood of an old woman's raincoat. At the time I thought it was another silly prank, but in retrospect it was quite funny.

'Aaargh! That's so COOL. That's the . . . the most beautiful thing I've ever seen,' Ali gasps, pretending to gush with joy. 'The craftsmanship! It must have cost at least . . . a POUND.'

'Seventy-five pee. With a staff discount.' I grin. 'Don't say I'm not good to you.'

'Wow, I shall treasure it always.' Ali pulls it onto her wrist and admires it. 'Well, when you FINALLY invite me up to stay, I'll wear it and you can show me around. Introduce me to a few men in kilts and we'll do the Highland fling. Do they still toss cabers?'

'Oh yes. Everyone says "och aye the noo" and all the blokes are called Jock. You can't move for little haggises running around with miniature bagpipes,' I say, jokily, even though I find Ali's version of what goes on in Scotland surprisingly irritating.

169

'We should get deep-fried Mars Bars too. Have you ever had one?'

'No,' I reply, am about to say, 'They're just for tourists' before I remember that I don't belong there myself. Oh what do I care? I've left all that behind me now. I take another swig of beer and look around the room, which is white and clinical, illuminated from all sides with halogen. Above the mirrored bar is a designer chandelier, which looks like a huge cut-glass sneeze suspended in mid air. The glare coming off it is dazzling and disturbing – a giddy, melting disco ball.

'*So do you think he's like you?*'

'What?' I ask Ali.

'I said what's the matter with you? You seem really preoccupied.' Ali's face is creased with concern. God, she's so pretty and *clean*. Her gaze is clear, as lively and twinkling as the crystal chandelier, surrounded by the dark chestnut mane of a well-groomed racehorse. If I lived on a macrobiotic diet for the rest of my life I could never look that healthy. She's a ripe young plum and I'm a wizened old prune.

She leans forward conspiratorially.

'Is it a man?' she smirks, and suddenly I'm back with Val in the staffroom.

'NO!'

I can't tell, I won't tell, I'll never tell. I study the ashtray.

'Oh come on. It is, isn't it? You've been sitting there mooning ever since you got here. Is it that guy last night?'

'NO!' I say again, folding my shredded beer label into a tiny vicious square. 'Definitely not.'

Ali gives me a lady-doth-protest-too-much look that makes me want to kick her in the shins. Why am I

170

being like this? We're supposed to be having a good time. I'm supposed to be showing her that I'm brilliant and that my life is going swimmingly. Most of all I'm supposed to be looking for Richard. Instead I'm stumbling around in a hungover trance having minor panic attacks over blackboards and light fittings, and Richard is as far away as ever.

'Honestly, it's not HIM. I'm fine, honestly. I've just got a terrible hangover,' I tell her, cranking up a smile. 'I'll liven up when I get this down me. Anyway, how are YOU? How's married life?'

I give her hand a friendly squeeze, which is meant well, but ends up seeming forced. The diamond on her wedding ring is huge. The big event was last year, on Ali's twenty-fifth birthday, but I couldn't go – I was working and couldn't get the time off. Now I can't even remember what job I was doing.

I'm a terrible friend. Terrible.

'Oh, fine. I suppose we've settled down, y'know. We just stay in and pig out on the sofa and watch DVDs, that kind of thing. It's nice. It's making me fat, though.' she says happily, pulling at a non-existent roll of lard on her perfectly proportioned belly. 'I'm letting myself go.'

'Yeah, course you are.'

'I mean, don't get me wrong, I'm *really* happy, the happiest I've ever been.'

I lean back on my chair, keeping up the smile, desperately trying to be pleased for her.

'It's just that it's not very glamorous sometimes. When Liam's off abroad doing exciting work stuff and I'm sat in the gallery all day, I feel like I'm getting into a rut. That's why I was so glad when you phoned to say you were coming. You're always moving around and trying out new things. You never stay still for a minute.'

'Well, that's only because I'm incapable of sticking at anything,' I say matter-of-factly, thinking of Kelly in her satin drawers, accusing me of crimes against professionalism.

'Balls. You're independent, that's all. Why stay in one place? Why not have adventures? You're a free agent.'

A free agent. I ponder this for a second and light a cigarette. What does that mean, anyway? It's just another way of saying you're on your own. And finding Richard was supposed to be an adventure, but it doesn't feel like one. It feels like some kind of mission, forced on me by the universe, like martyrs whose sole purpose in life is to be shot with arrows or imprisoned in caves or whatever it is martyrs get up to – a cross to bear.

'Yeah, but you've got a great job and a great husband. I hate everyone at my work and I have to wear a horrible uniform that makes me look like Jimmy Krankie,' I say, neglecting to mention that I now actually like Camp David, at least in his off-duty incarnation. And Fiona, too, come to think of it.

'I bet you look gorgeous in it,' Ali assures me. 'And there are thousands of people who would kill to get their hands on such upmarket merchandise as this.' She presses the button on the garter and two trendy mullets nearby cringe as the insane Scottish bleepy music starts up. A vivid image of David prancing about in the staff room, pops abruptly into my mind, giving me a jolt of weird, misplaced glee. 'Also, it's an ideal opportunity to sit on your tartan arse all day telling people to fuck off.'

I remember telling her about Pierce Cocksucker on the phone, and smile.

'That was an isolated incident.'

'Even so, it sounds like fun.'

'How do you work that out?'

'Aw, come on. You've got a funky little flat, no responsibilities, you go out and dress up as whatserface from ABBA and fall over. You're out there, doing what you like, seeing what fits. And you've always been the sort of person exciting things happen to.'

This is bizarre. Maybe the beer is starting to work, because I feel a sneaky glow of pride. Could it be that Ali is envious of *me*? *She* was always the one who had it made: the ideal husband, the fabulous house, the nice job, the state wedding, the cutting-edge kitchen appliances. I watch her for a moment and wonder whether she's just trying to make me feel better. Poor Jane, she's probably thinking. She obviously hasn't got any friends and she's going through some kind of crisis. And she's got hair like a dead badger.

'Anyway,' I stutter, embarrassed. 'You've got loads going on. And things might happen to me sometimes, but they're not always fun things.' I trail off, thinking about the diary and my ludicrously ill-conceived plan, wondering whether I'm just kidding myself. What am I doing?

'Are you hungry?' Ali asks, downing her drink. 'I'm starving. I think maybe I've got worms.'

'Maybe you're pregnant.'

Ali pulls a face.

'Huh, maybe YOU are,' she goads.

'I doubt it. I've got cobwebs in my knickers.'

'You know, picking the label off your beer is a sign of sexual frustration,' Ali teases, nodding towards the pile of tortured silver confetti I've made. I look at the powdery residue between my fingers with a sting of shame.

'Let's go to Café Bleu,' I say decisively.

Café Bleu is pristine, unlike me, a high-class restaurant with starched napkins and bulbous wine glasses. The acres of white tablecloth and vases of stargazer lilies give me a nervous thrill. Not only is Richard handsome, intelligent and sensitive, he must also be RICH.

Ali, unfazed, walks in, but I'm painfully aware of my flaws – a glued on lanky wig, clothes that have seen better days, no make-up save the remnants of last night's, the deathly pallor of a recently embalmed corpse. Am I seriously expecting Richard to fall at my feet? Why didn't I pay more attention to my appearance? I should at least have had a proper wash or worn an evening gown or gone to the hairdresser. What was I thinking?

'Do you think we'll get a table? I mean, it's Saturday night,' I whisper, suddenly wondering whether this is such a great idea.

'Well, if we don't ask we won't get,' Ali says.

'It's posh, isn't it?'

'Hmmm. Probably not as much as it'd like to be,' she sighs with the world-weary aura of someone well acquainted with five-star cuisine – mints on pillows, calf's testicles and all that jazz. I'm just Super Noodle girl, what would I know?

The fresh scent of mussels fills the air. Tables are carefully spaced around a circular bar, staffed by people in black waistcoats. In vast lumpy pots, sprays of what look like orchids stick their pink and orange tongues out at the diners. Babs would have a fit. Along with the heady aroma of seafood, I think I also catch a whiff of my shoes, which have chosen this exact moment to rejoice in smelling like wet kippers.

This isn't what I envisaged at all.

I didn't have enough time this morning to get a Richard-slaying outfit sorted out. I was going to have my hair in a chignon and wear a sleek, black Audrey Hepburn-style dress. At least I should have got changed in the pub or put some lip gloss on. How can I expect him to be attracted to me if I stink of fish? The thought that he might be in here fills me with clattering terror. Every other table might have a potential Richard on it, sitting with friends, tipping his head back and laughing, signing a credit-card slip, toying with his food, then he'd catch my eye and stop what he was doing.

I daren't look too hard, what if he really IS here? His dark, dark stare could be across this very room. We could meet tonight. In a matter of hours we could be together. Oh it's exquisite. It's terrifying. I feel hopelessly ill-prepared, clunky and out of place, and I'm so full of Lithuanian beer that I need to go to the toilet.

'We'd like a table for two, please. Is there anything available?' says Ali, stepping up to the counter. Her manner is polite and professional, firm but fair, completely self-assured in a way I could never be.

'Have you booked?' says somebody who I assume is the maître d'. He has an angular nose that looks like it was whittled from a carrot.

'No, but do you think you could squeeze us in?' she asks.

'I'm afraid we don't have anything tonight, girls.'

His hand is resting on the guestbook, which is held open at tonight's page by an elastic band. Even if he isn't here, somewhere in that book must be Richard's name, perhaps a contact number. The thought makes me itch.

'Are you sure?' I blurt out. 'Isn't there anything at all?'

He glances distastefully at me.

'Hold on a minute,' he sighs, going off to talk to someone else, a tall man with curly hair. He doesn't seem to be in any particular hurry. While he's away I sneak a look at the guestbook. I flick through it as casually as I can, as if it's a passing interest, like inspecting the silver dish of matchbooks next to the cash register or looking at the clock. I can't see Richard's name anywhere.

'What are you doing?' Ali asks.

'Oh nothing.' I smile at her stupidly. 'God, this place is so up itself. Don't you think he was really rude? I thought he was rude.'

Ali shrugs and steals a mint imperial.

'Sorry, but we're full.' Carrot-nose simpers, hauling the guestbook out of my reach and replacing the elastic band with a snap of irritation. 'I'm afraid you'll have to go somewhere else.'

'Oh, OK,' I say, secretly relieved.

I hold my breath and turn to face the diners. The men all look like second-division footballers, sitting opposite chain-store dolly birds with ceramically straightened hair. You can smell the styling products. They snack on baby pizzas and fish glistening with dribbly, unidentified sauces, and talk about whatever it is people like that talk about. Cars, probably. Or sunbeds. Richard must have just come here on the off-chance, for a business lunch. A one-off in a city he doesn't know? Whatever it was, this place just isn't him.

'Don't worry. We're too stylish and exciting for this place anyway,' says Ali supportively, leading the way back out with a composed, unconcerned look on her face.

'Where shall we go?' I ask, feeling lame and helpless. I want Ali to click her red shoes together and take me to Richard, so then I can sort this out once and for all and get on with . . . with what exactly? A wave of fatigue threatens to knock me over. Behind the glass, Café Bleu carries on, suddenly meaningless. Where would he be?

'Let's go this way,' Ali says.

Out here, Saturday night is gearing up. A crowd of stocky morons in party shirts weave their way past us, trailing a toxic cloud of aftershave and testosterone in their wake. Over on the river is a huge ship, which seems also to be a nightclub, decorated in fairy lights and pulsating with cheesy chart music.

'*He could be anywhere*' Dan had said, helpfully. A passerby drowns out the memory with a cry of, 'Show us yah norks!'

As we make our way down the Quayside, dotted with hens and stags reeling, yelling and drinking, semi-naked girls and men with too much gel in their hair, I can't help thinking that this is the last place I'm going to find Richard. *I like beautiful things*, he said, on the 11th of January. He wouldn't be able to stand it here. The lardy female flesh is too like raw meat, the bridges are too solid and ugly, shot through with rivets as mean as bullet holes. Richard is *refined*. Why would he live in a flat overlooking a bunch of cattle markets full of slappers in stilettos? Eventually we pass the flat where I'd imagined he might stay. The occupants are in, and someone is pulling wooden Venetian blinds down, a nondescript guy with a beard and a bald head. In the corner is a mundane black uplighter probably bought from an out-of-town furniture store, and behind him a TV glows green – he's watching a football match. He's soon obscured by narrow lines, and then one by one he flips the blinds shut. Click. Click. Click.

'If we go up there we'll be trapped in the Biggmarket which is the last place we want to be, believe me,' Ali says, sidestepping a group of middle-aged men in the same fancy shirts as the boys, but stuffed to bursting with beer bellies.

'Oh Jesus, look at this lot,' I mumble.

'Hor-reet girls', says one, who must be at least fifty-five, with a fat neck and a network of broken capillaries on his nose. 'Do ya like flowahs?'

'What?' Ali barks.

'Well, get tu-lips roond this,' he says, pointing at his crotch. The others crease up laughing.

Ali and I look at each other wearily.

'God, your Dad's so embarrassing,' she deadpans.

'I know.'

We turn right and trudge up a steep hill, back into the centre of town, against a tide of people. The bars and restaurants are packed, windows sweaty with condensation. I'm weighed down with disappointment, struggling to keep pushing forward. I want to impress upon Ali the importance of the diary, the fact that this stranger feels like a missing limb, that I'm not sure I can live without him, but I don't even know where to start looking.

Help me!

I want to wail, falling to my knees in front of all these fake tans and over made-up faces, beating my chest like a wounded ape.

We're all looking for the same thing aren't we?

Soon we come to a wide, pedestrianized shopping street, and at the top is an ominous stone column. Around it are heaving bars and predatory gaggles of girls.

'What's that?' I ask.

'Oh, that's the Monument. It's kind of a meeting place.'

My mouth goes dry.

The restaurant receipt in the back of the diary. 'Monument – 8 p.m.'

Richard was here.

He stood by this statue waiting for someone. Sarah Arseholen? Perhaps I've just retraced his steps. Then, clear as day, I can imagine him, the wind blowing his hair into his eyes, a look of detached amusement at the circus of drunken madness around him, as steady and upright as the column itself.

Suddenly every man I see could be him, an arched eyebrow here, a jawline there. A sea of potential darkhaired handsome strangers where before there were only mutt-faced slobs. But before I can get a good look, Ali takes my arm and guides me towards the yellow mouth of a Metro station.

'I know somewhere you can ALWAYS get a table,' she says, tap dancing her way down the steps, 'and the service is second to none.'

'Wow! You've got red hair! I didn't recognize you. How you doing? Long time no see.'

Liam clambers up off the sofa, unfolding his long, lean, catalogue-model body, which is clad in expensively battered jeans and a T-shirt with a drawing of a drum kit on it. He fixes me with his azure eyes, runs a hand through his blond, chipped, Brad Pitt mop, smiles his flirty, mischievous smile. He makes everyone in the world swoon, and he should be just my type, but some kind of receptor in my brain must be blocked as I'm impervious to his charms. Just as well really.

'Yep. Dyed it,' I twitter stupidly, giving the impression that I fancy him even though I don't. It seems to be the reaction he's used to. I wouldn't want to disappoint him.

'It's striking, isn't it? I didn't recognize her either,' Ali says, taking off her raincoat and slinging it on a chair, a round, chrome basket thing that looks expensive.

I gaze around the room. The house was apparently a wreck when they bought it last year; now it's full of light and paintings and knick-knacks placed just so. (Was that when I stopped phoning Ali? When she started taking about dado rails and plasterboard? It's possible.) Once upon a time Ali shared a flat in Manchester with Liam, and back then we all seemed to live the same way – posters torn from magazines tacked to the walls, cheap, scratchy threadbare carpet used by landlords the world over, domestic hygiene a low priority. Ali has obviously moved onto the next level while I'm lagging behind, paying £400 a month for the previous occupant's welded-on grease.

'Town was horrible,' Ali says.

'It's Saturday. What do you expect, snooch?'

Ugh! Urrrh! He calls her snooch!

'So *I* thought,' she says, advancing towards him with a minxy look and draping her arms round his broad, lifeguard shoulders, 'you could make us girls something to eat. You're always saying what a great chef you are.'

She looks over at me and winks, but it feels like I'm intruding on a special moment and I look away, studying the grain on the stripped floorboards. I hate being around couples. They always want you to indulge their intensely personal lovey-dovey banter. Why don't you just shag each other in front of me and have done with it? Sadists.

'Oh, that's your game, is it?' he murmurs saucily. 'Well I might be able to rustle up something from the fridge. What do you fancy, Jane?' He says it in the same provocative tone, his hand resting unselfconsciously on Ali's hip.

I stare at him blankly until I realize he's talking about food.

'Er, whatever you've got,' I chirp. Jesus, why can't I just behave normally? 'Shall I go and get some wine or something?'

'No, no it's fine. We've got plenty,' Ali says, disengaging herself and heading for the kitchen. 'Red or white?'

'Don't mind. I mean, either . . .'

'So, Jane, how's the tourist business? Still packing them in north of the border?' Liam enquires.

'Er, yeah, I suppose so. It's very . . . you know. Challenging.'

'Good stuff,' he says, rubbing his hands in professional mode. 'I love a challenge.'

'The house looks fantastic,' I tell him in the same annoyingly upbeat tone I can't seem to shake. This place puts me on edge. It's a three-storey museum of everything I haven't got.

'You haven't seen it, have you? Looks good, doesn't it? It was a total nightmare but we got there in the end. Want a tour?'

'Sure.'

I follow him through the wide hall. I can feel myself starting to wither. Compared to my cramped dingy cabin this house is a gleaming ocean liner, and I know it's only going to make me feel more inadequate. Meticulously spaced photographic prints line the whitewashed walls. One of them is a picture of a woman standing by the side of a desolate road. She looks distressed, wearing an ill-fitting full-length crimson wig, thumbing a lift that'll never come.

'This was all partitioned off,' Liam says, pointing to an elaborate arch. 'It's bizarre what people did to these houses in the Seventies. Every single interesting thing got covered up with chipboard.'

The searching eyes of the woman in the photo seem to follow me as I walk past, making me shiver. Two steps ahead of me Liam is in full swing about the irresponsible treatment of Victorian cornicing.

'They'd even blocked up the fireplaces – in the bedroom we took off this ugly box surround with a gas fire and there was this beautifully tiled hearth behind it. Who knows *what* they were thinking?'

'Yeah, that's . . . totally mad.'

Liam really is great looking – a naturally blond, handsome Andrex puppy, guileless and entirely unaware of how cute he is. You could put him in a watering can and stick him on a greetings card. He's sweet and loyal and makes the beds, and I couldn't wish for a better husband for Ali. And from where I'm standing he's got a great arse. It's just not what I want, that's all. Bit dull. Too sensible. Talks about cornicing. Too clean cut. Unasked for, Dan's shaved sealskin scalp flashes in front of my eyes.

'And this is the kitchen. Ta-da,' says Liam, fanning out his arms. The room is enormous and modern, the purring engine of the house, glistening with chrome.

'Wow! It's amazing. It's huge!'

Liam elaborately explains about knocking walls through and extending the back of the house as I take in the sights: one of those double fridges with an ice-cube maker, endless cupboards lit from the inside, a stainless-steel cooker hood and six-ring hob, an old-fashioned sink with a wooden drainer, a windowsill of fresh herbs. Across the room I can just about make out Ali, pouring red wine into three oversized stemmed glasses, not unlike the ones in Café Bleu. To complete the magazine centrespread, Stinky, their black cat, curls around her legs. It's so out of my league, I can't even bring myself to covet anything in particular. It's like watching a programme about how much money celebrities make – all those millions are meaningless to a loser like me.

'Liam, there's some chicken in the fridge and salad stuff,' she says, crossing the vast plains of terracotta tile, probably handcrafted in Tuscany by blind potters, to hand me my drink.

'Thanks, Ali.' I smile, trying to appear sophisticated and devil-may-care, as if I'm wearing a black poloneck. 'How's Stinks these days?' I bend to pet the cat, but it stretches and gives a big pointy-toothed yawn, then starts vigorously attacking its arse.

'Ooh, you're hungry,' I say, and it stops to glare at me accusingly. The hatred in its yellow eyes is so unexpected that I look away.

'She's mental, as usual. The other day she fell off the top of the wardrobe. I thought cats were supposed to land on their feet but she did a kind of nosedive. I think you banged your head, didn't you, Stinkapuss?'

'How about chicken salad then?' asks Liam, heaving masses of organic lettuce and cherry tomatoes and long red peppers from a salad drawer the size of a child's bedroom.

'Great,' I say brightly.

'Chicken plus salad – chicken salad,' she ponders. 'Very imaginative. I thought you were supposed to be a chef.'

Ali and Liam share a comedy glare and she starts to laugh. He looks exaggeratedly hurt. 'Oh I'm only joking, sweetie. Your chicken salad is the best thing in the world ever.' She backtracks, and hugs him as he pretends to whimper like a little boy.

Is it me? I wonder, leaning on the granite counter with my glass of Pinot Noir, or is this real? Is this what people do? Having grown up in a house where the most popular form of communication was to shout and throw pans at each other, I'm not familiar with this particular version of domestic bliss. It seems as if they might be using a secret instruction manual hidden in a compartment of the Shaker dresser by the front door. But this, it would appear, is love. It must be. Ali cuffs Liam playfully on the arm and tells him to get on with it, their smiles are genuine, and their complete inability to keep their hands off each other isn't for show, as far as I can tell. They're doing none of it for my benefit.

Anyway, they were destined to be together from the start. The day they met had a historic, golden quality to it. It was the end of an era – graduation time and we were moving out. I was working in a bar and going to a dismal flatshare in Levenshulme with a girl from the art college (whose project, I later found out to my horror, was to recreate the smell of her own vagina), and Ali was going away for six month's work experience in a gallery in Milan. I remember her coming back to the practically empty house and hyperventilating with desire. She was on her way back from the launderette and this handsome mirage rose up ahead of her. He walked past and apparently gave her look of such instant, awe-inspiring adoration it almost made her faint. Admittedly, she was a bit impressionable at the time – she'd just read *Wuthering Heights* and she hadn't had a shag for ages – but she said even though she didn't know who he was, she couldn't bear it if she never saw him again.

I know how that feels.

She didn't see him again, not for six months anyway, but when she returned from Italy, Liam, unbelievably, was the first person she saw when she got off the plane. He was working as a junior architect on a project at the airport. There he was, fantasy made flesh, wearing a hard hat of all things – the Diet Coke guy sprung to life. Bingo. They've been inseparable ever since. Life just goes smoothly for some people.

Ali makes an isn't-he-just-a-totally-adorable-big-fucking-dipstick face and advances towards me.

'Come on. Let's leave him to his culinary master-piece. I think he's on his period.'

'I heard that,' he mumbles, as we leave the room, and she giggles, the irrepressible laugh of someone who's happy. Proper relationships, I drearily realize, are a foreign country to me. From her perch on top of the bookshelf, Stinky watches me with regal disdain.

Much, much later on, the three of us are sitting at the expensively rough-edged kitchen table (no doubt made by local craftsmen in the pine forests of deepest Norway). In front of us are the remains of Liam's unexpectedly tasty chicken salad, traumatized crumbs of walnut bread and three empty bottles of wine. Over in the kitchen area, Stinky is having a mad half hour chasing ghosts, with his bell tinkling wildly. It's a touching and wholesome domestic scene. I'm drunk again. Surprise surprise.

'Jane once got off with a guy with one bollock.' Ali announces, completely out of the blue.

'That's not true,' I protest.

'Oh I think you did.'

Liam puts his head in his hands.

'I didn't see it, honestly. I didn't get that far.'

'You would have done, though. What was his name again? Colin?'

'Callum,' I say darkly.

'How come he only had one? Did he have to get it cut off or something?'

'I don't know – you were the one who told me about it – for all I know it was probably . . . bollocks. Huh huh.' I grin. My mouth feels like a piece of elastic. Everything is fuzzy and warm and nice.

'HA!' Ali shrieks with laughter, eyes shining, her face the same colour as the wine. 'Geddit? Bollocks.'

Liam, feigning boredom, sighs theatrically and slowly gets to his feet.

'Well, I hate to break up this very important UN Council meeting, but do you want coffee?'

'Ooh, yeah. Do you want coffee, Jane?' I nod. 'Hey,' she shrieks, grabbing my arm. 'Do you remember God? He was ace. Aw, what a guy. Now he DEFINITELY had two.'

'Not him again. You should have married him instead,' says Liam, without a trace of bitterness or jealousy, cranking up the stylish eggshell-blue coffee machine. Poor Liam, having to listen to this crap.

'Aw, yeah. He was lovely,' I say, misty-eyed at the thought. 'God. God, God, God.'

God was a six-foot slice of thrilling masculinity with Johnny Depp's cheekbones and lips like a blowfish who was a regular at the Freezer, our favourite haunt. He used to wear a Ramones T-shirt and tattered jeans so tight you could have measured his manhood with a ruler. (Come to think of it, we once nearly did.) All this was enough for him to attain mythical status with us. Then Ali got off with him and found out that his name was Derek. We thought that was hilarious, but now it seems kind of sad. After all, God, the supreme being, the pinnacle of male potency, was just some guy called Derek.

'He wasn't marriage material,' she slurs, pouring more wine into my glass. 'He belonged to no-one. He was all-powerful. Rowwwwwr! Now who else was there?'

This conversation could go on for ever. The past, what there is of it, seems strewn with unsuitable men. At college we treated them as entertainment, as if they were supporting cast members in our fabulous slutty show. Sometimes they were just our audience, watching us in awe or disgust, as we dressed like lunatics and made unladylike jokes. We wanted to impress and scare them, and we never took them very seriously. They were sloppy cider kisses in a club or terrible fumbles, or funny stories to tell, or pretty trophy boys to put on a pedestal. I can't even remember half of them.

'I never got off with anyone like God.' I sigh as the coffee machine whirrs in the background. 'I always seemed to get the weirdos and the lepers.'

'Matt wasn't a weirdo. He was nice.'

Matt hazily comes to me through a veil of wine – kind, sweet, always following me and apologizing for stuff he hadn't done. He once came round on his bike with a bunch of flowers for me. After that he could do no wrong as far as everyone else was concerned, but then they didn't have to talk to him or watch his drippy expression from across the table.

'But I wanted excitement,' I whine. 'He was a total pushover.'

'I used to LOVE him. I was SO jealous when you brought him home.'

'Really?'

I get a brief pang for long-lost Matt. Come to think of it, he *was* lovely. He was tall, sandy-haired and handsome and he looked very cute on his tiny BMX bike. It was the first time anyone had bought me flowers –

daisies from the garage, nothing fancy – and I was so pleased. I still remember the smell of them when he gave them to me, the intoxicating, sugary scent of pollen forever linked with the excitement of meeting someone new. But in the end, he lasted about as long as they all did. In fact, they outlived him by about three days.

'He was an engineering student,' I tell her sadly. 'It would never have worked.'

'So what? You were a picky tart, you were,' says Ali. 'There were tons of people after you, but it was always "Ooh, he's got a big nose" or "He's too friendly" or "He's too boring." You only ever went for the ones you couldn't have.'

'Rubbish.' I'm starting to feel high-pitched and strange, as if I'm being strangled.

'OK then.' She smiles, enjoying herself. 'What about poor Dave from Southside Records? He wasn't an engineering student. He was cool. He was soooo sweet and he used to make you tapes and whenever we went into the shop he'd let us come into the back and he'd make us a cup of tea. He thought you were the coolest girl EVER, and you couldn't be bothered.'

'Yeah, well, he was strange. You never heard the tapes. He liked some really weird stuff.'

The coffee machine comes to a shuddering, ominous climax, and all is quiet, save for the delicate tinkle of Stinky's bell.

Liam comes to the table with two cups of hot black coffee.

'Thanks, Liam,' I say, trying to seem delicate and gracious, even though I'm getting increasingly flustered.

'So who are you onto now?' Liam asks, sitting back down.

189

'Dave,' says Ali decisively. 'Record-shop boy. Very nice. Jane, however, wasn't interested. She refused to go out with him because she said he was autistic.'

Liam guffaws.

'No I didn't,' I protest.

'Yes you did.'

Oh fucking hell, OK, yes, I did.

Of course, there was nothing wrong with Dave, nothing that a good shag wouldn't have cured. His tapes weren't strange either. He was actually quite sexy. He had black curly hair and blue eyes and he looked like a Merchant Ivory Italian peasant goat herder who might surprise you from behind in a poppy field. In fact, he was really hot. But I was too busy fancying Nick, who was in the year above me at college, a monkey-faced ladykiller with an entourage of trendy friends who sang in a crap band called the Broken Rocks. I once attempted to ask him out, but lost my nerve halfway through, stuttered, blushed and ran away. Immediately after that he started going out with a girl who looked like a porn star, with jugs like the Alps.

'Face it, girl.' Ali smiles. 'You like the thrill of the chase.'

She could be right. I examine my split ends, which in the light of Ali's kitchen seem shockingly red.

'Are there any biscuits or anything?' Ali enquires.

'Tsk, what did your last slave die of?' Liam grumbles.

'Aw, come on, we're reminiscing. We need sustenance. And more wine if you've got it.'

Liam gets to his feet on command and starts rifling through a cupboard. The oversized kitchen clock reads half past midnight. It's far too late for coffee and I've got to get up early. I'm starting to wonder whether I'm a very good judge of character. But Richard isn't Nick.

Nick was just a silly little kid with big nostrils and a Mick Jagger complex. This is serious. And I like Richard for what he is – complex, intense, vulnerable – not for what he looks like, or because he's in a band, or because he's got trendy friends. I just need to find him, then I'll be able to see the situation more clearly. I'm going into it with my eyes open. It might not work out – he might not like me, or he might have a wife or something – but I can't just ignore this. And what if it does work out? He might be in York, and when I get off the train he'll be there, looking intensely adoring, blown away by a vision of flame-haired beauty (I'll take a bath in the morning), and we'll get a great kitchen with a six-ring hob and eat wild mushroom risotto until it comes out of our ears.

I look around the kitchen at Ali and Liam's life, the life they've made together – photographs and cookery books and a bunch of keys thrown in a dish, Liam's jacket hanging on the back of a chair, Stinky's food bowl surrounded by stray pieces of Go Cat, Post-its stuck onto the fridge saying, 'Buy more milk' – casual, trivial things, but with an aura of permanence.

I need someone to hold me in their arms and make no impossible demands. I need a home.

There's no reason why what happened with Ali and Liam can't happen to me.

'I think I'd better go to bed. I'm knackered. And my mum wants to meet me in Leeds at half past eleven.' I say, lying through my teeth.

'But it's so early. Oh don't. Stay up,' Ali screams. 'We haven't even mentioned Country Jim or Big Alan or the Gimmer Twins.'

A parade of vague faces and haircuts flash faintly through my mind. Just boys. Nobody life-changing, nobody important. All I really want to do is talk about Richard, this new, significant other, not dredge up half-remembered idiots from years ago. But I can't. If I have any more wine my tongue is going to get looser and I'll probably end up blabbing and giving myself away completely. They probably think I'm such a bore.

'I'm sorry, Ali. I've been really crap. I'm just so tired.'

'Aw! Why don't you stay longer? Couldn't you arrange to meet your mum later? We could go to the seaside or something,' Ali suggests, ripping into a packet of Reese's Pieces.

'I'd love to,' I say. 'But God, you know what Babs is like. She's had the whole day planned out for weeks. Come up to Edinburgh, both of you, and we'll go out properly soon,' I say, 'I'll show you around. I'll take you to, er, Arthur's Seat and the Botanic gardens to see the really big plant.'

What am I talking about? I don't want them to see my horrible flat, my manky work, my dust, baked-on grease and tartan straitjacket. What do I have to offer these sparkling, gorgeous people? A singing garter and a sour face, that's all.

'Great, we've got an invite. At last,' says Ali, triumphantly. 'How many times have I moaned about not seeing Jane enough?'

'You're always moaning.'

'I'm sorry I haven't . . . it's just, things have been difficult . . .'

'It's FINE, Janey. I'm only teasing. I'm just glad we found you again. We were worried about you.'

Ali has such a sincere, sympathetic expression on her face that I want to blub. It's like Sophie's office all over again. I pray I can keep it together. My life is fantastic. I'm single and loving it and my entire existence is just one big whirl of cocktail parties, shoes and romantic intrigue. You never know what I'm going to do next. I'm a free agent.

'Well, we should come up and get a hotel for the weekend sometime soon. I've got the car so we could go off and explore,' Liam chips in brightly. 'I've always quite fancied myself in a kilt.'

'Ooh, I'd fancy that TOO,' Ali says, seizing on the idea.

'Yeah, cool,' I say gaily. 'Let's do that. And next time I see you I won't have a hangover, promise.'

'Yeah, drunky monkey. And stop flashing your chuff an' all.' Ali laughs and reaches across the table to give me a hug. Compared to her warm, fleshy body, mine feels like a dry, gnarled twig, about to crumble into dust all over the nice terracotta tiles. 'Night, night. You're in the spare room on the second floor, next to the bathroom. Do you want me to show you?'

'No, I'll find it. Thanks so much for the dinner, Liam, it was magic.' I stand up awkwardly and hug him too, a static little embrace.

'Any time, darlin'.'

'You've got a good one here – great chef.'

'Hmm, I thought the chicken was a bit DRY, myself,' Ali says, in a snooty restaurant critic's voice.

'WHAT?' Liam thunders in mock disgust, hooking her under the arms and dragging her off the chair as she squeals delightedly. Stinky darts out of the room, terrified.

'You're going OUT!' he booms and carries her out of the back door, slamming and locking it as Ali, a blur behind the darkened etched glass, makes muffled, giggling protests.

'That'll teach her,' Liam says, grinning, his even white teeth like perfect, rounded pearls.

'Night Ali!' I yell, laughing as Liam opens the door a crack and she pours through it, rampaging and kicking him in the shin.

'You bastard.' She laughs. 'Oh, I've got a stitch.'

'I'm going to bed, you nutters.'

I leave them to their good-natured wrestling and hollering, so jealous of the fun they're having that I might just die, and head down the hall to get my bag from the living room. I pass the photograph of the deranged female hitchhiker and catch my breath. I realize that the reason it freaks me out is that she's me. Frozen in time, lurid hair flapping in the wind like a broken gate – she's neither here nor there.

I don't know what time it is, but birds sing outside, and I hear the plumbing shudder into life as someone somewhere turns on a tap. I lie motionless, staring rigidly at the shelves stacked with box files and Liam's books on architecture – Le Corbusier, Mies van der Rohe, Frank Lloyd Wright – books so heavy and glossy you could barely lift them to read. The latest iMac sits on the desk. On the wall there's an African mask from one of Ali and Liam's many adventures, probably their tailormade honeymoon safari to the Gambia, with disturbing bug eyes and a mouth like a hollowed-out sausage. The dressing table is just so, with complimentary guest toiletries. Two sweet-smelling bath bombs in a heavy cream-coloured dish, a tub of Johnson's Baby Powder, half a bottle of Anna Sui perfume, a polka-dot tooth mug with two brand-new toothbrushes sitting at jaunty angles. So many pretty, clean, new things. In the silver eye of the oval mirror I can see my lumpy shape under the quilt, the blot on the landscape.

I think I'm going to go back to the Monument one last time. But if I really listen to my instincts, I don't think Richard lives here. Perhaps work brings him to Newcastle, meetings with clients, or, I don't know, maybe even a woman. I squirm and roll over, putting my hands under the cool pillow. Please God, not that.

The bed is ridiculously comfortable, but I'm filled with tension. The thought of actively looking for Richard today, free from the pretence of visiting friends, fills me with fear. Walking around strange cities, a waif with matted hair, an anorak and a grubby vinyl bag with the Swissair logo on it, my shoes emitting fishy pongs. What if he rejects me? Nobody would blame him if he did. Worse still, what if he's disappeared off the face of the earth?

How do you know he's the man in the photograph?

Oh shut up.

Ali said I liked the thrill of the chase, but she couldn't be more wrong. I'm just a magnet for ludicrous situations, the person who gets singled out for reasons unknown. Maybe it's my face or something, but at college I was constantly getting approached by people selling drugs or being invited to parties by complete strangers. All I had to do was turn up somewhere and things would go goofy. I couldn't even go for a wee on Oxford Road without getting arrested. It's always been the same. At a schoolfriend's party, a sketchily qualified hypnotist called Barry Bernardi chose me from the very back of a crowd of thirty-five excitable children and made me dance like a chicken for ten whole minutes. I was the only girl in school who got flashed at in the park, and it happened twice. When I was five a woman came up to my mum in the supermarket and asked if I'd audition for a toilet-roll advert (she said no). During my driving test my instructor touched my knee and I crashed into a fence and killed a seagull (I failed). Good luck, bad luck, stupidity, serendipity; it all falls at my feet utterly at random.

This is just the latest instalment, a diary on a train. It could lead anywhere.

The familiar black book is poking out of my bag, a mysterious slippery eel. Who are you?

I stroke its glossy cover, running my fingers over the indentations and grain of the cardboard.

I think Ali knows something is going on. After all, in that bar I wasn't too subtle about denying I had a man, and she's always been able to see right through me. Oh well, who knows, she might meet him one of these days. I briefly entertain myself with the thought of Richard and I pulling up in front of their house in a sleek car, quite the best-looking couple in the world, hauling Louis Vuitton luggage out of the boot and exchanging a passionate, toe-curling kiss before greeting Ali and Liam (dwarfed by our movie-star radiance, of course) and sweeping through to their poky little kitchen with a bottle of something fabulous from our wine cellar.

I sit up in bed, and the person in the mirror stares back. Oh Christ. I'm momentarily shocked at how red my hair is, as if I'm a victim in little snotty-nosed Piers' colouring book. I hear the bathroom door being unlocked and the rhythmic thump of Liam's heavy footsteps going down the stairs. Mugs clunk in the kitchen, Stinky crows for his breakfast. I check the time on my mobile – 9.03. Better think about getting up.

Right. Richard. Let's see whether you can help me out here. Give me some advice. I close my eyes and turn to a page in the diary, and it falls open on the sensitive, stunning drawing – all light and shade and fluid lines – of a fellow train passenger with his face turned to the blank sky. '*Keep looking,*' it says underneath, and my heart flips.

He amazes me; it's like he's talking directly to me.

I wish I could draw like that.

Only a negative, closed mind would think that Richard was . . . all those awful things that Dan said he was. I don't care what anyone thinks, anyway, he's a genius. He's prophetic, intelligent and wise, and I just *have* to meet him. I mean, it's like he says, the week starting the 4th of February: *We don't have many chances for happiness. There are a finite number of opportunities, yet people disregard them all the time. I must do it too. After all, happiness presents itself to me so rarely, that I'm not even sure I would recognize it if it slapped me in the face.*

Well, Mr Miles, I know happiness when I see it, (I think), and I'm going to go out and get it. I'm going to do everything I can to find you, even if it means strapping a sandwich board to my chest and shouting your name through a megaphone. I'm not going to miss my opportunity. I get my notebook, an amateurish mess of lame scribbles compared to his, and set out my highly technical and well-thought-out plan.

SUNDAY (TODAY)
1. Go to Monument and look round Newc for last time. Go to YORK and find the shop where he got the credit note. The owner might remember him. Also there may be an ADDRESS.
2. E-mail Sarah Olsen. DO IT OR YOU WILL END UP SAD AND PATHETIC

3. At home, get York phone book and rip out M pages

MONDAY
1. LONDON. Get hotel. Phone every Richard Miles in the phone book on off chance. Put ad in *Time Out*?
2. If this doesn't work repeat on TUESDAY MORNING. If that doesn't work –

I hear a sound in the hall and pause, my pen halting as if on the edge of a precipice.

'Jane?' Ali knocks softly on the door.

I quickly shove the books under my pillow and pretend to have been asleep.

'Yes?' I say, making my voice sound croaky.

Her black head appears, slightly ruffled. She and Liam have probably been enjoying gymnastic sex all night long.

'Do you want a cup of tea?'

'Yes please.'

'What time are you going?' she whispers. 'Why am I whispering?'

We both laugh. I feel a flood of fondness for her. Suddenly there doesn't seem any need to play silly games of one-upmanship, pretending that my life is as wonderful as hers.

'Sorry if I was a bit weird last night,' I say.

'Don't worry about it. I had fun. It's just good to see you.'

'I've been really stressed lately,' I stutter. 'Work's been a bit shit. There's a lot going on – you know how it is.'

Kelly, fat fists on hips, springs up like a jack-in-the-box: '*You ruined my presentation!*'

'You'll get there in the end,' Ali assures me.

'Yeah,' I reply, unconvinced.

'I mean, not everyone has the guts to go off somewhere and start from scratch. It takes time to get a new life sorted out. But I think it's doing you good. I don't know, you seem more . . . mature or something.'

'How do you work that . . . ow!' I ask, sitting up on my elbows, the hard diary making its presence rather painfully felt.

'What?'

'Nothing – my elbows are creaking – must be more mature than I thought. Gosh, I'd better go soon, it's after nine.'

'I'll get the tea, grandma,' she chirps, and goes downstairs.

So that's what I'm doing, building a new life.

Doesn't sound too bad.

In fact, when you put it that way, the search for Richard seems almost noble, a quest for happiness rather than a deluded fool stalking a man in a photograph. I struggle to my feet and open the curtains. The street is deathly quiet, but the trees sway in unison, bathed in a light breeze, and in the clear morning I can see the school across the road is quite beautiful, a rusty brick building set in manicured green grounds. I stay there for a while with my nose pressed against the glass, smelling the pure air coming through the windowpane and letting it seep into my skin. Soon I feel light and airy and strong. I can do this.

Outside, a lone magpie swoops by and settles on the school's weathervane. I'm tempted to salute it, but I don't.

Right then.

It's time for action.

I stride to my bag and pull out some fresh clothes. All I need is a vest, a pair of jeans, lucky pants, a quick shower and a train ticket.

'I'm going to be in Edinburgh before you know it, waving a map around and being an annoying tourist,' Ali says, standing at the front door, wearing a long jumper with endless sleeves and not much else. 'I'm going to get a big tartan top hat and come in and embarrass you at work.'

'I think they've seen everything already,' I say dryly, wondering what time it is.

'Sorry you couldn't stay longer,' says Liam warmly. 'It's nice for her indoors to get a bit of company, you know. Stops her from hitting the tranquillizers.'

'Shut up,' yelps Ali, eyes wide with amused shock. 'He's terrible. Sorry about him. Maybe I should just cut my losses and come with you,' Ali ponders, folding her arms tightly around her chest.

'Oh I didn't mean it. C'mere,' he says wrapping her in a bear hug and nuzzling her neck. She purrs contentedly. I think I can actually see her knees start to give way.

'Anyway, much as I'd love to watch you two shagging, I've got to go.' I smile, hitching my bag onto my shoulder and starting to open the complicated brass latches on the door.

'Sorry. We'll see you soon anyway, when we come to visit,' she chirps, flushed and not sorry in the slightest.

What the hell. Let her see my mildewed bath and my scabby woodchip. What difference does it make? Maybe she could come into the tourist office and kick Kelly for me and Liam could build me an extension.

'Yeah, that'd be cool.' I feel so calm and in control now, a different person. 'Give me a ring,' I say.

'OK,' she promises. 'Oh, I forgot, I got you a present. Hang on.'

I stand uselessly as she goes to the kitchen.

'Say hi to your mum from me.' Liam smiles idly, burying his hands in his pockets and exposing a strip of suntanned midriff. The last time Liam met my mum was when they came through to see me during one of my tedious shifts at the florists, way back when Ali first started going out with him. Babs completely fell apart at the seams and started wittering on about nothing and fell over a bucket of carnations.

'I'll tell her. She fancies you, you know.'

'Does she? Well, she's a good-looking woman. Must run in the family.' He grins, wiggling his eyebrows Groucho Marx style.

'Yeah, we're all such gorgeous top models that none of us get out of bed for less than ten grand,' I say, rolling my eyes. When I stop rolling them, Liam is looking at me with a fond smirk playing on his lips.

'What?'

'Nothing. It's just you've got no idea, have you?'

'What do you mean?' I ask, starting to feel a bit unsure. 'No idea about what?'

We wait a bit longer. I need to leave soon if I'm going to scour Newcastle and go to that shop in York. Then I have to go home to see Babs and Becks. I'm suddenly struck by panic. Why on earth would Richard be hanging around by the Monument on a Sunday morning anyway? And what if I'm late and that shop closes early? What if it's not open at all? I should just go straight to York. But what if he's here? I gnaw at my thumbnail.

'There,' says Ali, thundering down the hall with a black piece of plastic in her hand. 'It's just a cheap piece of crap,' she explains, 'but I thought it'd give you something to do on the train. It helps you navigate the tricky path of life,' she says, Mystic Meg-style.

In her outstretched palm there's a magic eightball keyring. Exactly like the drawing in Richard's diary.

It's a sign.

This must be my lucky charm.

'You ask it something and shake it and the answer to life's mysteries appears in the window,' she says.

'I know,' I murmur, fascinated, holding the globe and watching the minute blue triangular die swish around in the murky liquid. 'Thanks,' I say, overwhelmed at the supernatural appropriateness of the gift. 'It's really cool. Thanks, Ali.'

I hug her close, my face pressing against the warm perfumed wool of her sweater for what seems like a long time.

'Oh, yeah, it's really expensive and rare,' she drawls from over my shoulder. 'Calm down – I got it in a cracker.'

Embarrassed at my over-the-top response to such a throwaway present and not wanting to arouse any suspicion, I decide to cover my tracks with a fake comedy outpouring of emotion, and grab Liam, too, enveloping them both in an over-the-top group hug.

'Oh I'm so touched,' I burble. 'It means so much to me. Waaaa!'

Liam laughs.

'Go on. Ask it something,' Ali suggests.

'Oh, I dunno what I'd . . . look, I really better go – I'll miss my train. I'll do it later. Thanks for having me. I'll see you really soon. Bye,' I say, kissing her on the cheek and hugging Liam. 'Take care of yourselves.'

'Byeeee,' they say in unison.

'You know how to get into town, don't you?' Ali asks as she lets me out. The air has a cold, brisk edge. It's a day to get things done.

'Yeah, it's fine, I know the way. See you soon.'

I walk down the path, and when I turn around at the gate they're both standing in the porch, waving, perfectly slotted together in a *Little House on The Prairie* pose. I wave back and walk away, clutching the key ring.

I'm a free agent, an independent spirit with purpose and poise, on my way to find the answers to life's mysteries. Soon, everything will become clear.

I shake the eightball.

Will I find him? Will I find the man of my dreams?

An air bubble appears at the window and the answer slowly bobs to the surface.

Suddenly the clouds split and pale beams of sunshine pour through the bushes and stream onto the pavement, forming a dappled, heavenly glow.

'Signs Point To Yes'.

As I walk towards the Metro station, feeling lighter with every step, Stinky darts across my path, a black streak against the bright pavement.

Part Three

YORK

I get off the Metro at the Monument and decide to walk down to the station. It's only about 10 a.m. and a street sweeper hums through the square, hoovering up the remains of last night's debauchery. Bottles, cans, paper greasy with leftover chips, a starburst of surprisingly colourful puke. Most of the shops haven't even opened yet, and the only people around are old couples up early and looking for something to do, backpackers and students just off the train and workers about to start their shifts. It's strange to think a city could be this quiet.

I sit down at the Monument and light a cigarette. The statue is covered in pigeon shit and a few birds hover around my feet, gurgling and cooing. Richard was here. He might not have been here for very long, but he was here. I open the diary and turn the restaurant receipt over in my fingers. I look again at the printout and the numbers on the credit card (would the bank give me an address? Or would it look suspicious if I asked?). It might not mean anything. The question is, where is he now?

I stare at the tip of my fag, willing Richard to appear. My cigarette suddenly tastes foul, instant cancer, and I grind it out on the stone, causing a shower of sparks.

OK, I think, as I set off slowly towards the station. It's your last chance. Richard, are you here?

The street sweeper carries on its mechanical duty, a white-haired couple look in the window of Comet. Seagulls the size of Alsatians swoop down to pick up soggy pockets of pitta bread and discarded burger buns. The place has a closed-up, redundant feeling to it, like an out-of-season seaside resort.

Time to go.

I wander through all the carriages – Smoking, the Quiet Coach, right down to First Class, but he's not on the train. Instead it's populated by day-trippers, noisy families playing cards and student travellers reading the latest bestsellers. At least I'm in his world, though, seeing what he sees. I bet he looks out at this scene all the time. The flat warehouse roofs by Newcastle station, its bridges, masterpieces of engineering, stretching down the muddy river, then later on a sign which urges me to 'Trust In God', and later still, the Komatsu truck factory, with banana-yellow diggers lined up perkily like Tonka toys. You never know, my seat could once have been his, and he'll probably know this month's issue of the GNER magazine off by heart – God knows I do – 'Ulrika Bares All.' '10 Things You Didn't Know About Peterborough', 'Win an action-packed day trip to Berwick-upon-Tweed'. Maybe he also nearly died of boredom eating the bland ham sandwiches and pre-wrapped muffins that taste of foam insulation. Maybe he takes a Walkman and listens to music to drown out the interminable beeps of text messages and inane chatter from the other passengers. Maybe he listens to Starlette, the feminine hygiene band he went to see. I looked them up on the internet, only to find a bunch of bad Nineties people in shimmering trousers describing themselves as 'jazz funkateers'. I'll have to knock THAT out of him when I find him.

So my journey passed entirely without incident, apart from a terse, urgent phone call from Babs, asking what I want for tea. The thought of her gravy-soaked dinners, served with overcooked vegetables and frozen roast potatoes from a series of interlocking Pyrex dishes bought sometime in 1979 made me feel sick until I got to York.

Oh, yes, and I thought I saw someone who looked like . . .

But it wasn't. Just a guy with a shaved head, one of millions.

After the grit of Newcastle, York is a picture postcard, and the day is encouragingly warm. I take off my jacket as I stride purposfully around the ancient city walls, trying to find the shop Richard went to, trying to catch a glimpse of a dark-haired, handsome stranger. Today I feel in control, as if I could meet him head on and not slip in a puddle of drool. For the millionth time I imagine how it would go. Maybe it would be a fairly ordinary encounter, which might become more meaningful over time. There might be no love at first sight at all, maybe we would be friends first. 'Oh, Richard, shut up!' I'd shriek, thumping his arm, as he took the piss out of me for getting excited about the diary. 'It's just a piece of shit,' he'd say casually, embarrassed. As I already know his secrets, there would be an easy-going, say-anything quality to our conversations. Maybe one day he'd buy me an ice cream – no, no, not an ice cream – a hotdog or something pretty graphic and loaded with sexual connotations, and I'd be stuffing myself, looking to any other onlookers like a hideous pig, but he would think I was cute, then stop in his tracks and realize that he loved me.

But his photograph snaps into my head, his striking, devilish, dark features, full of smoky mystery and intent, and I know that I couldn't manage the friendship part if I tried. Maybe – and this would be much more interesting – we could HATE each other at first and have a corset-busting *Gone With the Wind* style argument, loaded with blistering tension, featuring the kind of feisty wordplay that leads to ridiculously wild humping. 'Hi, my name is Jane, I have your diary.' 'Oh really, how odd, I er . . .' 'I hope you don't mind, Richard, but I found it on the train and I couldn't help looking at it. You really are a clever, fascinating man.' 'What do you think you're doing reading my diary, you nosy bitch!' 'Oh well, that's gratitude for you – fuck you, then, you pig!' 'No, Fuck you!' 'NO! fuck me!' 'Right then, I will!' He'd grab me and fling me . . .

The fantasy splutters out.

Oh, shut up, Jane, that's just totally stupid.

I keep walking, the early afternoon sun pleasantly warming my shoulders. I feel buoyant and silly and fizzy, like I've had a glass of champagne at lunchtime.

In the oldest part of town, tourists sit on tables outside cafés and peer into shop windows with studied fascination. Everything is geared towards keeping them happy, from the gift shops stacked with miniature English cottages and *Wind in the Willows* shit to the prim tearooms advertising Yorkshire tea and home-baked scones. The streets are narrow, some are cobbled and closed to cars. A relentless parade of pressed

212

slacks, backpacks, baseball caps, beige raincoats, checked golf wear and clip-on sunglasses passes through the tight pedestrian walkways. I could spot a tourist a mile off. I can smell them. I'll probably end up serving them all next week when they follow the well-worn trail up to Edinburgh, adding to their collections of bad ornaments, guided tours and extravagant three-course meals. Some of them are such gutbuckets they can barely squeeze through the streets, with tent-like T-shirts straining to hide spectacular sausage rolls of fat. (Fiona likes sending the tubby ones on tours she knows will involve walking, climbing stairs and general physical exertion. Once she convinced a twenty-stone woman to go on a horse-riding course in the Trossachs.)

A bubble of laughter rises up in me, threatening to pop out of my mouth.

OK, stop messing about. You have to find this shop.

I have a good feeling about this. I gently take the receipt from the diary, as if carefully extracting a tooth, and look at the address on the credit note. Kaleidoscope, 3 Lowgate, York, YO1 6BG. They might be able to lead me directly to Richard. The place must be around here somewhere – it's hardly a huge city. I follow the herd, behind a woman whose bum roams free inside the trousers of her saggy pink tracksuit. I must be in a good mood because the woman's behind reminds me of Kelly, and I glimpse her in my mind's eye, shuffling around awkwardly, a prissy ginger Womble in skin-tight satin flares, and feel a twinge of sympathy for her. Only nineteen. Probably never even been kissed. Well, I doubt it, anyway. Who'd kiss that ratbag?

Bet Richard is a good kisser. He looks like the kind of

man who might grab the back of your head while he does it, too.

There are all kinds of ways I might meet him, and believe me, I've examined every eventuality. Some versions are pathetic rescue fantasies, some are plausible, some ridiculously far-fetched. In one convoluted version I get my bag snatched and the thief, (played by, I don't know, Tim Roth or someone), pushes me over into his arms by accident, and Richard is my knight in shining armour, retrieving my bag and knocking the assailant out with one punch. We go for a stiff brandy somewhere private and he puts his arm around me until I stop shaking, then snogs my face off by a roaring fire. In another I see him standing over a bridge on his own, looking upset. I say something smart and snappy, along the lines of 'Don't jump' (ha ha) and he tells all about the awful split with his girlfriend, Sarah Arseholen, and I listen and nod and understand deeply. He doesn't know why he's telling a stranger all this, but then I give him the diary, tell him I found it, and we both throw it in the river, a symbolic offloading of the past, and he's permanently indebted to me. Then he snogs my face off. Today, in this weather, another one springs to mind. I sunbathe by the river and when I open my eyes he's there, standing over me, captivated by my resplendent form, his attentive face smiling down at me. When I imagine that scenario, for some reason I feel the urge to bite his bottom lip.

Despite the warm day I feel a shiver race through me.

God, I'm obsessed.

I'm a stalker. Crazy Jane, rooting through the bins.

'*Keep Looking*,' Richard said. Always dangling a

carrot and being mysterious. What a *dreamboat*. What a *hunk*.

Right, Jane, come on, this is a practical mission. You need to find him before you can molest him on river-banks. Find Lowgate.

I should have bought a map from the machine in the station, but I didn't think I'd need it. I wish there was a map to help me find Richard. His house highlighted with a red circle, and an arrow pointing to me, saying 'You Are Here'.

Walking a bit further I spot a man who must be in his sixties, a Yorkshireman if ever there was one: fishing hat, checked shirt, a varnished walking stick with a silver handle, tarnished with fingerprints.

'Excuse me? Do you know where Lowgate is?'

He regards me with an incurious country gaze.

'Well I don't know,' he says in a thick American accent.

Oh.

'I'm just a tourist.'

'Oh.'

'Are you on vacation here?'

'Er, well, no. well, I suppose so . . . I . . . I'm just looking for a shop.'

He nods sagely, glancing at my clothes, as if he thinks I could do with some new ones.

'Thanks anyway,' I say, walking away cluelessly in the direction of God knows where. York is a maze of archways and alleyways. I walk up a side street, past a bakery called The Buttery, which is closed and boarded up; a pub, the Saracen Arms, which promises dubious live entertainment, and now I'm out onto a main road. The traffic is heavy, and ahead of me there's a blue sign directing cars and lorries towards the A1(M).

I'm lost.

I wish I could find the tourist office.

Then, in an inconspicuous corner, suddenly I see Kaleidoscope, sitting in the middle of a small row of shops selling meat, bicycles and feminist literature. The frontage is painted a gruesome purple, the colour of Kelly's lip gloss. It's one of those places specializing in imported Indian tat and stoner accessories. The window display is made up of *Alien* head ashtrays, jewelled boxes made by blind ten-year-olds in sweat-shops, bedsit throws, joss-stick holders in the shape of urns, tie-dyed crocheted cardigans and crap bongs. Packs of striped tights are arranged in a fan-shape around a tray of nose rings.

Wait a minute, is Richard a Goth?

I check the credit note to see whether I've gone mad, but no, this is it. 'This credit note is to the value of £50 and can only be used by the authorised signatory. Goods cannot be refunded or exchanged. Does not affect your statutory rights.' Dated 11th of June, it expires at the end of September and sounds very official for a place that looks like a hippie's armpit. Underneath there's Richard's lovely signature, a fabulously insane scribble that I've pored over for hours, trying to decipher his true personality. Richard bought something from this shop and I have no idea what or why. It seems like a mistake to me.

It's open, at any rate, which is a blessing. I push the door open and wind chimes tinkle above me. The smell of incense and stale tobacco hits me in a mouldy, intoxicating wave. It takes a minute for my eyes to adjust to the darkness, but when they do, I can make out a pallid girl sitting behind the counter, reading a magazine called *Skin 'N' Ink*, featuring a fabulously decorated man with a peacock emblazoned on his back. She looks up briefly.

'Hiya,' she sighs, barely conscious.

'Hiya.' I walk to the counter, my purposefulness out of sync with the comatose atmosphere. She bristles slightly as I approach and reluctantly lays the magazine to one side, like she's squaring up for a fight. I wonder if that's what I look like when I'm at work.

"Scuse me,' I venture, noticing her hand is shaking. By her wrist is an ashtray, containing snuffed-out roaches. She's stoned off her box.

'I wondered if you could give me some information,' I say, sounding like a policewoman. 'I'm looking for someone.'

'Oh aye?' she asks, raising one plucked eyebrow so high that I'm waiting for it to slide off her head completely.

'Yes. I found this credit note and I'm trying to find the person who it belongs to.'

There's a silence.

Nothing.

She stares vacantly at a point just past my right shoulder.

'Do you have any records? An address, or anything?'

I give her the note and she looks at it uncomprehendingly for about two hours.

'You can't use this,' she drones.

'No, I know. I found it and I want to return it to the owner. Do you have any details of him on file?' I tail off, looking hopelessly at the disarray behind the counter. Bits of paper are scattered everywhere, and there seems to be some kind of recycling centre by her feet containing yellowing newspapers and empty tins of Kit-e-Kat.

'What's 'is signature say?' she mumbles, peering closely. Her hair is dyed the same ugly purple as the shop front and she needs her roots done.

'It says Richard Miles,' I say with forced patience.

'Richard Miles,' she ponders. 'Richard Miles.'

The sound of someone else saying his name makes me flinch. It's as if she's wandered into my bedroom and started messing around with my possessions.

'Richard Miles . . .'

Stop saying it.

'Yes. Erm, he's sort of good-looking.'

Her mouth turns up at the corners in a knowing smile. I realize I'm blushing.

'Good looking, eh? Hmm. Don't get many lookers in here.'

She sits and thinks for ever, traces of puzzlement wandering across her pale face every so often. I pass the time by looking at the selection of Zippo lighters on the counter. A brass belt buckle design with 'Born to be Wild' stamped into it. Bart Simpson saying 'Ay Caramba!' A fluorescent green leaf with 'I Love Weed' printed underneath in blurred writing.

This place is shite.

She still doesn't respond. After a while I wonder whether she's forgotten I'm here.

'So do you remember anyone?' I ask encouragingly, and she jolts as if electrocuted. Recovering herself, she busies herself rhythmically smoothing down the folds of her magazine.

'Well, there wa' this one bloke,' she offers, more alert now. 'He bought Nelly.'

I follow her eyes to a corner of the shop where there's a glass display case containing tacky belly-button jewellery of every conceivable type.

'Nelly?'

'The elephant.'

'Pardon?'

'The wooden elephant what used to sit there by the window. She wasn't for sale, but he wanted her. Said it was a present for some woman, a singer or something, someone I'd never heard of. Wouldn't take no for an answer, made a right scene. Then he brought it back,' she says, her tone turning nasty as the details take shape in her blitzed mind.

'He said he didn't want it after all, so I give 'im a credit note. He wanted his money back, but I wasn't gunna budge. Then after he'd gone I saw it wa' broke. Wouldn't stand up straight so I 'ad to throw it out.'

She snatches the credit note off the counter and eyes me with a needle of suspicion.

'Do you know 'im? If you do, tell 'im from me he's a fucking bastard.'

She returns to her magazine, the conversation clearly over. On the back cover is a close-up of an arm, tattooed shoulder to wrist with a snake.

'No,' I say, 'that can't be him.'

'I'm sure he was called Richard Miles.' She recites with eerie decisiveness, her gaze not shifting from the page.

I stand there for a moment. Elephants indeed. What would a man like Richard want with something like that? She rocks slowly back and forth, her mouth moving as she reads. She's obviously mad.

'Well, thanks for your help.'

'You're welcome. 'Ave a nice day.'

The glare of the sun stuns me as I leave the shop, the wind chimes clinking discordantly behind me. I stumble away, wondering what to make of it. Why would Richard go there at all? It seems so out of character. I shield my eyes and retrace my steps back to the safe haven of the tourists, with their reassuring, uncomplicated demands. I'm dehydrated. My head is spinning.

I find the most touristy café I can, a genteel overpriced tea room called Miss Merriweather's. It's a sea of white candyfloss hair and tanned bald patches the colour of pennies. Everyone clinks cups and brandishes sugar tongs while murmuring sedately. A dumpy teenage girl with blue sticking plasters attached to nearly every finger comes to greet me.

'Are you on your own?'

'Yes. On my own.'

As always, as usual, I'm on my own.

She allows herself a tiny smirk, as if being alone and desperate is somehow amusing. I half expect her to start pointing at me and saying I smell. Fuck you, dumpy drawers. She leads me downstairs into an oak-panelled room and sits me on a tiny table with a lone carnation in the middle of it. I order tea and a scone and try to figure out this weird Richard business. Over in the opposite corner a group of fashionably dressed young people have afternoon tea and take the piss out of the old-fashioned trimmings, suddenly erupting in a gale of supercilious har hars.

Nelly. It couldn't have been Richard who bought the elephant. I have his diary. I have his thoughts. He's just not . . . a wooden animal kind of guy. But he DID go there, and he did spend fifty quid. What on if not something like that? Harley-Davidson belt buckles? Although it was only a minute ago, I try to remember if there was anything tasteful in there, but all I can see is her arched eyebrows and scuzzy purple roots. A present for a singer, did she say? Is Sarah Arseholen famous or something?

Oh, but she was hammered, she didn't know what day it was. She must have got him mixed up with someone else. I mean, she can't work there all the time – if she did the place would probably crumble to the ground in a slagheap of cat-food tins and smouldering joints. And even if Richard WAS the one she was talking about, she probably misunderstood the situation. It took her long enough to figure out what I wanted, and even then she didn't quite get it. Chances are she could have hallucinated the whole thing. Her mind is probably a zoo of flying elephants and glow-in-the-dark badgers.

Even so, a tangle of unease sits in my gut.

Where are you, Richard? What are you? Help me out here.

The waitress comes back and lays my twee little teapot and scone in front of me with exaggerated precision.

'Thanks.'

She doesn't answer. Her face looks like it's made of pastry, dusted with cinnamon freckles. She's miles away, probably thinking about the end of her shift. Again, Kelly, like some pestering apparition, looms up in my mind, snapping the lid shut on her compact with a fastidious flourish.

'You don't know anyone called Richard Miles, do you?'

'Eh?' she asks dumbly, as if responding to a far-away voice.

'Richard Miles?'

I dig in my bag and show her the photograph. She stares at it and shakes her head.

'No. Phwoar. Wish I did, though,' she quips, bustling off to clear the next table.

Yeah.

Phwoar.

So do I.

I pick the raisins out of my scone, laying them at the side of my plate. I line them up in order of the stations on the mainline: Edinburgh, Newcastle, York, London. There are no more clues here, just a train ticket that doesn't really mean anything, other than that he bought a single to York on the 10th of June, and the ramblings of a madwoman. As far as I know he might not have been back since. London is the next place, the most likely place, I suppose. I squash the last raisin in line with my thumb and it spreads out in a flat, juicy splodge. London is so big. How will I ever find him there?

Knowing my luck he's probably back in Edinburgh.

The well-heeled twentysomethings have finished their ironic, hilarious afternoon tea and scrape their chairs back with a disorganized clatter. The lead rah-rah, a prematurely middle-aged-looking lad with a thick neck and high shirt collar says something funny and they all laugh heartily and head up the stairs. One of the stragglers gets a wallet out of his jeans pocket and puts a crisp twenty on the table. He's tall and wiry, blue-eyed and eager to please, with a shaved head that reminds me of . . . He turns round and smiles, an impertinent and not wholly unattractive smirk. The hairs stand up on the back of my neck.

I blink hard and look at my plate.

'Come on, Charlie, it'll be starting soon,' says a girl with an unbelievably posh accent.

When I look up they're gone.

*   *   *

It appears that Babs has a new look. She's now more Venus fly trap than chrysanthemum. Her blond perm has been replaced with an impish crop, and she's lost some weight. Her limbs look like spider's legs, clad in a black tight jumper and black ski pants. She could be a dancer if it wasn't for her complete inability to dance.

'PILATES!' she bellows, doing a twirl. Her bum is small and pert and wouldn't look out of place on an eight-year-old boy.

'It's transformed me. I got a video from Rita. You know how bloody boring she is about all that stuff, but once I started I couldn't get enough. You should try it. My God, Jane, your hair is *red*. What's all that about?'

'Dyed it,' I mumble.

'Are you going through one of your phases?' she asks suspiciously, holding the box of chocolates I've bought her between thumb and forefinger like a smelly old sock. I didn't want to get her flowers – she sees enough of them. Now it seems that chocolates are a no-no as well.

'No. Are you?'

'Oh Jane,' she gushes, her face flooding with affection. 'It's so good to see you. My little prickly hedgehog.' She grabs my cheek and pulls it irritatingly. If she wasn't my mother I'd kick her up the arse.

'Where's Becky?' I ask, disengaging myself and going through to the kitchen.

I'm shocked to find that it's completely changed. Instead of the old units stacked with Pyrex dishes and the tiles with the naff fruit-basket print, there are eggshell-blue cupboards and black and white chequered splashbacks. The layout is entirely different – I don't recognize the place.

223

'Hey, when did you change this?' I ask. I feel surprisingly betrayed.

'Haven't you seen it before?' she asks incredulously. 'I told you we'd had it done. In MAY, Jane. We had all the hassle with the people from the company, don't you remember? I nearly phoned *Watchdog*.'

'May?'

'DUH! You're in a world of your own, you are. Tunnel vision,' she says cheerily, putting the chocolates on the table. Babs goes over to the new hob and briefly stirs a pan. 'Becky's just gone out to get us some wine. Now, dinner will be ready soon so if you want to get scrubbed up.' She opens the oven with a squeak and a blast of hot air fills the room, accompanied by the comforting, yeasty smell of baked bread.

'Oh and there's a letter from your D-A-D by the phone. He remembers he's got one daughter, anyway,' she hollers over the sound of the cooker buzzer going off. With slumped shoulders, I drag myself into the hall. On the window sill by the leaded front door is a scarlet envelope waiting ominously, like a Valentine.

Hello, Dad, you errant swine. My yearly update on his far-flung activities, followed by the promise to meet up soon, which never quite materializes. I feel a pull of something like longing, but it isn't really that, it's more like menstrual cramp. I rip it open and pull out a card featuring a teddy bear holding a clutch of balloons. (What does he think I am? Five?)

Dear Jane, Sorry I haven't been in touch for so long – things have been hectic to say the least – I've just come back from Australia (ever the adventurer!) and New Zealand, where I took a tour of the barrier reef with Mike Bowes and a couple of Kiwis I met

224

in Auckland. Very impressive and beautiful place, better than Leeds any day of the week! How are you? Have you got a job yet? Got more travels up my sleeve later in the year – you know how restless I get. Maybe I'll pop in and see you. Doug Weston and his wife Therese have just bought a place in Aix-en-Provence and we're talking about starting up a vineyard . . .

Oh shut up. Just leave me out of it.

I throw the card aside and hike up the thickly carpeted stairs.

My old room has long been turned into a guest room, but it still has the claustrophobic, hormonal atmosphere of a teenage girl's lair. The bedcovers are different, scattered with babyish daisies on a magenta background, and the surface of the bedside table is no longer a cesspit of mouldy coffee mugs, tissues and Tampax. But on closer inspection my pre-college, younger self is still going strong. A poster of Jarvis Cocker, which makes me weirdly embarrassed now, is still tacked to the inside door of the built-in wardrobes. Down the side of the chest of drawers are the glow-in-the-dark Hello Kitty stickers that not even wire wool and paint stripper could remove. On the dressing table there's the old willow-pattern soapdish filled with rings and necklaces, including my freakishly tiny baby bracelet and a *Blue Peter* badge I got for collecting 500 milk bottle tops for the Ethiopia Appeal in 1987. It seems bizarre that I was once a girl who was in love with the world, cheerfully recycling tin foil, born with wrists the circumference of a carrot. I sit on the bed and fight the urge to be small again. Summer evenings with the light slanting in, absorbed in rearranging my doll's house or orchestrating a Barbie orgy, with nothing in particular on my mind.

I take the diary out and examine the tube tickets and the screwed-up, tattered business card. Copley and Weir publishing, something illegible Brewer Street, London W1. I think I'll make that my next port of call. In my notebook I cross out Number One in my list of York plans and realize that I haven't e-mailed Sarah Olsen yet. I underline it and write 'Monday' next to it, tentatively circling 'Get phone book for York and rip out M pages.'

Where will I get a phone book for York at this time on a Sunday?

It occurs to me that my plan is crap.

'Beck, I mean JANE! Becky's here, come down and see her,' my mum shrieks from the foot of the stairs. I hear the muffled sound of Becky's, bored, flat voice and the clattering of baking trays being pulled out of the oven. Becky always sounds unimpressed, even when she is. You could put a unicorn in front of her and not get so much as an 'Oh, right.'

I put the diary in the drawer, out of harm's way.

'Coming.'

On the way to the kitchen I pocket the card from my dad, resisting the urge to make it into a paper aeroplane and aim it straight for the bin. With a twinge of bleak irritation I notice that the only phone books Babs has are the Yellow Pages and a directory for Leeds West. I'll phone directory enquiries – they might have him listed.

'Hello, stranger,' says Becky, leaning casually against the new breakfast bar, long-limbed and dressed in a black low-cut top and trousers. Her pose is a bit too contrived – she's putting on the cool act for me.

'Hiya, Becks,' I say, not wanting to appear too

pleased to see her. 'Why are you both dressed like burglars? Have you been doing pilates as well?'

Becky curls her lip.

'What are you on about?'

'I was telling her about RITA,' Babs shouts, as if we're standing in the other room.

'Oh, right. No, I haven't.' Becky sniffs, raiding a drawer for a corkscrew. 'Your hair's very, er . . . interesting. Have you dyed it for anyone special?'

A chill seizes my stomach.

'No,' I say defensively. 'Do you need any help, Mum?'

'No you're all right. Sit down, I'm dishing up.' Babs clangs a pan of pasta into a colander and it slops out in a big yellow pile, causing a mushroom cloud of steam. Becky pours me a glass of wine, glug glug glug. It should be a touching family scene, except nothing in this room makes me feel at home. This is a more streamlined version of my old family, who were flabbier round the edges, with worse haircuts. It reminds me of *Back to the Future*, when Michael J. Fox comes back from the Fifties to find his house and his parents transformed. Except I had nothing to do with this particular makeover. I push my fork into the wipe-clean tablecloth and yearn for the Pyrex dishes and smell of gravy.

'So what are you here for?' Becky asks.

'I just needed a holiday,' I reply. 'What are you here for?'

Becky pops her eyes and sneers.

'Now girls, be NICE,' Babs soothes, putting a bowl of pasta in front of me. It's certainly not what I'd expected. Homemade tomato sauce, olives, capers, anchovies, garlic bread with rosemary (not from a packet), real parmesan rather than the powdered stuff

227

that stinks of cat sick, salad with basil and cherry tomatoes instead of cucumber and egg. What the hell is going on? When did Babs discover herbs?

'This looks nice,' I say. 'You don't normally cook stuff like this.'

'Well we used to eat so much rubbish,' she says, passing me the bread. 'I got turned on to healthy eating by a woman who came into the shop and I've not looked back since. When I think about all the bad fats we used to eat . . . Mince, bacon – fried with lard! Ooh, it turns my stomach. Now I can't even have milk in my tea.'

'Everything's changed since you left, Jane.' Becky smiles, a condescending edge to her voice.

'So it seems,' I mumble, feeling left out.

'So how are things in the land of tartan bagpipes and cabers?' Becky simpers.

I chew my food thoughtfully, wondering if I could spit it at her without Babs noticing. Patronizing cow.

'What cabers? There aren't any cabers. If you mean Edinburgh, Becky, it's fine,' I say, sounding a bit too snooty. 'The tourist office is really busy at the moment, but they let me off for a few days. They're very understanding.'

Becky makes a face, but I suddenly realize it's true. Sophie didn't have to give me time off or send me to London. And even if Kelly hates me, she still covered for me. The way she hauled those brochures out of sight and locked them in the cupboard was genius. Heroic, even. She must be able to pull trucks with those arms.

'It just doesn't strike me as being the kind of job you'd do, that's all. I mean, it's a bit dull, isn't it?'

When I look at Becky I see a family resemblance that

temporarily nauseates me. Our eyes are the same dark brown, our lips curve the same way, we're the same bothersome skin type (oily in all the wrong places). As boring as working in the florists? I want to say but hold my tongue.

'No. Actually, it's not.'

Becky shrugs and takes a huge mouthful of salad. Camp David dressed as John Travolta, Fiona with a pencil up her nose, Val coughing up blood, Kelly preening herself, Sophie's boobs hanging out covered in glitter, Dumb Paul, the Spanish tourists, Susan Chaterrrrgh, the lady-boy old women and even Pierce Cocksucker scroll leisurely through my mind. I cheerfully rip a piece off the garlicky loaf.

'It's pretty entertaining.'

'And it's great about the presentation tomorrow, isn't it?' Babs says joyfully, grasping my wrist.

'What?'

My mind goes desperately blank.

Babs' encouraging smile is frozen, waiting for my response. Becky watches me closely.

'The presentation in London, dummy,' Babs screams, pushing me in the arm with alarming force. 'Honestly, what's up with you? Are you on DRUGS? So, are you nervous?'

'Oh yeah,' I splutter. 'It's really scary. There's going to be about, er, thirty people there. It's called Edinburgh – Tradition and Invention,' I say, brilliantly recalling the title of Kelly's talk at the travel fair.

'Ooh! And where is it exactly?' Babs probes, impressed.

I stare at the salad bowl on the table, trying to figure out a convincing London place name. Lettuce lane, tomato road, olive street, salad, green salad, green . . .

'Green Park.'

'Ooh,' Babs coos, amazed, even though she has no idea where it is.

'Yeah, but still, I'm surprised you've lasted with this job for so long. Last I heard you hated it,' Becky chips in.

'I don't hate it,' I say, trying to spear a caper with the tine of my fork and pretending it's her head.

'You said you hated Edinburgh and that everyone was "up themselves", and that as soon as you could you were going to get another job,' she continues argumentatively.

Yes I did say that. Becky stares at me, the clear, unashamed stare of Somebody Who Is Right.

'I know, but . . .'

'In fact, I thought you were coming home for good this time. Mum said you sounded really depressed the last time she talked to you, and we thought you'd be ready to pack it in, didn't we, Mum?'

Babs looks uncomfortable and sips her wine, temporarily fascinated by the right-hand corner of the room.

'Well, you did sound a bit depressed, love.'

'Oh,' I say, crumbs jamming in my throat. I try to swallow, but the bread seems to have turned into something indigestible: cotton wool or Fuzzy Felt.

There's an embarrassed silence for everyone but Becks, who tucks into her dinner with renewed vigour, filling her big fat cheeks with food.

'Well, you're so far away, and you never tell us anything,' says Babs helplessly.

'Sometimes I have to admit I get worried. I hate to think of you sitting in your flat on your own, doing something you don't like . . .'

'I do like it,' I protest, my voice thick with dough.

'Good, GOOD! I'm so glad. I mean you're doing so well at the moment and it really seems like you're getting into your stride. Just you stick at it,' she says, breezy and upbeat but not particularly convincing. Her fingers clasp my hand, but they're fluttery and uncertain, and it's not the reassuring gesture she intended. Her eyes flit uneasily to Becky.

We eat in awkward silence.

My appetite has shrivelled.

Well, there's no place like home.

Obviously, everybody's just waiting for the day I mess up and come home with my tail between my legs. It would be just like me, after all. Never had a job that's lasted more than six months, always unsettled, always thinking about moving on before I've even arrived. It was a miracle I even finished my degree. In the second year I wanted to take a year out to go travelling, but Ali convinced me otherwise. If I'd gone grape picking in Bulgaria or opium harvesting in Azerbaijan, or whatever crazy adventures I'd seen in Sunday supplement travel articles, I doubt I would ever have gone back to college. When I was younger my after-school classes fell by the wayside with monotonous regularity. Ballet for three weeks, tap for two, modern dance for a month, piano for a month and a half, and in the orchestra for three whole months – a world record – until the oboe lost its thrilling appeal.

'Oh, I forgot, Mrs O'Connor finally agreed about that wreath. Now it'll just be 'Reg', not 'Reginald'. The size she wanted it wouldn't have fitted in the hearse,' Babs murmurs. Becky grunts in agreement.

'Poor old girl. Not thinking straight, I suppose,' she adds for want of something to say.

231

'How are things at the shop?' I ask, hoping to clear the air of my terrible failings.

'Oh, fine,' she says, switching on a sudden artificial brightness. 'You know, the usual. Quite busy. Been lots of weddings, recently, haven't there, Becks?'

'Hmm.'

'You'd think with the amount of divorces people wouldn't be so bothered, but they're lining up to get hitched these days. More fool them.' She laughs, bitterly, laying her plate to one side.

I meet Becky's eye across the table.

'I saw you got something from Dad. What did it say?' Becky asks. Her face is flushed and guarded.

'Oh, you know. Not much. Been to Australia and New Zealand and Outer Mongolia. Lots of stuff about some people we've never heard of. Sorry I haven't been in touch but I don't give a fuck . . .'

'JANE! Wash your mouth out,' Babs scolds rather limply as she gathers up the dishes and takes them to the sink.

'Well at least you got a card,' Becky moans, grumpily drawing squiggly lines in her leftover tomato sauce with a fork.

'You can have it if you want. It's got a teddy bear on it.'

'Did he mention me?'

'Er . . .' I falter.

'Who wants pudding?' Babs yells, making more noise than necessary, banging cupboards and clattering bowls. She opens the fridge and takes out an enormous tacky Sara Lee cheesecake in a foil dish, decorated with chocolate curls and red gooey cherries.

'I thought you were into healthy eating, Mum,' I say, as she plonks it on the table.

'Yes, well. SOD IT,' she says, cutting a large, savage slice.

Later the heating clicks and the clock ticks and the TV carries on in the corner. I'm in a stupor, barely able to have a single thought. The sofa is a spongy, dralon monster that's slowly eating me. Flip flip, goes Babs' slipper against her heel. Becky is on the phone in the hall, talking to some friend, probably reluctantly turning down an invitation. 'My sister's here. I've got to stay in.' Groan, moan. Babs has a cigarette on the go and is holding it glamorously aloft, as if she's a movie star or a passenger on the Orient Express. Her once luscious lips, concertinaed by years of dragging on filters, are puckered into a pout. I'm desperate for a fag but she'd kill me, and even so, I don't know whether I could get it together to smoke it. A sad, leaden feeling is weighing me down, and I can't remember why I'm even here. Along with the sofa, the indistinct burble of the TV and the airless heat coming from the radiators, the knowledge that I'm not approved of by anyone in the world beats me down in a single heavy blow, stunning me into silence. You seem depressed, says the brass deer on the mantlepiece. You can't stick at anything, says the black hole of the unlit fireplace. We're worried about you, laments the lolling head of a single gerbera, slotted neatly into a glass vase on the bookshelf.

'Ha! He's a CARD, innie?' Babs guffaws as somebody says something not very hilarious on the telly.

Up on the top shelf of the bookcase is a photo of me and Becky when I was fifteen and she was twelve. We're both at equally unwieldy stages of our development – Becky has funny little-girl breasts under her

233

T-shirt and I've got braces like the perimeter fence in *The Great Escape* – but we're totally unselfconscious. We're just being ourselves. We're beaming. I've got a 500-watt smile, braces or no braces. The last time I smiled like that was . . .

Babs lets out a hoot of laughter at the antics of some blokes on a DIY show: 'Tommy, you've just got to put two and two together and the rest'll fall into place, mate.'

I try to organize my brain to think about tomorrow but my plan slips and slides around in my head. London. I'll have to leave early so as to be in time for my 'presentation'. Then what? Something about an ad in *Time Out* . . . directory enquiries and, oh yes, the publishers. I need to go to the place on the business card. Somewhere on Brewer Street. It makes me tired. When I try to think of the logistics all I can see is a squashed raisin.

Becky, off the phone now, mooches into the living room and sits at the other end of the sofa with a dull, padded thud.

'It's so nice being here with my two girls,' says Babs, craning her neck to look at me. 'I wish you could stay longer, Jane.'

Between us, Becky stares at the television, face impassive. I send a watery smile across to my mum.

'I'll come back for longer next time,' I say, and Becky glances fiercely sideways.

'I'm going to make a cup of tea,' she harrumphs, springing up from the settee in one agile movement and stomping out of the room.

'What's up with her?' I ask when she's gone.

'She's just in a funny mood,' Babs hisses confidentially, tapping her cigarette on the side of a large crystal ashtray. She returns to the TV, as if she's explained everything. In the DIY show a bombsite of a bedroom is being decorated, the cracks filled and papered over, everything made new again. 'Once this is sorted you'll be able to relax.'

I feel peculiar, an anxious mixture of boredom and twitchiness. I don't want a showdown with Becky, but I can hear it brewing. I can't move my body off the sofa, but my legs are aching and restless. The kettle is rumbling in the kitchen but Becky has thundered upstairs.

'She doesn't like hearing about your life. She starts thinking that maybe it's time to move on,' Babs casually volunteers, blowing a puff of smoke in a thin blue jet. 'She's not as resilient as you; she doesn't go after things like you do. She's a sensitive little flower.'

I give a snort of derision. 'She is not.'

'Deep down she knows she shouldn't be here,' says Babs, ignoring me. 'What? You think she wants to work in the bloody SHOP for the rest of her life?'

She stretches her leg and whirls her foot in a circular motion. It's a lazy, languorous gesture that reminds me of Stinky the cat.

'I thought she was happy,' I say.

It's time for Babs to snort derisively.

'Don't be daft. She's miserable as sin. Shuffling around all day looking like she's chewing a wasp. She's twenty-three! She should have better things to do than hang around with her mother. She should be out in the world, making a go of things.'

I stare at the swirling pattern of the carpet, an ugly cream and brown mess that looks like it's stained with coffee. Does she really think I'm resilient?

'She's probably better off here,' I say glumly. 'It's not like the world's much fun.'

'Well I'd rather she made an effort – she's been really depressed lately and it's driving me up the bloody wall. I blame that letter. Fancy sending something to you and not to her. What was he thinking?' she flashes angrily.

I become aware of the card in my pocket, the sharp edges sticking into my skin.

'I don't want it.'

'You don't want it, I don't want it, none of us want it, but *we* can cope with it, can't we? She still hasn't got over it, Jane. Ten years it's been, and she still can't get to grips with the idea he isn't coming back. I don't know what to do. I've not had a squeak out of her for days.'

'I'll talk to her,' I mumble.

'Please,' Babs says with an imploring look, giving me a twinge of grown-up solidarity. We're just two people talking, not mother and daughter. She needs my help. And although I'm concerned for my sister's welfare, I feel a gleam of pride that I'm suddenly not the useless one any more.

'I will.'

'Maybe you can do some good. I'm not so worried about you. You might go on about how you get fed up and all those people at work are horrible, but I don't think you're that unhappy. I can tell things up there aren't THAT bad. Who's that bloke? Camp Kenny? He sounds like a laugh.'

'David.' I smile, tickled that she remembered. Images of him skitter through my mind. David grinning in his white suit, fluttering around me when I fell, buying me all those drinks, telling me to get off my arse and do some work. He was really nice to me at the club. No, things aren't THAT bad.

'Becky never meets anyone,' Babs whispers. 'Apart from Tracy what's-her-name from the deli shop next door. And between you and me, she's like a frigging wet weekend in Wetwang.'

I laugh and Babs laughs too, a throaty, sophisticated bleat that sounds like a creaky trap door. My mum's great. I watch Babs, sitting there in her armchair with her More menthol cigarettes, her pilates video stashed in the TV stand, her sultry black outfit and her new haircut, and feel a stab of admiration. Her hands are snagged with thorns and there'll always be a red line where her wedding ring used to be, but she's too bloody-minded to fail.

'By the way, I forgot to ask, how's Ali?' she says, settling back in her chair.

'Oh, she's great. Everything's great. Liam, too.' I say. Ali, beaming and radiant in that long, shapeless jumper flashes before my eyes, and I don't get the slightest urge to stove their heads in for having the cheek to be happy. Maybe I am growing up, after all.

'Ooh, he's a lovely boy, he is.'

'He said to tell you hi,' I tease.

'Ooh!' she squeals.

'Put it away, Mum. He's far too young for you.'

'Ah, what do you know?' she says. 'He is lovely, though. He's what they call a Light Man.'

'Mm,' I mutter, fiddling with a tassel on the sofa cushion.

'Rita once went to a Korean fortune teller in Brisbane,' she says, leaning in. 'You know, when she was going through a tricky patch with Don – you know her husband, runs the fruit shop on Gosforth Road, used to give you free satsumas . . .'

'Yes, go on,' I sigh.

'And SHE said that there are two types of men – light men and dark men – and that Don was a dark man. You see, the DARK ones are the moody, complicated ones, the ones who never know what they want, the ones with the big IDEAS. Like your father. Oh, they're mysterious and attractive at first, but you can't live with them. They don't open up – they drive you mad.'

'Right,' I say as I ponder Rita's highly scientific theory. 'Wasn't he the one who ran off with Becky's English teacher?'

'YES! You see. DARK,' she warns. 'Take it from me, don't get mixed up with 'em. Liam is light, so Ali will always be OK.'

'Right, well, whatever Rita says.'

I wonder about the dark properties of Richard. Is he one of them? No. He's an open book, surely.

'You don't know who he is,' says Dan in my ear. *'He could be anyone.'*

Babs reaches for yet another cigarette.

'Want one?'

'Er . . . no.'

She gives me a sly, knowing look and sticks it in her mouth.

'When you met Dad, how did you know you were in love?' I blurt, immediately cringing at sounding so corny. She stops and looks at me incredulously.

'Why? Are *you* in love?' She smirks.

'No. I'm just curious.'

'Well . . .' She clears her throat and examines the ceiling. 'I thought I was in love with him, but now I think I just fancied him really. He was so attractive,

238

with his big brown eyes and his big everything else. Everyone thought he was wonderful, and when I found out he liked me, I couldn't believe it. I was impressionable, swept away on the romance of it all. It was the Seventies, you know. I wasn't thinking straight. But reality has a habit of catching up with you, whether you like it or not.'

I idly trace the immaculate line of Richard's profile on the arm of the sofa. When I look up she's peering at me intently.

'Stop trying to be mysterious, Jane. You're like bloody cling film. You've got a boyfriend, haven't you? What's his name?'

She suddenly reaches over and starts tickling me, making me giggle uncontrollably.

'Come on. Tell me.'

'Stop it. I haven't got a boyfriend.'

She lays off me and goes back to her cigarette.

'Liar.' She grins. And for a moment it feels like she already knows. She knows everything and it's all going to be OK. The clock ticks on the mantle, drumming out a steady, comforting heartbeat.

'Do you really think I'm doing all right?' I plead weakly.

'EH? Oh, yeah.' She says, yawning.

'I'm not unhappy,' I venture. 'Things are looking up.'

'I know. Isn't that good? I think you might have found your calling at last.'

'Huh. Don't know about that.'

'Well, you never know. It's about time you settled down somewhere rather than just floating around. You haven't had the best of luck, but I reckon you're finding your feet. You're a stubborn pain in the arse and you won't give up without a fight,' she drawls jokily, hauling herself out of her chair and playfully mussing up my hair as she walks past. 'Do you want a cup of tea?'

In the kitchen the kettle lets out a high-pitched, jubilant whistle.

'Yeah.' I smile, running the soft thread of the cushion tassle through my fingers. It feels like warm sand.

R–I–C–H–A–R–D. I write his name on a Post-it note, first in lower case, secondly in capitals and then in a pitiful imitation of his signature. Through my open bedroom curtains the streetlight forms a puddle of orange on the carpet. Outside, the residents of Ashlea Road sit and watch television in living rooms unchanged for years. Directly opposite from us the Fletchers go through their evening rituals. They've had the same slatted office blinds and rickety mirrored dressing table in the bedroom for as long as I can remember. Me and Becky used to watch Pauline Fletcher getting changed and scream with horror as she stood in front of the mirror, examining her flabby bits. Pauline had a touch of the amateur porn star about her – she was always prancing around in a state of undress and behaving inappropriately at Christmas parties. She had a huge crush on my dad. I see her now, thankfully wearing a bathrobe, bending over to take something long and pink out of a drawer. As she flicks the blinds shut, I suppress an outraged giggle. Gordon is stationary on the chair downstairs, his face lit by cathode ray, an appalling brass plate mounted on the wall behind him like an oversized medal honouring twenty loyal years as a couch potato.

Next door a blurred, naked silhouette moves behind

the steamed-up, frosted glass of the bathroom. Vicki Morrison's husband having a shower – he works nights. I can just make out the pixellated curve of white arse cheek as he rubs himself down. On their darkened square of front lawn a rusted tricycle lies forlornly on its side. I notice that Vicki has bought one of those granite house nameplates you see in key-cutting shops – number 12 has now been re-christened 'The Mews'. Classy. The frustration I used to feel when I looked at this street used to drive me insane, but now I don't live here any more it all seems quite entertaining. 'Hi, Gordon.' I say under my breath. 'Your wife's diddling herself upstairs while you watch *Newsnight.*'

I get another piece of paper and idly practise Richard's signature again. I know the peaks and troughs off by heart, but however hard I try I can't copy it. Eventually I decide to write my own name in his style. Jane Darling, I write, but it looks like a cardiac monitor gone haywire. Jane Da— No, it's just not flowing enough. Jane Miles, I scribble, then immediately cross it out and screw the piece of paper into a little ball. Don't be so ridiculous. I aim for the wastebasket on the other side of the room.

OK, if it goes in, I'll find him tomorrow.

I throw it and it goes ridiculously wide, knocking over a tacky ceramic bull Lizzie bought for me in Spain when we were 13, which has somehow survived the guest-room clearout. The bull sets off a domino effect on the dresser, sending a London snow globe to the floor with a loud thump.

Oops.

Becky bangs on the wall.

'Sorry!'

The idea of talking to Becky about anything at the moment isn't particularly attractive. She's such a moody bitch.

So I do a bit of procrastinating and open the diary. The Keep Looking drawing, the funny picture of the duck, the Valentine's day sabotage plan, the sheep, the argument with the human potato, the pleas to find someone who understands him – I know every inch. I've seen it so often I could recite it standing on my head. I need new material. I long to have another photograph, another angle apart from the pensive, monochrome profile. I want to see what he looks like from the front, I want to know what he wears, what he likes to do, what his favourite colour is, how he really looks when he smiles, how he walks and moves and holds his pen. Is he right- or left-handed? Was he popular at school? Does he know any good jokes? What does he have for breakfast?

I peer at the photograph of the handsome man who has fallen into my lap. But the frowning brow and the fine bones have faded into something wearily familiar, something I've examined so thoroughly that it could never offer anything new.

I lie down and close my eyes, but my ability to picture him is exhausted. I bump into him on the street, but I can't imagine the pressure of my shoulder against his chest, I can't smell his skin, I can't recall the sensation of his safe hands grabbing my arms to steady me. I put him on the train, sitting across from me, but when he turns round to face me, he mutates suddenly into Dan.

I snap my eyes open in a panic.

Richard, don't desert me.

The eightball keyring nestles in the front pocket of

my bag and I shake it, waiting for the liquid to settle. Will I find him? The dice upturns and takes an age to decide, suspended for a while in its ominous little window. Finally it rights itself.

'Better Not Tell You Now'.

Agitated, I pace the room. This isn't good. This isn't good at all. I shake it again. The dice swims, goes under, flips over.

'Concentrate and Ask Again.'

No!

One more time, one more time. Will I find Richard?

'Reply Hazy – Try Again Later.'

Piece of shit! I throw it onto the bed and it bounces onto the pillow, finally resting in an obscure corner behind the headboard. I know it's just a toy, just a silly diversion, it doesn't have anything to do with the inner workings of the universe, but still, it could have had the decency to be on my side. I take a deep breath and exhale slowly. In the bathroom my mum is running a bath. I can hear her singing in a high, reedy voice along with the five millionth playing of 'Angels' coming from Becky's stereo.

Directory enquiries. Just phone directory enquiries. Duh!

I sneak downstairs and steal the cordless phone, which is lying on top of a pile of takeaway menus. I should have done this long ago. Why didn't I? Kneeling down at the side of the bed, as if to pray, I prepare to write down the thousands of numbers possibly connected to Richard.

'Hello. I need a multiple search. I need the numbers for every Richard and R. Miles in the London area,' I say in a low voice filled with intent.

At the other end the operator drearily taps at his

keyboard, failing to recognize the profundity of my situation.

'There's one entry for Richard Miles and 27 R Miles.' He drones.

'One?'

'Yes.'

'Only one?'

'Yes.' The operator sighs, bored out of his mind.

Is that him? Is it as easy as that?

'Er, can I have all the numbers, please? Just to be on the safe side. Thanks.'

How can there be only one Richard Miles listed in the whole of London? How can that be? It seems such an odd phenomenon that I wonder if it's a mistake. Surely it's a common enough name. The computerized voice starts with R., moves on to R.A., R.C., R.F., and then there it is, MILES, Richard. I draw a starburst around the number, underline it again and again just to make sure I'm not dreaming, and sit back on my heels, marvelling at it. As I stare at it, the number seems to get bigger, the pen lines get thicker and denser and after a while I have to turn away. It's so significant that it's almost like looking into his eyes.

How could I have been so dumb? One phone call. One Richard.

I can hardly breathe.

My chest is tight.

Should I do it? Should I do it now?

'Jane?'

My mum pokes her head round the door.

'Are you all right? You look a bit flushed.'

'Er, yeah . . . no, I'm fine. Just doing my homework for tomorrow,' I say, feeling caught out and covering the notebook with my elbow.

'What time are you going? I'll give you a lift to the station if you like.'

'Oh, that'd be great. Thanks.' I do a brief bit of scatterbrained mental arithmetic – a presentation would start around ten and it's about two hours away . . .

'The train's at eight,' I say, not knowing whether it is or not.

She cocks her head to one side, putting on a sentimental pout.

'I wish you could have stayed longer. I miss having you around, with all your bad moods and your gob ons. Come 'ere.' As she advances to give me a hug, I stand awkwardly upright, closing the book shut. Her body feels fragile and birdlike, but her grip is strong.

'Did you and Becky have a little chat?' she asks warily, holding me at arm's length.

'Not yet. I'll go in a minute.'

'I'd really appreciate it. Night, love.'

Babs plants a dry, smoky kiss on my cheek.

'Night.'

When she's gone I pace the room, a nervous wreck. Sod Becky. What am I going to say to Richard? How can I play it cool? Every line I think of makes me cringe and want to hide under the bed.

'Hello, you don't know me, but . . .' 'Did you leave a diary on the train?' 'Hi my name's Jane Darling and I . . .' 'Richard Miles? Jane Darling here . . .'

ARGH! My name is so stupid! Jane Darling, girl reporter. Jane Darling, the jolly-hockey-sticks heroine in a *Bunty* annual, scoffing midnight snacks in the dorm. Why can't I be called something more dignified? I could just say Jane, I suppose, keep it mysterious and enigmatic: 'Richard Miles? My name is Jane. Meet me

245

tomorrow at nine under the clock. I'll be wearing a pink carnation. Be there.'

Oh God, this is hopeless.

I watch as Gordon staggers out of his chair, possibly worse for wear, and switches off the TV. The Fletcher house is soon plunged into darkness, save for the soft diffused light coming from the boudoir.

I can hear my heart pounding. The number broods in the notebook, breathing, alive, quietly waiting.

Be practical, Jane.

You can't phone people at 11 o'clock on a Sunday. He'll probably be asleep if he has to commute. If it is him at all, which you really don't know for sure. Oh but it is. It is him. It has to be. I can feel it, pulling at me, an irresistible current. Should I phone it? No. Tomorrow I will call that number, and by the magic of telecommunications we'll be brought together. I'll hear his breath in the receiver and his voice will sing into my ear, and whatever happens then will be in the hands of fate.

I retrieve the keyring from behind the bed and give it one more shake. Will we speak to each other tomorrow?

The dice wallows in the water and bobs decisively to the surface.

'No.'

Oh shut up.

Becky's tastes are teenage to say the least – pop-compilation CDs with shiny, primary-coloured covers scatter the floor and Justin Timberlake gleams asexually from the cover of a magazine. I knock and wander in. Becky is lying on the bed, still wearing her shoes and sulking.

'Hiya,' I say.

'Hiya,' she mumbles.

'Are you OK?'

She shifts on the mattress, hiding her tired, splotchy face.

'Becky, what's the matter?' I move towards her, stepping over a pink, glossy book lying open next to a dirty dinner plate: *The Modern Girl's Guide to Being Fabulous*. The room smells of girlish, sweet perfumes – candied peaches and strawberry shortcake. I notice, with vague resentment, that she's got a brand-new DVD player.

'What's wrong?' I accidentally step on a CD and the plastic case cracks under my foot.

'Oh why don't you just go away,' she suddenly cries, her voice like the creature from the black lagoon, deep and unrecognizable. She's lying coiled and tensed up, a venomous snake ready to strike.

Taken aback, I stumble back to the door.

'Sorry . . .'

'You flounce in here after MONTHS and act as if you own the place and go, "Ooh, blah blah. The tourist office is *so* understanding, I've got a presentation, I'm so happy and successful, la la la . . ." she mimics, spewing bile. 'Why don't you fuck off?'

'Eh?'

I listen as she accuses me of having more successful hair than her, of being the prodigal daughter, of getting to do what I like while she has to stay and look after Mum. I also, apparently, have 'fancy Edinburgh ways'.

'Have you finished?' I say when she's finished. She's crying now, the wretched sobs of a toddler. Oh grow up. On her wall are pictures of school friends she hasn't seen for years. Her bedside table is a crèche of Beanie Babies.

247

'Look, Becky. Why don't you move out? Living here isn't doing you any good. You don't have to look after Mum; she's fine.'

She glares intently at the duvet cover, which is patterned with a complex mass of tumbling rosebuds on trellises.

'What would you know about this family? You only come back home when you want something. What is it this time? Money? Were you hoping Daddy had sent you a big fat cheque?'

Here we go.

'Look, if this is about the card, then you're welcome to it. It's crap. All he cares about is himself.' I take it out of my pocket and throw it across to her. The teddy bear with the balloons is folded in half but looks at home in the insipid flowery garden of Becky's bed.

When she sees it, she immediately starts wailing.

'No,' she cries, sitting up wildly and throwing the card back at me. 'All he cares about is YOU!'

'That's not true,' I yell, slipping effortlessly back into sibling rivalry – 'Is so!', 'Is not!' 'Is too!'

'Yes it is. I haven't seen him ONCE since he left. He took you to McDonalds, remember?'

'Becky, that was nearly ten years ago.'

'So?' she sniffs, fat tears plopping down her face.

I recall the fateful day my father took me to McDonalds. He talked excitedly about his plans, some of which were to involve us at some conveniently far-off point. 'Just you wait until I get settled,' he said, as I picked the sesame seeds off a cheeseburger and looked out of the window at people standing at a bus shelter in the rain, all wearing the same miserable, thwarted expressions. 'You can come out to France/Germany/Florida to visit, and we'll go water

248

skiing/horse riding/swimming with dolphins.' I was sixteen and he was a 48-year-old acting like a teenager. He'd left us in the winter and this was April, and he looked odd. His dark brown hair, tipped with dashing silver grey, was slightly askew, and he kept rubbing his eyes as if he hadn't slept. 'You understand, don't you, Jane?' he kept saying. 'You understand that I can't stay.' I didn't understand, but I thought it was important to seem grown up about it. As we sat there I remember a woman turning her head to stare at him through the window, quite unashamed. He had a lined, crumpled glamour about him that women found attractive. A dark man.

'I can't believe you're still talking about the Unhappy Meal,' I say. 'He fed me a pack of lies and then buggered off. It wasn't like it was a brilliant experience.'

Becky snuffles like a pig and throws her head onto her pillow dramatically.

'You're his FAVOURITE. Daddy's girl,' she whines accusingly. 'I had to bend over backwards to get him to even NOTICE me.'

'Oh that's bollocks. Remember when I went to the roller rink with Vicky Smith and when I got back you'd gone to Scarborough with him? You were away overnight and you went to see Orville and all I got was a broken stick of rock.'

Becky considers this at length, carefully examining the Artex on the ceiling while Robbie croons in the background.

'He prefers you because you're just like him,' she says flatly.

'What?'

'Going off on . . . whims.'

Whims.

Such a funny little word. Insubstantial, short-lived, over before it's even begun.

I think of the diary and my stomach sinks. I think of how I treated Dan, leaving him standing under that streetlight in the rain, and I feel terrible. All he wanted was to make sure I was OK. All I wanted was to run away – going everywhere, getting nowhere.

'You only just got here,' said Fiona, looking dismayed. '*He could be anywhere*,' says Dan for the zillionth time.

Is Richard a whim?

Oh my God, is this some fucked-up Freudian thing? Do I fancy my DAD?

No. Er, no. That's not it.

But the depressing thought remains. This is exactly the kind of thing my Dad would do. My plan is so half-baked and impulsive that I didn't even think of phoning directory enquiries until about five seconds ago. I'm one step away from starting an imaginary vineyard with Doug Weston and his lovely wife Therese.

Becky stares at me, knowing she's hit a nerve. Her moist eyes sparkle with righteous indignation, but my expression must be grave, because she starts to falter.

'I didn't . . . It's just . . . it's just that . . .'

'He doesn't prefer me. He doesn't want either of us,' I say, battling on through my confusion, wanting to be mean, savouring the bluntness of the words. It makes me sick all of a sudden: the pathetic snivelling child in her arrested-development bedroom, leeching off Mum.

She doesn't answer. She just lies there sniffing.

'He's not here any more and that's it. He's not going to come back and take you to McDonalds for a fucking milkshake. He isn't going to get back together with mum, either, not now or ever.'

'NO!' she wails.

'Did you really think that? After all this time?' I shout, the words clanging harshly. 'Forget it. Get off your arse and do something with yourself. You need a life of your own. Leave Mum to have hers. How can she meet anyone new with you hanging around?'

'NO!' screams Becky, leaping up from the bed. She tries to push me out of the room, but I stand firm, grabbing her shoulders and forcing her back towards the bed. Then something happens to her body. The strength in her arms snaps and instead of pushing her, I'm holding her up. Becky's face is streaming. She hangs limp, bending oddly from the waist as if she's winded. Her breathing comes in hiccups. I wonder briefly whether she's going to be sick.

'It's over, OK?' I say finally.

She pulls away from my grasp and collapses on the bed.

'I miss him, too, but he doesn't miss us,' I volunteer, feeling winded myself. 'He's too busy exploring the Barrier Reef with Mike Bowes.'

'Who?' asks Becky, curious despite her advanced emotional state.

'Oh, I don't know.' I say, giving up and collapsing on the bed next to her. My legs don't seem to want to support me either any more.

There's a pitiful silence. I pull a tissue from a Forever Friends novelty box at the side of the bed and pass it to her. It's half empty. Becky must do an awful lot of crying.

'Do you think we'll ever see him again?' she asks, blowing her nose with terrifying force.

'I don't know.'

She looks so young and wide-eyed, her cheeks raw

251

with streaks of dried salt. I'm supposed to be the capable big sister, strong and protective and good at mopping up tears, but I feel like jelly, a big coward. Poor Becky, living this lonely little half-life of floral bouquets and watching TV with Mum, physically unable to move on all because she's afraid, because she thinks he'll change his mind and everything will be OK again. It strikes me as so sad that for a moment I can hardly speak. When I was twenty-three I was peeling my face off the carpet after the millionth party and my dad could go to hell.

I take her hand. On her thin, blue-veined wrist is a bangle I bought her for Christmas last year.

'You need a break from all this. Come and visit me,' I tell her shakily. 'I'm not going to be like him. I'm staying in Edinburgh for a while. I can get you a key cut for the flat if you like.'

She looks down at our entwined hands, so alike you couldn't tell them apart.

'I'm always going to be around whether you like it or not,' I say. I meet Becky's eye and there's a sarcastic flicker between us. I smile, aware of the slushiness of this beautiful Hallmark moment.

Her hand breaks away from mine and she sticks her finger down her throat and makes gagging sounds.

'I mean it. Come up and stay. You might like it, instead of sitting in your bedroom smelling your own farts,' I whine. 'Although I should warn you that in Scotland it's compulsory to wear tartan doilies and eat shortbread. I'll introduce you to some awful up-themselves people with fancy Edinburgh ways and it'll be fun. We can even go out dancing – although not to any of the crap you like.'

Becky turns away grumpily from me, but I catch a

glimmer of amusement at the corner of her mouth. She gives me a half-hearted kick.

'Shut up,' she warbles, wiping her nose again and reducing her tissue to a stringy, sopping mess.

'Well I'm sorry to break it to you, but your taste in music sucks,' I inform her, absently wiping a recently escaped tear away and turning down the volume on Robbie, who's busy loving angels and ruining our tender, sisterly tête-à-tête.

'Hey!' Becky shrieks, lobbing a pillow at me. With a surge of energy I bat it back and it narrowly misses her, knocking over a lamp.

'Oi! Keep it down!' yells Babs from the bathroom.

'Sorry, Mum,' we both call in unison. There's a mischievous pause. Becky chucks the pillow at me, but I catch it.

'Right, stop it now. That's enough. I'm going to bed,' I say, putting on mature, responsible airs and moving out of the door into the hallway.

Just when she thinks I've left, I come back in and skim it across the room, catching her on the side of the head.

'Ha ha!'

I shut the door triumphantly and start back down the hall.

'Jane? Jane?' I hear Becky call in a small, faint voice from behind her door. I'm not falling for that one. Then the door opens a crack and her head pokes out. Her expression is serious and remorseful.

'What?'

'Thanks for . . . well, you know. Pep talk.' She mumbles, embarrassed.

I realize that I'm quite touched.

'S'OK,' I reply, feeling humbled.

'God, you're SO gullible.' She grins, opening the door to reveal the pillow and smacking me full in the face.

'Go to bed.'

I go into my room, feeling infinitely adult and like I've actually done something useful for a change. I set the alarm for six thirty. I don't even look at the diary. I don't want to think about tomorrow.

Lying down on the bed, I shut my eyes and realize that I'm absolutely knackered. Sleep soon comes washing over me.

Drifting out of the ether comes a sunset. Vivid oranges and crimsons fringed by silhouetted palms on a sandy beach. An indistinct figure is waiting for me in this clichéd version of paradise, and I edge closer towards the distant form. Soon I'm standing next to him. We say nothing. All I'm aware of is the slow swoosh of the waves and the wilting palm trees and this warm, calming presence. After a while, something strange happens to the scene. I notice a glossy sheen on it, and realize I'm at the travel fair, looking at a poster. I turn to the figure. He grins from ear to ear, watching me.

'Come on,' Dan says. 'I'll show you around.'

Part Four

LONDON

Babs unlocks the doors of her Vauxhall Astra with a piercing beep. It's a dim, grey morning, far too early for breakfast or decent conversation. I've had to keep the charade alive by getting dressed in professional-looking clothes; a black skirt and white shirt, black work shoes, flimsy 15-denier tights. I keep my battered leather jacket slung over my arm and when Babs starts fussing, I vow that I won't wear it in front of any influential people. As I get in the car bound for the station, dread settles in my guts as if it's the first day of school. I may as well be doing the presentation for real, I'm so nervous. Today I'll speak to Richard. Today, for better or worse, this is going to be sorted out. It was supposed to be a joyful occasion, the first day of the rest of my life. I didn't realize it would make me feel so grim.

'Now, have you got everything? I don't want you leaving any important papers behind,' Babs clucks, throwing her handbag on the back seat and strapping herself in.

'Yes,' I say in a dull voice.

'Right, we'd better go if we want to beat the traffic.

Have you got your belt on? You get fined if you're not wearing it.'

'Yes,' I say in an even duller voice. 'I'm twenty-six years old. I know that people have to wear seat belts in cars.'

'Ooh, who rattled your cage?'

She starts the car with a cranky splutter and revs the engine, then puts it into reverse. From the upstairs window, Becky, dressed in an oversized Donald Duck T-shirt, waves as we turn into the road. I wave back and see her thumbing her nose at me as we set off. She looks different. She's smiling, for a start.

'So is everything OK with Becky? I heard her laughing on the landing. I thought I'd never hear that sound again,' Babs says, flipping her left indicator.

'Yeah, we had a talk.' I say, not feeling like elaborating. My mouth tastes like dead rats and I want to go back to sleep.

'So, was it positive? Is she still upset about him?'

'Who?' I ask.

'Your dad, you dozy arse,' she shouts and turns the corner into Leeds Road.

'Yeah, but she'll get over it. I told her to stop waiting for him to come back because he's never coming back and that she should get a life and stop getting in your way.' I yawn, a deep, extravagant yawn that fills my lungs to bursting point and makes my eyes water.

'Did you?' gasps Babs. 'You didn't.'

'Yeah. She took it better than I thought she would. She seemed to understand. I told her to come up and see me in Edinburgh. I think she will.'

'Wow. She wouldn't take that off me. Thanks, love,' she says, her voice distant and amazed.

'I told her that you'd never get a new boyfriend with her in the way.'

'JANE!' Babs shrieks, trying to lamp me.

'Mum, watch the road.'

'Cheeky cow,' she scolds.

She drives for a while, pretending her nose is out of joint.

'Well, I hope you're all set for later on,' she says eventually. 'This presentation thing must mean you're doing really well. It's a big day, for you, isn't it?'

'Yeah,' I reply.

We come to a standstill at the traffic lights. On the right-hand side of the road is Barbara's Blooms, my mum's empire, with its dark green shutters and florid gold lettering on the sign. A mountain of stuffed council refuse bags is piled by the door.

I glance sideways at her proud face and feel awful.

She's so good and kind, and what am I? Selfish. Running around after complete strangers and lying to everyone.

I unzip my bag to get a stick of chewing gum and the corner of the diary pokes me in the delicate skin on my wrist, as if to remind me of its importance.

At the moment I don't even want to see it, it makes me feel sick. I shut the bag quickly and examine the tiny herringbone patterns on my smart work skirt. A gaggle of kids cross the road, wearing the familiar grey and black uniform of my old school. Their blazers are pressed and ties straightened, their brand-new white socks from Woolworths are almost luminous against the sombre drizzle of the morning. This must be their first week. The ticking of the indicator sounds portentous, like a time bomb.

It's a big day all right.

I'm such a fake.

'Mum . . .'

'OH! Will you look at that . . .' she says, turning her head and clocking the refuse sacks. 'I told that bloody Howard not to put his rubbish outside my shop. I swear I'll swing for him one of these days.'

The light turns green. We start moving again, this time much faster.

There's a snarled-up silence as Babs stews, consumed by her hatred of Howard. We pass the Texaco garage and come to a busy junction. I can't tell her about the presentation. Not today. Not now.

'Becky said I was like my Dad.'

'Eh?' she says, feeding the steering wheel through her hands and turning expertly into a stream of fast-moving cars.

'She said I was always going off on whims.'

There's a pause as Babs switches lanes.

'You,' she says firmly, 'are not like your dad. Not in that way. I mean, you know, you're stubborn and wilful and you don't know what's good for you, but you're definitely not as daft as him. You'd have to go a lot further than Edinburgh to match his bloody whims.'

If she knew I was about to get on a train to find someone I didn't know from Adam on the strength of his diary, she'd beg to differ. It's ludicrous. I may as well take my lunch packed in a handkerchief and skip off to London to see the Queen.

Babs sighs and switches on the radio, her previous good mood soured by inconsiderately positioned rubbish bags. The brash blare of a morning breakfast show fills the car with croaky, tired DJs trying to be funny.

'Ooh, I can't stand that lot,' she mutters, tuning into

Terry Wogan instead. The traffic near the city centre is at a profoundly slow crawl. It's a quarter to eight.

'You're going to MISS the TRAIN. I knew we should have left earlier,' she screeches in exasperation, craning her neck to see the cause of the jam.

'It's OK,' I say, suddenly too tired even to speak. I get a flashback of the taxi ride with Kelly on that fateful day. If we'd got the train we were supposed to get, there would be no diary. I wouldn't even be aware of the existence of Richard Miles. It would have ended up in lost property, his thoughts and ideas for ever forgotten next to mislaid briefcases and umbrellas with bent spokes. The thought gives me a weird, uneasy feeling. I get the sensation that my stomach is slowly curling up at the edges, like one of those cellophane fortune-telling fish.

'Anyway, Jane, stop worrying about stuff like that. Just carry on with what you're doing and everything will be OK,' Babs says. 'You're doing great. And if it doesn't work out, then whatever – come back home. No one's going to think any the less of you.'

'Yeah.'

Maybe that's true. Fiona said that you could start again without running away, but surely you can run away without starting again. It's just a holiday. Disappear and then come back, with a suntan, or a story, or a broken heart. Nobody thinking any the less of you.

But this doesn't feel like a holiday.

The vanilla magic tree swings back and forth on the rear-view mirror like a hypnotist's watch. There's something about the heat in the car that makes me feel as if I'm back in the womb. Outside the world looks forbidding, scary and unknown. Rain spits at the side window, and beside us I notice a filthy van with 'I wish my wife was this dirty' written in the muck. The driver sees me and winks, a hopeless, mechanical gesture. I don't feel ready for today. I don't feel at all ready.

I want to go home.

Oh God, I think, with a pinch of alarm. I didn't take that rubbish out before I left. My flat is going to stink when I get back. Queenie's going to be calling environmental health.

'I'm sure the traffic's got worse,' Babs is saying. 'It's because they won't let them build that bypass.'

I wonder how they're getting on without me at work. I bet Kelly's made up. I wonder if they're talking about me, laughing away in the staffroom. 'Did you see the nick of Jane the other night? Talk about pished. Dan said she was sick outside.'

Then I remember Dan asking my name, concern written all over his face. Everyone seemed genuinely shocked. Sophie, David, Fiona, even Kelly. But why was Dan first on the scene and not someone I knew?

Then I remember.

Dan was the one who tried to catch me.

It was his arms I fell into, then I slipped and hit my head and things all got fucked up.

'Hurrah!' Babs exclaims as the invisible obstacle is cleared and the traffic starts moving freely again. 'We'll get you on that train after all.'

I can see the station at the top of the hill, looming up inevitably, and resign myself to fate yet again.

Copley and Weir Publishing is not the grand building I'd expected, covered in glass and steel and buzzing with importance. It's a flat over a falafel shop in Soho, where Turkish men in red and white aprons stuff cones of pitta bread full of hummus and salad for two quid a pop. There are three buzzers – one for Copley and Weir, one for someone or something called Sandford and one for a company called Atomic! TV. Maybe if it was bigger, with a waiting room or a welcoming reception you could see from the street, I wouldn't mind going in, but the door is inconspicuous and impenetrable. Only someone with proper business there would even know where it was. As I stand there awkwardly, the deep-fried scent of falafel sinking into my clothes, a motorbike courier pulls up at the kerb and confidently strides towards the door, holding a box. I jump out of the way and he presses one of the buzzers. 'Delivery,' he barks into the intercom and the door opens.

'You want in?' he mumbles from behind the smoked glass visor of his helmet.

'Er, I . . .'

He doesn't have time for indecision and goes in anyway, thumping the door shut behind him. The sound slams through me and jangles my nerves. This is silly. What would I say to the receptionist? 'Do you know Richard Miles? He might have been here once, or know someone who has.' For all I know he could have been the motorbike courier.

I go across the street to a coffee shop and hang around. Through the plate-glass window the morning sun evaporates the rain and sends beams of refracted coloured light onto my hands. The table is scattered with sugar crystals, like tiny flecks of diamond. Richard *might* work over there. He might be at his desk now, staring at his screensaver or taking an important call. He might be drinking the same coffee as me, except in a takeaway cup. He might come out at any minute.

The number for the only Richard Miles in London is still in my notebook, but every time I reach for it something gets in the way. On the train – packed with commuters, none of them him – I tried to call it, but then we went through a tunnel. By the time we'd emerged the tannoy was blurrily announcing King's Cross and everyone started shifting in their seats, ready to get off.

Anyway, there'd be no point, he'd be at work.

Steam hisses sharply from the spout on the coffee machine. A glamorous waitress dressed in pink stands idly behind the counter, drawing on a napkin. The acrid smell of roasted coffee beans fills my nostrils.

Across the road, so near and yet so far, the door to Copley and Weir remains firmly shut.

I'm so tired.

I close my eyes.

'What are you doing tomorrow?'

With a jolt I come to, knocking my spoon off the saucer.

You've got to focus, Jane. Get your priorities straight. If you want a bed for the night you'd better get yourself a hotel. If you want to find out where Richard is, you'd better get off your arse and go across the road. If you want to speak to him, you'd better phone that number. With unthinking, dreamlike blankness I get to my feet. The waitress in pink doesn't look up, but I leave a tip anyway. Hauling my bag over my shoulder I leave the coffee shop. I stumble across the street, nearly getting run over by a passing cab, and stretch a zombified finger in the direction of the buzzer.

'Copley and Weir?' a tart female voice asks abruptly, and I realize I have no idea what to say.

'Sorry to trouble you, but can I come up? I have an enquiry,' I mutter.

'Do you have an appointment?'

'I'm trying to find someone,' I flounder. 'Can you just let me in for a minute?'

There's a crackle and a muffled silence. I think I hear an agitated sigh through the metal slats of the intercom, then mumbling, as if she's put her palm over a receiver.

'What is this regarding? Is it a publishing query?' another, louder female voice asks.

'No, it's just, I'm trying to find someone. I found one of your business cards in a diary belonging to this person and er . . . I wondered if you could tell me if he works here.'

A pause. Another motorcycle courier by the kerb noisily fires up his engine.

'What's his name?' the voice asks reluctantly, with a vague hint of curiosity.

'Richard Miles,' I practically yell over the racket.

Another pause, this time longer. Mumbling in the background, something like, 'it's not a good time?' 'Not again?' I can't hear.

'I'm afraid we can't help you.' The voice declares, snapping back into professional mode. 'And tell Mr Miles that these kinds of tactics do not work. The answer is still no.'

The intercom cuts off with a sharp burst of feedback and the motorbike screeches away, right on cue.

I press the buzzer again, twice.

Nothing happens.

I stand there, feeling stupid, looking at the peeling sticker for Atomic! TV – a tiny clipart drawing of a radio aerial, emanating zigzag bolts of electricity in all directions.

Eventually, when it becomes clear that nobody will

ever answer the door again, I set off, heading towards Charing Cross Road.

That was really odd.

What did she mean? Was Richard pestering them? They must have thought he'd sent me there, but for what? I walk past the falafel place. Garlic, cooking oil and diesel combine to form a bitter, thwarted smell.

At the end of the street I look over my shoulder. A tall man with dark hair and a dark suit is cutting swiftly across the road. His walk is brisk, practically a run. I don't see his face, but there's something about his haphazard movement – his jacket flapping black and dramatic like the wings of a magpie that makes me think it could be Richard. The possibility propels me towards him. He takes a left turn into an unnamed street, body-swerving a group of tourists, and I follow, metres behind him. He's running now with all the tenacity of an escaped convict; he must be either horrendously late or have just robbed a bank. He's heading for the Tottenham Court Road underground stop. It's him; it has to be, I think, tube tickets dancing merrily in my mind. Tottenham Court Road, Copley and Weir . . . Jane, your plan may be crap but you might just have found your man . . . he slips across a busy thoroughfare, dodging cars with ease, but I'm left stranded on a traffic island, separated from him by a huge articulated lorry. Written on the side in big green letters is 'Holms of Edinburgh'. Get out of the fucking way. I try to skip behind it, but then the traffic starts moving again and I'm cut off. Then I spot him, a split second of lean dark frame disappearing into the bowels of the tube. I find an opening in the road and run and run, pushing past irate commuters who wish me dead and shout at my back, but I don't care. I haven't had any breakfast, I can't breathe and prickly stars are forming in my field of vision, but I don't care, I'm pushing on down the endless stairs into the station. He's going through the turnstile as I fumble for my ticket. Where did I put my ticket? I can't find it I can't find it. He's turning right onto the Northern Line and I'm stuck. Oh thank God, it's here, I'm here, you're here. Richard, don't go. I feed the ticket into the slot but it's bent and 'SEEK ASSISTANCE' flashes in red light. An image of Kelly getting tangled up with her trolley-dolly bag careers into my mind. I remember smirking to myself at the time, but this is NOT funny, not funny at all. A surly attendant inspects my ticket and opens the side gate with a slow, deliberate movement that verges on the sadistic, but then I'm free, a greyhound out of a trap, and I bolt down the escalator, towards the platform, hearing the rumbling, vast sound of a train approaching. I dash onto the southbound platform, but it's not arriving, it's leaving.

It's leaving!

I watch it go.

I'm temporarily winded by exertion and the scorched air current coming up the tunnel. 'Morden 0 mins' says the orange LED of the oncoming trains sign, and then it flickers off, like a small death. It occurs to me, in a flash of wild hope, that maybe he's getting the northbound train, and I rush onto the opposite platform, but it's empty, apart from four African women in batik robes, a boy with a rucksack, and an old man picking his teeth on a bench.

He's gone.

Vanished into the guts of London, a teeny black dot on the multicoloured arteries of the tube map, getting further and further away from me.

Shit.

I stand there, panting, sweating, my chest pounding. It's such a bitter blow that I don't know how to react. I feel like I should do something epic, like down a bottle of whisky, throw myself under a train or join a convent. That was HIM! I KNOW it! But I just stand there, swaying gently and staring blankly at the brightly coloured robes of the African ladies. One has long-necked birds, one has tessellated patterns like the test card, the third has turtles and the other a glorious stampede of elephants.

I see the shop assistant in Kaleidoscope: 'He bought Nelly. Made a right scene . . .'

A train whooshes towards the platform in a gale of warm, litter-strewn wind. For want of anything better to do, I get on it.

'Check out is at midday, breakfast is from seven thirty to nine thirty, doors are locked at eleven thirty p.m. Ring the night bell and the porter will let you in,' says the receptionist at the Cloisters Hotel in a monotonous voice. He seems as if he should be the bellboy, with his waxed hedgehog hair and festive sprinkling of zits. Glued to the grimy computer monitor, he doesn't bother to look up. A faded silk flower arrangement sits on the counter, like something in a Christian reading room or a church hall – sun-bleached yellow roses tumble down in a depressing clump. The place is entirely, desperately brown, the colour of a smoker's lung, but at least it's cheap. Gareth Gates hands me a Yale key attached to an oversized plastic fob (also brown), and I'm dispatched to Room 13.

Lucky me.

The radiator, boiling hot and possibly connected to the fires of hell, fizzles in the corner. It must be about 30 degrees in here. I sit on the bed, a saggy monster with a brown counterpane, and look into the pock-marked mirror.

Hello, Jane.

You really are a lunatic.

What are you doing?

Then I think of the dashing man running through London like a knife through butter, and a fiendish thrill goes through me. I'm sure that was him. If this is a whim then I must remember to have more, and sod the consequences. Here, the whole idea of looking for Richard starts to make more sense. This is his city, I can feel it, he's a real person and I'm going to find him, because I have to give him back what's rightfully his. The adventure is beginning properly now, it's not just a pipe dream. I'm on the right track. And let's face it, I'm entitled to some excitement and intrigue. So far all I've had are home truths.

I might not have caught him this time, but I think I'm getting warmer.

Warmer and warmer.

God, I'm roasting.

I open the window and change out of my stupid work outfit into a clean vest and jeans. A quick investigation of the bathroom reveals no cockroaches, only an uninspiring beige suite. I don't really know for sure, but this strikes me as the kind of hotel used by dubious women who advertise in phone boxes. Although it's fairly clean, everything in it seems grubby. At the end of the bed is an old-fashioned Bush TV with a dial, and on the wall there's a print of a girl in a flowery dress sitting on a rocking chair. A billboard outside the window, advertising a new kind of car with ABS brakes, is the only indication that it isn't 1973.

I empty my bag onto the bed. My possessions look hearteningly modern and cheerful compared to the dreary room. I pick up the notebook and switch on my mobile, psyching myself up to phone Richard. He might have gone home – maybe he was running because he left the grill on or something. Anyway, if not I can leave a message for him to call me back. The thought makes my stomach lurch with exquisite agony.

'Welcome to Orange,' says the phone's blue screen, offering the most cheerful sentiment I've heard all day.

Wait a minute. I've got a new message from . . .

KELLY.

Eh?

'Hello Jane – hope you're having good hols, very sorry about Sat nite. Things at work OK see you next wk – K'

I stare at it in wonder.

Kelly is apologizing. Very sorry. Suddenly, unexpectedly, I'm crushed by loneliness. Then I realize, with a vague horror, that I've missed her. I actually wish she were here with her silly trolley and her vomit-coloured lipstick. I need to see an unfriendly face. Her prissy Womble ways, fuelled by youth, insecurity and fear, might settle my nerves. And you never know, her practical mind might devise a way to get me together with Richard. She could be the co-ordinator for my addled love life, kicking it into shape for me, pushing me firmly towards my goal. 'You make a good double act,' Sophie said, and I cringed at the time, but maybe I need a straight woman after all. For all her naïvety, Kelly would know what to do in a crisis. I want her to pick me up and haul me off like that box of brochures and put me somewhere safe. Either that or she could give me a guided tour of my emotions with her laser pointer.

Right, Jane, stop stalling and do it.

After a long pause and a lot of deep breaths, I decide to call him. No point in putting it off any more. The girl in the flowery dress watches my dramatic, life-changing moment vacantly. My hands are shaking, but I manage to dial Richard Miles' number. Out of all the phone calls I've ever made, this is the most important. I feel like I'm about to speak to the president. My tongue has gone dry.

There's the ringing tone.

One.

Two.

Three.

(Is he in?)

Four.

Then, in a deep, masculine, steady voice – like whipped cream and velvet, raindrops on roses and whiskers on kittens – Richard says hello.

'Hello,' I reply, stunned.

'Can I help you?'

My heart swoops into my mouth. Can he help me! Argh! I'm talking to Richard. My throat feels suddenly constricted and my tongue has swelled up to twice its original size.

'Er . . . yes, I . . . are you Richard Miles?'

Of COURSE he is! Duh! Of all the stupid questions – keep going . . .

'It's just that I found your diary on the train the other week and I wanted to return it to you. If that's OK.' My voice is coming out unnaturally high-pitched and polite, a call-centre employee on helium.

There's a silence at the other end. I can't judge it, I can't think clearly. My mind can only focus on the fact that I'm speaking to him. I'm speaking to Richard.

Eeeeeek!

'Er . . . I'm not Richard Miles,' the voice says coldly.

'You see,' I say, about to launch into a well-rehearsed explanation of events.

Then his words sink in.

'You're not?'

'No. He used to live here, but I don't have a forwarding address.' I hear a faint Brummie twang in the deep masculine voice, and the click of a mouse in the background. Suddenly he sounds like the most mundane person in the phonebook. I can almost smell his stale socks.

'What did you say about his diary? You found it?'

'Yeah,' I say glumly, blinking rapidly at the brown bed.

'Sorry. No idea where he is.'

'Oh.'

'Bye,' he says.

'No. No, WAIT!' I shout alarmingly. 'Are you sure, because . . . because.'

If this is the last resort, if this is my last chance, I think I'm going to cry, or explode.

'Are there any clues? Did he leave any clues? It's really important. When, when did he move out?'

'Oh, a while ago. About six months.'

'Would the landlord know his address?' I gasp.

'No, he skipped out without paying his rent and nobody's seen him since. Look, who is this?'

'Left without paying? That doesn't sound like the kind of thing he would do.'

'Do you know him?' he asks.

'Well . . . no . . . Did you meet him? What does he look like?'

'I don't—'

'Please!' I squeal, grasping my notebook and ripping the page.

273

'Honestly, I never met him. He wasn't here when I moved in. I only know his name because of all the mail I get for him.'

Tears blur my vision. The end of the room seems very far away. Richard. My Richard. What's happening? Is he in trouble? Could he be dead after all?

'It's vital that I track him down. Would he be in the phone book under any other name? I mean, does he have a middle initial?' I demand with mounting urgency.

'Look, I really don't know.' He sighs, getting completely sick of the hysterical woman on the phone.

'Please?'

'Right.' He sighs, annoyed. 'There's a letter here. Hang on. I'll just go and have a look.'

With that he puts the receiver on the table with an irate clunk. I check my list. R.A., R.C., R.G. Maybe directory enquiries didn't update his previous entry or something, maybe he's also listed under his new number.

'C. His middle initial is C. Is that OK for you?'

'R.C. Yes,' I whimper.

'If you find him, will you tell him there's a ton of stuff for him sitting here. If he doesn't want it I'm going to throw it out. I've had nothing but shit through the door for him for months,' he snaps.

'I will,' I say in a whisper. 'Thank you. Bye.'

I hang up.

OK. Keep it together, Jane.

So his middle initial is C. Middle C, music to my ears. Before I can analyse the conversation or torture myself about what it could stand for (Charles? Colin? Cedric?) I find R.C. on my list and dial it.

Everything seems turned on its head, racing on

without me. I can't keep up with the pace. Another ringing tone.

One.

Two.

Three.

'Hello you've reached Richard Miles,' says a low, professional-sounding recorded voice. 'I'm not here to take your call at the moment, but you can get me at the office on 5555474 or leave a message after the tone. Thanks.' Beeeeep!

I scramble to write the number down and hang up before I inadvertently leave a sinister heavy-breathing message. I think I might be about to have a heart attack. Fireworks snap crackle and pop above my head.

He was called Richard, too. R.C. is Richard. This can only be a good thing.

I fumble for a cigarette and inhale, the cool smoke forming a temporary vacancy in my addled brain. Is it him? It could be. Why wouldn't it be? I walk around the bed three times, smoke the cigarette down to the filter, throw it out of the window, go to the toilet, count the tiles in the bathroom, look out of the window again at the advert for the car with ABS brakes ('Adventure awaits,' it promises, and my heart skips a beat). I turn on the TV and flick through the channels – Des O'Connor, *Neighbours*, a black and white film featuring Lana Turner in a sweater with two ice cream cones stuffed up it, *Watercolour Challenge*, the news – then turn it off again. One last time I walk around the bed.

OK. Here I go again.

I call the office number.

'Richard Miles,' says the voice, casual but busy. He's probably in the middle of something death-defyingly important. Stock market, hiring and firing, selling pork bellies, closing a deal. I immediately wish I'd left it until later.

'Oh er . . . hello, I er . . . you don't know me, but er . . .' I begin, eloquently.

'What? Hello?'

'Hello,' I say, desperate and shaky. 'My name's Jane Darling.'

Something sticks in my throat and for a moment I'm rendered speechless.

'Well hello, Jane Darling,' Richard Miles says suavely.

My eyeballs feel like they're about to pop out of their sockets and ping across the room.

'Could you tell me, did you . . . did you leave a diary on the train recently?'

There's a pause.

'A diary?' He considers. 'Well let's see,' he says, in a playful tone. 'Yes I did as a matter of fact.'

'Oh, good God, I mean . . . good,' I gasp. 'You see, I found it, and . . .'

I have no idea what I'm going to say next. And what?

'You found it,' he repeats evenly. 'And did you read it?'

It's my turn to pause. The radiator shudders sympathetically.

'Sort of,' I admit. 'You're a hard man to pin down,' I say without thinking.

Oh God, did that sound creepy? Oh God!

'Well you're very naughty, Jane Darling,' he scolds, playing games with me. 'So you've got my diary and you know all my secrets. That makes things rather tricky. Are you going to give it back to me?'

'Yes,' I squeak. In the back of my mind a voice is screaming, 'He's flirting. He's flirting with you.'

276

'Tell you what, why don't we . . .' There's the sound of a photocopier or fax whirring in the background and he breaks off. 'Why don't we meet up?'

A choir of angels pipes up and sings hallelujah.

'You're not from London, are you?' he says.

'No, I'm from Leeds.' ('And I LOVE YOU!')

'But you're in London now?'

'Yes. I'm in' – all practical information has disappeared out of my head and I struggle to retrieve it – 'Islington.'

'Right. You know the King's Arms off Essex Road? On Mariscal Walk?'

'Yes,' I lie, not knowing the King's Arms from the Queen's Arse.

'Meet me there at eight o'clock,' he pronounces coolly. 'This is all very intriguing. Oh, how will I know you?'

'I'm tall and I have long red hair. I mean, you'll just . . . you'll just know,' I say meaningfully, making a reference to his diary entry.

'Mmm. Interesting,' he replies, sounding very interested indeed. A cramp of desire grabs me in the loins and I almost fall off the bed. 'I'm looking forward to it already. See you then, Miss D.'

The line cuts off and I'm left hanging, one leg dangling off the bed in a paroxysm of lust and amazement.

I've got a DATE. I've got a date with RICHARD.

She shoots she scores.

He called me Miss D! I stuff my fist in my mouth and roll helplessly around on my back like a beached seal, squealing.

The girl on the rocking chair gives me a flowery thumbs up.

277

Oh, I was right about this all along. Sometimes you just KNOW.

Oh!

I sit up and look at the photograph of Richard. There's a renewed peace in his face, and he looks more beautiful than ever. Some of the tension in his jaw has evaporated and he seems almost serene. He's real. He's real. The thought that, in a matter of hours, I'm going to be sitting across from this man makes me feel weak. And he flirted with me. Those words came straight from these lips. Richard's lips! I haven't felt like this since Gayle Gibbon's gorgeous brother illegally took me on the back of his motorbike when I was fifteen. It was so romantic and dangerous and deeply, thrillingly sexual, with him in his leathers and the big throbbing engine and stuff. I thought I was going to expire then, but now . . . oh GOD!

I scan the diary, the rising and falling handwriting that mimics the cadences of his voice. Now I know what it sounds like, I can picture him reading it, as if he was in the room with me. A delicious shiver runs down my spine.

I flick to the week ending the 24th of March, my favourite page, the one with the 'people are sheep' quote and the little drawings of mesmerized ewes blindly following an invisible force, and start to read the familiar words.

Then I stop mid sentence and notice something I've never noticed before.

On the right-hand side of the page, hurriedly written in blue biro, is a phone number. Next to it are three modest little letters: D–A–N.

My flapping, flustered heart sinks into a steady beat. Dan.

DAN.

How the hell did that get there?

Then I remember – he must have done it when I was in the alleyway, when I was decorating the wall with Jesus Christ Superpuke.

An image of his sealskin hair and worried brow immediately clouds my enthusiasm. He's like a concerned parent, pointing out the consequences of my actions, when all I want is to have some fun.

'Go away. Not now. Don't spoil this for me,' I say out loud, tentatively closing the diary in case he should burst out of it, holding a copy of the Bible and a rod of iron. I sit there eyeing it warily.

'*You don't know him. He could be anyone.*'

Shush. Shut up, not now.

OK, pull yourself together. Like Babs said, this is your big day. You can make mistakes and come home, and you're not like your father. Just enjoy it. Enjoy the moment. I look in the mirror and stick my tongue out at the girl staring back. Oh dear. The much-advertised red hair has faded, my skin is covered with a fine layer of city grime and my clothes are all shit. I'm going to have to take some emergency measures.

I haul myself to my feet and make a grab for my bag and jacket. On the chest of drawers where the brown plastic key fob is sitting, the number 13 glints gold in the afternoon sunlight. Trying to physically repel a brand-new, unwelcome feeling of unease (thanks a LOT, Dan), I throw the key fob in the air and catch it, then lunge out of the door into the long, dingy hallway, past the fire stairs, past the maid's trolley and into the streets of sweaty swinging London.

The woman at the make-up counter, plastered in foundation the colour of Kia-Ora, peers incomprehensibly at my skin. Her desiccated blonde doll's hair tickles my cheek. She sighs and I smell what she had for lunch – something featuring onions, coffee and fags.

'You're a type two,' she decides finally.

'OK,' I say, feeling like I've been successfully diagnosed.

I would normally avoid a place like this at all costs. The glittering entrance hall of the department store is choked up with a million fragrances and I've got a dull headache and seared nostrils, but tonight I want to look like a fair maiden. I want to float into that pub in a heavenly, feminine haze and steal his heart. Or at the very least not look like a dog.

I detect the familiar odour of Kelly's Eau de Skunk coming from a far corner. A woman who looks like she has lost the will to live is liberally spraying it on unsuspecting punters. Apparently it's called Play Girl. I resist the urge to snigger.

'Do you moisturize?' Kia-Ora demands, brushing pale concealer onto my dark circles.

'Sometimes.'

This is not the right answer. She frowns and gives a sharp intake of breath.

'You SHOULD. Morning and night. Use the all-in-one moisturizer along with the anti-shine anti-UV balm to keep the shine under control.'

'OK,' I say dumbly, not really listening.

'After this we'll start with the eyes,' she says, briefly flipping up a piece of plastic on the counter and showing me a palette of colours. 'I think you'd suit a dramatic look.'

'Whatever you say.'

'So what I'll do is I'll put Slate Rain on your upper lid and Smokey Robinson on your lower and finish it off with kohl and some lash lengthener.'

No idea. She may as well be speaking in Urdu.

'Yeah. OK.'

She goes back to putting my face into some sort of pleasing arrangement. I look up at the lights in the mirrored store and drift into a daydream. The King's Arms. Richard is there, leaning against the bar in his dark suit. He turns round slowly and sees me and the look on his face is poetry – he might have been expecting someone ordinary, he might have thought it was a joke, but now he realizes that this is serious, this is the moment he's been waiting for. The girl with red hair has come to him at last. I'm a vision, of course, sprinkling fairy dust and magic moonbeams on the dog-eared carpet as I stride in slow motion towards him. Our eyes meet in one glorious, unbreakable thread.

'Hello, Richard.'

'Hello, Miss D,' he says, his jaw still on the floor.

Kia-Ora is looking at me quizzically and I get the impression she might have said something.

'Sorry, what?'

'I SAID,' she says, 'is this for a special occasion?' She mixes two identical grey eyeshadows together on the back of her hand, forming a worrying bruise.

'Oh . . . yes,' I reply, flustered. Then, before I can stop it, 'I've got a date.'

'Really?' she grins. Her teeth are pointy and catlike. 'A first date, yeah?'

Kia-Ora's gummy curiosity makes me want to spill the beans. Now I've heard his voice and confirmed his existence, what's the point of keeping him a secret? He's a legitimate possibility, nothing to be ashamed of. It's not like he's my imaginary friend. We're two living breathing people going on a date, having a drink, maybe dinner and a movie.

'A blind date, actually. A very blind date.'

She listens in amazement as I spill my story. The diary, the search, the sighting, the phone calls, the final contact. I tell her what he looks like and she swoons along with me, we dissect the good fortune of finding him so quickly, the million-to-one chance of something like that happening, and find ourselves speechless, gazing into space. By the end of it, my head is sparkling with the sheer craziness of it all. It feels so good to have a confidant. Kia (I feel like we know each other now) is gratifyingly impressed.

'That's so EXCITING,' she gasps. 'I can't believe it. You're not telling porkies, are yer?'

'No.' I laugh, my newly made-up skin reverberating with feverish heat.

'Wow.'

'What you gunna wear?' she asks.

'I've bought a dress.'

'Ooh!' she squeals, raking her hands through the

rattling contents of a nearby plastic drawer. I want to squeal too.

There's a pause as Kia gets a kohl pencil and removes the cellophane hygiene seal with a sharp, hot-pink fingernail.

'That's SO exciting. Look down,' she says, and I dutifully lower my eyes. 'So where are you meeting him then? Is he taking you somewhere posh?'

'The King's Arms in Islington.'

She nearly pokes my eye out with the pencil.

'Eh?' She draws back, retracting her neck and giving herself an unattractive double chin. Confusion reigns supreme on her tangerine face.

'What? Is there something wrong?'

'Well, it's . . .'

She stops dead and seems to change her mind. Her tone is immediately bright and breezy and she fixes on a professional smile.

'It's a bit, I don't know . . . it's just not posh. That's all. Still, I don't suppose that'll matter when you two get together. Sounds like you're made for each other. Look down for me a minute,' she gabbles too quickly all one sentence.

I look down.

What's up with her?

'Now the next thing we'll do is lips. I think a pale, Sixties-type shade – maybe Sweetheart Kiss or Lady Marmalade,' she chatters, wielding the liner.

'Er, OK.'

'You're gonna knock him dead. These colours really suit you – and we've got a special offer on at the moment where you can get three shades for the price of two.'

'Oh. Right.'

There's a long, tense pause. The acoustics in the store sound dense and compressed. The hubbub of the café, the whirr of the lifts, the muted conversation, cosmetic adverts playing relentlessly on video screens, all mashed tightly, uncomfortably together. I feel light-headed.

'Do you think it's wise to go on your own, though?' Kia asks eventually. 'I mean, you don't really know who he is.'

Oh God. Not you as well.

'It'll be fine,' I say, my words sounding harsher than I'd intended. Every time I tell somebody about this I end up regretting it. Why did I open my big mouth?

'If I were you I'd take your mobile,' she murmurs, so quietly I hardly notice she's said it. 'Look up.'

Mascara is dutifully applied and my lips are given a going over with gloss.

'There. All done,' Kia says, showing me her handi-work. I look done, but I feel undone.

'What's wrong with the King's Arms?' I ask.

Behind her smile I see her wincing.

'Nothing,' she assures me. 'Just ain't the Ritz, that's all.' Then she starts banging on again about moisturizer.

'Now,' I think I hear her say, 'would you like to buy the anti-shine anti-UV anti-shite retinolizing flange cream?'

'I'm trying so hard, but I'm lost. I'm unravelling.' I trace the wobbly line of the G down into the scribble of ink with my fingernail.

He didn't sound like he was unravelling on the phone. He sounded more than together. Maybe that's his cover, though – suave, debonair, hiding his loneliness behind a mask.

My own mask is staying on, despite the best efforts of the rumbling radiator. On the TV, Richard and Judy wind up their show with the promise that tomorrow there will be a feature on 'How To Snag Mr Right'. I smile thinly. I wonder whether Judy feels the same about her Richard as I do about mine. My Richard, however, is a God. The photograph sits on the bed, looking like a publicity shot for a movie star.

Argh!

I'm going to meet him.

A spasm ripples through my shoulders. I want Lizzie to be here – she'd understand. When we'd write letters to our idols there was the same fizzy thrill as this. Pink envelopes stuffed with Holly Hobbie paper, fragranced with a squirt of Loulou perfume (Lizzie had seen this kind of thing done before – in *Grease*), then the final S.W.A.L.K lipstick mark ceremonially applied to the back before it hit the postbox. OK, so we were eleven and we didn't even have pubes, but we were convinced that Mark Owen/Luke Perry/New Kids on the Block (not my choice, I hasten to add) were just waiting to drop everything and fall in love with us. And although our wild fantasies only extended to chaste moonlit kisses, we were racked with a deep, soulful ardour we couldn't begin to articulate. It made us dizzy, it hyped us up like amphetamines, it made us swoon and laugh and lustfully lick the covers of magazines until we made them soggy. I still remember the creeping disappointment when we realized our boyfriends weren't going to reply, or the bitter sting of an impersonal fan-club letter stamped with a photocopy of their signature. They didn't know, or care, that we loved them.

This time, though, it's a sure thing.

I've got a reply with bells on. I've got a DATE.

Eek!

I'm not eleven any more, though. On to practical matters. It's nearly six o'clock. Essex Road train station is one stop from here and the A–Z reveals Mariscal Walk to be three streets behind that. I could go there on foot, but I don't want to misjudge the distance and turn up late with damp armpits and red cheeks. The horror.

For the millionth time I check myself in the mirror. I run a brush through my damp hair, rinsed through with Cherry Blossom dye using acrobatic skills – bent over backwards in the shower for fear of ruining my perfectly made-up complexion and Sweetheart Kissiness of lips – and pray that it won't kink. My new dress, a seemingly white, virginal number with a slutty plunging neck from Topshop, lies on the chair like a limp ghost.

With nearly two hours to kill, I decide to text Kelly to show there are no hard feelings, even though she tried to knock me out. Now she's 500 miles away, Kelly has become a strangely benign influence. Her infuriating pinched mouth and pedantic attention to boring details seem almost endearing. I'm suddenly struck with an odd yearning to be in the staff room, amongst the fag smoke and coffee grounds, listening to Val's tedious stories about discharge.

'Hello Kelly. Thanks for text – sorry too. Having good time in London. Got a date! Speak soon, J x'

I press send and go back to worrying about my appearance. I've never gone to so much effort for anyone. I was always the scruffy one at weddings and funerals, refusing to wear a nice skirt, having a tantrum if Babs tried to separate me from my favourite trainers, a nasty pair of dirty pink and white Nikes that once mysteriously ended up in the compost heap, under a layer of carrot peelings and egg shells. This isn't like me at all. I put on the white dress, which, to my dismay, has taken on a different personality between leaving the shop and coming back to the hotel. I looked like the Queen of the Elves in the changing room, but now I look like I'm about to sing a duet with Kenny Rogers and open a theme park devoted to my tits. I try to rein in my boobs and cram them under any spare material, fiddling with fastenings and pulling at straps until it feels like a straitjacket. After about half an hour I finally manage to avoid looking like a whore and sit down, exhausted, red cheeked, with damp armpits and sweaty palms. Great.

It's only 6.02.

'What's the worst that could happen?' says the teenage boy on the Dr Pepper advert just before a dreadful calamity ensues, involving his date, her father and a dog.

Richard gazes into the middle distance, impatient, looking for something.

Oh, Richard.

You don't have to wait much longer.

I gaze up at the light fitting, a frosted glass shade that could have been specially chosen for its depressing qualities. On the nightstand there's a brown leatherette folder containing the fabulous facilities the hotel has to offer. I open it and find a single leaf of yellowish paper inside. Welcome, Bienvenue, Wilkommen. Dial 9 for an outside line. Parking at rear. Enjoy your stay in London. Thankyou, Merci, Danke. A decade of grimy fingerprints fringe the edges of the page. He's not coming back to mine, that's for sure.

OK, Jane, concentrate.

Here's what's going to happen. You're going to sail into a black cab at approximately two minutes to eight, and probably get to the pub at five or ten minutes past eight (it wouldn't do to look too eager). You will take deep breaths and try not to faint when you see him. When he asks you if you'd like a drink, you will say, 'White wine, please,' in your most gracious, ladylike voice. You will talk honestly, but not too intensely, about your feelings when you read his diary, and perhaps you'll both laugh about the wrong turns and dead ends along the way. 'Sarah Olsen,' he might scoff. 'She's fifty-five with a hare lip and a wooden leg.' After that, who knows what?

I get to my feet and smooth down the back of my dress. I don't want to risk a cigarette; he might not like women who smell like ashtrays. The swell of rush-hour traffic roars through the window. Room 13 has a beautiful view of some metal bins, industrial tins of cooking oil and a back alley, overgrown with dock leaves, bind weed and nettles. Behind the brick-walled yard and sloped roof of the hotel kitchens is a row of garages with 'No Parking' written across the shutters in spray paint. Beyond that is the main road. A multi-coloured stream of cars whizzes by constantly. The 'Adventure Awaits' billboard is one of those revolving, slatted ones. I'm so tetchy and stuck for something to amuse myself with that I work out it turns every 55 seconds – Bargain flights, London to Pisa £89, Rome £79, Milan £69. Getta Pizza The Action! – After that, there's a sexist beer ad featuring the bronzed midriff of a woman with a bottle-top wedged in her belly button. 'Great Body', screams the tagline. Then, finally, before Adventure Awaits comes back round again, there's just a statement – white capitals on a black background. I have no idea what the poster is supposed to be advertising but it says, '*Go Home*' with a chilling finality.

I turn away from the window, suddenly cold.

On the TV, the cast of *Hollyoaks* are screaming at each other. I catch sight of myself in the mirror. I look scared to death, hollow-eyed and stricken.

On the bed my phone beeps sharply and I jump out of my skin.

Oh God no, please don't let it be Richard cancelling tonight. He hasn't got my number, but please don't let it be him anyway.

It's Kelly, of course, returning my text.

'A date?' It enquires. 'Who with? Dan?'

I stare at the green screen and turn the phone off, resuming the obsessive brushing of my mane. My scalp hurts as I drag the sharp bristles through my hair again and again, but I don't stop until the unsteady feeling subsides.

'Mariscal Walk?' The taxi driver asks.

'Yes, it's . . .' I picture the tiny road in the A–Z, with its abbreviated name squashed into the narrow capillaries of the map, too short and inconsequential to warrant much of a mention.

'Yeah, I know where it is. It's only round the bleedin' corner.'

'Yeah, I know,' I say in the same tone. 'It's just I'm in a hurry. Can you take me to the King's Arms, please?'

'The King's Arms,' he repeats slowly.

I meet his eye in the rear-view mirror. His gaze falls to my chest, which I cover up with the lapels of my leather jacket. Fuck. Off.

'Right,' he says eventually, and wheels insolently

into the evening traffic. If I could see the rest of his face I bet he'd be smirking. I can tell by way the oily hairs are sitting on his neck and the angle of the folds of flesh at the back of his big fat head.

I fix my attentions on the street. It's a sunny evening. Long shadows stripe the pavement and a gang of young kids, all colours and sizes, gather outside the off-licence on the corner. A suntanned couple wearing matching three-quarter-length combats stroll by, carrying Sainsbury's bags. Nobody is in a hurry, not even me, really. When I left, the clock said four minutes to eight.

The Magic Carpet kebab shop, Organotron Whole-foods, Janelle Afro hairdressers, a fancy bar called Merge and a record store crappily named Slip Da Disc go past through the window. Does Richard live here?

Only one way to find out.

Suddenly, before I've even had a chance to settle into my seat, we're at the tube and turning the corner.

Shit!

My heart starts palpitating as we draw up to Mariscal Walk. In a panic I clutch my new handbag and some-thing sharp sticks into my hand – oh GOD, the price tag! £3.99 in the sale. If Richard had seen that it would have been awful. What else have I got attached to me? Lipstick on my teeth, a sign saying 'Kick me' on my back? I rip off the tag and give myself a vicious paper cut just as we arrive at the King's Arms.

From the outside the pub looks fine. A sign advertising Live Football Saturday 1 p.m. – Arsenal vs Man U spoils the romance a bit, but otherwise, it's a pub, the same as any other.

But it's not, it's got Richard in it. The thought leaves me short of breath. Part of me wants to run away screaming. Mind you, he might not have arrived yet. It's only eight o'clock and here I am, keen as mustard with my knockers hanging out. I delicately smooth the white material of my dress over my knees, trying to buy some time.

A horrible thought occurs to me, Does this look like a wedding dress?

'Here we are then, the King's Arms,' says the driver touchily when I don't move. 'Three pound, please.'

I give him the money and get out as slowly as I can. As he leaves he gives me a look I can't quite read, but I know it isn't complimentary.

Walking towards the pub, I'm hit by the smell of wet dog. I glance at the sign over the entrance. JOHNNY FARRELL – licensed to sell beers, spirits, blah, blah. Behind the frosted glass doors, I hear a cheer and a thumping sound, then the clack-clack-rumble of pool balls being released from the undercarriage of the table.

Kia-Ora was right, it ain't the Ritz. So what is it? I'm starting to get jittery. Richard claimed to like beautiful things, but perhaps it's got a different kind of beauty – local colour or something. That would be typical of Richard, arranging to meet somewhere unconventional, to test whether I was up for the challenging job of being his . . . his friend. I inhale deeply and prepare to go in. Ziggy's, with the strains of 'I Will Survive' pounding up the stairs, looms up in my mind. At least behind those doors there were familiar faces. I wish Camp David or Fiona were here to give me moral support.

'*What if you find him and he's a total nutter?*'

I straighten my dress again and push the handle.

As I walk in, everyone turns to stare at me. The beady, sunken eyes of the pool sharks, the idle staff behind the bar, the crow-like, coiffured old woman sitting by the toilets, the cluster of red-cheeked pinstripe suits quaffing pints of lager, the hard-faced women draped over the cigarette machine, dressed as if touting for business. Richard is nowhere to be seen. The room is suspiciously quiet.

I freeze, frantically trying to decide whether to leave.

'Awright, luv,' says one of the pool sharks, an anvil-headed git with a plaster cast on his wrist. 'Are you the entertainment?'

'Oi, Maysey, shut it,' says a man behind the bar, maybe Johnny Farrell, licensed to sell beers and spirits. He's as bald as a peeled lychee, but tinged with angry pink, either sunburn or high-blood pressure. He smiles a toothless grin and beckons me over.

'Come in, darlin'. Don't worry about 'im – we don't bite.'

From here I can see Johnny is dripping with bright gold chains and tattoos. He might not bite, but I bet he owns some kind of angry dog that does. He busies himself with stocking a fridge full of bottles, as the barmaid, a girl with a droopy but curiously high-handed expression, whispers something to him and looks warily at me. I cross the pub, but I'm not the beautiful vision I wanted to be. The dress has turned me into Dolly Parton again, and as I walk my feet stick to the carpet. The City boys all stare and shuffle like a herd of cows. I want to go home, I think pathetically. I want to lock myself in my poky flat in Edinburgh and stay there, listening to the comforting sound of Queenie bottoming her cupboards or hoovering her pelmet. Put some make-up on, she said. You might meet the man of your dreams.

'What'll it be?' says Johnny, with businesslike cheer.

Close up, he looks like he's broken a few bones in his time, mostly other people's. His nose is flattened, a splodge of Play-doh squashed by a child's thumb. This doesn't seem like the kind of place for white wine, so I get a gin and tonic. When Johnny sets the weedy, flat drink in front of me, his knuckles say 'HATE'.

'Two pounds eighty five, luv.'

I fumble with my money. Droopy never takes her eyes off me. Where's Richard?

Avoiding the gaze of the old crow woman, I find a table and perch as delicately as I can on the seat. I keep my face firmly fixed on the contents of my bag. I open my purse, count my money, scan my credit card, press buttons on my mobile, inspect my lipstick, and read the diary intently. The pool sharks have returned to their game, but when I look up, the one who isn't Maysey is watching me closely, holding his cue like a soldier with a bayonet.

I wait for five minutes, which seems close to two hours. Maysey and his friend talk about me and erupt in a gale of bronchial laughter. Tearful, blubbery anger rents at my ribcage. How could Richard put me through this ordeal? Why couldn't we meet at a bright, unthreatening All Bar One, or a Wetherspoons pub full of comfy sofas and newspapers on sticks? Is this some kind of sick set-up? At that moment, all my excitement about meeting him evaporates. When I see him I might just smack him in the mouth.

Another five minutes. Maysey wins the game and racks up another set.

Break. Maysey's shot. Stripes.

No Richard.

I break my no-smoking rule and get a cigarette.

He's stood me up. He's playing games with me.

Richard, how could you do this to me, you bastard? After all we've been through?

My heart sinks to my shoes as I fiddle with my lighter. The gas fizzes and the blue flame dies and I can't get it to catch. I keep at it – the last thing I want is to get up again and attract more attention by asking for matches. My vision is blurry. I watch the tiny pinwheel on the lighter turn uselessly. Zip zip zip.

'Let me get that for you, Miss D.'

A deep, sexy voice fills my head.

For a second I don't dare find out the source. But I know it's him.

Richard is here.

(I didn't mean what I said about you being a bastard!)

Everything seems warm, liquid and dreamy. Finally, finally we're going to meet. It's just too much. I'm suddenly aware of every breath, eyelash and blood vessel, every muscle, vein, nerve, corpuscle and bone. Energy is flying through the air at breakneck speed. I see the grain on the table as if it's magnified, I hear vibrations from the street as if they're minor earthquakes. I turn my head, feeling the same momentum that powers the pool balls along the tired green baize towards each other, where they meet, in a thunder crack, then fall apart.

I meet his eye.

His big . . .

Bloodshot . . .

Grey . . .

bug eye.

'Sorry I'm late,' says the man standing over me.

He's about forty-five, with a paunch and a shock of sandy-coloured hair that makes him look like an overgrown schoolboy. I give an involuntary intake of breath, which lights my cigarette and draws a rush of smoke straight into the depths of my lungs, starting a coughing fit. As I hack and splutter, the man Who Says He's Richard Miles watches me dreamily, waiting for me to finish retching my guts up. He has rubbery fish lips and skin like Spam.

'Sorry . . . I . . .'

I take a slug of gin and nearly empty the glass. It tastes like paint stripper.

'You're . . .' I wheeze, gasping for breath, and hoping the sharp sensation catching at the back of my throat will go away soon, so I can recover some dignity and tell this weirdo that he is definitely NOT the Richard Miles I'm looking for.

'You're not Richard Miles,' I manage in between coughs.

He puffs up his chest proudly.

'I think you'll find I am. Let me get you another drink. Gin and tonic, is it?'

He doesn't wait for an answer and saunters to the bar, with his hand agitatedly jiggling in one pocket, as if he's playing with a bunch of keys or pocket billiards. He's wearing a nasty unfashionable grey suit, cut too high and tight on his pear-shaped hips. Horror sets in. Behind the bar, Johnny greets him with a familiar 'Awright, my son,' and even Droopy manages a smile. One of the City boys slaps him on the back and they share a confidential word. Richard turns round, then winks at me suggestively.

Oh my God. This is all wrong.

I've got to get out of here.

He's not Richard.

He's not.

'How do you know he's the man in the photograph?'

asks Dan, his words ringing in my head as if he were right next to me, talking into my ear in the nightclub, making the hairs on the back of my neck stand up.

'*How do you know?*'

Oh, Dan, I'm sorry.

Shit.

I'm unable to move. I'm struck with a sense of impending menace. He looks like the kind of person who would tie you up in the boot of his car and do unsavoury things to you in an abandoned cellar for a week. I find myself desperately wishing I had a can of mace or a plank of wood with nails in it. The thought that he might be Richard taunts me as I flick quickly through the diary. But how could someone like THAT write a diary like THIS? It's not possible.

Is it?

He waddles back over, carrying a pint of bitter for himself and another G & T for me, this time in a ladylike, stemmed glass.

'There you go, Miss D,' he says in an Estuary twang. 'If I'd known you looked like this' – he glances at my cleavage, which seems to be some kind of sport in this neck of the woods – 'I'd have suggested we meet in a more . . . discreet location.'

The way he says 'discreet' (with the T accentuated, loaded with vile innuendo), makes my skin crawl. His protruding watery eyes, the gritty colour of oysters, take in my hands, my dress, and end up firmly stationed between my breasts again. How could this be happening?

'You're not the Richard Miles I'm looking for,' I snap haughtily, scratching my opposite shoulder and covering my chest with my arm.

'Whoa,' he says, putting his hands up in a gesture of

surrender. 'I am Richard Miles. You can see my ID if you want.'

He takes out a battered leather wallet and produces a card. It's a monthly pass for the underground. Richard C. Miles. There he is on the photo, staring catatonically, like a frog on a lily pad.

'And you say you left a diary on the train?' I ask, feeling suffocated by this weird scenario, wondering how I can play it and still keep cool.

Just don't give too much away, I tell myself. Keep your trap shut. Don't show him the diary until you're sure it belongs to him. He can't be Richard. It's a coincidence. A really nasty one, but a coincidence all the same.

'Yeah,' he says casually and takes a sip of his pint. A repulsive frosting of creamy foam lingers on his lip. 'I'm always losing stuff. But I found you, so I reckon that more than makes up for it.'

Maysey and his scary friend are bursting with curiosity over at the pool table. 'Good old, Ricardo', they'll be thinking. 'Scored with a bird who phoned him up out of the blue. Jammy sod.'

'And . . . what was in it?' I demand, hoping he won't tell me the truth.

He exhales, half sigh, half whistle.

'Now you're asking,' he says. 'Just thoughts really.'

'What colour is the diary?' I ask, heart pounding crazily.

'Er . . . black . . .'

(Well, that could be a guess.)

'What kind of thoughts?'

'Eh? Oh, I dunno. Bollocks mostly. The first thing that comes into your head.' He looks wary, but covers it up by taking another drink.

I look at his stubby fingers, fat and knuckleless. They don't look like they'd be capable of drawing beautiful pictures and articulating interesting ideas. He's a Neanderthal. He's having me on.

'Let me see your handwriting. Let me see your signature,' I insist.

'Listen, Miss D, this is no way to start a friendship,' he says smoothly. 'I didn't have to come here, did I? I lost my diary and you found it. That's great. Now can't we just have a little drink? It'd be nice if we could get to know each other better. I think we've got a lot in common, you and me. There's no need for histrionics.'

The word 'histrionics' freezes mid-air. Richard used it when he was talking about his girlfriend, the Jane Asher wannabe who so wanted his babies. God knows why anyone would go within ten feet of him. A spasm of revulsion ripples through me.

'So tell me, Miss D, are you visiting London alone?'

'No,' I lie. 'I'm staying with a friend.'

'Really? And where do you live?'

'Edinburgh,' I squeak.

'Know it well,' he says, nodding his head sagely. 'I do a bit of work there on and off. Got an office up there. Do you know the Pentlands?'

'Yes,' I reply. At the side of the bar, next to a sign that says, 'Glass Wash Area – No Loitering,' Johnny Farrell is loitering, arms folded, staring into the middle distance, probably planning a murder.

'It's a lovely bit of countryside, that. Lots of history, very interesting place. I'm thinking of writing a book about it, actually. Trying to drum up some interest in it, but you know how it is, very competitive market. If it's not a spy novel or one of those crap bird's stories about shopping they don't want to know,' he says, taking two short, angry sips of his pint.

My head feels numb.

Copley and Weir?

'Oh yes,' he says, as if responding to a question. 'Beautiful city. I can't be doing with all that festival nonsense, though. Gets on your nerves after a bit, doesn't it?

I gulp, dry-mouthed from nerves and cheap tonic water.

Richard hates the festival.

'Still, you can see why so many people go. Whenever I'm there I like a good Scottish breakfast in the morning,' he says, massaging his flabby belly. 'Sets you up for the week, that does. You can't beat it.'

'Do you go up by train?' I ask pleasantly, as my world falls slowly apart at the seams.

'Sometimes. I prefer flying though – five or six hours on the train and your arse is killing you, if you'll pardon my French.'

Oh, so maybe . . .

'I found the diary on the train.' I say sharply, seeing a light at the end of the tunnel.

'Did you?' He looks gormlessly into the middle distance. 'Maybe I did get the train last time. Trains, planes and automobiles, that's me! I get around, what can I say? I work in entertainment – you know, management, looking after performers on the cabaret circuit, a few actors. Prima donnas the lot of them. Low-rent stuff, not very glamorous, but I don't get time to do anything else; I'm up and down the country wiping arses all the time. Always passing through. But maybe things are changing,' he adds wistfully. 'So . . . can I have it back?' he asks after a stilted pause. 'Come

299

on, you big tease, I don't want anyone knowing my secrets.'

I look down at the bag by my side and for a moment, feel like throwing it at him and leaving the whole sorry mess behind.

'It's not yours,' I announce plainly, hoping that he'll admit it was all a big joke, hoping that he'll backtrack and say, OK, it's not my diary, but got you going, didn't I? I want to leave but two chairs and the lumpen body of Richard Miles are blocking my exit.

He raises his wispy, almost invisible eyebrows, but doesn't look particularly bothered.

'How do you know that? You don't know that, do you? Eh? Anyway, forget the diary, I'm not interested in the diary, darling. I can get another one of them. I'm interested in you. What did you say you did?'

'I didn't.'

He draws back and exhales, shaking his head. His moist lips stretch across his small square yellow teeth in a slippery smile.

'You're hard work, you are. Tease,' he repeats, attempting a flirtatious look. 'You give the boys a run for their money, don't you? Worth it in the end, though, I'll bet.'

He shifts in his chair. Oh God. He's so utterly slimy that I keep expecting to see a slug trail on the seat. Or worse.

That's enough. I can't stand this. I reach into my bag, overcome by the need to escape. Find out for sure and get out.

'Do you know this person?'

My hands shaking, I hold up the black and white photograph and he glances at it.

'No idea,' he shrugs.

'It was in your diary,' I reply accusingly. (Got him!) 'Why don't you know who it is if it's in your diary?'

Richard C. Miles seems entirely unfazed.

'Maybe it was something to do with my work . . . I don't remember.' He pauses, grasping his temples as if to stave off a headache. His next words come out low and slow, considered and convincing. 'I get sent lots of photographs. Hopefuls send me publicity shots all the time.'

My throat tightens. It's plausible.

Then a sly, amused, weaselly expression spreads across his face. 'Oh Christ. Did . . . did you think that was me?'

'*He could be anyone.*'

'Well . . .' I stutter, not knowing the truth from fiction any more, not wanting to be in this horrible pub, not wanting to talk to this disgusting stranger with the bug eyes and damp top lip. Get out, get out, get out. Johnny Farrell glances over and frowns. Terror seeps through my veins, rising in a sickening tide. Maysey bashes his cue on the floor in a repetitive rhythm. Thump thump thump thump, like tribal drums before a sacrifice, and Richard laughs, an unhinged, nightmarish laugh.

'Bet you're a bit disappointed, eh?' he says, beside himself with mirth. 'Jesus, I would be.'

I start to stand up, unable to stay where I am, and grimly decide I have to make a run for it. He wouldn't come after me. He wouldn't know where I lived. Anyway, his legs are too short, I could outrun him any day of the week.

'Hey! Where you going?' he says in desperation, clasping onto my bare arm with his fat fingers.

'Look, I'm sorry, Miss D. I didn't mean to offend you.' His tone is wheedling and apologetic. 'The last thing I want to do is offend you. We've only just . . . Sit down and at least finish your drink.'

I stop. The pub seems suddenly empty, and nobody in here is on my side. The carpet consists of acres of unswept, swirling leaves, russets, oranges and mud browns. The women by the cigarette machine are gone and the City boys – Richard's friends – have dwindled to a pair, talking inconspicuously in a huddle. Johnny has disappeared in a puff of smoke. Nobody is at the bar, not even Droopy. Apart from the sinister hushed click of pool balls, the only sound is the constant perky chatter of the fruit machine, programmed to bleep, flash, and play Casio keyboard tunes to itself all day long. I feel strange and doomed and alone.

I sit down in a stupor. This ghastly little man could very well be Richard. I admit it. I didn't know who he was, I assumed all kinds of ludicrous things, and this is the payoff. His fingers have left white indents in my arm. I want to get a wire brush and scrub them off.

'Now, I might not be a pin-up, Miss D, but I'm not a bad boy, once you get to know me. Give me a chance and you might find you prefer the more mature approach.'

Shakily I take a drink.

'You're very beautiful,' he says in a whisper, drawing closer. He smells of sickly aftershave and leather and something else – something cheesy. 'I'm not used to beautiful strange women calling me and asking me out on dates.'

'I didn't ask you.'

'Ah,' he says, shushing me with an infuriating soft-ness. 'I haven't finished. I feel like you've come to rescue me. I feel like we've got a kind of connection, don't you? I think that deep down, you're intrigued about me too. You wanted a bit of excitement, same as me, don't you, Jane?'

Hearing him say my name makes me feel like throwing up.

'You wanted an adventure to take you away from the daily grind. That's why you were drawn to me when you read my diary – the thrill of the new, the thrill of the chase. That's why you came all the way down here.'

'No.' I think of Ali, sitting at the kitchen table, saying the same thing.

'Aw, don't deny it. Why else would you have phoned me up? Anyway, we're all a bit like that, aren't we, Jane? But you, you were brave enough to pursue it, and I'm glad, because now you're here and we can have an adventure together.'

He leans on his elbow, leering at me.

'Trust me,' he murmurs, gazing into my eyes in a vile, lustful way. 'I'll take you to places you've never been before.'

'I'm going now.'

'You're beautiful,' he says in a thick voice.

Under the table his fingers make a last ditch grab for me, reaching up my skirt and squeezing my inner thigh.

'Get off me!'

I almost scream and jump up, upending the glasses on the table. Bitter flies into the air and splashes onto the skirt of my white dress, staining it brown. The pool sharks stop in their tracks. Most of the beer has gone onto Richard. I watch it drip onto the floor, forming a foamy lake by his cheap shoes.

'For God's sake,' he says in a low, vicious tone, wiping his trousers and fussing over it with the hem of his jacket. 'What the hell did you have to go and do that for?'

'You're not who I'm looking for. You're a fucking pervert,' I gasp, my voice shaking with fear and anger.

He looks over at the bar, embarrassed, and snorts with overtly loud laughter, a dry, malicious sound.

'Ha! Why am I a pervert? I'm not the little slag who chases round after strangers with her tits hanging out, am I? You want to get Johnny to pay you a few quid for your trouble – he's always on the lookout for new girls.'

My body seems to have seized up. I can't speak.

'Look at yer, in your white dress acting like butter wouldn't melt. Cock tease. If you phone people up begging for it, then that's what you get, love.'

I realize that my bag is in my hand, the strap wound tight against my knuckles. Blindly, I swing it high in the air and smack Richard C (for cunt) Miles across the head. He's shocked, I notice, as the black, sharp corner of the diary catches him above the eye and slices his brow in a neat red slit.

Before he can retaliate, I'm running out of the pub, my legs almost giving way with fear. Blood is rushing in my ears, I can barely see.

'Bitch!' he yells from behind the peeling, scratched doors of the King's Arms, but I'm already halfway up the street, my stained white skirt flapping behind me like a vapour trail.

I don't stop running until I get to the hotel. The lobby, which looked so dreary when I arrived, is suddenly as welcoming and forgiving as home. The dry flower arrangement, the brown decor, the bell boy/receptionist with the acne, they make sense, compared to the horrors of meeting Richard. I take the lift up one floor and fumble with the lock to Room 13, opening the door and then barricading myself in with the chest of drawers. What if he saw where I went? What if Johnny comes after me? And Maysey and his friend – they were witnesses. Who would they defend? Him or me? They had pool cues, but I bet they had more besides. Maysey didn't get a broken wrist from doing macramé, that's for sure.

I try to catch my breath. The air is suffocating, the heat from the radiator trapped by the closed, grimy window. I open it and shut it again. Someone could easily climb onto the roof of the hotel kitchen and shimmy up the drainpipe to get to the window.

I turn on the TV for some sense of normality and step out of my dress. I never want to see it again. It smells of him, of his stinking beer and stinking fingers. I throw it in the bath and turn on the taps full blast.

He wouldn't come. He didn't follow me. He was such a nasty flabby toad that he would have had a heart attack. Still, the last thing I should be doing is standing around in my underwear with the curtains open. I turn the bath taps off and fill the sink, locking the bathroom door and dunking my head in the scalding water. The instructions on the pack of Autumn Scarlet said it lasted 8 washes, plus the Cherry Blossom. I scrub furiously, methodically lathering and rinsing again and again until the water runs clear and the worst of the red dye is gone. Gingerly stepping out into the room, I find jeans and a T-shirt, and sit on the bed with my knees drawn up to my chin. And I wait, tracking the tiniest noises in the corridor. I find another lighter in my bag and smoke five cigarettes in a row. I wish I had some booze to give me courage, and to get rid of the foul juniper taste of the gin, but I don't want to risk being seen in public. God knows what would happen if he saw me. He might decide to hit me with something more dangerous than a diary. He was insane.

I pull the bottom of my T-shirt over my knees. I can't believe his horrible hands touched me. The thought of his nicotine-blond hair and cold, fishy eyes is so hideous I can't bear it.

I try to swallow, but there's a rock in my throat.

Soon, involuntary tears fall onto the brown bed-spread, raining slippery black droplets onto it.

Running after strangers with your tits hanging out.

He was right about that one.

What am I doing? What did I expect?

Still the tears come, and a balloon of grief swells in my chest. I'm really crying now, heaving and wailing, just like in Sophie's office, tears of self-pity more than anything – self-pity, disgust and a dismal unease. I think back to last week, when I didn't know who Richard Miles was. What did I have to cry about then?

Nothing, that's what.

Now I know why that Kia-Ora woman made a face and tried to cover it up – the King's Arms is a knocking shop. I went to a glorified brothel to meet a total stranger. And what do you know, the man of my dreams, the man I've been wasting my time obsessing about, wasn't a dark, handsome knight in shining armour waiting to fall into my arms at all. He was just a slimy little toerag who couldn't believe his luck, waiting to get in my knickers. Could the diary have been his? How the hell do I know? I don't know anything about him, I never did. He's a figment of my imagination, a bunch of train tickets and receipts. Dan was right. I can't begin to imagine why I didn't listen.

The photograph sits in front of me, mocking me. It

could be an agency photo, an Equity still. I peer closely. Is he an actor? It's lit like a stage set, with him looking meaningfully in the distance – the photographer could be asking him to cup his chin in his hand. Everything frogface said could be a total fluke, an elaborate deception, and the photo could still be Richard, but so what? Neither people I spoke to had any time for him, and Copley and Weir couldn't disguise their contempt either. Maybe Bug Eyes was *nicer* than the man in the photograph. Maybe behind his smouldering looks he's a complete bastard, whoever he is.

Well I'm sick of him. I don't care what he is or what he looks like. I don't want him. I hoist open the window and throw the photo out.

I want it to plummet to the ground and into the earth's core, but of course it doesn't, it flutters gracefully and irritatingly downwards, caught in a gentle breeze. When the photo settles by the bins at the back of the hotel, it doesn't even have the decency to land on its flip side. The face just turns its dreamy attention to a crate of empty bottles, and lies there, forever waiting, set in stone.

Whatever, I never want to see a diary again. It's spoiled and pointless. It's not the answer.

A gritty, thin wind, carrying the smell of car fumes and kebabs wafts into my face. I hate this place. The unfamiliarity of the grotty back yard makes my head spin. I need to go home. I miss my flat. My stupid, low-ceilinged, multi-coloured cramped flat that tries to dent my skull every chance it gets. I miss its smell, a faint Victorian smell of mildew, mixed with new gloss paint and the scorched metal of convector heaters. I need to go back to where my stuff is, to climb up the stairs and bump into Queenie and have an innocent, inane conversation. I don't even care whether she thinks I'm a hooker, either – nothing could make me feel as cheap as I do now. I need my own space, with my car-boot-sale lamp and the outfit from Ziggy's still sprawled across the floor, that bottle-green vest and those split silver trousers with the crocheted hat sitting on top like a doily. Friday wasn't that bad, was it, Jane? Nothing was THIS bad, was it? You went out, had a laugh, danced, met a nice boy, a boy who wanted to show you around and eat ice cream, not stick his hand up your skirt . . . Susan Chater liked your presentation. You showed old ladies a good time and helped people out. Fiona said you were a rising star and David bought you a drink. Kelly said sorry and admitted she was wrong. Sophie told you a joke and complimented you on your hair. What was wrong with ANY of it?

The image of Dan holding the jacket and diary in the dreary shadows of the alleyway fills me with deep remorse. He was nice and sweet and actually *existed*, unlike Richard, who could still be anyone. He just wanted to make sure you were all right, but you wouldn't give him a chance. And you walked all over him, you stupid cow.

Kelly was never the problem. Or the tourist office. Or Edinburgh.

You're the problem.

You.

I glare at myself in the mirror and pull at my hair. The red tint clings on for dear life. My department-store makeover is streaked and ruined, making me look every inch a slut. Look at me. What an idiot. Taking the wrong fork in the road, getting out of my depth. Deluded, wrong-headed, vain Jane. You were the one who was lost and unravelling. Asking the universe for signs. Making decisions with a cheap plastic toy, when all the time, the signs were blazing neon, right under your nose, pointing the other way.

I hear the rattle of a crate being knocked over in the yard and slam the window shut. Through the grime I see a man from the hotel bar coming out for a break. I hide behind the thick, heavy curtain and watch as he takes a chocolate bar from his pocket. His face is tired and drawn, pockmarked with scars. He sits down wearily on a nearby crate and tears the black and red wrapper with his teeth. Noticing the photo he reaches out to pick it up, and looks at it for a while, puzzled. In one single movement he screws up the photo and tosses it aside, then takes a ravenous bite of chocolate, chewing steadily. It doesn't mean a thing to him.

Nor me.

I stand there for ages, fingering the scratchy fabric of the curtain. Behind me the TV cackles to itself, showing a documentary about plastic surgery. A woman with two black eyes and blue marker-pen lines under her chin says how thrilled she is with her face lift. The next shot is of a psychologist, sitting in a study lined with books.

'Unfortunately these days, people are easily seduced by appearance.'

I gingerly take the diary out of my bag. It feels hazardous to hold, like uranium. I want it to be put in a sterilized bag and incinerated by people in protective suits. I don't even want to touch it in case it contaminates me again – in case I give into it again. But I open it.

Fumbling through the deceiving, flowing text and junky, sickening pieces of paper, I find what I'm looking for.

There's no indecision this time, no nerves, just a sense of purpose.

Five rings.

One. Two. Three. Four. Five.

'Hello?'

Background noise swells up and engulfs his voice.

'Hello. It's Jane.'

The reception cuts out and then the noise comes back in again, a cacophonous tide.

'Hello?' the voice says again.

'Hello, Dan?' I say, louder, more desperately, feeling as if I'm drowning. 'It's Jane.'

Through the fuzz a light seems to click on.

'Jane?'

'I just wanted to say—'

'Wait a minute . . . I can't hear you . . . I'm at a gig,' he yells. 'Hang on.'

I hear the thumping of a drum kit and squall of distortion, and his breath over the top of it, an almost inaudible hiss. Then the noise tails off, as if muffled by a blanket.

'Hello?' he says eventually, loud and clear.

'I'm sorry, Dan. I just wanted to speak to you.'

This suddenly seems a bad idea. I'm the wet girlie girl who calls at three in the morning. I can barely keep it together. My eyes are sore and blurred and I feel as if I've been hit in the face with a mallet.

'I'm . . . I'm sorry about the other night. I just wanted you to know,' I whimper.

There's a short pause. For a wounded moment I wonder whether he remembers who I am.

'It's Jane,' I falter. 'From Ziggys?'

'Yeah, I know,' he says kindly.

'I was a real bitch, and all that stuff about the stupid

310

diary – I'm really sorry. I didn't mean to act like that. I think I must have gone a bit insane.' I glare at it and tear a strip off a page.

'Are you OK? You sound a bit strange.'

'I'm all right.'

As soon as I tell this blatant lie, my chin starts wobbling and the tears start to flow.

'Are you crying?' he asks.

Oh God. I try to muffle my pitiful sobs, but the force of it is too strong. Great, Jane, great.

'I am SO, SO sorry,' I say, repetitively. 'You must think I'm a lunatic.' My voice is see-sawing all over the place. 'I didn't mean to bother you. Go back to your gig and have a good time. I'll maybe see you around sometime, OK?'

'Wait,' he says so urgently that I flinch. 'What happened? Did you meet that guy? Did he do something to you?'

The fact that Dan not only remembers the whole sorry mess but actually cares, fills me with such grateful relief that it sets me off again. No matter how hard I try to stop, the tears come down in torrents.

'It was horrible. He tried to . . . to . . . put his hand . . .'

'Where are you? Are you on your own?'

I wipe my nose.

'Where are you?' he asks again.

Through strangulated gasps I manage to get it out.

'I'm in London. In a hotel in Islington.'

'Right, OK, I'm in Camden,' he says purposefully. Behind him, a door opens and loud music comes crashing out. A dim and distant memory of Dan telling me he was coming down for an interview floats up in my brain. Something about a magazine. I picture him,

311

his fine face, clear eyes and concerned brow, looking reassuring and capable, like a doctor. Why didn't I trust him?

'What's the hotel called?' he shouts.

'No! No . . . it's OK.' I shout back, not wanting him to come here, to go out of his way, to see me breaking down in this seedy room, whimpering and carrying on and dribbling all over the brown blanket with the faded woman in the rocking chair peering from the wall. 'I'm OK, honestly. Don't, please. I'm going home tomorrow morning. I'll phone you when I'm back in Edinburgh.'

'But . . .'

'Really,' I snuffle. 'I'll be fine. I just phoned to say sorry. I didn't mean to act the way I did the other night. I don't know what's the matter with me. I've just . . . I've just lost my way a bit. I'm really not like this at all . . .' I trail off.

'It's OK,' he whispers. 'It's OK.'

A warm sensation floods through me, making me slow and sleepy.

It's OK.

'I want to er . . . see you again. I won't be mental this time, I promise. Can I take you out for ice cream?' I say in a croaky voice.

'I'd like that,' he says.

'Will you take me to see the big plant?' I ask pathetically.

I can hear him smiling. Either that or sticking his finger down his throat. Shit, he probably doesn't even know what I'm talking about.

'Dunno,' he says, being cool. 'Might be washing my hair.'

'You haven't got any hair.'

'Oh well . . . OK, then. Seeing as it's you.'

312

I stay there for a while, with the hot receiver of my phone glued to my ear, not wanting him to go.

'Jane?' Dan finally asks. 'Where is he now?'

'Hey?'

'The guy with the diary.'

'Don't worry,' I tell him, wiping my damp face. 'He's not here. He never really was.'

I wake up with the TV still on and the phone by my side. It takes me a minute to figure out why the door is blocked by a chest of drawers, and then I remember in a sick rush of grey bug eyes, fat fingers, swirling leaves, pool cues, tattoos and flat gins. The dress is still in the bath, immersed in beery water. I cover my puffy, tear-stained face with my arm. My skin smells of fusty bed sheets, smoke and my own astringent perfume, the DKNY stuff that Becky bought me last birthday in a Boots-style box set that made my heart sink. Now it's the smell of the King's Arms, not mine, and I know I'll never wear it again.

It's eight-thirty. I'll be on the train at eleven o'clock and be back in Edinburgh by four. Tomorrow I'll be back in the tourist office and things are going to change for the better. Instead of being miserable, dreary Jane with a stick up her arse, shuffling around with holes in her tights and grunting at everyone, I'm going to smile and make jokes and laugh at my mistakes and ask people questions about their lives, rather than obsessing about mine. I'll be a total laugh riot. I'll do what Sophie wants and draw an interactive map of Scotland on my bum and tap dance through the office with novelty Edinburgh snowstorms stuffed down my bra. The new Jane will delight and surprise, not frustrate and disappoint. I might even wear a jaunty hat.

Well, I'll try to make more of an effort, anyway.

I go to the bathroom and scoop out the dress, which is billowing helplessly in the bath like a fallen parachute. God knows what I was thinking – it's an awful dress. I wring it out as best I can, bundle it up into a damp ball and stuff it into the plastic bin. Then I take a scalding hot shower, washing out all traces of Richard C. Miles, the Smokey Robinson eyeshadow and as much as I can of the red dye. It all slides down the plughole in a gratifying stream of discoloured, faintly rusty water: a bad dream fading from memory. When I step out I wrap myself in a rough hotel towel and scrub until my skin is tingling.

I'm clean.

I'm new.

I stare at the phone on the bed and break out into an entirely goofy grin.

Suddenly I'm struck with a ravenous appetite, and the Cloisters hotel breakfast seems like the best idea ever. I'm starving. I feel like I haven't eaten for weeks. I shove my hair into an untidy ponytail, clamber into some jeans and a T-shirt. In the light of day, a cool, cloudless September morning with no shadows lurking in the corners, the idea of Richard doesn't frighten me any more. Even if he were sitting in the dining room threatening to cut my throat with a butter knife I wouldn't run. Besides, if I don't have sausages in the next five minutes I'll die.

Passing the maid's trolley, piled high with dirty laundry, I take the lift. It's lined with smoked brown mirrors that reflect every angle. Maybe it's a strange effect brought about by the glass or the dim, fly-speckled light, but I look different. Even in this grubby, coppery haze I look better. Then I figure out what it is.

I look cheerful.

'Morning,' says the spotty receptionist with a smile.

'Morning,' I say, right back at him, returning the smile. He seems tickled and blushes, busying himself with some papers and a stapler.

I cross to the dining room, following the smell of breakfast. The room is set out like a canteen, with the same smoked glass mirrors as the lift. Couples sit vacantly chewing slices of white toast at brown tables. Clumps of tourists stare into space, consult guidebooks or drift past on their way out to see Big Ben. None of us belongs here, we're all just passing through on the way to somewhere else. The only real fixture is the food, which could have been there since Roman times. Slabs of petrified bacon and soggy fried eggs lie on stainless-steel trays under copper heat lamps, with a sign, possibly considered futuristic in the Seventies, saying 'self service'. Even though it doesn't look too hot – 'It ain't the Ritz. It ain't the Ritz,' says Kia-Ora, like a parrot – I'm so outrageously hungry that I could eat the tables and chairs. I pile a plate high and find a single table. As I walk towards it, I can sense people looking at me. Maybe they can see my tentative transformation. Or maybe my flies are undone.

Either way, this morning I feel different, as if something fundamental has altered. This is how it was after I lost my virginity with Jamie Leonard in his stinky teenage-boy bedroom when I was 18. The rowing machine covered in dirty clothes and the bomber burns from a thousand joints speckling his windowsill didn't exactly do much for me, but we did it anyway and I was glad to have the burden lifted. I thought Babs and Becky would notice when I turned up for my tea without my virginity, but they didn't. I remember feeling a twinge of disappointment. Babs was quick enough off the draw when my first period arrived after an irritable day trip to Mother Shipton's Cave – while I was in the toilet contemplating foreign, disturbing stains, she was running up and down the stairs yelling, 'My baby's a woman!' – but on this particular occasion the sprouts were passed and nothing was said.

I shift in my seat. I want someone to ask me why my skin looks so blooming, and why I appear to be in such fabulously rude health today. And I would say . . .

What would I say?

Even though it's appallingly greasy, the food is the best thing that's ever passed my lips. Every mouthful makes me feel ridiculously vital and alive. The coffee comes in large china cups that seem shaped to fit my hand, and I sip it slowly, feeling warmth seeping into my bones.

Over at the buffet, the bulb in one of the heat lamps flickers for a split second and comes on brighter than before. The man who screwed up the photo is clearing plates from one of the tables, unaware that he did me a huge favour. I imagine the photograph, in the back of a bin lorry, being chewed up by mechanical teeth. I study myself for signs of regret, but none are forthcoming.

I finish my coffee and go back upstairs.

As I come through the door, the diary is lying out on the floor face down, open where I left it. I type Dan's number into my phone and press Save. I brace myself and take one last look at Richard Miles. Now even his name seems pompous and self-important. My fingers curl around the edges of the diary. Look at it, this skimpy little book, always poking me in the arm and sticking its sharp corners into my chest, announcing itself loftily, but never really revealing anything. Good as a weapon or a drinks stand, useless for anything else. I can't believe I hung on to it for so long, chasing around looking for its owner like Cinderella in reverse. What did Dan say? 'self-indulgent' 'adolescent' 'weird pictures of women'. I flick through the book and stare at the drawings – accomplished, yes, but angular and unhinged. The long-necked cats that I'd found amusing and endearing are just freaky, and the women, well-upholstered with gigantic knockers, I see now are fantasy heroines, copied from comic books, their Wonder Woman hotpants and wristbands replaced by floating dresses and feminine charms of Richard's choosing.

'She's beautiful, a girl with long red hair, a fair maiden . . .'

What a crock of shit.

He can't spell, either.

'historyonics', 'gloryfied', 'acessories', 'your' instead of 'you're'. Duh. I go to the page surrounded by drawings of catatonic sheep, and the rant I once considered so feisty and entertaining is like the ramblings of a grounded teenager locked in his bedroom, a kid who hates everything because it's not fair. I flick through the book, page after page of random scribbles, the outpourings of somebody far removed from me. A curiosity, perhaps, intriguing and mysterious, but so what? What's in it for me? Whether it belongs to a prince or a frog now seems completely irrelevant.

One by one I take the receipts and tickets from the

back of the diary and lay them out on the bed, just like I did on my living-room floor the day after I found it. Even then the patchwork map looked meaningless, but now it's laughable. How on earth did I think I was going to find him? A ticket for a crap band – Jazz funkateers – should have known! – some tube and train tickets, evidence of nothing but travel, the Kaleidoscope receipt – the woman with the purple roots comes to me in a murky glimmer: 'Owes me fifty quid. Fucking bastard.' – and the enigmatic Sarah Olsen, of course, the person who could have solved this entire mystery without me even having to leave the house. If he is the Richard in the pub, she might be one of his 'clients', a depressed ageing redhead who gets a fiver an hour to sing at working men's clubs. If I'd e-mailed her that day she might have saved me all this unpleasantness, not to mention money. Why didn't I do that? Because I didn't want to take the risk that she was his girlfriend and my dreams would be shattered.

Ha.

I gather everything up and stuff it into my shoulder bag. Picking up my phone and key and taking one last look out of the filthy dust-caked window, I leave Room 13 for good.

The bellboy's fingers tremble as he hands me the credit-card slip.

'Thank you very much for choosing Cloisters,' he squeaks. 'Have a good day.'

'And you.' I smile.

As I walk towards the revolving doors, I take the diary – the scraps of useless paper, the doodles, the tickets and spelling mistakes and the self-indulgent whining – and chuck it in the litter bin next to another vile dried-flower arrangement. The clattering plastic lid sounds like applause.

Hurrah.

Goodbye, Richard. Nice not knowing you.

Emerging from the brown lung of the hotel, I feel as if I've been given electric-shock therapy. I'm suddenly, spectacularly, cured. Everything seems super-real. The buses are bright red, the shop windows are dazzling, the air has a crisp edge I can almost touch. A couple of miles away is King's Cross, and five hours beyond that is Edinburgh. I climb into a lushly upholstered, beetle-shiny black cab and let it speed me towards the beginning of my new life. Crowds spill through the glass doors of the station and I'm caught up in an irresistible flow of people. There's my train, a dark-blue bullet stretching far off into the distance. Platform 8, the 1100 hours to Edinburgh Waverley – no more knot of tension from wondering if Richard will be on it, no more fretting that my life might change in the blink of a dark smouldering eye, no more poring over that daft book. Nothing else to think about but a crap buffet, a nice view and the million new things that might happen at the end of the line. I take my phone out of my pocket and sigh with relief. I think maybe I'll call work.

The train is still fairly empty and I wander slowly to my seat, listening to the staff-room phone ringing out. Eventually, a camp-as-Christmas voice answers and I'm flooded with silly affection.

'Hiya, David. It's Jane.'

'ARGH! Janey Waney! Awright doll. You're alive. We thought we'd have to start scouring the brothels! What happened to you on Friday?'

'Hm, yeah, sorry about that,' I mumble, throwing my

bag onto the table and cradling the phone with my shoulder. 'It was your fault for making me drink that horrible pink bollocks . . .'

'Ooh,' he bellows, resurrecting the ghost of Frankie Howerd. 'Leave my bollocks out of it!'

I groan and sit down. The engine hums happily and the air inside the carriage feels clean and calm. I dangle my leg across the aisle seat, stretched out like a cat in a sunbeam.

'So how's everything? Is Sophie still drunk?'

'Och, don't even GO there. You know she took Paul home?' he gabbles, taking a deep breath, ready to fire off a barrage of gossip. 'Well, he came in Monday looking like he'd been *buggered* – the TORMENT on his wee spotty face, I couldnae bear it! I swear to God, she's broken him. He was walking like John Wayne. Oh MAN, can you imagine what it would have LOOKED like – her big glittery boobies jiggling about and his botty pumpin' away . . .'

'DAVID!' I squeal, far too loud. A man across the aisle frowns at me over his paper.

David is cackling away at the other end like a deranged monkey. I recover myself and whisper an apology to the disapproving man, who is still glaring at me. Miserable sod.

'Hey, do you think she's up the stick?' I hiss.

I'm enjoying this. Why was I so stuck up about David before? I briefly notice that the train is full of people who seem pinched and depressed, gazing out of windows in a dazed, hopeful trance.

'Oh, I never thought of that,' David suddenly erupts. 'Hey, she HAS been looking peaky these past couple of days. Oh MY GOD! The baby'd be a total DAMIEN! It'd have really gelled Lady Di hair, dirty great knockers, acne and talk about monthly targets,' he creases up with laughter, beside himself. I'm laughing too, happy to join in, happy to be a part of it at all.

'Anyway,' he says, gasping and swallowing. 'Enough about that, what have YOU been doing? Fucking off on holiday when it's our busiest time of the year, ya lazy trollop.'

'Oh, nothing,' I say distractedly. 'Nothing much. I'll tell you about it when I get back – do you want to go for a drink later?'

'Eh? Oh, aye. Let's. Ooh, can we go to Los Caballeros? They've got a buckin' bronco.'

'Hmm, yeah. I was maybe thinking of something a bit more sedate than humping a rocking horse.'

'You speak for yourself – I have to take what I can get. When you coming back?'

'I'm setting off now, so a few hours. Oh, and ask Fiona and Kelly if they want to come.'

'Kelly? Are you sure?' asks David, his tone half wary, half incredulous.

'Yeah.'

David pauses. There's a high voice in the background.

'Oh GOD, Queen Sophie would like to speak with you now,' says David in ceremonial tones. 'I'll go and ask Fee and Smelly. See ya later.'

The receiver is passed. Sophie sounds like she's eating something fairly substantial, like a side of beef or a pillow.

'Nnnng . . . Guh! Jane – lovely to hear from you. You know, you've made an old woman very happy. Good news,' she says, her smooth telephone manner muffled by food. 'Susan Chater LOVED your presentation at Destinations so much that she'd like both you and

322

Kelly to go down to London on the 4th of November to help represent Edinburgh and drum up business at the British Travel trade fair. It's absolutely THE most prestigious event in the travel calendar and I'm sure you won't let us down!'

'Really?' I ask.

I'm actually going to have to give my imaginary London presentation for real?

'Yes, and you get four-star hotel accommodation over two days. It's a great honour. Last year some awful tarts from the airport desk went down and made a right hash of it, so Susan has high hopes. Anyway, must dash. See you tomorrow bright and early.'

'Yeah, bye.'

Jesus. That's odd.

There's static and shuffling, and even weirder after all that's happened, the polite, *friendly* tones of Kelly come down the line.

'Hello, Jane.'

'Hiya, Kelly. How are you?'

'Did you get my text?' she asks immediately.

'Yeah. It's all OK. Let's just forget about all that other stuff, shall we?'

'Yeah.'

'Good news about the trade fair, though, isn't it? I'll make sure I don't mess it up this time and start talking about wounds.'

Kelly attempts a laugh. 'No, it'll be good. So how's London? Did you have a nice time on your date?'

'Oh,' I falter. David is in the background, having kittens, yelling, 'What date? What DATE?'

'I . . . it wasn't so good.'

'Why, what happened?' she asks, sounding confused. 'I thought you were going with Dan—'

How does she know about Dan? I only talked to him for ten minutes at the club.

'Er, no, it wasn't with Dan.' I tell her. My cheeks are reddening. 'It was a blind date with this other guy . . . but he was a nightmare . . . I got upset and phoned Dan and he wanted to come and get me and he was really sweet . . . it's all a bit strange . . . Listen, I'll tell you about it when I get back. Do you fancy a drink later? Is Fiona coming, too?'

'Er, yeah, she said she would,' she says, sounding befuddled.

'I'll come into the office when I get back then.'

'Where are you now?' she asks with sudden urgency.

'King's Cross. Why? The eleven o'clock's just about to go so I should be in Edin—'

'OK,' she says brightly, cutting me off. 'Got to go. See you then.'

The line goes dead. What's she being so weird about? Then I remember that the office must be outrageously busy. I think of the lines of tourists queuing up, blank expressions and soaking umbrellas, desperately needing to know what to do with themselves. Then I think of my tartan skirt, hanging on the back of my bedroom door, and smile. *How long is the Royal Mile?*

Later on I'll take Kelly out and we'll have a proper conversation. I'll even feign an interest in Will Young, or Care Bears, or whatever it is she's into. Then I'll go back to my flat and take Queenie a present in return for her rock-hard fruitcake, and thank her for being so kind, caring about my welfare when I didn't. I'll make my peace with the jutting-out walls and mottled chipboard, and we'll see whether we can't all get along.

'Excuse me,' says a male voice behind me.

Something about it sets my teeth on edge. It's posh, clipped and eerily familiar.

Just as I crane my head over the seat, a sharp point whacks me full in the shin, closely followed by someone trying to push past me. A shockwave of jarring pain hits and my reflex sends my leg flying upwards. My foot connects with something soft. I swing my injured leg under the table out of harm's way and sit up straight on the aisle seat, turning fully to face the owner of the voice, but he's too busy bending double, whining, clutching his nuts.

'Oh no. Oh, I'm sorry,' I gasp, embarrassed. My shin is killing me, and a fierce red dent is forming just below my knee. The briefcase he skewered me with is on the floor, papers spilling out of it like a tickertape parade, so I uselessly scramble to pick them up. He slowly, angrily lifts his head.

'You idiot,' he spits, breathlessly.

'I'm . . . sorry, I'm just . . .'

'What did you have to stick your leg in the aisle for, you stupid woman?'

His eyes meet mine, blurred with discomfort and rage. I see his face properly and I'm hit with a sickening stab of recognition.

The thick dark hair, the James Bond features, the smell of money – I've seen him before.

High cheekbones, dark suit . . .

Oh God, oh my GOD.

It's . . . it's . . .

Pierce Cocksucker!

Still bending over, he flicks my hand away from the papers, and I loll backwards in my seat, rubbing my leg. As he turns round to rescue more sheets of A4, I see his pinstripe arse sticking out and notice that his left hand is firmly lodged between his legs, nursing his knackers.

'Are you OK?' I say, biting my lip, trying not to laugh at this well-deserved twist of fate. Pierce doesn't answer.

'I know you,' I tell him loudly. 'I work in the tourist office in Edinburgh. You were really rude to me when I was trying to book you a hotel.'

Pierce, straightening up and adjusting his tie, sends me a not-very-convincing withering look. An exasperated sweat has broken out on his forehead.

'I'm SORRY?'

'Well so you should be,' I continue, 'but I forgive you.'

'I . . . I haven't got a clue what you're talking about,' he says uncertainly, still wincing with pain.

'I apologize too, for telling you to eff-off,' I say gravely. 'It was very unprofessional of me and I should have known that you were probably feeling disorientated after your journey. After all, we at the tourist office are the first point of contact. Come in any time and I'll personally see to it that you're given top priority in our accommodation service.'

Pierce stands there, staring at me with a bewildered expression, a forelock of hair falling over one eye. He doesn't know whether to run screaming or punch me. This is great. With the wind knocked out of his sails, he seems completely harmless. I wonder why he got me so wound up. He's a total pushover.

'Anyway, my name's Jane. What's yours?' I beam flirtatiously.

Pierce's posh public-school brain seems to be taking a long time to engage. He keeps opening and closing his mouth. Any minute now springs are going to burst out of his head like a broken sofa.

'Er,' he manages to say. 'Peter.'

'Really? I had you down as more of a Pierce. Anyway, no hard feelings, eh? As I said, it's all water under the bridge.'

He gapes at me in wonder, and with as much dignity as he can muster, wobbles off unsteadily to the next carriage. When he gets to the automatic doors, he turns round and throws me a look of confusion mixed with something else – a hint of curiosity maybe? – before disappearing in the direction of first class.

A burst of guilty, ridiculous hysteria threatens to escape and I clamp my hand over my mouth. A playground chant starts up in my head. 'I kicked Pierce in the nu-uts . . .'

Bless him, the big arsehole. I hope he finds what he's looking for – a hotel, a girlfriend, a new pair of bollocks, whatever.

'Could all passengers not intending to travel please leave the train as this service is about to depart.'

The stations are announced. York – purple roots, raisins and wooden elephants; Newcastle – monuments and posh restaurants; Edinburgh – not all tartan and shortbread, but full of secrets under the surface, if you know where to look.

I shift in my chair. Good, no diaries shoved down the side of this seat.

I look out of the window at the heaving crowds and last-minute passengers dashing to get on board. It's strange. I feel steady and centred, like the eye of the storm, while everyone is running around in a state of nervous collapse, weighed down with baggage, taking their problems out on each other, making assumptions, sending out waves of unadulterated hatred and

327

desperation. Maybe I'm a proper tour guide at last, equipped for any eventuality, with access to a map.

'Excuse me, is this seat taken?'

An out-of-breath voice pours into my ear.

I turn around.

'No, it's . . .' I begin.

Then I stop.

He's so real it's a shock to see him, like looking at something under a magnifying glass. So much detail. The long lashes, the eyes – bleached blue in this light – the earnest trust-me-I'm-a-doctor expression. A few freckles here and there, which I know I'm not going to get tired of looking at. All of it is in front of me, three-dimensional, bursting with life.

He's here.

Not a ghost, not a photograph, not a psychopath.

Dan.

Dan is here. How did he know where to find me?

My mouth goes dry with surprise. He looks so substantial. It's almost hard to look at him properly, like blinking into the sun.

Before I can even think to stop it, a loony grin creeps across my face.

'Hello,' I say.

'Hello,' he says back, sliding into the seat opposite me. He smells of sugar and spice and all things nice – warm skin and soap. I briefly wonder whether the diary gave me some kind of temporary brain damage. How could I have passed him up? Was it something to do with the blow to the head?

'I've been looking for you,' he announces with mock seriousness.

'Really?'

'I've been in this station since eight o'clock. People were starting to think I was a rent boy.'

'Really?'

My smile is so wide it's verging on the cheesy (pull yourself together).

'Then as soon as you get here I don't even see you. You've changed your hair. Again,' he says, reaching out to touch the ends of it. A shiver goes through me, but he stops mid-air and draws his hand back.

'Looks better. I didn't like the red. Made you look like Noddy Holder.'

'Gee, thanks.'

We sit there grinning at each other, like two crazed hyenas.

'Why were you waiting for me?' I ask eventually.

'Well, you said you wanted to see me again, didn't you? Kelly tipped me off that you were on the eleven o'clock train.'

'Kelly?'

'She's my spy. She told me she'd just spoken to you.'

'Oh, so that's why she was being weird. Is she your pimp or something?'

'Nah. It's just a little arrangement we have. She sets me up with girls by knocking them unconscious on dancefloors. Except you got away.' He glances shyly down at my hands, which I realize are shaking. 'Anyway, I think she wanted to make up for what she did to you at Ziggy's. Although I reckon she did you a favour. It's not every day you fall into the arms of a handsome rogue like me.'

'You dropped me,' I remind him.

'I tried to pick you up later on, though, didn't I? But you were having none of it, I seem to recall.'

'Well, I can't help it if you look gay, can I?'

329

'Well I can't help it if you're daft, either. Urgh.' He says, mimicking my shrill drunken Leeds accent. 'Ah've got curry on me wellies.'

I kick him under the table and he laughs. A calm, balanced, happy feeling descends on me as I take in Dan's lanky frame and beaming smile. Sitting opposite him feels fine and familiar, like crawling into my own bed. A clean sheet.

'So are you going to stop running off, then?'

'Yeah. Definitely. Absolutely.'

'You're not keeping that diary in your knicker drawer are you?'

'No. It's in the bin.'

'Good. I'll have no woman of mine buggering off to London to chase strange men,' he lectures theatrically, leaning forward.

I raise an eyebrow.

'I'm not your woman.'

He gives me a dirty little smirk. I sneer and stick my tongue out at him in a pathetically unconvincing gesture of defiance.

'That's what I like about you, Darling. You're so feisty.'

'Fuck off.'

'And so well spoken.'

'Fuck off,' I say, laughing.

'Wash your mouth out.' He smiles.

There's a high-pitched bleeping sound and the doors close. I'm already far from the polluted, greenhouse air of King's Cross. Dan's sandy sealskin hair glitters in the sun, turning it to gold. His tanned forearms give me a frisky, heady feeling, like the first day of the holidays.

'Right then,' he says. 'So where do you want to go?'

'Anywhere. Nowhere. Doesn't matter.'

330

Over the tannoy the guard is babbling on about restaurant carriages and buffets, and the other passengers are talking and rustling newspapers. Dan reaches his hand across the table and examines my ragged fingernails. His lips are set in a neat pout, curling up at the edges, idly amused. Eat your heart out, Brad. He fixes me with a sizzling blue stare.

'Tell you what,' he says. 'Let's go home.'

'Good idea,' I reply, wrapping my fingers around his. As the train pulls away, Dan kisses me, and in that split second we're gone.

THE END

A GIRL COULD STAND UP

Leslie Marshall

'A LOVELY TALE OF TEENAGE LOVE AND
COMPANIONSHIP IN A WORLD WHERE ALL
ADULTS SEEM INSANE'
Time Out

When six-year-old Elray reaches up to touch the moon in the
Tunnel of Love, she narrowly escapes a freak electric current
that claims the lives of both her parents. Suddenly orphaned,
she is left stunned and mute, until two loving but
undomesticated uncles step in.

Cross-dressing Uncle Ajax insists on being addressed as
'Aunt'; Uncle Harwood is a macho photographer, full of
swagger and fond of drink. When the deceptively sweet Irish
lawyer Rena moves in to mount a lucrative lawsuit against
the fairground, the eccentric household becomes the very
model of family life reinvented.

'A PAGE-TURNER THAT WILL DISARM AND CHARM. A
STAND-OUT TALENT'
People

'SHE IS THE HOMER OF DYSFUNCTIONAL FAMILY LIFE.
THIS IS THE BEST FIRST NOVEL I'VE READ IN YEARS'
Edmund White

'UTTERLY REAL . . . RENDERED WITH TRUTHFULLNESS
AND CHARM'
Los Angeles Times

'AN ATMOSPHERE OF CRAZY CHEERFULNESS . . .
UNDERCUT BY MOMENTS OF POIGNANCY . . . A
PLEASURE TO READ'
Daily Telegraph

'THIS QUIRKY NOVEL IS A MUST FOR KATE ATKINSON
AND JOHN IRVING FANS WHO ARE FOND OF A
SURREAL READ'
Glamour

0 552 77190 2

BLACK SWAN

CAN YOU KEEP A SECRET?

Sophie Kinsella

Emma is like every girl in the world. She has
a few little secrets.

Secrets from her mother:
1. I lost my virginity in the spare bedroom to Danny
Nussbaum while Mum and Dad were downstairs
watching *Ben Hur*.

. . . From her boyfriend:
2. I'm a size twelve. Not a size eight, like Connor thinks.
3. I've always thought Connor looks a bit like Ken. As
in Barbie and Ken.

. . . From her colleagues:
4. When Artemis really annoys me, I feed her plant
orange juice. (Which is pretty much every day).
5. It was me who jammed the copier that time. In fact,
all the times.

. . . Secrets she wouldn't share with anyone in
the world:
6. My G string is hurting me.
7. I faked my Maths GCSE grace on my CV.
8. I have no idea what NATO stands for. Or even what
it is . . .

. . . until she spills them all to a stranger on a plane.
At least, she *thought* he was a stranger . . .

'BRILLIANT READING'
Heat

0 552 77110 4

BLACK SWAN

LONG GONE ANYBODY
Susannah Waters

Where do people go when they disappear?

That boy you went to school with, the girl who shared
your university room for a term, the neighbour you
glimpsed through the curtains – where did they
go when they left?

A nineteen-year-old runs away from her life and keeps
on running. Haunted by the unexplained departure of
her mother four years earlier, she is looking and not
looking. Adopting one identity after another – female
escort, apple-picker, cashier, canvas girl in a travelling
circus – she is afraid to slow down for fear of what, or
who, may catch up with her. When anonymous
postcards start to arrive at every place she goes,
she is finally forced to confront the fate of her
long-gone mother. Can this runaway-girl
escape the same end?

In a compulsive and moving novel riddled with family
secrets, a predictably happy ending is never a
guarantee. But one thing becomes certain; people
can only ever save themselves.

0 552 77221 6

BLACK SWAN

UP ALL NIGHT

Carmen Reid

Welcome to a week in the life of Jo Randall – but this is no *ordinary* week.

There aren't enough hours in the day for Jo, overworked newspaper reporter, mother of two, and newly divorced after ten years of marriage. She's close to cracking the biggest scoop of her career – a cover-up with serious implications for her own family. If she knocks on the right doors and asks the right questions (with a little help from her outrageously smart friend, Bella Browning) then a real exclusive could be hers . . .

But how will Jo meet her deadlines when her distractions include two needy daughters and a Barbie birthday party to organize, her pompous ex-husband, his new 'girlfriend' and the romantic intentions of a scruffy but delicious young super-chef?

Time is running out, but who needs sleep when you can stay Up All Night . . . ?

0 552 15164 5

CORGI BOOKS

A SELECTED LIST OF FINE WRITING
AVAILABLE FROM CORGI AND BLACK SWAN

77084	1	COOL FOR CATS	Jessica Adams	£6.99
77115	5	BRICK LANE	Monica Ali	£7.99
99934	2	EVERY GOOD WOMAN DESERVES A LOVER	Diana Appleyard	£6.99
77186	4	ALL INCLUSIVE	Judy Astley	£6.99
77105	8	NOT THE END OF THE WORLD	Kate Atkinson	£6.99
99947	4	CROSS MY HEART AND HOPE TO DIE	Claire Calman	£6.99
99954	7	SWIFT AS DESIRE	Laura Esquivel	£6.99
99898	2	ALL BONES AND LIES	Anne Fine	£6.99
99656	4	THE TEN O'CLOCK HORSES	Laurie Graham	£5.99
99890	7	DISOBEDIENCE	Jane Hamilton	£6.99
77179	1	JIGS & REELS	Joanne Harris	£6.99
77110	4	CAN YOU KEEP A SECRET?	Sophie Kinsella	£6.99
77164	3	MANEATER	Gigi Levangie	£6.99
77104	X	BY BREAD ALONE	Sarah-Kate Lynch	£6.99
77216	X	EAT, DRINK AND BE MARRIED	Eve Makis	£6.99
77200	3	NO WONDER I TAKE A DRINK	Laura Marney	£6.99
77190	2	A GIRL COULD STAND UP	Leslie Marshall	£6.99
99939	3	MY SECRET LOVER	Imogen Parker	£6.99
15164	5	UP ALL NIGHT	Carmen Reid	£6.99
77145	7	GHOST HEART	Cecilia Samartin	£6.99
99952	0	LIFE ISN'T ALL HA HA HEE HEE	Meera Syal	£6.99
77173	2	BROTHER & SISTER	Joanna Trollope	£6.99
77155	4	LIFESAVER	Louise Voss	£6.99
99864	8	A DESERT IN BOHEMIA	Jill Paton Walsh	£6.99
77221	6	LONG GONE ANYBODY	Susannah Waters	£6.99
77101	5	PAINTING RUBY TUESDAY	Jane Yardley	£6.99